CW01667606

JOSIE BONHAM

THE RAKE'S RESCUED BRIDE

First published by Pitcheroak Press 2023

First edition

ISBN: 978-1-913856-08-3

This book was professionally typeset on Reedsy.
Find out more at reedsy.com

CHAPTER ONE

April 1807

Lucy Vaughan stared out of the window at the Shropshire fields and hedgerows, barely seeing them. The hired coach rattled along at a steady pace. It was well worn but clean and the springs were better than those of the family coach they were following. They would soon be home, not that Rugeley Hall had ever felt like home after Mama had taken her off to London at the age of seventeen. Not once in five years had they visited Rugeley Hall during the London season, until now.

Lucy sighed. "I still can't believe that Papa would rent out our London house for the rest of the season without consulting us."

"It shows how desperate for money he is. I knew your father would ruin us one day." Mama's voice shook and she stared at the floor. "He can't leave the gambling alone. I have no idea who he's lost to this time. He'll be in a foul temper."

For which Mama would suffer. Lucy frowned. "I've never known him be anything else but bad tempered. Perhaps we should have refused to come back?"

Mama sat up straight. "I thought about staying in a hotel

until James and Susan returned but that would have caused talk. I don't want your prospects ruined because of Papa's actions."

Lucy snorted. "Since I'm not interested in finding a husband that wouldn't have mattered. But if Papa was in one of his temper tantrums he'd have arrived in town with the coach and dragged us back here."

"I know. He won't be happy that we've hired a second coach to get all our belongings home, because of the cost."

"Don't worry, I've hardly spent any of this quarter's allowance. I'll give Papa enough money to keep him quiet for a while but make sure I have sufficient to pay the servants' wages and settle the tradesmen's bills. The family carriage wouldn't have been big enough for us, two maids and all of our clothes. We left a lot in storage in the attics as it is."

"True." Mama chewed at her bottom lip. "But you know what your father's like."

"Only too well. He never considers anyone but himself. I feel dreadful about letting Grace down with all the work at the orphanage. There wasn't even time to explain it to her. I made something up for Mrs Craddock."

"Best that you didn't tell them the truth. People will assume Papa is ill or something rather than ruined."

"Grace would have kept it to herself. I'd have felt better if I could have told her in person why we had to leave."

"I shouldn't worry too much. Mrs Craddock sounds very efficient."

"Yes, she is. It was lucky that she'd already volunteered to help. She'll do a good job. I shall miss working with the orphanage though. Especially with the employment exchange for pupils and former pupils going so well." Lucy sighed. "I wonder how long we'll have to stay here?"

Mama twisted her hands together. "I don't know but I wish Aunt Susan and Uncle James had been in London."

"I can't see them missing the London season for too long. We'll soon hear from them."

"I suppose so. Apparently, Uncle James is working on something really important for the government and even his secretary doesn't know where they are at the moment."

Lucy frowned. "That's unfortunate. We don't want to spend any longer with Papa than we have to."

"Uncle James's secretary said he would get the message to them as soon as he knew where they were."

"I hope that doesn't take long. Peter wrote to me a while ago. Papa tried to get him to agree to break the entail on all the Vaughan estates and properties. If he hadn't refused, I expect Papa would have sold the London house rather than rent it out."

Mama's face drained of colour. "I'm sure your father was trying to find out the terms of your Great Aunt Agatha's will from Uncle James at Christmas."

Lucy's mouth dropped open. "Why would he do that?"

"To find out how much Peter was left in order to exhort money from him." Mama looked away from her and stared out of the window.

"I don't think you need to worry. Peter wrote that he was going to stay with some friends so Papa couldn't keep badgering him about the entail. He'll have the sense to keep out of the way until Papa has solved his money problems."

"I heard from Peter not long before we had to leave London. He said nothing about the entail but he did say he intended to go up to Scotland with friends at the end of April. Papa won't be able to find him for now. I have this awful feeling that Papa has lost so much money this time that even Uncle James won't be able to sort him out."

Lucy sat bolt upright. "Heavens above, Papa hasn't borrowed money from Uncle James, has he?"

Mama's face took on a pinched expression. "Quite a considerable sum over the years. Your father thought Aunt Agatha's money would go to me rather than you two. I suspect he's been borrowing against that expectation. If he's trying to break the entail on the Rugeley Estates he must be desperate. Renting out the London house won't be enough to rescue him. I dread to think what he'll do."

"I don't see what he can do."

"Neither do I, but I have a feeling it was a mistake to come back here."

CHAPTER TWO

May 1807 Shropshire

The meagre fire in the blue drawing room of Rugeley Hall did little to tackle the chill of an unseasonably cold day. Lucy rose from a threadbare sofa which had long since faded to an indeterminate colour, more grey than blue, and strode around the room. How could Papa have allowed the Hall to fall into such a state? This had been an elegant room once. Now the carpet was dangerously worn in places, the furniture was almost beyond repair and there were dark stains on the cream and gold wallpaper that looked suspiciously like damp patches. She walked across to where her mother was staring at the needlework on her lap.

"Mama, I don't believe you have set a single stitch in twenty minutes or more." She sighed. "What are we going to do? Papa has been in a foul mood for the last few weeks but he was so animated last night when he said he was going to find me a husband. I don't want any sort of a husband but if I did, he wouldn't be one chosen by Papa."

"I'm so sorry, Lucy," Mama said. "Stand firm. Legally, your father can't force you to marry at your age."

That might be true but what would he do to Mama if she refused?

"It doesn't make sense." Lucy shook her head and frowned. "How would marrying me off help when he's relying on my allowance to keep the estate and house going?"

"Your Great Aunt Agatha left a large fortune, as you must have realised from the size of your allowance. I expect he's hoping to do a deal with a suitor when settlements are discussed to divert some of your share to him," Mama said. "I've sent another message to your uncle's secretary telling him we need Uncle James urgently."

Lucy stopped pacing. "You don't think Papa has someone in mind, do you? I wanted to have it out with him this morning but he had already gone out and no one has seen him since. It's not like him to be up before noon let alone before breakfast."

Mama twisted her wedding ring round and sighed. "Try not to say anything until you have to. You know how easily he flies up into the boughs. Susan and James should be back in London by now. I hope they come soon."

"They can support me but Papa would be within his legal rights to keep you here."

Mama's face took on a pinched expression. "Once your Uncle James is here, I can't see your father stopping us going away with him and Susan."

"I'm not so sure." Her voice rose until it was little more than a squeak. "So, there we have it, my own father wants to sell me off to the highest bidder. No one could have ever accused him of being a doting father but that's a new low even for him. I wouldn't put it past him to try and blackmail me into it by threatening you."

"Hush, Lucy. I think I can hear him coming." Mama's eyes looked too big for her face.

Lucy nodded. She threw herself down on the sofa next

to Mama, who was trembling, and took her hand. Heavy footsteps sounded in the hall. The door was flung open and her father stomped inside, looking rather unsteady on his feet. His face was red and bloated. If he carried on drinking like he was then Mama would soon be a widow. She might be an unnatural daughter but in some ways that would be a relief. The way Papa was going there would not be much left for Peter to salvage when the time came for him to inherit.

Lucy was careful to avoid eye contact with him. It was all very well Mama saying he couldn't force her to marry but as soon as she gave any indication that she would refuse all hell would break loose. Footsteps came towards her until she was forced to glance up. Papa tucked his thumbs into his pockets and rocked backwards and forwards from his heels to his toes in front of her. Lucy's stomach clenched. This looked ominous.

"What the deuce are you doing wearing that old gown, Lucy?" Papa's face went redder than ever.

"There's nothing wrong with this gown."

"Why does nobody in this house ever listen to a word I say? I meant exactly what I said last night. Let me repeat. It's time you were married and if your mother won't look to it then I must. Go and put something more fetching on. If you're quick you have time before dinner. Get your hair dressed in a better style while you're at it." His voice rose to a yell.

Lucy threw herself against the back of the sofa as if she had been hit. Never say Papa already had someone in mind and he was on his way? She exchanged a glance with Mama, who looked terrified.

"This is my warmest gown and it is perfectly adequate for a family dinner."

So much for her resolution to be careful not to say anything that would upset him. If he had already got someone in mind and had invited them to dinner, he could at least have the courtesy to tell her directly.

"Look at me when I'm talking to you. Not your mother. I'm still master in this house although sometimes it doesn't feel like it." He glared at Mama with such a venomous expression that Lucy shivered.

Papa's hands balled into fists and he took a step towards Mama who flinched. "You and your precious family think you are so superior don't you. I've found a handsome lord for the girl when you haven't managed to bring even one suitor up to scratch."

Papa leaned towards Mama and smirked at her. Her whole body seemed to shrink. Then he spun around to face Lucy.

"He's coming for dinner. Go and pretty yourself up and be down here in half an hour. I'll take him into the library if he arrives early." He marched off before Lucy could reply, colliding with the door frame on his way out.

Perhaps it was as well Papa hadn't given her a chance to speak. He was three parts foxed and looked angry enough to hit Mama in front of her if she had refused. Something he had managed to resist up until now. She and Peter had been nearly grown up before they had realised what was going on, although it had explained a lot. If anyone could be excused for drinking to excess it was Mama, who rarely drank alcohol. Somehow, she had managed to protect them from Papa's temper enough to give them a decent childhood.

Lucy squeezed her mother's hand. "I'll go and change. It will be best to humour Papa until Aunt Susan and Uncle James arrive to rescue us."

She walked up the stairs feeling drained. What was she to

do? There was a limit to how long she could stretch out a courtship, if Papa meant to allow her one at all. This was all happening too quickly. Was she being unrealistic to think she could take charge of her own destiny? Plenty of young women were forced to marry men of their father's choosing. Why should she be any different? It wasn't what Mama wanted for her but Papa had looked murderous. If she defied him there would be violence. Perhaps she should give in and accept this man if he wasn't too dreadful? Unless her aunt and uncle arrived soon it might be her only course of action.

Emma, her maid was waiting for her in her room and helped her to change into one of her smart London evening gowns. A blue silk which had the highest neckline of any she had brought with her. She rejected a shawl of Norwich lace in favour of a thick, fawn coloured woollen one. She refused to shiver her way through the evening just to keep her father happy. Somehow Rugeley Hall always felt cold, even in the middle of the summer.

Half an hour later Lucy made her way slowly down the stairs. She reached the hall and hesitated at the sound of male voices coming from the blue drawing room. Her father must have taken the suitor in to meet her. He wouldn't be best pleased that she wasn't already there. She pushed the door open and marched in. A few steps into the room she froze and couldn't stop her mouth from dropping wide open. Her worst nightmare was playing out in front of her. Papa was making small talk with Lord Parfitt of all men.

Not him, anyone but him. The room spun around her. The man who had plagued her so much for the first part of the season that she couldn't go to any social function without him pestering her. The man with the worst reputation in London.

All but the most desperate of doting Mamas did their best to make sure their daughters were never in the same room as Lord Parfitt. She closed her eyes and prayed that Uncle James and Aunt Susan would arrive soon. She took a deep breath and carried on walking, being careful to avoid all eye contact with either of the two men in the room. Her mother saw her first, her own shock was mirrored in Mama's face.

Her father gave a hearty laugh. "There you are, Puss. Lord Parfitt here says you're well acquainted. Friends even." He rubbed his hands together. "What could be better? I told you I'd found you a good match."

How could Papa look so satisfied with himself? A tight ball of anger settled in her chest. He must know what Parfitt's reputation was like.

Lord Parfitt jumped to his feet and bowed low. She avoided his gaze. He walked up to her and lifted her chin with his hand. Mama looked horrified but her father grinned all the more. She forced her eyes open to meet Lord Parfitt's gaze and then wished she hadn't. The triumph in his eyes made her feel sick. He would be a handsome man if it wasn't for the sneer that always marred his features. The over-scented cologne he was wearing increased her nausea. She tried to step away from him. In response he tightened his grip on her chin until it hurt.

"Don't I get a smile? I said earlier in the year I intended to speak to your father."

It was no good, there was no way she could pretend to be happy with Lord Parfitt's attentions. He'd realise what she was up to if she did after the way she had managed to evade him for the first weeks of the season, with Bertie Lovell's help. She would have to think of a better way to delay any marriage ceremony. The vicar in the village was elderly and had the living from her father. He'd be no help if they tried to force her to marry Parfitt. Banns took three weeks but she knew of cases where people had simply bought a licence from the bishop. She stayed silent. Parfitt went red in the face.

"I shall expect a bit more civility than this when we're married," he said in a harsh voice. His eyes ran over her figure and he licked his lips.

Lucy suppressed a shudder. This couldn't be happening. So that was why Parfitt had disappeared from London so suddenly. He'd come to find Papa, despite all her efforts to repulse him. She had assumed he'd lost interest when he had disappeared without a word. Any thoughts of going through with the marriage if the man had proved reasonable to make life easier for Mama wouldn't fly. Mama would blame herself if she got mixed up with Parfitt. Her head swam again. No point trying to think now. All she could do was to concentrate on getting through the evening and escape from Parfitt's company as soon as possible. Finding a plan would have to come later.

Papa staggered to his feet and gave a forced laugh. "She's just a bit shocked to see how well I've done for her, Parfitt. I think she was afraid I'd picked out some country bumpkin instead of a London swell, with a title to boot. Let's go in to dinner."

Papa caught Mama's arm and marched her into the dining room. Lucy went to follow them but Parfitt put a hand on her shoulder.

"Not so quickly. I think you owe me a little kiss." He leaned towards her until Lucy could feel his breath on her face. A strong smell of brandy hit her. Her best hope was if he had far too much to drink and managed to turn his curricle over on the way home. Assuming he had driven himself. Parfitt caught her chin again and held it steady. There was nothing she could do when he plonked his lips on hers. His spare hand kneaded her bottom. How could Papa do this to his own daughter? She kept her mouth stubbornly closed and eventually Parfitt gave up.

He pulled her arm so hard it wrenched her shoulder. "We had better go in to dinner but I'm warning you to stop repulsing me or it will be the worse for you." A lascivious smile played across his face. He dropped his voice to a silky whisper. "Or perhaps not. It might be fun to force you. Perhaps I'll try you out after dinner."

He licked his lips and laughed. The sound went through her. She jerked her head as far away from him as she could get. He laughed again and pulled her towards the dining room. Dinner passed in a blur, the few mouthfuls of food she managed to swallow tasting like ashes. Drake, their elderly butler, caught her eye as he stopped to top up her wine glass. Parfitt was looking at Papa, who was holding forth at great length about a horse of his he expected to win at Newmarket. Lucy shook her head but nodded towards Lord Parfitt's empty glass. Drake grinned at her and filled it to the brim.

Cheered by this small act of defiance Lucy managed to eat a fruit tart from the final course. Drake filled Lord Parfitt's glass twice more and winked at her the second time. She was not without friends but what could servants do against an influential man like Lord Parfitt? He was also physically powerful, tall and athletically built. A shudder ran through her and the last piece of tart stuck in her throat making her cough. She gulped down the wine left in her glass to sooth it. A wall of warmth hit her stomach. Perhaps she should have drunk more to numb the fear engulfing her.

Mama took advantage of the gap in the conversation to lead her out of the room.

"We'll leave you to your port, gentlemen."

Mama scuttled into the drawing room and shut the door behind them. "We don't have much time. I don't trust Lord Parfitt not to ravish you tonight to seal the bargain."

Mama was shaking but her face was set in determined lines. Lucy collapsed onto the sofa in front of the fire.

"I can't believe this is happening."

Mama sighed. "It's as I feared. Papa has done some sort of deal with Lord Parfitt. Parfitt's devious, he might even have set Papa up to lose money to him to get to you. He made such a nuisance of himself trying to court you."

"Surely even Parfitt couldn't be that devious. And most of Aunt Agatha's money will have gone to Peter."

Mama smiled at her. "Believe it or not, Aunt Agatha was just like you when she was young. She never intended to marry until Uncle Gerard swept her off her feet. She believed in equal treatment for women and I'm confident half of her money is in the trust for you. I'm not sure but I think she tied yours up until you're five and twenty, apart from a generous allowance, unless you marry younger. The executors of her will are sworn to secrecy. I expect she was hoping you would find your own Gerard without the fortune hunters circling you."

"And Papa gets a share of it if I marry the delectable Parfitt."

"Not if I can help it. I've told Drake to send Emma to your room. She'll sleep on a truckle bed with you tonight. Let's get you locked up so that dreadful man can't get at you. The doors in this place are far too sturdy for anyone to knock down. If Parfitt marries you, it will be over my dead body."

Lucy stifled a cry. There was a danger Mama wouldn't survive whatever happened. She had often wondered how dangerous father's temper was and his current behaviour was far from reassuring.

She caught her mother's hand. "What about you tonight? Papa is in such a volatile mood."

"Don't worry about me. My maid is waiting for me too. I'll be barricaded in until the morning. I'm hoping your aunt and uncle will appear tomorrow." Mama twisted her hands together. "They should be back in London by now and they should have got my last message."

"I don't expect Lord Parfitt to be around too early tomorrow. I'll walk through the woods to Mayford Castle first thing. I wish we knew who has inherited it. I'll try and sneak in a back way and see if any of the old staff are still there. They might help me hire a coach to get us away from here. In case Uncle James and Aunt Susan don't arrive in time to save us."

CHAPTER THREE

A frantic knocking at the huge front door made Lucy halt so sharply that she had to grab the banister to save herself from falling headlong down the stairs. Who would bang on the door like that other than one of Papa's cronies? She glanced at the grandfather clock in the hall and gasped. Seven o'clock was far too early in the day for one of them to be about. Could it be Lord Parfitt, despite Drake's efforts to get him foxed yesterday? Her heart leapt into her throat. Most likely, she had to get to Mayford Castle somehow. It was her only hope if it was him.

The knocking became louder. Fiddlesticks. If this was Parfitt, calling this early meant he was local or else staying in the area. She leaned over the banister. Drake appeared from the nether regions of the house and shuffled to the door, buttoning up his tunic as fast as his rheumatic fingers would let him. He reached for the bolt at the top of the door.

Drake shook his head and grumbled loudly enough for Lucy to hear him from the first-floor landing. "What kind of God-fearing person arrives at this time of the day?"

What kind indeed? Lucy drew back a little and pulled the hood of her dark red cloak over her head to cover her blonde hair. With only her eyes and the cloak protruding above the banister she should be hard to spot in the shadows. Her body trembled but she stayed where she was. She grimaced. Any friend of her father would never be acceptable to her, but Parfitt was another level of unacceptable. Besides, she would much rather dwindle into a spinster than marry anyone after seeing the horror of her parent's marriage.

Drake bent down with a curse and pulled the final bolt back. He tugged at the door until it swung open with an ominous creaking sound. Yet something else that urgently needed attention at the Hall. Papa had really let the place go. Lucy held her breath at a roar from a tall, sturdily built man, wearing a black riding coat, who pushed past Drake, leaving the old man swaying. Yes, that was Parfitt. What a way to treat a loyal servant.

"Out of my way, man. Where's your master? I'm expected and I don't appreciate being kept waiting."

Drake hurried off without a word in the direction of the library. Lucy stared at Parfitt as he stomped after the butler. She dropped to the floor and leaned her back against the banister. No. No. No. There was no way she could ever bring herself to marry him. No matter what Papa did to her. She brushed away the tears running down her cheeks with the back of her hand. Now was not the time to give in to a fit of weeping.

Lucy forced several deep breaths into tight lungs until she felt calmer. She needed time to think and form a plan. She heard a door open and her father's voice intruded on her thoughts.

"Good to see you so early, Lord Parfitt. Come into the library, where we won't be disturbed." His voice sounded artificially hearty.

The library door closed with a snap and she couldn't hear

Parfitt's reply. Lucy stood up and hung over the banister. There was no one in the hallway, not even Drake. The hum of masculine voices from the library suggested Papa was deep in conversation with Parfitt. With luck, she had time to escape from the house and hide herself in the woods that separated their estate from their neighbour's lands around Mayford Castle.

The men's voices became louder. Perhaps they were haggling over her, as if she was a prize cow being sold at a livestock market. Lucy's mouth went dry. She gathered her skirts in one hand and ran down the stairs, holding onto the banister for support with the other. She crept closer to the library door until she could hear what they were saying.

"She'll come around. She just needs some time." Papa sounded as if he was pleading with Parfitt now. "James won't like it if he thinks she was forced into marriage."

"Stop snivelling, man. We haven't got time. You're in this deeper than me, remember."

Lucy shivered at Parfitt's menacing tone. What were they involved in? Good Lord, were they both in debt and intending to split her fortune? It was time to escape. She slipped through the servants' door, at the opposite side of the hallway to the library. There was no sign of Drake or any of the other servants and the kitchen was empty as she ran through it to the door leading out to the kitchen gardens. Good, the servants would be able to say they didn't know where she was with perfect honesty when father sent for her only to find she wasn't in the house. Lord Parfitt sounded furious. She hadn't expected her locking herself into her bedroom would go down well with him. That summons wouldn't be long coming.

Whatever hold Parfitt had over Papa it must be a strong one.

If it was about money, how much did Papa owe? He must know she wouldn't marry an oaf like Lord Parfitt without a fight. She quickened to a headlong pace until she reached the walled garden and closed the gate behind her, gasping for air. She was hidden from a casual observer glancing out from the house in here. There was no sign of anyone. Hardly surprising since old Tom was the only gardener her father still employed. He was probably having a nap somewhere. All the same she checked again while she caught her breath. There was always the chance that this was one of the days the young man who had been doing some casual work in the gardens showed up. She gathered herself and set off at a steady trot.

There was some way to go to the woods and complete safety, it was best to pace herself. Lucy sighed. She had loved those woods as a child and knew every inch of them, every hiding place and the easiest trees to climb. The woods where she and Peter had played and had so much fun with Bertie Lovell, when he came to stay with his godfather every summer and more often than not Easter too. Bertie who always seemed to be there when she needed him. And still was. He'd dogged her footsteps when Parfitt had pursued her at society events this season. Despite Bertie's wild reputation she didn't believe the half of what was said about him.

Sad to think that old Mr Mayford was now dead. They had always daydreamed that Mayford Castle would belong to Bertie one day. In reality, although Bertie was close enough to his godfather to call him Uncle Ambrose, the castle and the estate would be entailed. She gasped. Never say Lord Parfitt had inherited it? He must be stopping close by to have arrived so early. A sob escaped her. How would she bear it if he had?

It was a warm spring day. The sun rose higher. Lucy became

increasingly hot and sticky. She was glad when some clouds started to roll in, deflecting the heat of the sun. Keeping to the paths around the hedgerows reduced the chance of being spotted, but it made it a much longer journey. The biggest difficulty would be when she reached the lane bordering her father's property. She increased her pace, holding her hand to her side to ease the stitch that caused. She had to get to those woods before Papa came looking for her. At long last she reached the lane and leaned against the hedge to catch her breath. She heard the sound of horses galloping towards her and curled into a gap in the hedge.

Lucy kept her cloak wrapped firmly around her and her head down and tried not to breathe too loudly. The hoof beats drew nearer. It sounded like two horses. Fiddlesticks, was it Papa and Lord Parfitt? Her heart was thumping so hard it almost drowned out the sound of voices. But then she heard the unmistakable tones of the squire's two sons. They cantered past. She took some deep breaths and peered out cautiously from the hedge. There was no sign of anyone in this field with her. She walked along to where she knew there was a gap in the hedge with a matching gap almost opposite. She strained her ears. All seemed quiet. There was nothing for it but to risk crossing the road.

She pushed her way through the hedge, tugging at her cloak when it became snagged on a twig and pulling her hood back up firmly over her blonde hair. There was no sign of anyone approaching in either direction on the road. Lucy gathered her skirts, ran across and dived into the opposite field. Instinct took over and she started running straight through the field without bothering to waste time getting to the hedge dividing it from its next-door neighbour. She staggered on, her breath coming in short, frantic gasps. Nearly there now. The overhead cloud thickened and the temperature dropped, which helped.

With her focus firmly on a large oak tree on the edge of the woods she scrambled on as best she could. When she reached the first of the scrubby trees at the edge of the woodland, she threw herself down behind a clump of bushes and lay there like a wounded animal, catching her breath. The best hiding places were deep in the woods, close to Mayford Castle. She struggled to her feet and plunged in amongst the trees. Branches caught at her clothes, slowing her down.

She drew in big lungfuls of air and the earthy scent of woodland calmed her. The quickest path towards the Castle was quite steep. She trudged upwards. The undergrowth on either side of the path was thick. Although the path was wide and frequently used by the servants from the castle as a shortcut to the village, she could hide quickly if she heard anyone coming. The rustle of leaves in the wind and the songs of several species of bird were all she could hear.

The woods were more overgrown than she remembered, but then it was some years since she'd been in them. Once Mama had taken her to London, they had rarely stayed at Rugeley Hall. Preferring visits to Aunt Susan after the London season, well away from Papa. On the odd occasion when they had stayed for a few days she hadn't bothered to visit the woods without Peter and Bertie, who had been young men about town by then. She dragged her mind back to the present. Would there still be vantage points close to the Castle that weren't too overgrown for her to look for signs of anyone living there?

Mr Mayford had never mentioned any relatives, but would a nice gentleman like him want to admit to being related to a toad like Lord Parfitt? There were plenty of other places Parfitt could be staying in the area, perhaps even with the Squire. The Squire's wife was a social climber, the sort to make up to someone with a title no matter what he was like. Or was she just being hopeful? Lord Parfitt as a neighbour would be yet another reason to stay well away from home. Mama was pinning her hopes on Aunt Susan to rescue them. What if they were still away on Government business? Lucy kept walking. It didn't bear thinking about.

A restless wind sent the branches overhead dancing around, almost as if they were trying to catch her. Now she was getting fanciful. If the castle appeared to be unoccupied her best plan was to throw herself on the housekeeper's mercy. Not only would Mrs Hobbs conceal her for a while, she would ply her with tea and cakes. An important consideration for someone who had missed breakfast. Mrs Hobbs could be relied upon to keep her visit secret, assuming she was still the housekeeper of course.

Weariness overcame her and she was drawn to a fallen tree trunk deeper into the woods. She forced her way through the undergrowth and sat down on the end of the trunk, where she was hidden from the path. The remains of a branch jutted upwards and formed a back rest. What on earth was she going to do? Lucy leaned back against the branch and closed her eyes but inspiration stubbornly refused to visit her. It was tempting to hide there all day but her stomach growled at the prospect. With a sigh she rose from the tree trunk and fought her way back to the path.

The top part of the hill grew steeper and it was an effort to keep going. Living in London and keeping late hours had left her far less fit than she had been as a child. Why hadn't she noticed before? Anything was better than living with Papa but she was a country girl at heart. It was no use wallowing in self-pity. There had to be a way out of this mess. Perhaps she could persuade Mama to give up her crazy idea of finding her a kind husband, preferably with a title, and they could hide in the country somewhere. Kind men did exist but the risk of being mistaken in a man was too much to contemplate. Her future was hers to decide.

Lucy squared her shoulders and trudged on into a cooling breeze which seemed to be strengthening by the minute. The quality of the light had changed. She looked upwards through a gap in the trees at a sky black with unshed rain. Branches danced around her, leaves rustling, as if waving her on. The rustling grew louder and splashes of rain found their way through the spring canopy above. Oh fiddlesticks, it looked like a storm was brewing.

She reached the summit of the hill and battled on doggedly. Her legs were aching with the effort but the last thing she wanted was to be caught out in a storm. The splashes became a steady stream and the wind howled through the trees. What if it turned thundery? A distant rumble confirmed her worst fear. These woods with their huge oaks wouldn't be safe in a thunderstorm. She had no choice but to make straight for Mayford Castle and hope old Mr Mayford's servants were still there. A caretaker would be in residence who could let her in to safety if they had gone.

Lucy emerged from the trees to an enormous clap of thunder that sounded almost overhead. There was no sign of anyone at the front of the Castle. The rain was coming down in torrents. Head down, she ran around the side of the Castle towards the kitchen door and collided with someone running up from the direction of the stables. A solid masculine body enveloped her in a hug. She struggled to break free. Torrential rain coupled with tears of frustration obscured her vision but she could see enough to know that the man was wearing a black riding coat. Lord Parfitt! Lucy aimed a kick at his shin. She connected with a satisfying thud.

CHAPTER FOUR

"Ouch. Lucy, what was that for?" Bertie Lovell stood back, keeping a hold on Lucy's shoulders.

Lucy stared up at him and blinked. "Bertie! What are you doing here?"

"I live here, stoopid." He smiled down at her, amused at her surprise.

"But you're wearing a black riding coat like Lord Parfitt."

"What's that got to say to anything? Plenty of men in the Ton wear black riding coats. The rain must have addled your brains. Come on let's get to the Castle. We'll be drowned if we don't and I remember how much you hate thunderstorms."

Bertie put an arm around her and half carried her as they ran towards the kitchen. Lucy stumbled as he let go of her to wrench open the door. He picked her up and carried her over the threshold.

"You're shaking. I'll go and find Mrs Hobbs. We'll get you dry first and then we can have explanations." He put her down next to the kitchen fireplace, where a welcome log fire crackled merrily, and hurried off to the Housekeeper's sitting room.

Bertie pursed his lips. Lucy was in a real taking, but then she had always hated thunderstorms. That was a strange comment to make about his coat being similar to Lord Parfitt's though.

He stopped abruptly, with his hand raised to knock on Mrs Hobbs's door. Zounds. Had Vaughan summoned Lucy home to marry Parfitt? A repulsive individual but a fabulously wealthy one, unless he had suffered a serious financial reverse of some sort? And definitely not the right husband for a gentle soul like Lucy. He'd crush her. Not that Parfitt would get the chance if he had anything to say to it. Lucy was as good as a sister to him.

His heartbeat pounded in his ears and his hands formed themselves into fists. It had been sickening watching Parfitt hang about Lucy earlier in the season. The hell-hound had taken himself off with little argument in exchange for being let off his gambling debts. Which didn't prove anything about his financial situation though. Parfitt had always been a scaly cove when it came to money. Vaughan was the one with a tendency to live beyond his means from what Uncle Ambrose had said. Was Parfitt trying to buy Lucy in exchange for hauling her father out of the river tick?

He knocked on the door and it was swiftly answered by Mrs Hobbs.

"I'm sorry to disturb your morning break, Mrs Hobbs, but I need your help. Miss Vaughan is home and she got caught out by the storm on a morning walk. She headed here for shelter." Bertie's cheeks flamed. Mrs Hobbs would be thinking they'd had an assignation from his own rain-soaked clothing. "I've left her in the kitchen next to the fire but she's soaked through and shivering."

Mrs Hobbs jumped up immediately. "Oh, the poor dear. I remember how much she hated thunderstorms, especially here where we're so close to the woods. I'll send one of the maids to light a fire in the best guest bedroom and have the footman heat up some water for a bath. We'll have to dry her clothes as best we can."

"Thank you. We must talk about taking on some more staff soon. I rather think I'll make this place my main residence."

Mrs Hobbs's face lit up. "I'm so glad Mr Lovell. Now let's go and sort out Miss Vaughan, she was always such a lovely girl."

Bertie followed Mrs Hobbs to the kitchen, his face feeling hot. It would have been impossible to miss the speculative glance she had given him. They found Lucy standing so close to the fire it was a wonder she didn't scorch. She'd removed her cloak and let it fall onto the stone flags where it was already surrounded by a puddle of water. Even her hair was drenched, the weight of water pulling it partially loose from its pins, leaving her pinched face framed by strands of sodden blonde hair. The poor girl looked as if she hadn't slept well for days.

Cook was taking things out of the ovens making the kitchen fill with heavenly smells. She waddled across to them with a tray of freshly baked buns, which looked delicious. In no time at all Mrs Hobbs had Lucy swaddled in a couple of thick, woollen blankets and pulled a chair up to the fire for her. Cook plied them with buns and hot tea. Bertie's stomach reminded him he'd gone for his ride without breakfast. He was tucking into his third bun when Lucy sat back and caught his gaze.

"I'd forgotten how good Cook's buns were. I'm sorry I kicked you."

Bertie cleared his throat. "About that. Am I right in thinking that your father wants to marry you off to Lord Parfitt?"

Lucy crossed her arms tightly in front of herself, as she had done as a little girl when she was worried. Which, come to think about it, had generally meant she'd fallen foul of her father's temper. He caught his breath. The thought of a lovely, wholesome girl like Lucy paired off with a nasty rake like Lord Parfitt was enough to make him wish he hadn't eaten that third bun. He gave Lucy an encouraging smile.

Her lips moved into an answering smile but it was clearly an effort. "I'm afraid so. Papa's got money problems. He rented out our house in Town. We had to come home with very little notice. Then the other day he announced he was going to arrange a match for me. Uncle James and Aunt Susan were out of Town when we left. Mama has written to ask them to rescue us but I'm not sure if it will serve."

"Why not? He can hardly force you to marry."

"Papa could make it uncomfortable for me by threatening Mama if she doesn't persuade me." She looked away from him. "Husbands have the legal right to control their wives."

Hmm. Vaughan was definitely a rum customer but Mrs Vaughan's family was a powerful one. "Surely your uncle could apply pressure on him to leave you both alone."

"If he arrives soon, he might be able to get us away." Lucy shivered.

Bertie frowned. "If I know your aunt and uncle they will be here quickly."

"Uncle James's secretary didn't know where they were the first time Mama wrote weeks ago. He said he would pass the message on as soon as he could. Mama wrote again saying it was urgent when Papa mentioned marrying me off. Last night Papa announced that my future husband would be joining us for dinner."

"And Parfitt turned up?"

She nodded. "I'm afraid so. You can imagine how horrified I was."

"I can guess. Parfitt disgusts me. Any woman would baulk at the prospect of marrying him. I can't believe your father could expect it of you."

"It was a grim evening."

Lucy went so pale for a moment he thought she might swoon.

"Mama rushed us out after the meal before Papa could stop her and we ran upstairs and barricaded ourselves in our bedrooms." She shuddered. "I can't remember ever feeling so scared. I got up early to come here to see if I could get help to hire a carriage to get us away."

Good Lord, that didn't sound good. Lucy didn't scare easily. He caught her hand and gave it a squeeze. She flinched and rubbed at her shoulder.

Bertie's mouth dropped open. "Did Parfitt hurt you?"

"Yes. Papa contrived to leave us together in the drawing room before dinner. Parfitt got angry when I wouldn't kiss him and dragged me into dinner by one arm."

Blind fury thudded through Bertie's veins. He took some deep breaths. "Parfitt won't do anything to you while I'm here. Trust me. If all else fails, I'll throw you over my charger and ride off with you."

That brought a smile to her face, as he knew it would.

"Just like when we were children and played at castles and knights and you and Peter vied to win my favour!" Lucy smiled up at him. "I'm so glad you're here, Bertie."

Bertie grimaced. "I wish I had come straight here and not let my friends carry me off for a visit on the way."

"You're here now and I can't tell you how comforting that is. My only worry is whether your charger will be strong enough to carry both of us."

"Have no fear on that score. Max made me a present

of a magnificent, chestnut stallion when I visited him and Georgie."

Lucy's eyes lit up. "From the Hargreaves' stud in Ireland?"

"Yes. He's called Chalice and you will love him. What horse do you ride now? Still that lovely grey mare?"

Lucy shook her head and looked away from him. "Papa sold her when I went to London. I don't have a horse now."

"What! That's dreadful. I always thought your father was a bully but I never realised he was that bad. Is Parfitt staying at Rugeley Hall?"

"No, but he must be somewhere close by. He arrived early as I was about to go out to come here. I hid and he went into the library with Papa. I wasn't aware Papa even knew Parfitt." Lucy blushed a painfully deep red and stared at the floor. "You saw how Parfitt was pestering me in London. I was never so glad as when he had to go out of Town suddenly."

Lucy raised her eyes to his, she looked ready to burst into tears. It was Bertie's turn to look away, given his own role in sending Parfitt to the right-about. Despite being more than two years younger than him and Peter, Lucy had been fearless when they all played together. It was awful to see her so upset. Any sane woman with a grain of sense would be terrified of being married off to Parfitt. She hadn't looked so miserable since the time he had found her crying when her kitten had got himself stuck in a rabbit hole and she thought he might die.

His ten-year-old self had helped her then. Surely, he could do something for her this time. He stood and walked over to her chair, placing a hand on her shoulder. They were adults now or he would have hugged her like he had then, before helping her to widen the hole and lift the kitten out.

"I'm more than happy to do anything I can to help you. Remember that time when I helped you dig Mittens out of a rabbit hole? We did it then and we can save the day together now."

She squeezed the hand resting on her shoulder and gave him a tremulous smile that did something strange to his insides. "That's kind of you Bertie. I think this is a much harder problem than rescuing a naughty kitten."

Bertie had never heard Lucy sound so defeated. He smiled down at her. "We'll think of something. Where's Peter? He would back you up against your father."

Lucy shook her head and grimaced. "I'm sure he would but Papa has chosen his time well. Peter is touring Scotland with friends. We have no idea where he is. He is not expected back for at least a month."

"Your father can't physically make you marry Parfitt."

Bertie turned a little away so Lucy couldn't see his face. From what he knew of Parfitt that might not be true but there was no point alarming her. Once she'd warmed up and regained her equilibrium they could go through her options. He stared at the fire and shuddered. There was no way he was going to let Lucy be forced into marriage with that reprobate.

"He was so angry when he saw I didn't want Parfitt he could do anything if I don't comply." Lucy gave a weak smile. "If it was only me, I would be on that charger with you tonight. I fear he might do something dreadful to Mama if I ran away."

"I only arrived a couple of days ago and all I've had time for is to go around and say hello to the tenants. I fully intended to call at the Hall to see if you were there. What a blessing I didn't." Bertie stood up and stomped around the kitchen. "It's better if neither he nor Parfitt know I'm here. With Peter away it's up to me to help you escape."

Lucy gave him a tremulous smile. "I don't suppose you have a travelling carriage we could use do you? I can't leave Mama alone with Papa and Aunt Susan could be anywhere."

"There's bound to be one in the barns somewhere but until my new horses are delivered there are no carriage horses to pull it." Bertie frowned. "It's only a matter of time until your father finds out I'm here. I've visited all the tenants and the news of me being here is bound to get around the neighbourhood. We need to get you away quickly. Today if we can."

Lucy bowed her head and rubbed at her eyes. "I came over here hoping there would be some servants left who could hire a carriage for me. I think things will be coming to a head quickly. The problem is a hired carriage can hardly drive up to the house for us. I have to go back to fetch Mama. Have you brought a groom with you who could collect messages from me?"

"I'm afraid not. I rode Chalice here in easy stages. That's one of the reasons I accepted my friends' invitation as they are halfway between London and here. Max is arranging for Nat Overton's major-domo, Mr Bright, to find me some trained grooms as well as most of the horses I will need. They should be arriving fairly soon. I need to talk to Uncle Ambrose's old head groom, Warner, who is still here. I don't want to upset him but it's probably time for him to be pensioned off. He's too old to be delivering messages. I haven't even got my valet with me yet. I gave him some time off to visit his family."

"Oh dear. There is no one I can trust at home to bring a message to you and keep quiet." She sounded defeated.

Bertie sat down opposite her and took her hand. Lord she was still cold the poor girl. "I tell you what. Some of my old clothes are still here from when we used to go off on our adventures. I get fit even in London with lots of riding, walks and sessions at Gentleman Jackson's boxing saloon. I think I'll still be able to get into them. I'll disguise myself as a groom and come across later in case..." He stuttered to a halt and grimaced.

"In case my own father is planning to marry me off straight away now Parfitt is here? I fear it's all too likely. He's never been a warm father but I thought he had some regard for me until the last few days."

"Something like that." Bertie clamped his jaw so tight that it hurt. There was no way on this earth he was going to let an evil, duddering rake like Parfitt anywhere near Lucy.

Bertie's throat constricted. "Even if we get you away my Lord Parfitt is going to chase after you. I know it. His pursuit of you has been so determined and he's a man who can't abide not getting his own way. I don't want to alarm you but we need to take precautions."

Lucy's shoulders slumped. She met his gaze, her deep blue eyes bright with unshed tears. "Someone is bound to see you if you come to the house and there is little you can do on your own."

"Look at me, Lucy. Have I ever let you down?"

"No never. You have been as good as a second brother to me."

"We always made a good team the three of us."

Lucy smiled. "Eventually, once you and Peter finally gave in and let me go on your adventures with you."

"Well then, even two of us should be enough to outwit your father. Do you remember that big old oak tree with the hole in it where we used to meet up?"

Lucy nodded. "The one nearest to the kitchen gardens?"

"That's the one. I'll be there around five o'clock. If you can't get away at that time leave a message tucked in the hole in the tree."

"I suppose that might serve. Emma, my maid, is taken with the boy old Tom sometimes has to help with the gardening. She's a sensible girl. It wouldn't take her long to slip out to that tree. If anyone sees her, they'll think she's hoping for a glimpse of the boy."

"That's better. You're thinking more clearly now. I don't like the thought of leaving you with your father though. If you feel in danger of being whisked away to a church come straight here. We can worry about rescuing your mother later if that happens."

"Once I'm back I'll lock myself in my room and get Emma to send Mama to me."

"That's the ticket. I wish Bright would arrive with some grooms. I haven't even got a spare horse until he does."

"They must be coming soon surely." Lucy wrinkled her nose in thought. "It's a few weeks since you visited the Marquess of Hargreaves, isn't it?"

"You're right. They could arrive anytime. I've been drifting along putting off talking to Warner. I'll have that chat with him as soon as I've got you home. He might know of someone local with decent horses to sell that won't stand out like Chalice, in case we need to make a run for it across country. Chin up. We'll find a way out of this mess, all right and tight." He gave Lucy's hand another squeeze.

"I feel so much better now I know you're here to help me." Lucy smiled up at him and the pinched look that had haunted her face receded.

The door opened and Bertie let go of Lucy's hand. Mrs Hobbs entered followed by a young maid who picked up Lucy's sodden cloak and hung it near to the fire to dry.

"You look a lot better now you've had something warm to drink, Miss Vaughan. We've got a hot bath ready for you upstairs. We'll try and get your clothes dry while you're there." Mrs Hobbs turned towards the maid. "Molly here will help you."

Molly bobbed a curtsy. "Follow me, Miss. We'll soon have you out of those wet things."

"I'm not sure there is time for that."

Bertie shooed her off. "Off with you. It's not going to help anything if you catch a chill from getting drowned. Another half an hour or so won't make any difference."

"I suppose you're right." Lucy shivered. "I will feel better if I'm warm and dry."

Bertie watched as Molly ushered Lucy out of the room. "I'm making a lot of extra work for you here Mrs Hobbs. If you know of any suitable indoor staff locally, I'd like you to try and hire them."

Mrs Hobbs smiled at him. "I know of several girls who might be suitable and one young man who would make a good footman."

"Excellent. I've no idea how much servants are paid these days but I know Uncle Ambrose was always a generous employer. I'd like you to take these young people on as soon as you can and decide what level of pay would be in keeping with his example."

"Of course, Mr Lovell. It will be lovely getting the Castle as it should be, full of life again."

Bertie nodded. "Yes, it will. I imagine Uncle Ambrose

arranged pensions for the older members of staff."

"He did." Mrs Hobbs smiled. "Very generous ones too. Several of them have cottages in the village."

"Warner wasn't ready to retire I take it."

"I'm not sure, Mr Lovell. I know provision was made for him as soon as he wants to retire. I thought he would be but I have a feeling he has some idea of trying to get his nephew a job here as a groom first."

Bertie chewed at his lip. If Bright sent him a full complement of already trained grooms that could be awkward. "I'll have a chat with him, Mrs Hobbs."

Mrs Hobbs started to say something and then hesitated.

"What is it?"

"I think the nephew, Arthur, is hoping to do better for himself than a groom's job. His mother died a few months ago and he moved in with Warner, but the lad can read and write and he's clever. His father was a land agent but he died when Arthur was young. There are no relatives on that side of the family who would help him. Arthur told me he would love to get a job as a land agent or something like that himself. I shouldn't put you off employing him though, the lad needs a job."

Mrs Hobbs must be fond of the boy, judging by the hopeful look on her face. "How old is he?"

"About twenty I believe. He has a little money from his mother but she was an invalid for years. Arthur looked after her and a lot of the money went on doctor's fees. He's a good lad. In fact, the doctor offered to train him up as a junior partner but Arthur says he couldn't see himself as a doctor. He told me he takes after his mother's family and loves the land and horses."

"Which is why Warner thinks he would make a good groom I suppose."

"I think so. If you ask me young Arthur has spent too long in sick rooms for a lad his age and longs for something a bit more exciting."

"And who could blame him." Vague memories of seeing his father lying in bed looking frighteningly ill flitted through Bertie's mind. He couldn't have been more than five or six at the time but the horror of that sick room was still with him. Bertie rubbed his chin. "Hmm. I might be able to find him something else. If not, I'll take him on as an extra groom or whatever while he looks around for something better."

Bertie relaxed. That solved the groom problem. Uncle Ambrose would want him to look after all his old staff, even if it meant obliging one by employing a relative. He had been a great believer in loyalty.

Mrs Hobbs frowned. "As an extra groom?"

"I'm getting some grooms from a friend but I don't know how many and how qualified yet. I may not need any more. I must have that chat with Warner." Bertie grinned. "I've been putting it off, afraid of upsetting him. My new agent will be arriving soon. I met him in London and he seems a good sort. Arthur might be suitable if he wants an assistant. I'll sound him out."

"Thank you, Mr Lovell."

"If we're left with any spaces for a full complement of indoor staff, Miss Vaughan has links to a London orphanage. We may be able to recruit staff from there with initial training. See what you can do locally first. We might have to advertise for more senior staff." A sudden thought hit him. He grimaced. "Cook doesn't want to retire, does she?"

Mrs Hobbs laughed. "Not at all. She's worried you might bring in a fancy French chef."

Bertie shuddered. "Definitely not. I like good English food. I had enough of fancy dinners in London."

"Do you want to tell Cook yourself, Mr Lovell?"

Bertie grinned. "I'll leave that to you or she might think I'm ten years old again and give me one of her hugs. I'll escort Miss Vaughan home as soon as it's stopped raining. I'm off to the stable to make sure my horse is ready. It's lucky I only took him out for a short ride this morning."

CHAPTER FIVE

Lucy lay back in the bath with a satisfied sigh. This was the most relaxed she had been for over a week. It was comforting to know that Bertie was here and eager to help. The tension in her muscles eased as a sensation of calm swept over her. Molly was a quiet soul who kept in the background leaving her to enjoy the bliss of a few moments to herself. Emma was a dear but she never stopped talking. With so much on her mind sometimes all she wanted was peace and quiet to think. It was tempting to hide away at Mayford Castle and not return until Aunt Susan had appeared. The only problem being that her mother would bear the brunt of Papa's fury.

He had become more volatile than she remembered. His aggressive outbursts were less controlled and more frequent. And more dangerous. It was a terrible thing to be afraid of your own father. As a useful commodity she was safe for now but what about Mama? If Papa took out his frustration on her, would she get more than the odd bruise she had always tried to hide from her and Peter when they were children? Lucy shuddered. It seemed inevitable that she would.

"Are you getting chilled, Miss Vaughan?" Molly picked up a towel that was heating up in front of the fire.

"I was chilled to the bone, but I'm warming up now. I'll stay here a bit longer."

"In that case, I'll run down to the kitchen with your wet clothes and Cook will help us get them dry in front of the range."

"Thank you, Molly."

Lucy closed her eyes and concentrated on the feel of the warm water and the heat seeping deep into her frozen body. A few minutes calm was exactly what she needed. Then as soon as Molly was back, she really would have to get dry. The sooner she got back home the better, even if she had to borrow some clothes from the maids. With any luck Lord Parfitt would be long gone for the day. Once her father drank himself into a stupor later on, she and Mama would plan what they were going to do. Surely Aunt Susan must be in touch soon. Lucy felt herself drifting into a half waking state and jumped when there was a tap at the door and Molly came in.

"You were nearly asleep, Miss. Sorry I startled you."

Lucy smiled at her. "It wasn't your fault and I need to get out now anyway."

Molly put a grey and white bundle on the bed. "We found a maid's uniform that should fit you reasonably well, Miss Vaughan."

Lucy stepped out into the towel Molly held out for her and wrapped it around her body. Molly gave her wet hair a rub and then wrapped it up in another dry towel. Within a few minutes Lucy was ready to go back downstairs and face the rest of the day. She squared her shoulders and followed Molly out of the guest bedroom. Bertie had always been the lively one with lots of ideas, he would come up with something. If she could keep Parfitt at bay, he might be able to make enquiries about where

Aunt Susan was. Uncle James would be better still if Bertie could find him. He was about the only person Papa ever took any notice of. Lucy entered the kitchen to find Bertie coming in from outside.

Bertie smiled. "That's better you look much more like the Lucy I know now you've warmed up. Why don't we prevail on cook to make some more tea and find something else to eat while we wait for your clothes to dry out?"

"I think it would be better if I got back as soon as possible."

Bertie wrinkled his nose. "If you ask me, you'd be far better to slip into the house in the clothes you're wearing and go straight up to your room. Then no one need know you've even been here."

"I know what you mean, but by the time my clothes have dried out and I've walked all the way home it will be getting late. I need to get back before Papa has time to work himself up into a real temper. With luck he won't have noticed I'm missing yet. I rarely see him before dinner."

"Warner says Uncle Ambrose's old mount is still up to short distances with a light rider. Warner's nephew has been exercising him. Riding will be much quicker than you walking, especially if we canter down the drive and risk using the lane to the Hall."

Lucy sighed. "It would be a lot quicker and it would be wonderful to be on a horse again but I can't."

"Why on earth not?"

"I haven't got a riding habit with me or a side saddle."

"You used to wear Peter's breeches and ride astride with us not so long ago. I'm sure there will be an old pair of mine here that will fit you."

Lucy face burned. The elegant, athletically built young man

in front of her was a far cry from the scrawny youth he had been when they all played together. "We were children then. What if someone saw me?"

"It's hardly a busy lane and most people who do use it are my tenants. They would keep quiet if they did see you."

"I suppose you're right." Lucy chewed at her lip.

Bertie laughed and shook his head at her. "Of course, I'm right. How did you get to be so missish?"

"I'm not missish." Lucy resisted the temptation to stamp her foot. He was trying to help her after all but men had no idea how difficult life could be for females. "Simply cautious. I'll do it but on your head be it if we see anyone who won't keep it quiet. I suppose I could wear the breeches under my skirt."

"And keep them hidden in your bedroom in case we have to run away. Come on. Let's see what else there is to eat and leave Mrs Hobbs to get your clothes dry."

Lucy took hold of Bertie's arm. Good Lord, if they ran away together, she would be ruined. "You do realise that if you were seen with me wearing breeches and riding astride you might come under pressure to marry me, don't you?"

Bertie's mouth dropped open. "But we were brought up almost as brother and sister."

"We were children then. I haven't lived here since I was seventeen. It's different now. If we were caught running away together without Mama ..." Lucy's voice trailed off and she gulped in a huge breath.

Bertie stared at her. "Ah, I see. In that case I would have to marry you or you would be ruined. I'm sorry. I'd forgotten about all the ridiculous rules of society you ladies are bound by."

"I can't let you risk being forced into marriage against your will, it wouldn't be fair." Lucy thought hard. "What am I saying? I don't ever want to marry anyway, so it wouldn't matter if I was ruined. As far as I know my inheritance is tied up until I'm five and twenty but then I'll get full control over it. I'm sure Aunt Susan would hide me for three years until I can set up my own establishment, under a false name of course."

* * *

"I don't like the thought of you being ruined, Lucy. You would be safe with me and I'll have to marry sometime, I'd as lief it was you as anyone else if it came to it." Bertie kept his voice light and smiled at her.

Considering he had played the role of a rakehell so well for the past few years, most decent girls wouldn't look at him. What a fool he had been. He shook his head. "Let's not worry about that for now. It won't arise if we can get you away with your mother."

Lucy's body seemed to take on a life of its own, trembling violently. She wrapped her arms around herself and chewed at her lip. "Bertie, you don't understand. I don't ever want to marry." She collapsed onto a chair by the fire.

Bertie sat next to her and took her hand. She flinched and his stomach tightened. He let go of her hand immediately. It seemed she was afraid of men, which wasn't surprising given what her father was like. But now her fear extended to him. Lucy no longer saw him as her playmate of old but a grown man. Gone was the easy camaraderie they had enjoyed whenever they met up in London. With Parfitt pursuing her, he had made it his business to keep a close watch earlier in the season. They had seen each other more frequently than ever without a hint of constraint between them. A surge of anger went through him. He couldn't let this latest start of her father's ruin their relationship forever.

"It's alright, Lucy. You're safe with me." He used the coaxing tone that worked well with his cousin's children in the hope of banishing the stricken look from her face.

Lucy stared at him, wide eyed. "I know that, Bertie, but the thought of marriage to anybody terrifies me."

"Try not to think about it. Let's take things a step at a time. We can plot your escape on the ride over to the Hall."

Less than an hour later, Bertie gave Lucy a leg up onto Uncle Ambrose's huge, old bay gelding, Thunderer. He stood patiently as she arranged her skirts to cover the breeches she wore as best she could. He was confident she would manage such a large horse. Riding was something you didn't forget and Lucy had been a consummate horsewoman before she went to London. He waited until she was settled in the saddle and climbed up onto Chalice using a mounting stone. Chalice was full of energy and threw his head around, despite having been ridden earlier. It took a few moments to settle him.

He patted Chalice's neck. "Calm down old fellow. I know I'm none too respectable in these old clothes but it's in a good cause."

Lucy giggled. "You do look rather odd dressed like that on a horse of Chalice's quality. If anyone sees you from a distance, they'll think someone has stolen him."

"Zounds. I hope not. I've no desire for a chase. If it should happen, I'll head back home. You can ride on and leave Thunderer tied up somewhere as near to the Hall as you dare for me to retrieve later." He glanced across at Lucy. "Are you ready?"

Lucy gave him a smile that looked forced. "As ready as I will ever be. I dread going home. It is lovely being back on horseback though."

They trotted down the drive. Bertie let Lucy lead the way. Yes, she was perfectly comfortable riding Thunderer. The old boy still looked as if he had a fair bit of life in him. He pushed Chalice forward until he was alongside Lucy.

"Thunderer seems fit enough, doesn't he? Warner said his nephew's been keeping him exercised."

Lucy frowned. "He looks a bit familiar to me. I'm sure I've seen him in the stables recently. I wonder if Warner's nephew is the young man who's been helping Tom, our gardener?"

"The one your maid is sweet on? That would be useful if he was. I can't see anyone about. Let's give them their heads."

Lucy nodded and set Thunderer off at a canter. In no time at all they reached the back lane that led to Rugeley Hall. Bertie urged Chalice to the front as they turned onto the lane. He stood up in the stirrups.

"I still can't see anyone, let's up the pace a bit. Shout if Thunderer can't keep up with Chalice."

Bertie held Chalice to a steady canter for a few minutes then loosened the reins and let him speed up until they weren't far off a gallop. He'd checked this lane himself and it was in good, sound condition with no need to worry about rabbit holes or anything of that sort. He glanced behind. Thunderer was keeping up well. He gave Lucy a grin and let Chalice have his head. They kept up the pace until the big oak tree near to the kitchen gardens came into view. Bertie pulled up behind the big tree and Lucy soon joined him. This time the smile she gave him was genuine. The wind had brought the colour to her cheeks and her eyes sparkled. That was better. This was the Lucy he remembered.

Bertie jumped down and tied Chalice to a bush. Lucy had already taken one foot out of the stirrup. He risked leaving Thunderer untied and put his hands at her waist. He lifted her down and caught his breath as their bodies collided briefly. This definitely wasn't the young girl he thought of her as. Lucy had grown into an extraordinarily desirable young woman. He felt her stiffen and set her down quickly. She looked up at him, chewing at her bottom lip, with a wary expression in her eyes. Her attitude to him had changed since his offer to marry her if her reputation was threatened.

The old childhood camaraderie they had fallen into to begin with had started to slip. He could swear she had become more aware of him, as he had of her. His offer to marry her was what had spooked her though. If she had been any other woman, he might have thought his tactless assertion that he had as lief marry her as anyone else had annoyed her. But that wasn't it. She seemed wary to the point of being frightened of him.

"Be careful getting back into the house I'm going to wait here until I see you wave to me from your bedroom window. If you feel threatened in any way, wave a handkerchief and I'll stay put."

"Thank you so much Bertie. Don't worry, I'll be safe enough for now. I'll slip through the kitchen and up the servant stairs. Cook won't give me away."

"Take care, Lucy."

She gave him a smile and ran to the door in the wall which led to the kitchen gardens. As she reached it, she turned and gave him a wave, then disappeared inside. Thunderer whinnied and Bertie quickly caught his reins.

"Quiet now, old man." He rubbed the horse's nose and tied him up next to Chalice.

The truth was he could think of a lot worse women to marry and few, if any, better but marriage wasn't what Lucy wanted. He must be careful to hide his growing attraction to her if he was to keep her trust. He would have no hope of helping her if he lost that trust. Why was she so afraid of men? Was there more than her objectionable father behind her fears. Perhaps some bad experience with an overenthusiastic suitor?

He stiffened. Lord Parfitt hadn't violated her, had he? His hands tightened into fists as he fixed his gaze on Lucy's bedroom window. How many times had Lucy and Peter climbed down the ivy outside Lucy's window to join him on a night time adventure? He smiled at the memory. Would Lucy need to use that escape route again, perhaps with her mother in tow?

A hand waved from her window. He waved back. Lucy disappeared from view. There was no sign of anyone around. Keeping hold of Chalice's reins, he climbed onto Thunderer's back. That way anyone who saw him would assume he was a groom leading his master's horse home. They set off at a slow trot. If Parfitt had violated Lucy, he would never have been able to avoid gloating about it. Especially as marriage to Lucy appeared to be what he was after. Although it was possible the disgusting reprobate had run through his inheritance and was after her money.

Lucy had spent a lot of time with Grace Bamford since she had volunteered to help at the orphanage Grace was a patron of. Grace's radical views on women's rights were well known, which might have influenced Lucy. But it was more than that. Fear was behind Lucy's aversion to marriage. He would swear to it. Lucy's parents' marriage had never been happy. He suspected Mrs Vaughan had regularly suffered violence at her husband's hands. Could that be enough to make Lucy afraid of all men, including him if he wasn't careful?

Chalice settled down to being led better than he had expected. He urged Thunderer into a slow canter. There was a lot to do to set his plans in motion. He couldn't be fonder of Lucy if she was his sister rather than Peter's. Heaven knew he wasn't ready for marriage but, if that was the only way to save her, he could think of a lot worse fates than being married to a lovely girl like Lucy. She was the nicest person he had ever met, without being in the least bit wishy-washy. The important thing was to save her from Parfitt and any other men of his ilk her father might try and foist on her if she succeeded in scaring off Parfitt.

Back at the Castle's stables, Bertie helped Warner rub down the horses. Warner straightened up, holding his back, and studied Chalice. "A wonderful bit of horseflesh, if you don't mind me saying so, Mr Lovell."

"He is indeed. A present from my cousin, the Marquess of Hargreaves." Bertie stroked Chalice's sleek copper-coloured neck and fed him a carrot. "Chalice is from the Marquess's own stud in Ireland."

"Aye. You can tell he's quality. Brings back memories of when Mr Mayford was young. Loved his horses he did." Warner sighed and handed Bertie another carrot.

Bertie breathed deeply. This was his opportunity. He was fond of Warner, after all he had put him on his first pony and taught him to ride. His best approach was to tackle the problem of the nephew first, leaving Warner free to make his own decision about retirement.

"I plan to make Mayford Castle my main residence. There are bound to be quite a few vacancies for staff. What sort of position is your nephew looking for?"

"I don't rightly know." Warner scratched his head. "He's a clever lad and well educated. He's down at the Squire's today, tutoring his youngest boy before he goes to school. Our Arthur is good with horses but I think he wants something more. He's a good lad though. Been taking any work he can get."

Warner stared at the floor. I hope you don't mind me letting him ride Thunderer? The horse needs exercise and it's meant Arthur can fit in more work."

"I have no objection at all. Arthur certainly sounds like a young man who will do well."

"Aye. I hope so. I thought he might be up to my job here but I think the lad has ambitions to better himself. His father was from a gentry family." Warner watched him from under bushy brows.

Bertie smiled. "I'll do what I can for him, Warner. I have one or two ideas. What about yourself? A friend is sending me some trained grooms. I'm hoping you will agree to stay here, at least part time, to see them properly trained up to Uncle Ambrose's standard. I intend to keep a large stable."

A slightly built young man came into the stables. He gave Bertie a friendly smile and extended his hand.

"How do you do. You must be Mr Lovell. I'm Arthur Reid."

Bertie smiled back and took the extended hand. "I'm very happy to meet you, Arthur. You and I need to have a chat about what sort of permanent employment you're looking for but first I need your help with a rather difficult and sensitive matter. Could you come up to the house in say half an hour?"

"Of course, Mr Lovell. I'll go and get cleaned up. I've been busy doing some gardening this afternoon."

Bertie watched him go. With his slight frame and long, wavy hair he looked much younger than twenty. "Now where were we?"

"We were talking about my future here." Warner eyed him warily.

Bertie sighed, he still had no idea whether Warner wanted to retire or not. There was no way to avoid asking him outright.

"I understand that several of the older staff have decided to take up Uncle Ambrose's retirement offer. What I'm trying to ask you is how do you feel about your own retirement? Would you prefer to retire now, to stay working full-time, or would you be prepared to stay on part-time, settling in the new staff and then be happy to retire?"

Warner stayed silent for several minutes. Had he offended him?

A slow smile spread across the old man's face. "I'd like to retire once I've seen Arthur settled, or at least I will be used to the idea by then. I'll be very happy to help with the new staff first." Warner's smile became a grin. "I'm curious to see what your stable will be like when you have it all set up. But my old back is past doing too much work these days."

"Thank you, Warner. My new steward will be arriving soon. He can sort out the details of your retirement cottage and stipend. In the meantime, I'll pay you full wages even when you reduce your hours. Now, I'd had better get up to the house and have that chat with Arthur."

Arthur appeared in the kitchen, neatly scrubbed and wearing fresh clothes, a few minutes early.

"Come and sit down. This is the warmest place in the house at the moment." Bertie nodded at a flagon of ale. "Would you like some?"

Arthur nodded. "Yes please."

Bertie poured out the drinks and they both sat at the table nearest to the fire. "It's cold for the time of year. First things first. What is your daily rate of pay? I need your services for at least a few days."

"I don't rightly know, Sir. Whatever you think is reasonable." Arthur hesitated. "I would feel bad about leaving Tom, the gardener at the Hall in the lurch, but apart from that I'm free now. I finished my coaching sessions with the Squire's youngest boy today."

"I'm happy for you to carry on working at Rugeley Hall for now. Do you know anything about the situation between Miss Vaughan and her father? I would appreciate you keeping all this to yourself."

Arthur nodded vigorously. "I won't breathe a word of anything you tell me, Sir."

"Good. It's absolutely essential that her father doesn't get wind of the fact that I've agreed to help her. As far as I know, he's not aware that I'm even in the district. I'm hoping it will stay like that for a while."

"Miss Vaughan's father trying to marry her off is the talk of all the servants. She's very popular even though she hasn't been home for some time. They're all up in arms at the man her father has picked for her. I'm sure they'll do anything they can to help."

"Good. The fewer people who know of our plans the better, but having servants happy to see nothing might prove useful. A friend's steward is arriving soon, but I'm not sure when, bringing some grooms he's trained. There will be some horses he has picked out for me. The idea was that he would help me select any more horses I need." Bertie's scratched his chin. "I don't suppose you know of anywhere local with horses to sell in case I need some quickly?"

Arthur's eyes widened. "I do as it happens, but they're nowhere near the standard of the horse you brought with you."

"That's all to the good. I need some sturdy animals that won't stand out like Chalice would. People turn around to look at him. I need to merge into the background. How far away are these horses? "

"In the next village. I've been getting some work helping the vicar there write his sermons. He told me about a gentleman farmer who breeds decent horses as a side line." Arthur blushed. "I felt guilty about riding Thunderer without your permission."

"So, you thought about buying a horse of your own?"

Arthur nodded. "Yes. I had a look at them. He has some quite decent horses for sale. Uncle said he would check with you but was sure you wouldn't mind me riding Thunderer because he needed exercising. I left it for now."

"I don't mind at all. I'm grateful to you for keeping Thunderer fit. How far away is this farm? I brought some money with me if the horses for sale are suitable. Did they tell you what prices they were looking for? "

"All different prices but very reasonable. We could walk to the farm in less than half an hour if you don't want Chalice to be noticed."

Arthur gave him a questioning look. He seemed trustworthy and intelligent.

Bertie gave a satisfied nod. "Good point. Let's go as soon as we've eaten. I need to be back here by half past four at the latest. Two hours or so should be time enough. I might need horses sooner rather than later. I hope the farmer is around and doesn't mind people turning up without an appointment."

"I'm sure he'll be delighted. I did say I might be back and he said to call any time I was in the district."

"If he's in we may solve my problem." Bertie grimaced. "I know Lord Parfitt, the man who has thrown Miss Vaughan into a spin by his arrival. He's a nasty individual and I don't trust him." He sniffed. "By the smell of it the pie Cook has in the oven should be ready soon. Excellent. I'm hoping to buy at least four horses. We can ride one and lead one each if I'm lucky enough to get them.

"Are you planning to spirit Miss Vaughan and her mother away?"

"If that's the only option. Mrs Vaughan is waiting to hear from her sister, but don't repeat that to anyone, not even to Miss Vaughan's maid."

Arthur blushed a vivid scarlet." I'm sure she wouldn't say anything, but I will respect your confidence of course."

The door opened and Cook bustled in. "The pie should be ready now, Mr Lovell."

"Good." Bertie's stomach growled and he rubbed his hands together. Mr Reid will be sharing it with me."

CHAPTER SIX

Lucy's feet dragged as she walked through the kitchen gardens towards what had once been her home. A knot of tension settled in the pit of her stomach. It was reassuring to have Bertie nearby but just the thought of being in the same house as Lord Parfitt was enough to give any girl a fit of the vapours. Dinner would be another four hours yet. With luck Parfitt would have gone back to wherever he was staying to get changed. She stopped at the gate into the formal gardens, heart thumping.

There was no sign of anyone. She slipped through the gate and ran, head down, around to the kitchen door, taking care to keep her hood covering her blonde hair. If anyone saw her in this old cloak, hopefully, they would think she was one of the maids. She reached the kitchen door without incident and blushed as she remembered how she had cannoned into poor Bertie at Mayford Castle. He would have a good bruise where she had kicked him on the shin.

One of the maids looked up as she walked into the kitchen. Lucy shook her head slightly and put a finger to her lips. The maid nodded and carried on with what she was doing. Fortunately, there was a servant staircase directly off the servant's quarters that came out right by her bedroom door.

Once she reached it, she ran up the stairs as fast as she could go. She put her ear to the door at the top of the staircase for several minutes before she plucked up the courage to pull it open and run to her own room. She jumped in alarm when someone stood up from the chair near the window, then let out a relieved breath as she realised it was her mother.

Mama walked towards her and caught her hands, rubbing them between her own. Her face full of concern. "You feel cold. I'm glad to see you. I was afraid Lord Parfitt had spirited you away."

"I just about managed to avoid him this morning when he arrived. I tell you now, there is no way I will marry Lord Parfitt."

Mama locked the door and led her to the sofa with an arm around her shoulders. "I know that my darling. There is no way I will let that happen. I have news." Mama frowned. "Aunt Susan is hiding out with friends a few miles away, but it could be days before your Uncle James arrives. Susan on her own might not be enough to protect you from your father. If we go and stay with Susan there is a fair chance your father will find us."

Mama stood up and walked up and down in front of the fire, wringing her hands. "I'm not sure what to do for the best." Her voice trembled.

"I have news too. I took shelter from the storm at Mayford Castle and Bertie Lovell now owns it and has moved in. He's offered to help." Despite the tears that threatened, Lucy couldn't help but smile. "Even if he has to carry me off on his charger to safety. And I must say his new horse, Chalice, is a magnificent animal. From the Irish stud of the Marquess of Hargreaves no less."

"So, Bertie is here." Mama gave a smile. "Do you think he was serious?"

Lucy nodded. "Yes, he insisted he would help me to escape if that is the only way to stop Papa marrying me off."

Mama sat down, with her head in her hands. "Maybe that will serve. He was always a resourceful boy. I don't care what happens to me as long as you escape."

"Bertie's going to wait by that big old oak tree near to the gardens at five o'clock so I can tell him what's happening." Lucy shivered. "Where is Papa and where is Lord Parfitt now?"

"Lord Parfitt rode off about an hour ago in a raging temper. I believe he has a special licence in his pocket. Papa has assured him you will be here to meet him at dinner tonight."

Lucy threw herself onto the bed and lay back with a hand covering her eyes. This was worse than she had hoped. Perhaps Papa had realised that there was no point trying to persuade her. She sat up and propped herself against her pillows.

"He's going to try and drag me off tonight, isn't he?"

Mama stood and paced around the room. Her pallor did nothing to reassure Lucy.

"I very much fear so. I sent Susan a message asking her to come for dinner as soon as he said about Parfitt coming to dinner. I'm not sure the message got through. I haven't seen that footman since. I do hope your father hasn't lashed out at him."

"How far away is Aunt Susan?"

"She is staying with the Smart family. I think they are about three or four miles away at least."

"Assuming the footman went on foot, which he must've done since the only riding horse we have now is Papa's, he may not even have reached Aunt Susan yet. It's likely to take at least a couple of hours for her to get here. Papa won't know that I'm back yet. What time is it now?"

Her mother shook her head. "It's past two o'clock, but your father was in such a rage I told him you were back and lying on your bed with a headache. He believed me I think."

Lucy hugged her knees. "I wish I could be sure that he does believe that. Where is Emma? She might have managed to find out a bit more about what Papa is up to."

"She's down in the kitchens supposedly asking Cook to make a tisane for your headache."

"One of the kitchen maids saw me creep in. She's bound to tell Emma I'm back."

Mama lowered her voice. "I hope neither of them say anything to my maid. I have a feeling your father is paying her to spy on me."

Lucy gasped. "But Marie has been with you for years."

"I know, but most people can be bought. I've said nothing to any of the servants and especially not Marie."

"We can't take her then whatever happens. I'm confident that Emma is loyal to me and all the kitchen staff if it comes to that."

"I hope you're right. We need to do something quickly."

"Bertie should be at the oak tree in less than three hours." Lucy chewed at her lip. "He'll have his horse and I think he may bring a spare. I have a feeling he knows more about Lord Parfitt than he wanted to tell me and none of it good. He was disgusted when he found out he was the man Papa expects me to marry."

"Parfitt does have an unsavoury reputation." Mama grimaced and wouldn't meet her eye.

"We would have to leave Emma behind as well as Marie if we go with Bertie tonight. Emma has family nearby she could escape to. Bertie's horse could carry both him and me I think, leaving the other horse for you. Then we can ride over to where Aunt Susan is hiding."

Mama shook her head. "There are several things wrong with that. Your father is bound to seek me out before dinner. We would be likely to miss Aunt Susan if she has got the message about coming here for dinner. Our best plan is for me to try and hold things up to give you more time and wait for Aunt Susan to arrive. Your father's afraid of Uncle James. I don't think he would do anything too severe to me in front of Aunt Susan. It's a pity James isn't here but he's had to stay in London on affairs of state. It could be days before he gets here and I agree with you." Mama hesitated, wild eyed. "Papa intends to give you to Lord Parfitt tonight."

"I've never seen Papa so volatile." Tears welled up in Lucy's eyes. "I'm not convinced you'd be safe."

"If we both try and escape our chances are really low. If you go with Bertie and take Emma, if you can, you should be all right. Bertie has powerful family behind him. I'm sure he'd be able to find somewhere safe for you."

Mama stared at the floor and refused to meet Lucy's eyes. Surely Mama knew that Bertie would probably end up having to marry her, which wasn't what either of them wanted. A flash of heat flooded through her. But if he involved the Marquess of Hargreaves or even, possibly more likely, took her to London and sought help from the Cathlays it was a fate he wouldn't be able to avoid.

"You know as well as I do that if I escape with Bertie, even if I manage to take Emma with me, he will see me as compromised and feel obliged to marry me." Lucy couldn't keep the tremor out of her voice.

Mama sat on the bed next to her and took her hand. "It is a possibility, but you and Bertie were such good friends. I think you would be happy together."

Lucy pulled her hand away. "I've seen the way Papa has treated you over the years. I never ever want to get married to any man, even Bertie. I just couldn't do it and it wouldn't only be me who was compromised. I know Bertie has been really wild in recent years, but he's a good man at heart. I think it was his way of rebelling against that awful mother of his. I can't bear the thought of his name being blackened if any of this got out. Especially now, when he has the chance of a fresh start at Mayford Castle. He's respected in this area and if people thought he'd taken advantage of me he'd lose that. It's not fair to put him in that situation."

"Lucy, you have a stark choice. Either accept Bertie's help and risk putting him in a difficult position or face the likelihood of Lord Parfitt abducting you and marrying you forcibly. From what I know of him he is perfectly capable of that. Bertie is much too fond of you to want that to happen."

There was a knock at the door.

"Is that you, Emma?" Lucy said in a voice so strained that the story of her being incapacitated with a headache would be easy to believe.

"Yes, Miss."

"Wait a moment, the door's locked." Lucy climbed off the bed and ran across to the door. She almost pulled Emma inside and then slammed the door shut and locked it.

Emma nodded at the tray she was carrying. "Cook swears by this for headaches, you might as well drink it. If you haven't got a headache now you soon will have. Word is that your father is absolutely furious with you. That man who came, Lord Parfitt, was ranting and raving at him for quite a while before he went." Emma shook her head and smiled. "He would have been funny if this wasn't so serious."

Lucy flopped back down onto the bed. Emma sounded worried. "That's much as we feared. Do you agree with Mama that something is afoot today?" Her throat was so tight her voice came out as a whisper.

Emma put the tray onto a side table by the bed and frowned. "Yes, I do. Lord Parfitt is a dreadful man. You don't want to marry him. He assaulted one of the maids on his way out. Fortunately, the housekeeper was around and managed to rescue her. What are you going to do?"

"We can't quite decide. I know this won't go any farther. Particularly not to Marie. Bertie Lovell is in residence at Mayford Castle. He has offered to help and he's planning to be at that big oak tree near the kitchen gardens at five o'clock to make sure I'm safe."

Lucy gave a grim smile and looked across at her mother. "I've decided you're right. I'm going to have to accept Bertie's help. How are we going to escape the house without being seen? With Papa being in such a taking he'll have servants looking for me."

Mama sat down on the bed next to Lucy and took one of her hands. "Are you sure that Bertie will come mounted?"

"Perhaps not. His new horse is outstanding, the sort of animal that people would notice. He may decide to walk across."

Mama rubbed her brow. "I wish I knew where Susan was and if she got my message. Emma, can you ride?"

"Oh yes Mrs Vaughan. I can drive a pony and trap too."

Mama shook her head. "I managed to get the footman to check for me and the only horse in the stable is Mr Vaughan's mount. There is no carriage, not even his curricle, apart from the decrepit coach you had to travel here in. The footman said they used hired horses all the way to get to London. Mr Vaughan must have lost everything.

"Lucy, you must go with Bertie and take Emma if you can. There are some old clothes of Peter's that I left with the housekeeper. You won't be able to take bags with you. I suggest you both wear a pair of Peter's breeches under your skirts and put on warm cloaks." She pulled out a fat purse. "I've been saving up for something like this. There should be enough money to pay for a journey to London or wherever Mr Lovell thinks is best."

Lucy's heart raced. Until today she had hoped to reason with Papa but now the necessity of flight was all too real. She squared her shoulders. "You don't have to come with me if you don't want to, Emma. I think it might be your safest option though."

Emma's eyes gleamed. "Oh, I wouldn't miss it for the world, Miss Vaughan. I've been longing for some adventure."

"In that case you had better see the housekeeper for what you need, but not until we're nearly ready to go."

"I know what you mean, Miss. I'm not surprised you said that about Marie. Some of the other servants might be suspect too, but I'm sure the housekeeper and all the kitchen staff will keep their heads down and say nothing."

Mama smiled. "I can see you are a sensible girl, Emma. Once Lucy is safe, I'll make sure you are well provided for. Unless of course Lucy is in a position to offer you employment herself.

Whatever happens, you will receive a reward over and above your normal wages."

Emma blushed. "I don't need a reward. I couldn't bear to see Miss Vaughan anywhere near that horrible man, let alone married to him. I'm not sure about moving to a different part of the country permanently though." Her blush deepened. "I have a bit of an understanding with the young man who works in the garden sometimes. His mother has died and he's living with his uncle."

"We'll have to see what happens. It might be difficult to keep in touch with your young man."

"Don't worry about that, Mrs Vaughan. We'll write to each other. He's a clever young man is my Arthur and he means to better himself. Once he's got a job that pays enough to support a family, we're going to get married."

A broad smile lit up Emma's face. Lucy envied her certainty that she could be happy spending her life with a man. Perhaps her parents had been happily married. She pulled her thoughts back to the present.

"I think we're all going to have to go and meet Bertie later. It's lucky my bedroom is at the back of the house. If we climb down the ivy, we should be able to escape without being seen. The only difficult bit is staying out of view until you get to the kitchen gardens."

Mama shook her head. "My climbing days are over. I've already told you to forget me. I'll stay here to distract your father and wait for Aunt Susan to rescue me."

Lucy tried to argue.

"No, Lucy. My mind is made up. You'll have a much better chance of escape without me."

Emma coughed. "Why don't we leave the decision until

the last moment? I've never seen the master in such a foul temper as this. I'm not sure you would be safe staying here with Miss Vaughan gone. I wouldn't be surprised if he lashed out at you." She looked down at the floor. "Not that it is my place to criticise my betters."

Mama gave a hollow laugh. "You're worth a dozen of my husband, my dear." She glanced across at Lucy. "Emma's right. I would suggest you and Emma went now, but I wouldn't put it past your father to force his way in here to check up on you."

"Do be careful, Mama."

"Don't worry about me. I'll go back to my room and keep Marie busy, finding outfits for tonight. My room is at the front of the house. I'll keep a look out for Aunt Susan."

Lucy watched her mother hurry out of the room. "If I know Bertie, he'll be at least a few minutes early arriving at the oak tree. Why don't you take my best blue evening gown downstairs to press? It will give you an excuse to be going to the kitchens and you can ask the housekeeper for the clothes Mama mentioned. I'll lock the door behind you."

"Yes, Miss Vaughan. When I come back I'll knock three times. If I were you, I would try and rest for an hour. Let me help you out of those clothes and in to a nightshift. Then if your father does insist on seeing you there will be nothing to make him suspicious."

Lucy allowed herself to be undressed in a dreamlike state. All this worry and fear was wearing. As soon as she was ready the two of them walked to the door. They waited in silence for a few moments listening. Eventually, Lucy nodded and opened the door. She poked her head out. There was no one in the corridor. She signalled to Emma who disappeared through it. Lucy watched until Emma reached the door to the servants' stairs. She pulled her door shut with a satisfying thud and turned the key in the lock.

Lord, she was tired. The bed did look alluring. She climbed in and the next thing she heard was a considerable commotion downstairs. Three knocks sounded at the door. Lucy rushed over to open it and Emma tumbled inside. This time it was Emma who shut the door with a bang and turned the lock.

"There's a coach coming up the drive that looks like your aunt's travelling carriage. Mr Vaughan has seen it and he's shouting at your mother something awful," Emma said as soon as the door was locked. She started shaking. "He's red in the face and using language I've never heard before."

"Quick. Help me get into an old day dress. Something comfortable I'd wear if I was poorly. I'm going down. I can't bear the thought of what he might do to Mama."

"If you're sure, Miss." Emma ran to her closet and pulled out one of Lucy's favourite day dresses.

Within a matter of minutes Lucy ran down the servants' stairs, closely followed by Emma. Whatever Mama had said, she couldn't bear the thought of her mother being attacked. Too often as a child she had looked at her mother's bruises, which she'd hidden as best she could, and tried not to say anything. She opened the door at the bottom a crack and peered into the hall. The front door was open wide enough for her to see a single horse being led away by a groom. Drake hesitated by the door with his mouth open, seemingly not sure what to do.

Emma tapped her shoulder and whispered in her ear. "The carriage hasn't got here yet. That looks like Lord Parfitt's horse being led away."

Drake wasn't looking their way and he was one of the servants they could trust. She stepped out into the hallway. Emma was right. The coach approaching was Aunt Susan's. There was no sign of anyone else but the door of the library was slightly ajar and the sound of raised voices reverberated around the hall. Father was shouting and Mama's voice, pleading with him, filled the gaps when he stopped to draw breath. Lord, it sounded bad. Where was Lord Parfitt or whoever had arrived on horseback? Drake was still staring through the open front door as if mesmerized. Lucy crept across the corridor and stood next to the library door, signalling to Emma to stay where she was.

Father's voice roared out as if he was in pain. "I told you to stay out of this, Madam. Defy me by inviting that harridan of a sister of yours, would you? I don't believe for a moment that your sister is calling on us by chance. You'll pay for this. It's high time Lucy was married. I find her a perfectly good suitor, something you've failed to do in five years of living in London racking up huge bills, and you complain."

Lucy struggled to hold back a gasp as Papa raised a fist. Emma had ignored her instruction to stay behind the servants' door and put a hand on her shoulder, holding her back. Before Lucy could react, a man stepped out of the shadows and stood in front of Mama. His face wasn't visible. He could be Lord Parfitt from his build.

"Hold on there, man." Definitely Lord Parfitt. "I want a bride with good standing in society. Lord and Lady Hampton are good Ton. Lucy would be far less valuable to me if she is at outs with her aunt and uncle. If you understand me." His voice dripped sarcasm.

"What? Of course, I do." Papa slapped Lord Parfitt on the

back. "I'm angry at my wife questioning my decisions. That's all. Take my advice, make sure you stamp out that sort of nonsense right at the beginning."

Lucy took a step back as if she'd been slapped. As she'd thought, her own father was selling her off to the highest bidder. Parfitt was rich by all accounts but not well thought of in Ton circles. She sniffed. It was bad enough thinking Parfitt wanted her for herself, now it seemed all he wanted was her social connections. At least he might save Mama from a beating.

"Have no fears on that score, I fully intend to." Lord Parfitt's characteristic sneering tone sent a shiver down Lucy's spine. "I suggest you go and greet Lord and Lady Hampton and invite them to stay for dinner."

"As you wish, my lord." Papa lowered his voice so much that Lucy had to strain to hear him. "Hampton normally rides, I can only see a carriage. Lady Hampton is probably on her own. What about our plans for later?"

"Oh, for heaven's sake, Vaughan, stop fussing. I'm a patient man but you're trying my patience sorely. There will be time to sort that out later. Don't keep her ladyship waiting."

Emma pulled her into the shadows just in time as her father stormed out of the library and marched to the front door. Mama followed looking pale but unharmed. Emma and Lucy flitted across the hallway and back behind the sanctuary of the servants' door. Lucy held her breath for several moments but no one seem to have noticed them. She kept the door open wide enough to watch the hall. Father bawled out an order for footmen. One came running past Lucy and Emma and only just avoided a collision. He grinned at them as he ran out into the hall and stopped in front of Papa.

Papa's face became redder still. He jabbed a finger towards the footman "Where's the other one?"

"I don't rightly know, Mr Vaughan. I expect he's in another part of the house and didn't hear."

Papa stomped across to a bell pull and tugged it hard. "I don't pay you men to be in the wrong part of the house when I need you."

Mama's hands fluttered towards her mouth. If the missing footman was in Aunt Susan's carriage, he had better be careful not to be seen or Mama would be in even more trouble. The sound of wheels scrunching on gravel reached them and the coach pulled up. Mama rushed forward. Papa put a hand on her shoulder and pulled her back to stand by him. A footman in Aunt Susan's livery jumped down from the back of the coach and ran round to open the door for her. Mama slumped at the same moment as the hand was removed from her shoulder. She toppled to one side but managed to stay on her feet.

Aunt Susan took the footman's hand and climbed down from the carriage wreathed in smiles. "I'm staying with Lord and Lady Smart for a few days. I thought I'd surprise you with a visit."

Mama rushed forward and took one of her sister's hands. "How lovely to see you, Susan. A wonderful surprise."

Papa stepped forwards. He bowed and gave Aunt Susan a smile that look more like a grimace. "Yes, what a lovely surprise Susan. Why don't you stay for dinner?"

Aunt Susan gave him a considering look. "That would be delightful." She linked arms with Mama. "Let's go to your drawing room? Then we can have a cosy chat over a cup of tea." Aunt Susan swept into the house taking Mama with her, past a furious Papa who looked as if he was about to say something.

Lord Parfitt appeared in the doorway.

Papa caught up with Aunt Susan. “Allow me to introduce Lord Parfitt who is dining with us this evening, Susan.”

Aunt Susan flapped a hand in Parfitt’s direction. “No need to introduce us. We’ve met before in London.”

Lord Parfitt swept her a deep bow and gave an ingratiating smile. Heavens, Parfitt really did want to toady up to Aunt Susan. Perhaps he had annoyed a few too many people in London and was hoping to force his way back into polite society. He was the sort of person people ducked behind pillars to avoid, from what she’d seen of him in London.

CHAPTER SEVEN

Bertie enjoyed the walk to the farm selling horses, which lay just beyond the Mayford Estates at its shortest boundary. Arthur seemed a modest young man and Bertie spent the walk drawing him out.

"If you had a free choice of employment, what would you choose?"

Arthur walked on in silence for a few moments. "My father was the estate manager for a distant relative. I enjoy being outdoors and I think something like that might suit me." Arthur gave him a shy smile. "I would need some training before I could aspire to that sort of position. I'm ready to take on anything that's offered and try and work my way up. I still have some money left from Mama's savings. Father was a careful man and always put some aside."

Bertie nodded. "I was sorry to hear about your mother. I understand you nursed her for some time."

"Yes, I did. One day I was a carefree boy of fourteen then the next my father was killed in a riding accident. Mama was determined for me to have an education and we lived on her savings quite comfortably. There was enough to pay the local vicar to tutor me. He was going to try and find me work as a tutor, for families with boys to educate at home before going on to school, once I was older. Then, when I was sixteen, Mama took ill and I wasn't able to take on outside work. The vicar insisted on carrying on my education for free, bless him."

Bertie was quiet for a while. Then he smiled at Arthur. "I've always liked your uncle, a straightforward, honest sort of man. He gave my godfather very good service. I believe you are of a similar ilk. I'm determined to find you suitable employment, if not with me then with friends. My new agent should be arriving any day. I'll ask him if he would take you on as an assistant. I'm not making any promises as I don't know his circumstances. He may have sons or nephews that he's hoping to advance."

Arthur grinned at him. "I'm happy to do anything for now. If I'm lucky enough for the agent to take me on that would suit me very well. I've got an understanding with Emma, Miss Vaughan's lady's maid. We have a lot in common. She lost her father when she was young and her mother is living with an aunt not far away from Mayford Castle."

Bertie narrowed his eyes as a smile played around Arthur's mouth when he mentioned Lucy. It seemed Mrs Hobbs wasn't the only person mentally pairing him and Lucy off. They were likely to be disappointed.

"I doubt if Miss Vaughan will ever want to go back to Rugeley Hall. Although, I suppose the family link might make it easier for you to keep in touch with Emma."

"We'll be able to write. Her father was a vicar but it wasn't a very lucrative living and they had little in the way of savings. Emma's aunt took them in when he died."

Bertie was silent for a while as they marched along the narrow country lane. "It seems very harsh for Emma's mother to be turned off without some sort of provision made for her when her husband died. There's so much I don't know about being a landowner. Remind me to find out what livings I have responsibility for."

"Of course, Sir."

"I've had an idea. You're smaller than me. There are plenty of my old clothes at the Castle. There should be some to fit you. We'll be two friends travelling as two grooms. Once we've spoken to this farmer, you'll have to practice calling me Bertie."

"Don't the gentry call each other by their surnames?"

"Very often but all my close friends call me Bertie. We'll have to think up a history of how we met and your background, in case we meet anyone who knows me on our travels."

Arthur frowned. "You're convinced Miss Vaughan will have to flee then."

"I'm afraid so. Lord Parfitt is a reprobate and a scoundrel. I don't trust him to play fair and I don't want him anywhere near to Lucy." Bertie scowled at the thought. "How much farther have we got to go?"

"Not much more than ten minutes. When we climb that stile coming up," Arthur pointed further down the lane to a stile barely visible behind the thick hedge that ran along its length, "we might be able to see the horses, depending on which field they're in."

Bertie took a deep breath and followed Arthur over the stile. A lot was resting on this. They would be in trouble if they couldn't get some decent horses. If the horses were too good, would he have enough money? Arthur tapped his shoulder and pointed.

"We're in luck, the horses in this field look like the ones he had for sale. There's a couple not here, let's hope none of these are taken."

Some of the horses moved towards them. Bertie eyed them cautiously. "Are any of them likely to turn vicious do you think from memory?"

"Not that I remember. That grey mare at the back was a sweet horse. Very good natured." Arthur glanced at Bertie. "She would make a good lady's horse. Although she looks sturdy enough to carry a fair weight."

Bertie approached the horses slowly. A bay horse came towards him but the others trotted off. He patted the horse's neck.

"Hello boy, you look a strong animal. He ran his hands over the horse's flank. He stood quietly and allowed Bertie to run a hand over his legs. His coat was a bit thick but he looked healthy and well kept. The horse snorted and cantered off. "He's got a good action. They need a bit of work but they're perfect for what we want and will make good hacks later on. I wonder how much the farmer wants for them."

"I liked the grey mare the best and she was the most expensive. How much money have you got available?"

"Three hundred guineas of the money I brought with me. My next job was to arrange banking facilities in Stafford."

"You should have enough for all five of them with a bit to spare." Arthur went pink. "I do know Mrs Hobbs has the key to the estate strongbox. I've done a few small jobs around the house and she's paid me straightaway."

"Of course, why didn't I think of the strongbox? Let's hope there's plenty there. I wish I knew when the new agent was arriving. He could sort out the banking facilities. My man of business in London has written to the bank to make the arrangements." Bertie took one last look at the horses. "We had better move on to see the farmer. We don't want somebody thinking we are here to steal them. Did you have a chance to check their ages?"

"The farmer said they were all around four or five years old. I checked the teeth of all of them and I think that's about right."

"Good young horses then. That grey looks well bred. I'll see what we can get them for. I might have to leave that one behind in case there's not much money in the strongbox."

Arthur looked disappointed but said nothing. They strode across the field and over another stile.

Arthur pointed ahead. "That's the farmhouse but I think I can see the farmer in this next field. Yes, that's him." He raised a hand and a stocky individual looked up and waved back.

The farmer joined them and Arthur smiled at him. "Are all the horses in the field we've just walked through still for sale?"

"They are that. I've sold the other two but these are some good animals." The farmer eyed Bertie with interest. "Mr Lovell, is it?"

"Yes, I'm pleased to meet you." Bertie held out a hand and the farmer grasped it.

"Bert Eldridge."

Bertie laughed. "We have the same first name in common then, Mr Eldridge. Arthur here is working for me now. I'm going to make Mayford Castle my main home and intend to keep a large stable. A friend of mine is bringing up some horses for me but I need a few hacks for various members of the staff including Arthur. They all look good sturdy horses from what I can see. I haven't a great deal of time as I may have to go to London in the next few days on business. What price would you give me if I took all five off your hands?"

Mr Eldridge pulled at his ear. He glanced across at Bertie meeting his gaze. "They're all good young horses. As I told your man all around four or five years old."

Bertie waited patiently hiding a smile. They were good horses but it sounded as if business was fairly slow. The grey was probably worth as much as a hundred pounds and the others perhaps forty pounds or so each.

Mr Eldridge broke the silence. "How would three hundred and fifty pounds suit you for all five?" He gave Bertie a hopeful look.

Bertie pursed his lips. An opening gambit but it wasn't far off a fair price. Uncle Ambrose had always been generous with money, there would be something in the strongbox, assuming the lawyers who handled the transfer of the estate had kept Mrs Hobbs supplied with adequate funds to keep the household running smoothly. The farmer shifted from foot to foot. That looked promising and he needed the horses.

"How about three hundred pounds and you throw in a couple of old saddles and three leading reins?"

Mr Eldridge shook his head. "You're a hard man Mr Lovell but I've got some more horses coming to work on soon. I'll take your offer. They will be old saddles though." He raised his eyebrows and held out his hand.

Bertie took the hand in a firm grip and shook it. "There are plenty of saddles back at Mayford Castle but only two horses in them. They've already been ridden today and we couldn't carry anything as big as saddles. All we need is something good enough to get us back home."

"Fair enough, Mr Lovell." Mr Eldridge turned away but not before Bertie saw him grin. He pointed towards the horses.

"The chestnut and the bay horse are the most placid. You should have no trouble leading those two together."

With the deal clinched they were soon on their way. Even leading three horses it was a much quicker journey back to Mayford Castle than walking. None of the horses was excitable, although the grey mare had a tendency to shy at any sudden noises. Mrs Hobbs was down in the stables with Warner when they rode up to the Mayford Castle stables.

"Ah, there you are, Mr Lovell. I was hoping you'd be back soon. I've left a messenger being fed by Cook in the kitchen. He's from your new agent, Mr Roskelley. Mr Roskelley is staying overnight with friends not that far away. He said to expect him around the middle of the day tomorrow."

Warner took the horse he was leading from him and Bertie jumped down from his horse.

"That's bad timing, Mrs Hobbs. I'll have a think about what's best to do."

"What do you want me to say to the messenger, Mr Lovell?"

"Well, Mr Roskelley is going to have to come tomorrow, so just say we look forward to seeing him but I might be away."

"Thank you, Mr Lovell. I'll go straight back."

Bertie patted the neck of the horse he had ridden. "I might've paid just a little bit more than they were worth but I think these are some quite good animals. What do you think Warner?"

Warner tied up the bay horse Bertie had been leading and came back to collect the chestnut. "These two need a bit of tidying up but they're decent animals. Probably worth between forty and fifty pounds each I would say."

Bertie grinned. That was better than he'd thought. He took the grey mare from Arthur. "What about this one?"

"Now that is a nice little mare." He ran a hand over her. Pretty and she looks quite sturdy. Better bred than the others too. It's a while since I bought any horses but I'd say she was worth at least a hundred pounds."

Warner looked at him expectantly and Bertie grinned.

"The farmer had some more horses arriving and he accepted three hundred pounds for the lot. He even let us have a couple of old saddles but I can't say they were very comfortable. They got us home though."

"A fair price, Mr Lovell. I wonder when all these grooms are going to arrive."

"I do as well. I would much prefer them coming tomorrow rather than the new agent." Bertie scratched his head. "I'll have to think up a plan. I might have to leave Mr Roskelley to you."

"I've no objection Mr Lovell, but my riding days are over when it comes to showing him around."

"I know. Well, there's nothing like having to get used to something quickly is there. My London man of business found Mr Roskelley. If he's of the calibre I've been promised he should be able to cope, but it's not ideal."

"Don't worry Mr Lovell, I'll tell him about all the tenants. We may be able to get a boy from the village to show him around." Warner turned his attention to the two horses Arthur was holding. "They do look a good lot, Mr Lovell. Any idea how old they are?"

"I'd already looked them over, Uncle," Arthur said. "Mr Eldridge told me they were around four or five years old and I'm pretty sure that's accurate."

Warner nodded at Bertie. "You struck a good deal, Mr Lovell. Your uncle trained you well."

Bertie laughed. "It was a case of having to strike a tough bargain. I might have got them cheaper but I needed them if I'm going to rescue Miss Vaughan and the man has to make a profit."

"That's true enough. Your uncle didn't let himself be cheated but he was careful not to underpay. You're very like him."

"I'd like to think so, even though we weren't blood relations." In truth he dreaded to think how he would have turned out without Uncle Ambrose's influence.

"I hope you rescue Miss Vaughan. A lovely young lady." Warner smiled and looked away.

"So do I!" Lord not another one trying to marry him off to Lucy. "I had better get on. I'll speak to you later."

"I'll stay and give you a hand rubbing these horses down, Uncle," Arthur said. "If that's all right with you, Mr Lovell?"

"Of course, it is. I'm not sure how he's going to manage on his own until these grooms turn up. When you finish come up to the library. I think it's more than likely that we will have to set off on our journey before Mr Roskelley arrives." Bertie looked at his pocket watch. "We've got about an hour before we need to set off for Rugeley Hall."

Bertie ran up to the house and went in through the kitchen door. Mrs Hobbs was talking to the messenger, a young lad who looked like he might be a farmer's son. Bertie nodded to him.

"I'm sorry I don't have time to write a message, but tell Mr Roskelley I'm looking forward to working with him. I have to go to London on business soon. It may be tomorrow but I'll make arrangements for someone to be around to greet him if so." Bertie reached in his pocket and handed the messenger a crown.

"Thank you, Mr Lovell. I'll be sure to pass the message on. Thank you for the refreshments, Mrs Hobbs. I'll be on my way now."

Bertie watched him go. A well-spoken boy. Probably the son of Roskelley's friends. Roskelley must know the area, which would make it easier for him to find his stride.

"Mrs Hobbs, I may have to go on a long journey soon to escort Miss Vaughan to safety, possibly as early as tonight. I spent most of the money I had left on the horses I've just bought. I never thought to check what was in the estate's strong box."

"There's several hundred pounds in there, Mr Lovell."

"That's good. Mr Roskelley will be able to arrange banking facilities but that may take a few days. Set aside what you think you will need for the next week or two, plus a bit extra. I'll take whatever's left with me."

"Of course, Mr Lovell. I'll go fetch the key and bring the box to you." Mrs Hobb's voice was full of concern. "Where will you be?"

"In the library. I'm going spend a few minutes going through the estate books, just in case I'm here tomorrow when Mr Roskelley arrives. I don't want him to think I'm not interested."

Mrs Hobbs frowned at him. "It does sound serious about Miss Vaughan. I've told the staff to say absolutely nothing about her visit here today to anyone. I'm sure they can all be trusted."

Bertie grinned to himself. Mrs Hobbs sounded so determined none of the staff would dare to disobey her. "Thank you, I really appreciate your discretion."

Bertie hurried along to the old tower wing and ran up the steps to the library on the first floor. Things were getting complicated, but in one way it was good that Mr Roskelley would be around to look after the estate while he was with Lucy. His stomach churned. She had to be in danger with Parfitt chasing her.

Mrs Hobbs bustled in with a large key. "The strongbox is in the desk in the hidden room, Mr Lovell."

"That makes sense. Uncle Ambrose was always very careful." Bertie gave a wistful sigh. "I really miss him. Now let's go through and sort this money out." Bertie reached for the hidden latch to the secret room on the wainscoting of the library. It slid open almost silently. "I'm glad to see you've kept this well-oiled, Mrs Hobbs."

He was even happier to see the amount of money in the box. He left a generous amount with Mrs Hobbs for housekeeping sundry expenses and carefully stashed the rest away in the inner pocket of his coat.

CHAPTER EIGHT

Lucy waited until Mama and Aunt Susan disappeared into the blue drawing room. She reached out to pull the servants' door shut but Emma stopped her.

"Leave that I would," Emma whispered. "They often get left slightly open and no one will notice it. They might notice if it closes with no one going through it."

They reached Lucy's room without incident and Emma pulled the blue evening gown out of the closet. "Let's get you into your evening dress in case your father comes up to check on you."

"I suppose you're right but I still think Lord Parfitt intends to carry me off tonight."

"I'm not so sure now. He seemed awfully keen to be on good terms with your aunt. I wonder if he might have one attempt to persuade you to marry him willingly by pointing out what might happen to your family if you don't."

"He must know I wouldn't listen."

Emma put her head on one side, a serious expression on her face. "Not necessarily. If you don't mind me saying, I have a feeling your father has got himself in to serious debt. He was almost exploding with the effort of controlling his temper so as not to upset Lord Parfitt. Debt can pull a family right down."

"You could be right, but if I was to escape whilst Aunt Susan is here, I think Mama would be safe. How good are you at riding, Emma?"

"I'm a decent horsewoman. I used to ride with my brother when we were young."

Lucy sat down on the bed in her shift and cupped her chin on her hands. If you came with me Bertie might be able to get me to safety. If no one knows about it he can't be forced into marrying me."

"Perhaps he would like to marry you if you were good friends as children?"

"Yes, we were. We're still friends but as his friend I don't want to force his hand to do something that he wouldn't have wanted otherwise."

Emma looked away. "He might have been saving himself for you. Sometimes men need a little nudge. My Arthur has moved in with his uncle, who is head groom at Mayford Castle. All the staff there think the world of Mr Lovell. I wouldn't rule out marriage to him if I were you."

Emma sounded serious. Lucy shook her head so hard her curls bounced. "I intend to stay unmarried and content myself with charity works. My great aunt left me more than enough to live on as far as I know. I won't get it until I'm five and twenty but that's less than three years away. Aunt Susan and Uncle James are going abroad soon, they might take me with them."

Emma rolled her eyes. "If you say so, Miss Vaughan."

"Yes, I do. Now, what's our best plan?"

"What time will dinner be served?"

"Papa likes to keep town hours even in the country, especially when we have visitors. I don't think he will change the normal time of six o'clock."

"Good. I hid the clothes from the housekeeper in your closet when I slipped in with your dress earlier." Emma bit her lip as if worried about something.

"What are you thinking?"

"It's your hair. It's so blonde it stands out. There's a couple of caps in with the clothes. When we were in London, I noticed that some ladies are having their hair cut really short. I spent one of my free afternoons watching another lady's maid I was friendly with cut the hair of one of her charges. She let me have a go on the youngest sister who isn't out yet. It wasn't too difficult. I smuggled some scissors up as well. I could do a reasonable job of your hair. If I cut it really short you could put the cap on without worrying about any of it falling out."

Lucy laughed. "I like that idea. A new start and a new hairstyle. I wish I knew for sure whether Papa was going to come up."

"I see what you mean. If we went now and he did come to check on you, we won't have much start."

"If he hasn't come up in the next half hour, I think we're safe. We can climb out of my window and down the ivy."

Emma looked startled and Lucy grinned. "It's quite safe. Peter and I used to climb down it all the time when we were children. We would meet Bertie by the big oak tree near the kitchen gardens on some adventure or other. We used to climb up and down late at night with only moonlight to show us the way. Bertie will be there at five o'clock, we'll have full daylight."

"Our biggest problem will be avoiding the people Parfitt will send after you."

Lucy hugged her knees, thinking. "I've had an idea. Lord Parfitt has a morbid fear of illness. When he was pestering me in London, the only day that I managed to repel him from a morning visit was the one when Mama was ill with a cold. Run down to the kitchen and fetch a pepper pot."

Emma giggled. "What a wonderful idea. I'll be back in a trice."

"Leave the door unlocked in case Papa comes up. I think he will."

Lucy laid back in bed and closed her eyes. There was no guarantee that Papa would try and see her, but it would be just her luck if he came before Emma returned with the pepper. She forced herself to breathe steadily and waited. After what seemed an age, but was probably only a matter of minutes, the door opened to admit Emma, who shut it behind herself and turned the key in the lock.

"I made a big show of asking the laundry maids for some clean handkerchiefs because you have a terrible cold." Emma put a pile of clean, folded handkerchiefs on the bed and pulled out a pepper pot from her pocket. "Here you are. Cook made sure it was full for me."

Lucy sprinkled pepper on one of the handkerchiefs and held it close to her nose. She started sneezing straightaway and grabbed one of the clean handkerchiefs. "Heavens - that worked better than I expected." She picked up a fresh handkerchief and sniffed the pepper again. The results were even more dramatic. Holding a handkerchief to her nose she tucked the pepper covered one under her pillow.

"That worked well." Emma moved to clear away the used handkerchief.

"Leave it on the bed. I'll sniff the pepper again when I've

recovered. I'm praying my father does come up. I can't see Lord Parfitt pushing for a marriage for at least a couple of days if I can convince Papa I really am ill."

Heavy footsteps sounded outside the door. Emma moved as if to open it but Lucy caught her hand. "He'll be suspicious if we make this too easy," Lucy whispered.

The door knob rattled. When it didn't open, her father's voice boomed out. "Stop all this play acting, Lucy. You are marrying Lord Parfitt and that's all there is to it." He hammered at the door.

Lucy sniffed at the pepper covered handkerchief.

"Leave me alone. I've got a..." a sneezing fit took her, "cold."

"For Heaven's sake open this door," Papa shouted again.

"You'll catch it if you come in." Lucy made herself sneeze again.

"If you think having a cold is going to stop you getting married then you can think again. Now open this door."

Lucy sprinkled some more pepper on the handkerchief. She pushed the pepper pot under her pillow and held the handkerchief to her nose before hiding that as well and picking up a fresh handkerchief from the pile. She nodded at Emma, who walked across to the door and turned the key. Emma opened it with a flourish just as Lucy started a fresh bout of sneezing.

Lucy's eyes watered and she glared at her father. "My head aches, my eyes hurt and I can't stop sneezing. I'm staying in bed until I feel better."

"Don't be so childish. What's a cold between friends?"

A new spasm of sneezing wracked Lucy. Her head really was aching now. "This is the worst cold I've had in ages. It's all your fault. I'm so upset at you expecting me to marry whoever you choose. If I've got to marry then I will, but not Lord Parfitt."

Papa paced the room. "You will marry who I say you will." He sounded angry but a little worried, frightened even.

"No, I won't. I'm of age and you can't force me." Lucy called on her long-time ability to cry when she wanted to. The tears irritated her nose and she started sneezing again. She looked up to see Mama and Aunt Susan peering through.

Mama ran through the doorway. "Oh, my poor darling. You don't look at all well."

Aunt Susan grabbed Mama's arm and pulled her back. She winked at Lucy. "Don't go any nearer. There's a new type of influenza in London that makes people sneeze all the time. Some people have been really ill with it. It's best to keep Lucy in isolation and if I were you, I'd keep her maid away from the other maids as well." Aunt Susan kept her back to Papa, looking amused.

Papa knew when he was beaten. "I'll go and tell Lord Parfitt that you've got the influenza." He stormed out of the room.

Emma rushed to the door. "He's out of sight now." She closed the door gently.

"How did you manage that, Lucy?" Aunt Susan asked.

Lucy grinned at her. "Pepper."

"Clever girl. If your father thinks he'll get Lord Parfitt anywhere near you with suspected influenza I'll eat my hat." Quickly now, Lucy, what is your plan?"

"I won't be watched so closely if father accepts that I'm genuinely ill. Lord Parfitt won't want to risk the possibility of influenza, which will give me some respite from whatever plot they are hatching to marry me off to him. Bertie Lovell has inherited Mayford Castle and he's in residence. I sheltered there from the rain this morning and he's offered to help. He's going to be at the big oak tree by the kitchen gardens tonight because he had a feeling that, now Lord Parfitt has surfaced, things might move quickly. I'm going to take Emma and meet him."

Lucy blushed painfully. Aunt Susan must be aware that father could be violent but it was still shameful. "If Bertie can whisk us away, will you make sure Mama is safe?"

"Of course." Aunt Susan rubbed her chin. "I'll offer to stay overnight, saying I'm seriously worried about your health. If I send my carriage back to the Smart's house with a message your father won't be suspicious that I'm about to carry you all off."

Lucy closed her eyes. Would Mama be safe even for one night? No, she didn't want to risk it. "I don't want to leave until you've got Mama safely away. Legally Papa could keep her here."

"I can see what you're saying. Your Uncle had to stay London on urgent government business and your father is in such a temper he might not listen to me." Aunt Susan hesitated. "I know. I'll tell my coachman to start off on the route to the Smarts' house and then double back and hide out at the inn in the village until later tonight. Your mother will tell her maid not to wait up as she expects dinner to last until late since she has guests. We'll disappear as soon as we can."

"How will you get to the village without being noticed?"

"We'll walk. There's a nearly full moon tonight. We'll be unlucky to be seen. We'll start the journey back to London overnight. Your father will follow our trail if you're missed straightaway, but a long way behind. That will give you more time to escape. Where do you plan to go?"

"I haven't thought that far ahead. The safest thing might be for Bertie to take us to stay with the Cathlays in London. We can decide that later once we're safely away."

Mama put a hand around her shoulders. "I'll pray you escape. Bertie Lovell is a good and clever young man, whatever the Ton might think of him. He will keep you safe as long as you can get away from here without being caught. We had better go now."

Lucy detained her with a hand on her arm. "I don't trust your maid not to give you away before you've got far."

"Don't worry about us. Susan has got armed guards dressed as footmen. We'll take the two new footmen I employed when we arrived as well. They can be relied on. I thought they might come in useful. They're both boys from the village and I know their families well. We'll be well protected."

Mama squeezed her hand and kissed her on the cheek before turning with a sigh and making for the door.

Aunt Susan followed. She turned back before she reached the door and frowned. "Take care girls. This is a bad business. I wish you well but be assured if anything goes wrong your Uncle James will leave no stone unturned to rescue you. We'll call on the Cathlays as soon as we arrive in Town. I hope we're reunited soon."

Lucy fought back tears as the door closed behind them. When would she see them again? Emma locked the door and ran to the closet. She pulled out a bundle of clothes and the clothes Lucy had worn that morning, including the pair of Bertie's breeches. Lucy's face grew hot at the sight of them. Somehow, she could no longer see Bertie as the young boy who had befriended her, when her own brother would have left her behind.

He was the same kind person she had always known, but there was something scary about him now. All men frightened her if she was being honest. They were such unpredictable creatures, something Papa had taught her only too well. The important thing was to escape from Lord Parfitt. Emma would be with her and Bertie was the safest man she could escape with. He still thought of her as a little sister.

CHAPTER NINE

Lucy opened her window and peered out. The sky was clear and the ground appeared to have dried well after the morning storm.

"There's no sign of anyone. We should be safe to make our exit. You did lock the door, didn't you?"

"Yes, and I've checked it twice. There's still time to cut your hair off. I'm worried about your cap falling off."

"There's always a chance someone will come up to the room this evening to look for me. We can worry about a disguise later. Come on, I don't feel safe here now we're dressed to escape."

"If you say so, Miss Vaughan. I suppose you're right. I'll bring the scissors with me. I've tied them up in the bundle I made with my cloak. Can you tie it onto my back securely?"

Lucy checked the knots on the makeshift harness of Emma's bundle and tied it on. "There, that seems secure. Just be careful if you have to jump down the last bit not to land on the scissors."

Emma nodded and checked Lucy's bundle before strapping it to her back. "All secure. We'd better go. I'm not looking forward to climbing down this ivy."

"I'd go down first to show you how but I don't think you

would manage closing the window, there's quite a knack to it. We can't afford to have it coming open and banging. Every minute our escape goes undetected increases our chances of getting away safely."

Lucy leaned out of the window and put a hand into the nearest tangle of ivy and pushed at it. "See it's perfectly solid. Take your time and make sure you've got a good footing before you lower yourself down the next bit. Don't look down, breathe deeply and you will be on firm ground before you know it."

"If you say so, Miss Vaughan." Emma swung a breeches clad leg over the windowsill. She flailed around with her foot for a moment then let out a breath. "I see what you mean I've got a firm foothold now."

Lucy watched as Emma swung her other leg over the window ledge. The second leg flailed around for a moment and Lucy held her breath. Then Emma seemed to gain confidence and took her first step down, then another and another. Lucy's heart stopped thundering in her chest. The first time she had climbed down had been terrifying. Only the thought of Peter and Bertie laughing at her if she didn't make it had kept her going. At last Emma reached the ground. Lucy followed. Emma's clever idea of tying up their skirts and other items they wanted to take into bundles in the cloaks and fixing them to their backs was a great help. She must remember to adjust for the weight on her back.

She found good footholds and lowered herself until just her head and shoulders were above the window ledge and carefully edged the window closed. She pulled hard, praying it would catch straightaway. It did and she climbed down rather faster than Emma. All that practice as a child had come in useful. She jumped down the last couple of feet to stand by Emma and put a finger to her lips. This was the most dangerous part of their escape. If anyone loyal to Papa came round the corner of the house now, they were for it. There was no sign of anyone. She took Emma's arm and they ran across to the hedge that separated the formal garden from the lawns.

No one shouted. They reached the gate into the formal gardens and Lucy pushed Emma through and followed, pulling it shut behind her. She listened hard but there was still no sign of pursuit. They caught their breath for a few moments.

"Now to get down to the oak tree. Come on, Emma. I'm not sure of the time but I think we've got about twenty minutes. If I know Bertie, he'll probably be early. I hope so, we don't want to be standing around in case anyone has come looking for me."

She led the way through the gardens. Every sense was on full alert, listening and looking for trouble. They came out of the formal gardens but there was no sign of Bertie by the oak tree. Panic gripped her but she took a deep breath. "I hope Bertie's here soon. Our best bet is to go and hide behind the trees further on where we can see him come."

When they got close to the oak tree Emma stopped her when they heard a whistle. Arthur materialised from behind the tree, his eyes gleaming with excitement.

"I'm glad you're early. I've left Mr Lovell in the trees holding onto four horses." He took Emma's hand and led them towards the stand of trees that marked the start of the woods between Rugeley Hall and Mayford Castle. He led them through a gap and into a small clearing. Some of her fear left Lucy when she saw Bertie. There were some people in life you could always rely upon and Bertie was one of them. She smiled and ran towards him.

"Did your horses arrive then?"

Bertie grinned. "Not the ones that Mr Bright is bringing. We managed to buy these from a farmer that Arthur knows. They're all young healthy beasts and they should be good enough for what we want. Just looking at you I can see it's time to escape."

"I'm afraid so. We should be safe for a while unless father decides to visit my room again. Where are we going to go?"

Bertie handed the reins of two of the horses to Arthur. He threw Lucy up into the saddle of a bay horse and mounted a chestnut. "Back to Mayford Castle for now."

"But shouldn't we try to get as far away as possible?"

"I've been thinking about that. I've got a plan. We can talk about it when we reach the Castle safely. Remember the secret room? We can hide you in there for now in case there is an immediate pursuit. Let's not waste any more time."

"Agreed. The sooner we get away from here the happier I'll be. You can tell me what you've got planned when we are safely tucked away at the Castle." Lucy shivered.

"You're cold. It's not safe to stay here or I'd give you my coat and take your pack. Let's get going, we'll soon be at the Castle." Bertie led the way through some of the deepest parts of the wood.

There was sense to what Bertie was suggesting. He had always been the resourceful one. They could regroup at the castle and sort out what they were going to wear. Bertie might be able to find some coats that fitted. It would keep them safer if they could pass as young men. There might even be time for Emma to cut her hair. Her cap snagged on a low-lying branch and she just managed to save it with one hand. Yes, she definitely did need her hair cut. At least the horse seemed pretty placid. Having a hand taken off the reins hadn't given it any ideas.

They soon reached Mayford Castle. Bertie led the way around to the stables, where Mrs Hobbs was waiting with Warner.

"Can you take the ladies into the house please, Mrs Hobbs," Bertie said. "I'll help Arthur and Warner rub the horses down and join you in the kitchen as soon as I can."

He lifted Lucy down and a tremor went through her. She really was cold, she had better do as Bertie said.

"Thank you, Mrs Hobbs. We need warming up. We found some breeches but we couldn't find any coats to fit."

"I've thought of that, Miss Vaughan. I found some old grooms' liveries, left over from the days when Mr Mayford kept a larger stable. I don't think fashions for grooms have changed too much in the last few years. Right, let's get you into that warm kitchen. Cook is waiting to feed you up."

The thought of some of Cook's food was enticing. "That sounds good, Mrs Hobbs. I've been too nervous to eat all day. Besides which I was pretending to be ill."

Lucy and Emma strode up to the kitchen door with Mrs Hobbs. Cook was waiting for them in the kitchen.

"You young ladies look frozen come and sit by the fire. There's a nice vegetable pie here you can have and I'll make you a hot drink."

"Don't worry about anyone finding you here," Mrs Hobbs said. "I've got a boy up in the tower keeping a lookout."

They untied their backpacks and walked over to the big kitchen table in the middle of the room. Lucy sat down to a plateful of pie and was surprised how much she managed to eat. Two cups of tea later and she was feeling much more human.

Emma grinned at her. "That's the best I've seen you looking all day, Miss Vaughan. That cold cleared up quickly."

Mrs Hobbs brought a cup of tea over for herself and sat down at the table. "Do you think your father believed you were ill?"

Emma giggled. "Oh, she put up a marvellous performance, Mrs Hobbs. Aided by a pot of pepper I fetched for her."

Mrs Hobbs laughed and Lucy couldn't help smiling at the memory.

"I remembered that Lord Parfitt is terrified of illness. Aunt Susan turned up and suggested it might be influenza. I'm hoping that's put him off the idea of carrying me off to a church tonight and they don't look for me until tomorrow."

Mrs Hobbs nodded. "That was clever of you both. I'm glad to hear your aunt is with your mother."

"So am I. I wish we could have brought Mama with us but it wouldn't have been feasible. Aunt Susan has a plan to get them away after dinner tonight. I hope all goes well."

"Of course, it will, Miss Vaughan. Don't you get a worrying! You're going to need your wits about you to help Mr Lovell get you somewhere safe." Mrs Hobbs smiled at her. "We heard they had trouble with that there Lord Parfitt down in the village yesterday. He tried to have his way with one of the serving maids in the inn. The landlord and his son threw him out and banned him from the inn. He threatened them with all sorts. Not a nice man our Lord Parfitt. I don't know what your father was thinking, expecting you to marry someone like that. Being a lord doesn't make him a good husband for you. It's all round the village."

Bertie came in and joined them at the table. "Any more of that excellent pie, Cook?"

"I'll bring you some over, Mr Lovell. With a tankard of ale."

"Wonderful, Cook." He put a hand on Lucy's arm and gave it a squeeze. "Cheer up. We'll get you somewhere safe. It was lucky that Arthur knew about those horses for sale. Apart from the grey mare, they're unremarkable. I didn't want to ride Chalice, he's too well-known in the area now. If we dress you both as grooms, with Arthur dressed as if he's a friend of mine, it's going to be much harder for Parfitt to track us down. He'll be expecting a carriage."

Lucy nodded. "We thought we'd be better dressed as youths. Emma has managed to bring her scissors with her. If we've got time, she's going to cut my hair short."

"That's a good idea. We'll make time. It might be an idea to cut Arthur's hair short, he's wearing it quite long. It would change his appearance slightly, especially from a distance."

"Why don't I cut yours now, Miss Vaughan? We can sweep up what's cut off and burn it in the fire," Emma looked around, "if that's all right with Cook."

Cook walked over. "I'll pull a chair over by the fire for you and fetch a broom ready."

"Such a waste of all that lovely hair," Bertie said. "Never mind you'll soon be able to grow it again."

Lucy doubted it, her hair was so long, but she nodded and sat on the chair Cook positioned near to the fire. Emma fetched her scissors and set to work. Lucy closed her eyes as her blonde tresses fell in swathes to the floor.

Emma stood back to survey her handiwork. "There, I've cut it really short but it suits you. You definitely look more boyish."

Bertie swallowed the last mouthful of his pie and moved closer. "I don't know about looking boyish but it certainly looks fetching." He smiled at her.

Lucy felt herself go hot. Bertie sat back down and picked up his tankard of ale, as if he realised his comments had made her feel awkward. She watched Emma sweep up the pile of golden hair with a sharp pang.

"Oh, my hair. I suppose it's in a good cause. With it this short the colour doesn't stand out so much." She looked at Emma. "I think yours needs to be a bit shorter. Hand over those scissors, it's my turn."

Emma took her place on the chair. "Yes, it will be better short. But be careful how you cut the front." Emma looked worried.

"I watched how you cut mine, don't worry, I'll try not to make too much of a mess of it."

Cook fetched a looking glass. "Here you are, Miss Vaughan. So, you can see how Emma has shaped your hair, especially round the ears. She's done a good job of it."

Lucy studied her appearance. It did look quite smart, even if her head felt cold already. At least she'd have the thick cap to keep her warm. She set to on Emma with a will and chunks of chestnut hair fell to the floor. Cook was right, getting it looking tidy around the ears was a bit of a challenge. She left the front a bit longer, then Emma could trim it herself if she wasn't happy.

"There it's finished." Lucy fetched the looking glass. "What do you think? I've left the front a bit longer."

"That's not bad for a first attempt. I'll leave it a bit longer at the front so we don't look as if we've both had our hair cut at the same time."

The door opened and Arthur came in. "I've helped uncle with the horses, they're all settled for the night."

Lucy's eyes flew to Bertie. "Are you sure we shouldn't get going this evening?"

"Lord Parfitt is a wily old devil. I'd be surprised if he doesn't have someone check you really are in your room, even if they have to break the lock. If he does, it won't be long before he finds out you're missing."

"All the more reason to get as big a start as possible, surely."

Bertie grinned at her. "That's exactly what Parfitt would expect us to do. I know him only too well. He might not go near you himself if he thinks you're ill, but he won't take it on trust. He's been to the village and he's bound to have found out I'm here. This is the first place he'll look."

"I don't trust Mama's maid. She might realise if Mama and Aunt Susan get away before anyone looks for me. Besides if Parfitt does search here first, we need to be well away." Her voice rose. Tiredness threatened to overwhelm her. She ran a hand across her brow.

"Don't fret, Lucy. No one knows about the secret room except you, me, Mrs Hobbs, and now Arthur and Emma of course. Well, Peter too, but he's not here. I suggest we make up beds in there for you and you go to bed soon. We'll make an early start in the morning."

"But Bertie, we'll be in the same position in the morning. He'll still be right behind us."

"Possibly, but you could always hide away there all day tomorrow if necessary. We need to confuse Parfitt."

Lucy shook her head but she was too exhausted to argue. Perhaps Bertie was right.

Bertie moved across and took her hand. "Come on, Lucy, what do you say?"

"Well at least we might be a bit more rested tomorrow and

we should be safe hidden away in the secret room. I asked for your help, now I ought to accept it."

Bertie squeezed her hand and a warm feeling swept over her. If anyone could save her it was Bertie. She nodded.

"Good girl. Arthur, before you have your dinner, I think we need Emma to cut your hair as well."

Emma went pink but she picked up the scissors and pointed to the chair in front of the fire. "Let's get it done quickly, Arthur. Just in case that Parfitt man comes across now."

Arthur sat down and smiled up at Emma. She went even pinker and Lucy felt that surge of envy again. Life would have been so much simpler if she found some decent man to marry while she was in London. Whenever she'd found a man interesting, fear tugged her away from getting to know him better.

"I haven't long had my hair cut, Emma, Bertie said. "This is a fashionable style. Do you think you could cut Arthur's in a similar manner?"

"I'll do my best. Ready, Arthur? Let's get going."

Emma worked quickly and produced a good imitation of Bertie's haircut. She really was a talented girl.

Cook rushed over and brushed up the last of the hair. "I think Mr Lovell is right. Let's get you girls bedded down for the night."

"Good idea, Cook. I've already sent Mrs Hobbs to make up beds for them with a trusted maid. You stay here and feed Arthur and I'll walk upstairs with them.

Bertie helped them to carry all their things. Lucy had a good look round to make sure they'd left nothing behind. Mrs Hobbs had transformed the secret room.

"I hope you'll be warm enough, Miss Vaughan. I'll keep the

fire in the library made up as some of the warmth will find its way into this room being as the chimney is on this wall. Now have you got everything you need?

Lucy scanned the room by the light of a good-sized lantern. Molly was making up the second of two truckle beds. There were two chairs and a table laden with a pile of coats. Mrs Hobbs saw her looking at them.

"Those are some of those riding coatts that previous grooms grew out of. Once he let go of most of his stable, Mr Mayford found positions for all the young grooms and the spare uniforms have stayed in a cupboard ever since. I don't think fashions have changed much for those sorts of coats. With your hair short and the caps which you've brought with you, you should pass quite well as boys. No one but me Cook and Molly knows you're here. Oh except for the two boys taking turns at keeping watch from the top of the tower. I'm sure they can be relied upon to keep quiet. I'll call in later to see if you've got everything you need."

CHAPTER TEN

Bertie left Mrs Hobbs in charge and went back into the library. He spread several of the account books around to make it look like he was busy. The more he thought about it the more confident he was he had made the right decision. Lucy's urge to get as far away as possible was understandable but that would play right into Parfitt's hands. Even if Lucy's clever influenza ruse worked, which he doubted it would for long, she would be missed tomorrow, once Mrs Vaughan's disappearance was noted. Or even tonight if Lucy was right about her mother's maid.

Emma had done a good job with her hair cutting. Lucy would be much less conspicuous although it was such a shame to cut off that beautiful hair. His breath hitched. Something about the new style made him feel as if he was looking at someone else rather than his childhood playmate. He forced the thought to the back of his mind and made a determined effort to read some of the estate's papers. Mrs Hobbs came out a few minutes later.

"I've got them well settled, Mr Lovell. Miss Vaughan looks exhausted. She'll be a lot better for a good night's sleep."

"Yes, that was my thinking. I'm glad you thought of putting those boys at the top of the tower to look out though. Lord

Parfitt might come here at some point tonight. Can you send Arthur to me as soon as he's finished his tea? I want to get him sorted out with some of my clothes fairly quickly. I don't think we'll see Parfitt until after dinner at the earliest. Did you find those saddlebags I wanted?"

"Yes, I put them in your room. They're in good condition. Mr Mayford never bought anything but the best."

"Arthur won't recognise himself once we've got him kitted out. It's lucky that he's of a slighter build than me. If Parfitt does seek me out tonight, I can't decide whether to stay another day here or set off early tomorrow."

"I think Miss Vaughan would get really fretful if you stayed here. Besides, if Mr Roskelley turns up in the morning, I can always say you're riding out with him if Lord Parfitt comes again. Those girls look completely different with their hair cut and wearing grooms' clothes. They're both really slim. I found them a couple of mufflers to put round their necks when you go into places. I can't see them being recognised."

Bertie sat back in his chair and tapped his chin. "You're probably right. I think we should get going tomorrow. I've had another idea but I need to speak to Arthur."

"I'll go down and see if he's ready."

"Thank you. Now I'm going to seriously look at these estate documents. It's something I should have been doing all week. I do hope Mr Roskelley proves good."

Mrs Hobbs left and it wasn't long before Arthur came up carrying two tankards of ale. "Cook thought you might need some more of this."

Bertie laughed and took the tankard. "My biggest fear when I came here was that Cook and Mrs Hobbs might want to retire. We can rely on them to hold the fort."

"We can. I don't like the sound of Lord Parfitt." Arthur raised his eyebrows. "You seem convinced that he will pursue Miss Vaughan no matter what."

"He's a man who can never bear to be bested." Bertie frowned, then a smile spread across his face. "I have an idea. How far away do Emma's aunt and her mother live?"

"It's getting on for fifteen miles by the main roads but there are some cross-country bridle paths and lanes that make it less than ten miles." Arthur grinned. "I tried them out to visit Emma when she was allowed a few days to go and visit them last week."

"How reliable are these ladies?"

"Oh, very trustworthy and very sensible both of them. Do you intend to make our first stop with them? Emma's aunt has a haberdashery and dressmaking business on the edge of the village. It's quite a good size and it has stables at the back. It wouldn't be a bad idea to stay there."

"I wonder if Mr Vaughan knows where Lucy's family live?"

Arthur shook his head. "No, he's not been too interested in staff. He probably didn't even notice that Miss Vaughan had allowed her some time off. There's a link by stage coach from the village inn. I escorted her there so she didn't use transport from the Hall."

"Now that is good news." Bertie picked up his tankard and downed half of it in one go. Zounds. This was getting complicated. "There may be people at the Hall who know you've been living here with your uncle. If we spend the night with Emma's family, how would you feel about coming back here to look after Mr Roskelley?"

Arthur's face fell. "You might be running into danger. Wouldn't it be better if I stayed with you?"

"Believe it or not I'm an excellent shot. I'll take my pistols with me. I've also got a set of ladies' pistols and, since she spent so much time with her brother and me as a girl, Miss Vaughan learnt to shoot as well. I don't like leaving Mr Roskelley completely on his own apart from servants who can only give him limited advice. If you come back to help him it would feel much more courteous for me. It would also introduce you. Then if Mr Roskelley hasn't got any young relatives who he wants to train up I'm sure he'll be more than happy to take you on."

"I'd love that, but I still think I'd rather help to protect Emma and Miss Vaughan."

"I know this part of the world really well. There are plenty of inns we can stay at where I know I can trust the landlord."

Arthur ran his hand through his newly cut hair, looking worried. "That doesn't get them to safety though."

"When we're far enough away from here, I'll send a messenger with a letter to the Duchess of Cathlay, my cousin. I'm sure she and her husband will arrange somewhere safe for us to stay and send an escort. In the meantime, we can make for the house of a good friend of mine."

"All the more reason I should stay with you. I could be that messenger."

"I need you here to settle Mr Roskelley in." Bertie rested his head in his hands and thought hard. "That's true. Let's compromise. Stay with Mr Roskelley tomorrow to show him around and then tell him you've got an errand to run for me and will be back as soon as you can. I'll give you the Cathlay's address in London and you can catch the early morning mail coach."

"Yes, Mr Lovell."

Bertie smiled. "Don't look so poker faced at me young man. The more I think about it the more I like this plan. Parfitt will be along this evening, or tomorrow at the latest, to check if I'm still here. If I'm not and he comes across Mr Roskelley managing as best he can with no one to greet him he'll know for sure I'm with Miss Vaughan. He won't be so sure if he sees I've left someone to settle Roskelley in. I've been known for my careless ways in recent years. He'll think I've gone off to stay with friends now my agent has arrived to take the reins of Mayford."

Arthur still looked dubious but nodded. "I suppose so and the Cathlays will know you need help quickly."

"Good man. Watch out for anyone following you. When you reach Cathlay House insist on speaking to no one except the Duchess, or the Duke if she's out. I'll give you a letter of introduction to confirm you are working for me but leave you to explain everything. I can rely on the Duke to send out a search party if they don't hear from me quickly."

"Wouldn't it be better to speak to the Duke for preference?"

Bertie grinned. "If you're feeling brave. He's a formidable man. He won't let me down though. Right. Let's get you dressed in some of my clothes."

"We don't really need to do that now do we?"

Bertie chuckled. "Even more so if you want an audience with the Duke of Cathlay. Besides, first impressions count and you want to make a good impression on Mr Roskelley."

Arthur sighed. "If you say so. I know I should be more deferential."

Bertie slapped him on the shoulder. "Not with me. There's no reason why we shouldn't be friends. Land agents and their assistants often get invited to dinner and such like. Let's get you dressed. It won't hurt if you're with me when Lord Parfitt calls, so he knows you're working for me. I shall struggle to keep my temper with him and you can hold me back if necessary."

When they returned to the library, someone had cleared their tankards and put a tray with a decanter of brandy and several glasses onto a side table. Bertie pointed at the tray. "Would you like a brandy?"

Arthur shook his head. "I'd rather keep a clear head."

"Very wise but if Parfitt does show up, I'll have to offer him a drink."

Arthur frowned. "Why would you offer someone you can't stand a drink?"

"Arthur, you make me feel so old. That's the way society works. The niceties have to be observed even with people we don't like. Otherwise, it would be awkward when you kept bumping into them at social functions."

"I suppose so. I don't think I'd like living in the city, I'm definitely a country person."

"I'm beginning to think I am too. I'm tired of playing the family's black sheep. It's time I settled down."

Arthur looked puzzled. "How could you be the black sheep of your family?"

"It's a long story. I might tell you one day."

There was a tap at the door and Mrs Hobbs rushed in. "The boy up in the tower has just run down to tell me that a group of riders are approaching."

"Thank you, Mrs Hobbs. Can you let Miss Vaughan know?"

Mrs Hobbs knocked at the panelling and pressed the hidden control in the wainscoting. The door glided open. Mrs Hobbs slipped inside the secret room and emerged quickly. "I've told her, Mr Lovell. She wants a quick word with you. I'd better get downstairs ready to open the door."

Bertie knocked and went through into the secret room. "This is exactly what I thought would happen, Lucy. There is no need for you to worry. Arthur is with me and he's made a perfect young country gentleman. Especially with his new haircut. I wish we could leave the door open so you can hear what he says but better not, we don't want him spotting an opening."

Lucy was sitting on one of the truckle beds. She smiled up at him. Lord, she looked exhausted. It really was a good job Arthur would be with him. All he wanted to do was plant Parfitt a facer.

"I do hope Mama and Aunt Susan are safe."

"Don't worry. Your Uncle James is a powerful man. He has the ear of a lot of people in government. Even Parfitt won't want to upset him. I'm glad Parfitt's come tonight. It means we can get off really early tomorrow with much less chance of a search party being nearby early on. Most of his people will be spread fairly wide by then I should imagine."

"Where are we going to head for?"

"Arthur is going to escort us somewhere safe." Bertie glanced at the other bed. "Possibly to your aunt's house, Emma, where we can regroup and decide our next step. Do you think she would be able and willing to put us up?"

Emma grinned at him. "I'm positive she will."

"Good. We'll talk about that in the morning. Once we're safely hidden, Arthur will ride back here to look after Mr Roskelley when he arrives. He'll show him around then catch the early morning mail coach down to London and get an audience with the Cathlays."

"That's a good idea. If anybody can help it's the Duke of Cathlay," Lucy said.

Bertie laughed. "And the Duchess. I'd lay odds on my cousin Augusta finding you somewhere safe to stay for as long as you need. You try and get a good night's sleep. When I say early tomorrow, I mean early. Ideally Arthur needs to be back here by noon."

Arthur put his head inside the opening. "I think I can hear Mrs Hobbs talking to Lord Parfitt. We'd better get into position."

"Right. I'll send Mrs Hobbs in to check on you as soon as they've gone. Can you close the door behind me, Lucy?"

Bertie gave Lucy's shoulder a squeeze and returned to the library. He took a seat at the big desk. "Pull up a chair next to me, Arthur. Let's make it look as if I'm showing you some of the estate books. What do you know about crop rotation?"

Arthur laughed. "Not a great deal to be honest. I suppose now might be a good time to learn."

"I spent some time with my cousin, the Marquess of Hargreaves, recently. He taught me a lot about the latest theories on agriculture. So much to learn. From what my man of business told me, Mr Roskelley is quite an expert on this sort of thing."

They were settled into a discussion on crop rotation when there was a knock at the door and Mrs Hobbs opened it.

"Lord Parfitt to see you, Mr Lovell."

"Show him in, Mrs Hobbs."

Bertie stood and Arthur shot to his feet so quickly he had to grab one of the estate books to stop it falling off the desk. Parfitt strutted in, still wearing his evening dress. Good Lord, that fancy waistcoat would make even a hardened dandy hesitate to wear it. It had so much gold and silver embroidery it was a wonder he could do the buttons up. And what on earth was that overpowering cologne he was wearing? Revolting stuff. Watching him drool over Lucy at the beginning of the season had been more than he could bear. Parfitt glared at him and marched towards his desk.

Bertie fixed a smile to his face. "To what do I owe this pleasure, Lord Parfitt? Allow me to introduce my new assistant land agent, Mr Reid."

Parfitt ignored Arthur and carried on walking up to Bertie until they were standing almost toe to toe. Bertie stood his ground and waited.

Parfitt's nostrils flared and he bared his lips. "Stop playing with me. What have you done with her?"

Bertie ignored the menace in Parfitt's voice and smiled at him. "What do you mean, what have I done with her? With whom?" He rubbed his chin. "Not that I've done anything with anybody recently that I can recall."

"Don't take me for a fool, man," Lord Parfitt shouted.

Bertie took out his handkerchief and carefully wiped Parfitt's spittle from his cheek. "Ah, you mean the wench from the tavern, do you?" He adopted his silkiest voice. "A bit below my touch, my lord."

Arthur gasped and Lord Parfitt went so red that for a moment Bertie thought he might have a seizure and solve their problem. Parfitt raised a fist.

Bertie smiled at him. "I see you don't believe me. If it's fisticuffs you want, allow me a moment to remove my coat. I've been missing my sessions with Gentleman Jackson."

Parfitt dropped his arm with a visible effort. He rocked back on his heels. "Stop trying to be clever with me you unlicked cub. What have you done with Miss Vaughan? The lady is betrothed to me."

Bertie raised his eyebrows. "I don't believe you. The lady has more taste."

"Tell me what you've done with her or I'll have the magistrate on you."

"That's an interesting proposition." Bertie's smile widened. "He's already here. I'm the magistrate for this area."

"You would be! Now, listen to me and listen to me hard." Parfitt jabbed a forefinger at him. "Tell me what you've done with Miss Vaughan or I'll involve the Government if I have to."

Bertie gave him his laziest smile. "What makes you think I've done anything with Miss Vaughan?"

"She's disappeared from her room. She's nowhere to be found in Rugeley Hall. The only place she could have come is here. I demand to search it."

"Search away dear fellow, but you'll have to excuse me I'm rather busy, my new agent is coming tomorrow. Mr Reid here will show you around. I must say mislaying your betrothed was rather careless of you."

Both of Lord Parfitt's hands formed into fists but he turned on his heel and marched to the door. "There will be trouble over this, Mr Lovell. And don't think your illustrious relatives will be able to get you out of it this time. I wonder what your new assistant land agent would think if he knew the extent of your depravity."

Bertie narrowed his eyes. "I may have been rather wild in my youth but I've never sunk to your depths, my lord. Do you want Mr Reid to show you around or do you not?"

"You must have her hidden somewhere on the estate or you wouldn't be prepared for me to look around the house. Don't you worry, you won't get away with this. I'll have my men watching you."

"If I find any of your men on my estate I'll be sending for the constable, good day to you, Lord Parfitt."

Parfitt stormed out. Bertie moved to the door and watched him disappear down the stairs. Never had he been so glad that the hidden room had been a closely guarded secret for as long as he could remember. It was going to be awkward to get away. Parfitt was bound to post some of his men around. He heard the door open and then close with something of a bang. Mrs Hobbs's opinion of Lord Parfitt wasn't difficult to work out.

"I'm so glad you were here, Arthur. I came close to planting a facer on Parfitt but I wouldn't have put it past him to have had me hauled before the magistrate from the next district. If it's still old Mr Cosgrove he's not above taking a financial inducement to provide the right result for anyone rich enough."

Arthur shook his head. "What a dreadful man. You were right about him coming here tonight. How are we going to get away tomorrow without being seen?"

"I suspect Parfitt will send most of his men to all the posting inns in walking distance, particularly the one where the mail coach to London stops. That gives us an hour or two. The new horses are used to being out at night. There's a clearing in the woods not far from the stables. We can tie the horses up in there and leave our saddles ready for the morning. That will leave only our saddlebags to carry. I know all the paths through the woods. As does Miss Vaughan. We should be able to cover quite a distance before we need to come out of the cover of the trees. Whereabouts is Emma's aunt's house?"

"Past Mayford village and just as you go into Dunsford. I'm sure I can remember the tracks across country if we can get past Mayford."

"Good. I know all the paths to Mayford. I'm going to load up the pistols I've got now. Have you ever done any shooting?"

Arthur frowned. "I know the basics but I can't say I have had a great deal of practice."

"As long as you know how to handle a gun I might as well prepare a pair for you as well. And I mustn't forget the small pair for Miss Vaughan. Once I've done that we'll go and move the horses. Go and warn your uncle. Take care in case there are any of Lord Parfitt's men still about."

"Which of the five horses shall I leave behind? The grey one?"

Bertie pursed his lips. "How about you ride the grey horse and start off first in the morning to act as a decoy if Parfitt has left a man watching the Castle. Leave the grey in the stable tonight. I'll ride with the ladies through the woods. You take a more open route and we'll find you at the vicarage in Mayford."

"That might work. Where shall I wait for you?"

"The vicar is a good friend of mine. He'll let you in if you tell him Bertie Lovell sent you. I'll leave it to your discretion as to how much to tell him. Make a show of leaving your horse in his stables, anyone following you will assume you have business with the vicar. Then double back here."

"I can see a flaw." Arthur wrinkled up his nose. "What if someone is left to watch me?"

"Not that likely, but worth assuming there might be. I can leave the others with the horses tied up in the woods behind Mayford and slip around to the back entrance to the vicarage on foot to let you know we've arrived safely. I know where the road to Dunsford starts. Give us half an hour then follow us. We'll meet at the Red Lion, which isn't far from Mayford and I can find my way there without using the main road. The landlord knows me well, a result of my misspent youth. You can lead us across country from there."

"I don't like leaving you for so long but on those horses and dressed as grooms Emma and Miss Vaughan shouldn't stand out."

Bertie nodded. "This is not going to be easy but Parfitt is not going to defeat us."

CHAPTER ELEVEN

Lucy sat on the side of the bed and tried not to tremble. Any minute now Lord Parfitt would be the other side of the wall separating the secret room from the library. Not a pleasant thought. She turned the lamp, which was sitting on a small table between the two truckle beds, down low to be sure no light could find its way through any chinks in the wainscoting. The room was a velvety dark with just a little blob of light. She couldn't even chat to Emma to relieve the tension. What a nightmare this was. After what seemed a lifetime, there was a knock at the door and Mrs Hobbs came in carrying a tray. Emma reached for the lamp and turned it up. Mrs Hobbs put the tray down next to the lamp.

"Oh food. Those buns look wonderful," Emma said.

Mrs Hobbs smiled at her. "Cook's best. Mr Reid said Mr Lovell was magnificent the way he saw off Lord Parfitt. That man's a blustering fool. Is there anything else you want?"

Lucy shook her head. "No, I think we've got everything we need. Thank you, Mrs Hobbs. We'll eat something and then try and get some sleep."

"That's the best thing, Miss Vaughan. Mr Lovell says you'll be making an early start in the morning. I'll come and wake you up myself. Molly will be up in a few minutes to make up the fire so it stays alight. Leave the door open and you should get the heat in here." She shivered. "I would have liked to put you in a nice warm guest bedroom now Lord Parfitt has gone but Mr Lovell thought it best you stay in here in case he returns. Nasty man that he is."

Lucy hugged her knees under the covers. Nasty didn't begin to cover it, repulsive might be a good start. "It is cold in here but Mr Lovell was right about Parfitt coming tonight and he's right about being cautious. Lord Parfitt is the most devious man I know."

"I shouldn't say this but whatever was your father thinking of?" Mrs Hobbs grimaced and shook her head. "It should warm up in here with the gap left open. I'll ask Molly to bring up some hot bricks for you. You'll struggle to sleep with cold feet."

It would take a lot more than warm feet to get her to sleep but she thanked Mrs Hobbs. The woman was a treasure. Once Molly had arrived and put a cloth-wrapped hot brick in each of their beds Lucy snuggled down to enjoy the extra warmth. She could rest her body even if her mind insisted on worrying the night away.

The next thing Lucy was aware of was a hand on her shoulder shaking her gently awake. She opened her eyes to see Mrs Hobbs smiling down at her.

"Heavens, what time is it? Has Lord Parfitt come back?" Lucy sat up with a jerk.

"There's been no sign of him, Miss Vaughan. It's six o'clock and time to get up. Mr Lovell wants to be on the road before seven. I've left hot chocolate for you both and the men have packed some of Cook's buns in the saddlebags. Molly will be here in a moment to help you get ready. Did you sleep well?"

Lucy nodded. "I never expected to sleep at all but the last thing I remember is Molly putting a hot brick in my bed and me turning over."

"That's good. You'll need to have your wits about you today. You can rely on Mr Lovell. I'm sure he'll get you to safety."

"Thank you, Mrs Hobbs. I'm truly grateful for all you have done for me."

"My pleasure, Miss Vaughan." A smile played around Mrs Hobbs's mouth. "I hope we see you again very soon."

Lucy watched Mrs Hobbs disappear and groaned. Emma looked at her and burst into giggles.

"Mrs Hobbs is trying to pair you off isn't she, Miss Vaughan? Although I do think you could do a lot worse than marry Mr Lovell, even if it's not my place to say so," Emma said, sweetly.

Lucy climbed out of bed. "I'm not going to dignify that with a reply. Come on we must get ready quickly. I won't feel safe until we're well away from here."

Less than half an hour later they joined Bertie in the kitchen. He grinned at Lucy.

"I thought you'd be early." He turned towards Arthur who was polishing off a hunk of bread and cheese at the kitchen table. "As soon as you've eaten that you might as well set off. Don't rush though, dawdle a bit."

Arthur grinned at him. "Don't worry, I'll give any men Parfitt has posted plenty of time to notice me."

Arthur chewed his last mouthful and gulped down some ale. He winked at Emma as he rose from the table. "I'll see you at the Red Lion later."

Lucy watched him go and raised her eyebrows at Bertie. "What's our plan for today then?"

"Arthur will set off on the grey horse, which should be visible even in this poor light. He'll use the main road to the vicarage in Mayford village. If any of Parfitt's men are around, we're hoping they'll follow him. He'll stay there with the vicar until I creep around the back and let him know we've arrived."

"Arthur is known for helping more than one local vicar with their sermons. But won't anyone following him think it's strange him arriving so early?" Emma said.

"The vicar is a friend of mine and everyone in Mayford knows he's an early riser. He likes to get a spot of fishing in before he starts work sometimes. The rest of us are going to make our way to Mayford through the woods. There aren't many places where we'll have to go out into the open. I'll leave you in the woodland behind the vicarage and return once I've spoken to Arthur. We'll go across country to the Red Lion. If anyone was following Arthur they will probably have given up by then. It will look like he's going there for a good breakfast to a casual observer."

Emma chewed at her lip.

"What's the matter, Emma?" Lucy said.

"I'm a bit worried about the two of us being alone in the woods."

Bertie picked up two small pistols from a side table. "There's no need to worry, Emma. Miss Vaughan will carry these and she's a very good shot. I won't be gone long."

"I suppose that's something."

Lucy shook her head. "How do we know Emma's aunt will agree to put us up?"

"Arthur asked me that when you were asleep, Miss Vaughan," Emma said. "My aunt loves company and she's got plenty of room. I know she won't mind. She's got a huge barn at the back too which my uncle used partly for storage.

The other part is used as a stable but there's only one horse and a gig kept in it now. Uncle was a cloth merchant, which was what gave Aunt Maria the idea to become a modiste. She does very well."

Bertie put his hand on Lucy's shoulder and a rush of heat spread through her. He smiled at her. "We need a base to lie low for a day or two, Lucy. To give Arthur time to go to London to request help from my cousin Augusta and the Duke. Don't fret, it will all work out."

There was a teasing note in Bertie's voice. Lucy went to toss her hair, only to find that short hair didn't move much. "I'm not fretting. I think it's an imposition on Emma's aunt's good nature. That's all."

"Honestly, she won't mind at all," Emma said. "Especially if she gets to see Arthur again. She was very taken with him, as was my mother." She went bright pink.

Lucy smiled at her. "It sounds like they're hoping you two will get together. Should I start looking for a new maid?"

Emma's face went pinker still. "That's all for the future. It will be years before Arthur will be able to support a wife."

"I see." Lucy caught Bertie's eye. "What if we're followed? I don't want to be responsible for taking trouble to their door."

"Then we'll think of another plan. I don't think we will be followed. I know the landlord of the Red Lion. We can go in the back way straight into his private parlour and no one will know we're there. When the horses are rested, we can carry on, using the back entrance as before. Arthur will lead us on a cross country route to Dunsford. Come on. It's time we set off."

The horses were waiting patiently for them when they arrived in the clearing in the woods behind the stables. It was a dry day and the birds were singing. The perfect day for an early morning ride in normal circumstances, with the early morning light bathing everything in a warm glow. Bertie fixed their saddlebags and threw them both up into the saddle. Lucy watched Emma, she seemed reasonably at home on a horse. A surge of excitement rushed through her at the prospect of riding again.

"Ready?" Bertie whispered.

Lucy nodded and urged her horse to follow him as he led them out of the spinney and past a flock of sheep gazing peacefully in a field belonging to the home farm. They stayed close to the hedge until Bertie turned his mount into a narrow path. She looked behind and Emma was smiling. This was so much better than life in the city. Perhaps she could buy a house in a decent sized country town and find an impecunious relative to live with her. Such a pity she wasn't getting her inheritance until she was five and twenty.

The path was tight in places and she concentrated on guiding her horse. The noise of a cart's wheels on a road reached them. Bertie lifted an arm to call them to a halt. He waited until the sound receded and then walked his horse slowly up to where the path crossed a lane. He signalled for them to join him and they crossed the lane three abreast. Lucy's breathing felt forced as she looked around in case anyone was lurking but they were soon safely back amongst trees and this time on a wider path.

Bertie set his horse to a smart trot and Lucy followed. Emma rode up beside her. Lucy grinned. How she had missed riding. They weaved their way through a criss-cross of paths. It must be adding miles to the short trip to the village but it was definitely keeping them as hidden as possible.

After what seemed an age, but was probably no more than half an hour, Bertie called them to a halt in a clearing. It was much smaller than the one behind the stables at Mayford Castle. The trees almost seemed to be reaching out to touch them they were so close. The tapping of a woodpecker made her jump. Lucy shivered. Even the birds seemed less cheerful here.

"We're right behind the vicarage. I'll tie my horse up. You stay mounted, I'll be back as soon as I can." Bertie jumped down and disappeared into the trees.

Lucy removed a hand from the reins and felt the reassuring outline of one of the pistols in her pocket.

Emma pulled her horse to a halt beside her. Her face was taut. "I shall be glad when they join us."

Lucy nodded. "I'll face the way Bertie's just gone, you turn your horse round and watch the other way. If you hear or see anything, give me a whistle."

They watched in silence until Lucy's nerves felt raw with tension. She took some deep breaths to steady herself. If only Mama hadn't persuaded her to have another season in London, Lord Parfitt might not have tried to fix his interest with her. He had never noticed her before. On the other hand, if father was in financial trouble, he could have found somebody even worse, if that was possible.

Bertie appeared through a gap in the trees so suddenly that Lucy started. Her horse jinked at the sudden tension on its reins but she soon had him back under control.

Bertie smiled at her. "There's no need to look so worried, it's going to be all right, you'll see."

He untied the reins of his horse and scrambled into the saddle. "Follow me. We'll soon be joining Arthur at the Red

Lion. Then you can rest for a while and we'll have a proper breakfast."

About ten minutes later they emerged from the trees onto farmland. Bertie pointed to a gate in the hedge on the opposite side of the field they were in. "That's the back way into the Red Lion." He stood up in the stirrups and looked all around. "I can't see anyone. If we stay close to the hedge there's a path we can trot or even canter across the field on. Come on."

The path was sound and they were soon cantering. Now they were out in the open there was a gentle breeze and Lucy enjoyed the feel of it on her face. The horse had a decent action. After a rest it should be more than capable of carrying her to Dunsford. She felt almost relaxed for the first time in days. She looked behind her. Emma too seemed to be enjoying herself, although she had kept her horse to a trot. When they reached the gate, it was opened for them by a smiling Arthur. A young boy came up behind him and took the reins of Bertie's horse as he jumped down. In no time at all Bertie had dismounted and lifted her down from her horse.

Lucy's eyes widened. "That boy will think it strange if he sees you lifting a groom down," she hissed at him, more to cover her confusion at feeling his hands at her waist than anything else.

Bertie grinned. "Don't worry he's not looking this way."

Lucy shook her head at him. She led her horse through the gate and followed the young boy into a barn behind the higgledy-piggledy building that must be the inn. She called to Emma to follow with her horse. If they wanted to be thought of as grooms, they needed to act like grooms.

Arthur helped them to attend to the horses then led them through the back door of the inn and into a cosy, private dining room. Bertie was already there talking to a thin, middle-aged man with wisps of grey hair arranged around a bald head. He must be the landlord.

Bertie waved a hand towards them. "I might as well bring the lads in with me. They'll be working hard once we meet up with my friend's head groom who's bringing me what I hope are going to be some excellent horses."

Lucy's eyes narrowed when she saw the landlord exchange a knowing smile with Bertie.

"I'll be sure to tell anyone who asks where you are that you'll be returning soon with some horses to make you the envy of the neighbourhood, Mr Lovell."

Bertie grinned. "I'm hoping my cousin, the Marquess of Hargreaves, will have sent me some more from his stud in Ireland. I'm delighted with the stallion I had from him earlier in the year."

"You mean that beautiful chestnut. He's certainly raised some eyebrows." The landlord smiled. "If you should have any spare carriage horses that are calm enough to be rented out you might send them my way. As long as they're not too expensive."

Bertie's eyes danced. "I'll see what I can do."

The landlord nodded. "I'll leave you all to your breakfast."

Lucy raised her eyebrows at Bertie once the door closed behind the landlord. "Did I hear you agreeing to give that man a bribe?"

"I will certainly try and send a few carriage horses his way at a very good price. If any rumours about me disappearing at the same time as you should crop up, I know he'll do his best to scotch them. Which could prove very helpful. Besides which we're old friends. The number of times he covered for me and

Peter when we weren't supposed to be here were legion."

Lucy put her hands on her hips. "I see. Something else you two did without telling me."

"I'm afraid so. We would have taken you but it just wouldn't have been the done thing to let you go with us. It can't be easy being female sometimes, young ladies are so hedged about."

Lucy nodded. A spurt of anger shot through her. "And, if we marry, we become the property of our husbands. Not that you would know about such things." She couldn't keep a peevish note out of her voice.

Bertie threw back his head and laughed. "Anyone who has spent any time around Grace Bamford would be aware of that." His eyes met hers. "You do realise that if you married a decent man, he wouldn't hold you to that. You'd have far more freedom than you do as a single young lady."

"Perhaps, but I've seen too much of what can go wrong in a marriage." She lowered her gaze. Just talking about marriage made her feel vulnerable.

"We're not all like your father, you know." Bertie shook his head with a frown and went to help himself from the breakfast buffet laid on a table near to the window.

Lucy followed. She was surprisingly hungry. She filled a plate with ham and eggs, poured herself a cup of coffee and sat down at the dining table. She took a place as far away from Bertie as she could. It was strange how she felt so uncomfortable around him sometimes when they had always been such easy companions. Emma and Arthur were sitting side by side and chatting happily, totally engrossed in each other. The food on the plates in front of them was hardly touched.

It was obvious now that Bertie and Peter had grown away

from her sooner than she'd realised. Perhaps it was inevitable because, as Bertie said, women were treated differently to men. The pair had taken her all over the countryside with them when they were all schoolchildren. The scrapes they'd got into. She'd loved every minute of it. But looking back their adventures had dwindled as the boys grew older. She sniffed. That must have been when they were old enough to start frequenting places like this.

Now they were grown up there was bound to be a gulf between her and Bertie. They had such different life experiences. A sigh escaped her. She turned her attention to her breakfast. On a trip like this it was important to eat when you could, heaven alone knew when they would have their next meal. Bertie went over to the breakfast table and poured himself another cup of coffee. He put it down and walked around to where she was sitting.

"Allow me to get you another cup of coffee."

Lucy nodded. "Thank you."

Bertie's hand brushed hers as he reached for her cup. Lucy shivered and closed her eyes as a rush of heat ran through her. It was almost as if she was nervous of him these days. Had Lord Parfitt upset her so much that the slightest thing made her suspect the worst of a man?

Bertie's eyes met hers and he gave her a smile before walking across to fetch the coffee. He looked a little uncomfortable himself. Would they ever get back to being proper friends? Bertie put her cup down in front of her with a small smile but he didn't meet her eyes this time. He sat next to Arthur and drew him into conversation. It was annoying that those two seemed to be working out their course of action between them. Once Arthur had left them with Emma's aunt she might get more of a say. After all, she was the person most affected by this. She would insist he listened to her.

Her shoulders slumped. How could she be so ungrateful? Bertie was going to enormous trouble to help her out of this fix. He'd even offered to marry her to save her reputation. Surely that was the action of a true friend. Not that she would ever accept his offer. She was just feeling strange because of the stress of it all. Once she was safe, they could perhaps get their friendship back on track. Until he married of course. She couldn't imagine a wife would want her husband to have close female friends. For some reason that made her feel sad. Perhaps most people felt sad when it finally dawned on them that they had left childhood well and truly behind and had a whole new raft of responsibilities stretching in front of them.

Bertie and Arthur carried on their discussion until Arthur stood up and walked across to address Lucy.

"I'm going to leave first, through the front door. I'll start off down the main road as if I was going back to Mayford then turn off into a lane that leads to one of our tenants. From there I can cut across country and meet you in a few minutes."

Lucy's mouth tightened. This was a far cry from the days when both Peter and Bertie had often deferred to her for ideas. She forced a smile and nodded at Arthur.

"What a good idea, Arthur. We'll leave it a few minutes and then Emma and I will go and saddle up our horses ready for the ride."

Arthur gave them a salute and disappeared through the dining room door. Bertie moved over to sit next to her.

"Will you and Emma be able to manage?"

Lucy's foot itched. It would be childish to stamp it at him, tempting as it was, but she was going to have this out with

Bertie once they'd left the sanctuary of Emma's aunt's house. If living with a man meant that you were always told what you were going to do then she was very right not to want to get married.

"We're grooms. Saddling horses is what we do." Lucy couldn't keep a peevish note out of her voice. "Come on Emma, Arthur should be away by now."

Emma followed her out of the room and through the back door. She put a hand on her arm before they reached the barn with the horses.

"What's the matter, Miss Vaughan. You don't seem yourself today. I know it's worrying but I just have this feeling there's something else bothering you."

Lucy sighed. "I know I should be grateful for all his help, but I'm getting really tired of being told what to do. I'm perfectly capable of taking a part in making decisions."

"I'm sure Mr Lovell is aware of that. It's just that, in a situation like this, decisions have to be taken quickly. When it's only the three of us you'll be able to have your say, I'm sure."

Lucy nodded and marched into the barn. Fortunately, there was no one in there. The groom who had taught her to ride had insisted she learn how to look after horses well, which had set her in good stead for this adventure. Within a few minutes she and Emma had all three horses saddled up. She took the reins of the horses she and Emma were riding and stalked out of the barn. Bertie must have been watching for them. He sauntered out of the back door of the inn and waved goodbye to somebody in the hallway, probably the innkeeper. Lucy gave the reins of her horse to Emma and handed Bertie his.

"Here you are, Mr Lovell."

Bertie mounted the horse using a mounting block. Lucy helped Emma do the same and climbed on board her own horse using the block. The horse must have picked up on her mood. It danced around as she threw her leg over its back. Bertie moved as if to catch her reins. She frowned at him and settled onto the saddle, pushing her foot into the stirrup with unnecessary force. She stroked the horse's neck and took some deep breaths. The animal soon calmed down.

Bertie gave her a quizzical smile and set off across the field along the path by the hedge. She and Emma trotted behind him. What she would really like was the opportunity to see what her horse's gallop was like. That would shake the fidgets out of her. But that wasn't going to happen. Certainly not at the moment anyway when the last thing they needed to do was draw attention to themselves. Bertie led them to a bridle path and within minutes they met up with Arthur, waiting for them behind a bend in the path.

"I saw no one at all on my way here, Mr Lovell. We should be safe to stay on this path for a while. Then we'll dodge about a bit."

Bertie smiled at him. "Excellent. We saw no one either."

An hour later Arthur called them to a halt. "We're close to the outskirts of Dunsford now. Emma's aunt, Mrs Mitchell, owns the first house on the high street. If you all stay here, I'll dismount and slip in the back way to warn them you're on your way."

"Why don't I come with you, Arthur?" Emma said.

Lucy suppressed a grin. Arthur was as bad as Bertie. "That seems a sensible plan to me. Emma's mother and Mrs Mitchell are going to be surprised to see us. It will come better from Emma."

Emma jumped down from her horse and handed the reins to Lucy, before Arthur could object. "Absolutely. I know they won't mind but I'd rather explain it to them myself."

Bertie held Arthur's horse. They watched as Arthur and Emma walked across the field and disappeared through a gap in the hedge.

Lucy felt on edge. She glanced around but could see no one. This feeling of being watched was simply nerves.

She moved her horse closer to Bertie's. "Let's ride up by the hedge so we can't be seen from the road. We've had no trouble so far but I don't think we can take it for granted that will continue."

Bertie nodded and they edged the horses close to the hedge. "I know what you mean. We've been lucky as yet but this is just the first leg of the journey. The very fact that Parfitt has pressed on with his suit, considering you're so clearly adverse to him, suggests he will go to great lengths to try and find you. I have no idea what he's up to. I think it's more than just being determined to marry you. There is something behind this. Money is definitely involved and yet I'm not convinced it's the whole story." Bertie looked puzzled.

"I don't know what to think. I suspect that somehow or other Papa has managed to get himself deeply in Lord Parfitt's debt. I assumed that was by accident but I suppose you're right. Parfitt may well have set out deliberately to get him in debt in order to get to me. Strange thing is, whenever I have seen him in society in the past, he's always had a dark-haired lady on his arm. Why set his sights on me?"

"Don't underestimate yourself, Lucy. You're a very attractive young woman. I can understand any man falling for you. But Parfitt isn't just any man. He's the nastiest piece of work

I've ever come across. The sort of man most sensible people would cross the road to avoid. Let's not talk of this anymore. We don't want to paralyse ourselves with fear."

"Let's talk about our plans then. How long are we going to stay here and where do we go after that?"

"Ideally, we need to move on as quickly as possible. Originally, I intended to travel with Arthur, then it would have been a groom apiece. It would compromise you even more, but I do wonder if we would be less conspicuous leaving Emma with her family and carrying on just the two of us. At least until we can reach my friend's house."

Lucy closed her eyes and hoped that the heat rushing to her cheeks wasn't too obvious. The thought of being alone with Bertie was disconcerting. Their relationship really had changed. Could it be that he himself had become interested in her as a woman? It was a strange thought. A scary thought. She could never marry him but it would be awful to lose him as a friend. She bit her lip.

Bertie caught her gaze. "Are you so opposed to leaving Emma here you can't answer me?" he said, so softly a shiver ran through her.

"It's not that. I'd be ruined no matter what if this adventure was to become known. It would also be fairer to Emma." She gulped down a deep breath. "I can't rid myself of the notion that danger lurks. Are you sure you want to carry on with this?"

"Of course, I'm sure, stoopid. Good Lord, I could never look Peter in the face again if I didn't protect you from Parfitt."

Lucy nodded. "I shall miss Emma but leaving her is best. She's a competent horsewoman but she doesn't look entirely secure riding astride. If we had to flee pursuers, I don't think she would be able to keep up with us."

Bertie grinned. "The three of us had plenty of practice at riding like madcaps, didn't we? She'll be safer here. I like young Arthur a lot and he'll have a permanent position with me. I imagine he and Emma will marry as soon as he's settled in. A good match for both of them. He's from gentry stock and it sounds like Emma will have an inheritance from her aunt one day."

"They seem happy with each other. I'll be looking for a new lady's maid soon I expect."

Arthur appeared through the hedge and made his way across to them. "The ladies are frantically getting ready for us. They're so pleased to see Emma they really don't mind putting you up at all. I'd better get back now. I hope the grey mare is fit enough for all this work."

"That's a good point, Arthur. That lane you went down after the Red Lion is home to a second one of my tenants a bit further along. Don't worry too much about getting back quickly. Take the mare along steadily and stop at the first farm you come to - Weatheroak Farm - and give her a rest. It's not far from where we met you. Just turn left when you hit the lane."

Arthur nodded. "Then do you want me to call into the first tenant briefly so a casual observer would assume I'd been there all this time?"

"That's a good idea. You can warn both tenants about the new agent arriving today and ask them to spread the word."

"Right you are," Arthur said cheerfully. "The mare seems all right at the moment. I don't think she'll be too tired to get me home. But I'll ride Thunderer when I show Mr Roskelley around later."

"I can see you're an excellent rider. Take Chalice, he's a

horse that needs plenty of exercise."

Arthur's face lit up. "Thank you. I'll enjoy that."

"Considering I'm sending you on a long and arduous mail coach ride down to London letting you ride Chalice is the least I can do. Right. Best of luck. Hopefully we'll see you again soon. Oh, and one more thing..."

Bertie leaned down from his horse and squeezed Arthur's shoulder. "Be vigilant at all times and take those pistols with you on the mail coach. Get an inside seat if you can. I don't want to lose the best employee I've ever had before I've even signed him up formally."

Arthur flushed with pleasure. "I'll be careful. Look after Emma for me."

"We've decided to leave her here for now with her family. She's not as experienced a rider as us two and it will be safer."

A wave of relief washed over Arthur's face. "You'll have fun persuading her but I think you're right. Take care yourselves."

CHAPTER TWELVE

Bertie watched Arthur ride off. There was no one in sight and yet he couldn't shake off the feeling that they had been followed. The worrying thing was Lucy seemed wary as well. They were probably both just being nervous. He moved his horse closer to Lucy.

"Let me lead Emma's horse for you. That's one thing we haven't thought of. Will Mrs Mitchell mind keeping it in her stables for now?"

"Mention you're going to take Arthur on in a good position and she will do almost anything for you I expect." Lucy grinned at him. "Let's go and meet Emma's family."

Bertie took one more look around. "The hedge gets lower farther on. Let's dismount and lead the horses in."

It was awkward dismounting and holding onto two sets reins. Lucy had dismounted before he could. Lord, was he disappointed at not having an excuse to lift her down? Suddenly she didn't seem like Peter's little sister any more. There was no doubt that she was a very desirable young woman. But she'd made it plain she wasn't interested in marriage no matter what happened. He had better get used to accepting that. They reached the end of the field. Marrying Lucy seemed a good idea the more he thought about it. Once she was safely away from Parfitt, perhaps he could help her to see him in a different light?

Emma was waiting for them. "Let me take the horse I rode. Follow me, we can go straight into the stables."

Bertie managed to reach the stables before they did. There was no way he was going to let Emma rub the horses down at her family home where there was no one to see them. Emma led them into a barn-like stable. He tied his mount up to a post and took the other two off Lucy.

"I'll see to these if Emma will show me where everything is. You go with Emma and introduce yourself to her mother and aunt. I'll be with you soon as I can."

"Oh yes. I can't wait to introduce you, Miss Vaughan," Emma said. She pointed out where everything was kept and walked to the door of the barn housing the stables.

Lucy stood, looking undecided for a moment, but shrugged and followed Emma. Bertie smiled to himself. Lucy was cross with him for taking charge. She'd always had a mind of her own and she was no different now she was grown-up. She was infinitely superior to all the insipid beauties who were paraded in front of him whenever it he went anywhere near a Ton party.

He had to marry some time. Surely, he and Lucy could be happy together. She had been annoyed at him and Arthur deciding everything. It would be wise to make sure he at least let her think she was taking the lead on the next leg of their escape. Perhaps if she could see she would have some autonomy with him she might change her mind about marriage. He worked hard rubbing down the horses.

Emma came back in. "Aunt Mary says there's plenty of fresh fodder in the other half of the barn. There's no need to worry about the horses coming to any harm in here. Uncle used to keep all his cloth in the other side when he was alive. It's nice and dry. Let me help you feed them. Miss Vaughan seems to be getting on very well. But then I never thought she wouldn't. Such a lovely lady." Emma looked up at him before disappearing to fetch the fodder.

That young woman was far too clever. She'd noticed he was interested in her mistress. Seeing Emma and Arthur together had given him ideas and obviously Emma wanted everyone else to be as happy as she was. Arthur was an impressive young man and he'd be a fool not to employ him. If Mr Roskelley had someone else in mind for his assistant perhaps Arthur could be his secretary. If he could write sermons for clergyman a few letters should be no problem, although he did seem really excited at the prospect of working as a land agent.

Emma came back with some fodder and three carrots. Once the horses finished munching their carrots, Bertie tied them up loosely where they could reach the fodder and a trough of water.

"Do we need to change that water, Emma?"

"No, Aunt Mary said it's fresh. It gets replaced every day for Aunt Mary's carriage horses and the hacks the servants use." They had visitors yesterday and the water would have been changed when they left."

Bertie rocked back on his heels. They hadn't thought of Emma's family having visitors. Emma must have seen his face. She tapped him on the arm.

"Don't worry, Mr Lovell. Aunt Mary says she has no visitors planned for the next couple of days at least."

Bertie smiled. "Thank you, Emma."

He was asking for a favour to stay here. He could hardly

complain if Emma's family were the sociable type. Something they should have thought of. He'd already been thinking along the lines of staying no more than one night. An early start in the morning would be best. The horses seemed as sturdy as he'd hoped. He and Lucy should be able to put some miles on quickly with them before they had to stop to change. The more distance they put between them and Rugeley Hall the better. Just what was Parfitt up to?

Bertie walked into the house behind Emma. He ran a finger inside his collar. Lucy was right, they were imposing on Emma's family. They were also quite possibly putting them at risk. Word of Emma being at home would soon get out, especially as the family seemed very sociable. On balance though, Emma was still safer staying here. As soon as he was back from London, Arthur would be bound to make sure she was all right.

He was shown into a well-appointed drawing room where Lucy was being plied with tea and cakes. Two ladies stood to greet him. They were quite clearly sisters. Almost identical but not quite. The taller of the two moved towards him and held out her hand.

"How do you do, Mr Lovell. I'm Emma's aunt, Mrs Mitchell." She ushered her sister forwards. "This is Emma's mother Mrs Burnley."

Bertie bowed and shook hands with both of them. "It's a pleasure to meet you. You must be very proud of Emma. She's been a great support to Miss Vaughan."

Mrs Burnley smiled at him and narrowed her eyes. "She's always been a good girl, very capable. It was lovely to see her young man if only briefly."

"They make a good couple. I've been very impressed with

Arthur. Mr Roskelley, my new land agent, should be arriving today. If he's happy to have Arthur to work for him I intend to offer Arthur the position of assistant land agent. I can't promise anything yet, although I know it's Arthur's preferred role. It just depends what Mr Roskelley's circumstances are."

Bertie smiled. "But whatever happens I will find Arthur a good position. I haven't arranged a secretary yet and that might be something he would be interested in. I'd prefer to place him as Mr Roskelley's assistant. I think it would suit him very well. The Mayford Estate owns several cottages as well as one or two substantial houses, besides the agent's house. Whatever job I find for Arthur will come with accommodation." Bertie ground to a halt. He was babbling. Emma's mother seemed to have no argument with it though. She was bound to be happy to see her daughter comfortably settled.

"Won't you take a seat, Mr Lovell?" Mrs Mitchell said. "Would you like tea or something stronger?"

"I'm not much of a drinker Mrs Mitchell. Especially not at this time of day. A cup of tea would be lovely."

After polishing off two cups of tea and two pieces of cake Bertie felt more human. It was time to get down to the serious stuff.

"I hope you don't mind us imposing upon you like this, ladies. I'm sure Emma has explained the circumstances around our flight. I know this won't go any farther. I've known Lord Parfitt for a while. He's a thoroughly unpleasant individual and possibly even sinister. I was so keen to get Miss Vaughan away I never stopped to think that we might be putting you ladies in danger if we stayed here. Be honest with me. If you would prefer us to go now and find an inn for the night please say so." His voice tailed off. Lucy would be safer here.

Both ladies shook their heads vigorously. "Definitely not, Mr Lovell. There is no need to worry about us. I've kept on some of the people who worked for my husband when he had his cloth business. Let me introduce you to Harry." She tugged a bell pull and the young maid who had served the tea came in.

"Betsy, would you fetch Harry please. And tell him to bring William and Buster."

"Do you want them in here, Mrs Mitchell?" Betsy looked incredulous.

Mrs Mitchell laughed. "Yes please, Betsy. It'll only be for a few moments."

Betsy bobbed a curtsy and disappeared. The family seemed very prosperous. It was surprising that they had allowed Emma to become a lady's maid. Mrs Burnley must have seen his expression. She smiled at him.

"We weren't keen to allow Emma to become a maid but she was determined to have some adventures. We were visiting friends in London when one of them mentioned Miss Vaughan looking for someone. Nothing would do for Emma but to apply. I honestly didn't expect her to be considered with no experience so we let her have her head. Miss Vaughan is a remarkable young woman and she decided to offer Emma the job simply because she liked her. I knew Miss Vaughan and her mother were well liked and I could see no harm in it so we let Emma take it. She's certainly enjoyed working for Miss Vaughan."

Bertie smiled. "But I don't suppose you're too upset that she's met Arthur. His father was a land agent but I expect you know that. He's an excellent young man. Now about Emma. We can't justify taking her with us, it's too dangerous. We haven't told her yet. I don't think she'll be very happy about it!"

There was a commotion in the hall outside. Good Lord was that a dog barking? Betsy opened the door and ushered in two men and the largest dog he had ever seen. This must be Buster. He looked like he had a fair bit of wolfhound in the mix along with a few other breeds he couldn't place. The dog walked up to him and started sniffing. He looked harmless enough but he had heard of dogs like that being trained as guard dogs. He waited till the dog had had plenty of time to get used to him. Eventually Buster rested his head on Bertie's leg and Bertie stroked him between the ears.

"Aye, he's trustworthy all right, Mrs Mitchell. Buster can always sniff out a wrong 'un."

"He certainly can, Harry."

Buster started licking Bertie's face. He laughed and pushed him off gently. "I imagine you've got this dog well trained or else he'd be no use as a guard dog."

"I have that," Harry said. "Nothing ever gets past him when I tell him to stand guard."

The dog changed personality in an instant. He stood tall and bared his teeth.

Harry laughed. "Step down, Buster."

Buster curled up at Bertie's feet, once again the harmless family pet. Bertie let out a whistle.

"That's some dog you've got there." Bertie hesitated. "I'm a little concerned that some rather bad people might follow us here and put you in danger."

"Buster will keep everyone safe," Harry said.

"I may be wrong, I hope I am, but the sort of people who may be following us will almost certainly be carrying pistols and knives and anything else you can think off."

Harry pointed out the slight man standing next to him. He was the sort of man you could overlook. Bertie studied him, especially the way he was standing. He looked as if he could be an ex-military man.

"William here was in the army. There's nothing he doesn't know about fighting and he's a dab hand with the pistols himself. Don't you worry about us. We'll keep the ladies safe."

"I'm very glad to hear that."

William stepped forward. His eyes gleamed. "This takes me back to the army, this does. Waiting for the enemy to attack. Why don't I have a scout around? If someone was following you on their own, they wouldn't attack straightaway they would go and fetch reinforcements."

"Would you do that for us? I would really appreciate it. I've had the same thought myself." Bertie looked across at Lucy. "We both had a feeling today that we might be being watched but couldn't see anyone. It could just be anxiety but as you say someone on their own might be following us."

"I love a bit of scouting, I do. Harry, how about I stay here for now keeping guard and you take Buster around and see if he can find any traces of anyone?"

A slow smile spread across Harry's face. "I'm sure he'd enjoy that. He knows Mr Reid's scent." He pointed at Bertie. "And he's made himself well acquainted with Mr Lovell."

All eyes turned to Lucy. She laughed. "Why don't you come and say hello then, Buster. I like dogs."

Harry led the dog over to her. Bertie chuckled as he laid his head on her lap and raised big brown eyes to her face.

Lucy stroked Buster's back. "You really are a lovely dog, aren't you? And yet you can turn so fierce in an instant.

Looking at that innocent face who could believe it if they hadn't seen it with their own eyes."

Buster gave her an adoring look and licked her hand. Harry called to him to heel and he stopped immediately and stood up.

"Good dog, Buster. Now let's go and say hello to their horses." Harry looked at Bertie. "He's good with horses. There's no need to worry about him."

"I'm sure he's wonderful with them but take care. I've only just bought these horses and I have no idea how they get on with dogs."

"Don't you worry, Mr Lovell. Buster will have them comfortable with him in no time."

"I hope that's all right with you, Mrs Mitchell?" Bertie said."

"Of course, it is, Mr Lovell. Robert, our groom should be back soon. He's ex-army. If William does some scouting around the area once Robert's back, he can keep guard. Then Harry and Buster can go with him. You had better take Buster outside now, Harry. William, why don't you have a walk around our grounds with them until Robert comes back?"

Harry and William trailed out. Buster stopped to lick Bertie's hand before he followed them out of the door."

Mrs Mitchell laughed. "Buster really has taken a fancy to you. He's a very good judge of character." She looked across towards Lucy. "When you're ready to leave I could lend you William for the day to make sure you get away from here safely."

"That would be extremely kind of you," Bertie said. "We need to rest our horses but I think our best plan is to set off first thing tomorrow. Then if someone is tracking us and has gone for reinforcements, we've got time to get away. Arthur is catching the mail coach down to London first thing in the morning. He knows where I'm going to head for in the next few days. I'm relying on the Duke of Cathlay sending some of his people to assist us. If he should be away from home I know the Duchess, my cousin Augusta, will organise something in his stead."

Mrs Burnley and Mrs Mitchell exchanged a glance.

"Mary dear, Robert's very reliable. Could we release William for a few days to travel with them, until they manage to meet up with the Duke of Cathlay's people?"

Bertie shook his head. "I don't want you to leave yourselves vulnerable."

"I'd forgotten Robert was in the army too. He's a quiet man but very quick-witted. We'll be safe with him, Harry and Buster."

"In that case I'd be delighted to accept your offer. I'll provide a gratuity for them all but I hope you won't mind if I leave it until later, when I've had a chance to visit my bank. I need to keep what money I've got at the moment for expenses on the journey."

"Of course, Mr Lovell. Now I wonder where Emma's got to. She was making up beds for you with Betsy's help. Very willing is Betsy but she has a lot to learn. I'm looking for another maid to add to my staff." Mrs Mitchell grinned at her sister. "We didn't think Emma would last long as a lady's maid. We've really missed her. She's not a girl who can sit around with little to do, she likes to be busy."

Bertie exchange glances with Lucy and they both laughed. "Let's hope Mr Roskelley hasn't already got someone in mind for his assistant. I can see Emma would be wonderful as the wife of a land agent. There's always plenty to do helping the tenants." Bertie looked across at Lucy, who refused to meet his eyes. "As a single man I'm in sore need of someone who can work with the tenants' families for me. I understand Emma's father was a clergyman."

Mrs Burnley beamed at him. "Yes, he was. Even when she was little Emma used to come with me when we visited people in the village who were sick or needy. It's in Emma's blood."

Emma bounced into the room. "That's everything ready for you. What's in my blood?"

Bertie waited and let Lucy answer. "Mr Lovell was just saying you'll be perfect as the wife of a land agent, Emma. Especially when it comes to dealing with sick and needy tenants. Since you had experience of that as a clergyman's daughter."

"I hadn't thought of that. Yes, I would enjoy helping out." She smiled.

"Which is especially helpful, Emma as I have no wife to help with the task." Bertie glanced at Lucy again.

Unless he was much mistaken, she was blushing. Although she was sitting close to the fire so, perhaps, she had been blushing before and he hadn't noticed. Now why did he keep coming back to this thought of trying to persuade Lucy to change her mind about marrying him? Truth be told he was quite concerned about marriage himself. But then most of that was worrying about ending up with someone as self-centred as his mother. There was no danger of that with Lucy.

"That might not be for a long time, Mr Lovell. No land agent has asked me to marry him yet." A smile played about Emma's lips." You look tired, Miss Vaughan. Why don't you come upstairs and have a lie down. I can lend you some clothes and you can dress up and have a proper dinner tonight."

"Is Robert back yet?" Mrs Mitchell asked.

Emma nodded. "Yes, I just saw him coming through the kitchen door as I was talking to Cook."

"Good. Why don't you get him to fill a bath with hot water for Miss Vaughan? Then send him out to find Harry and William, who will be in the barn or our grounds."

"Oh no. I couldn't possibly put you to so much trouble," Lucy said. "We made a lot of work for you as it is."

"Nonsense, my dear. This will probably be the last chance you have to soak away your cares for a week or two I imagine. Off you go with Emma and we'll see you later."

Mrs Mitchell waited until the door closed behind them. "Now, you were saying about leaving Emma behind. That's probably wise. She rode as a young child but then our circumstances changed. It's only a year or so since she's had the opportunity again and we hadn't even got around to getting a proper mount for her. She would hold you up."

Bertie nodded. "She's a competent rider but we could see she hasn't got the skills we have. Besides that, I wouldn't feel right taking her into danger. We may be making too much of it but both of us know Lord Parfitt and the man is nothing if not persistent."

Mrs Burnley frowned. "As Emma's mother I don't want her going into danger. That said, I'm not entirely happy about Miss Vaughan being on the road dressed as a groom without another female. What happens if you come across someone you know?"

Bertie ran a finger around the inside of his collar and took a deep breath. "I've known Lucy and her brother a very long time. Since Peter isn't here and can't be contacted, I'm doing what I know he would. I've offered Lucy marriage." He shook his head. "I can't deceive you. Lucy is adamant she doesn't want to marry. Rest assured, if her reputation is compromised, I will do my utmost to change her mind. We've always got on well. I'm sure we would deal happily together." Bertie's face went hot. Did he have to sound so eager?

Both ladies laughed. "We thought you were sweet on her." Mrs Burnley said.

"I don't know about that, but I had a very unhappy childhood apart from the time I spent with Peter and Lucy. In all conscience I would have offered her marriage whatever happens after this adventure. I would be lying if I said I was completely indifferent to her. My problem is she still sees me as her childhood playmate. The three of us were inseparable. My mother didn't have time for me after my father died. I was sent to stay with Uncle Ambrose at Mayford Castle for all my school holidays, apart from the occasional Christmas when we were invited to Hargreaves Hall.

"My father died when I was very young. I wouldn't be the person I was now without Uncle Ambrose, Peter and Lucy. I owe them a huge debt of gratitude and if I can persuade Lucy to marry me I will. It seems to me that's the only way to keep her safe from her father's machinations, whatever happens with Lord Parfitt. I'm well able to support a wife. You can be comfortable that Lucy is in good hands."

"Yes, I think we can. It was good of you to share all that with us, rest assured it won't go outside this room. You must be tired yourself. Feel free to do whatever you want until dinnertime. Stay in here by the fire, have a lie down or go for a walk in the gardens."

"In that case, I'll go and chat to William and Harry if I can find them. I'm really grateful for you letting me have William.

That will be a huge help. Thank you, ladies."

Bertie made his way outside and soon came across Harry with Buster. "Have you had a chance to look around at all yet?"

"We walked around the garden the area behind the barn. No sign of anything so far. If someone is tracking you, I'd be surprised if they came onto our property. Robert's back. We'll walk around the surrounding fields in a minute." A gleam of anticipation shone in Harry's eyes.

"Do you mind if I join you?" Bertie patted his pockets. "I'm carrying pistols and I'm a decent shot."

Harry let out a loud laugh. "I'd think you were a fool going on this errand if you weren't. Come on. Let's go and find William."

Buster trotted along by Bertie's side and rubbed his head against Bertie's hand. Bertie stroked his head.

"Ee, that dog has really taken to you. I can see you're a dog man."

"My uncle always had dogs until the last one died a few years ago. There was a wolf hound I was particularly fond of. Once I've settled down at Mayford Castle, I think I'll get a couple of dogs."

"It would be a waste not to, the way Buster has taken to you. If you want help with training them, I'm your man."

"Thank you. I'll remember that."

CHAPTER THIRTEEN

Lucy lay back in the bath and let the heat wash over her. Emma's room was well appointed and it was a luxury to have a separate dressing room with space for a bath.

"Is there anything else you need, Miss Vaughan?" Emma called through the door.

"No thank you, this is lovely. I could make a habit of this, bathing every day. I don't know about you, but I haven't ridden for ages and I'm feeling quite achy already. I'm puzzled. If you don't mind me asking, Emma, why did you decide to become a maid? You seem really comfortable here and I can't believe you needed to look for work."

Emma plopped down on a chair just outside the room. "No not at all. My mother was completely against it but Aunt Mary said work never hurt anyone. Their father was a lawyer and they were gently brought up but my uncle was a hugely successful merchant. I can see why my aunt decided she preferred to work. They were never lucky enough to have children and she wanted something that would challenge her."

Lucy sighed. "I can completely understand that. Women in the upper levels of society can be so hedged about, it's insufferable. I don't know what I would have done in London without my charitable work. I hope it works out for Arthur. Bertie is too honourable to insist Mr Roskelley takes Arthur on as his assistant if he has young relatives he wants instead. He'll make sure Arthur gets a good job though. Then you'll have your own house to run."

"I hope so. I know Arthur has some money saved up and Aunt Mary is bound to give me a dowry. I would love it if we could live near here."

"I'm sure it will work out. How long have you known Arthur?"

"He's been with his uncle for getting on for a year. I met him not long after he arrived through our vicar's wife. Arthur had been doing some work for the vicar. We've been corresponding ever since I went to London with my mother and aunt." Emma giggled. "Don't tell my mother though, she wouldn't approve of me writing to a young man."

"I like Arthur very much but it's a short time to be certain that he's the one for you."

"Perhaps, but it feels right to me and we've been able to see quite a bit of each other since I arrived at Rugeley. I've got some towels warming by the fire when you're ready to get out. We're a similar size. I'll get a few gowns out of my wardrobe for you to choose from. You might as well have a good evening tonight. Heaven knows how long you'll be dressed as a groom."

"Surely I don't need to dress up for dinner?" Lucy groaned inwardly. Would Emma take that as a criticism of her family status?

"I definitely think you should dress up. My aunt and mother will expect it. I don't think you should rule out marrying Mr Lovell either. He's looked at you differently since you had your hair cut. Before he was just remembering you as a child I expect. It won't hurt to catch his attention. You never know, you might change your mind." Emma put her head around the door and grinned at her.

Lucy shook her head. "I've seen the hell my mother's been through with my father. I don't ever want to marry anyone."

"Now that's a silly attitude." Emma marched in hands on hips. "It's very insulting to men. Mr Lovell is a real gentleman. I can't for a minute imagine him treating a wife badly. You've known him for years, surely you must know that."

"Yes, Bertie is one of the best of men. I'm just repulsed by the whole idea of being married. Being the property of a man. Having him tell me what to do all the time."

"Now you really are being silly, Miss Vaughan. My uncle was a brilliant businessman but I can tell you my aunt was always in control. He deferred to her on everything. Except business decisions. Even then he often asked what she thought. All I'm saying is don't rule it out. And don't put him off so much that he never asks you again."

Lucy sat up so fast water slopped over the edge of the bathtub. "How do you know he asked me to marry him?"

"It doesn't take much working out, does it? Mr Lovell is a complete gentleman. If you go travelling with him for days and anyone finds out your reputation will be ruined in your social circle. He's no fool and will know that. Besides, he obviously thinks a lot of you and if you're married to him, you can't marry Lord Parfitt, can you. It stands to reason." Emma sounded exasperated.

Lucy clamped her mouth tightly shut. She simply couldn't cope with this at the moment. It was all far too confusing. Perhaps Emma was right about not making it too difficult for

Bertie to ask her again, in case she changed her mind. She shuddered. Marriage was so final. She soaped her hair and then ducked under the water to rinse it clean. If Papa was short of money, was it beyond him to kidnap her and try to marry her off to someone else if Lord Parfitt backed off? Possibly not. Would she ever be safe if she didn't marry? She shook her head so hard drops of water spread across the room. Bertie deserved better than to be trapped into marriage to save her from a cruel father.

"I think I'll get out now, Emma."

Emma disappeared from view and came back with an armful of towels. She placed one on a chair and held one out to Lucy. "Here you are. Now your hair is so short it will soon be dry if you sit in front of the fire for a few moments and give it a good rub."

Lucy rubbed herself dry. Emma pulled a thick dressing gown out of a closet and handed it to her. She sat down close to the fire. With the length cut off her hair her head was a mass of blonde curls. She rather liked it. It was already three parts dry simply by giving it a good rub with a towel. Her long hair had taken hours to dry.

"Short hair suits you, Miss Vaughan. I'll show you to the best guest bedroom. There's a nice fire going in there too. Betsy got it going earlier before we made the beds."

Emma showed her to a pleasant room with rich red damask drapes and a four-poster bed with matching hangings. The fabrics were stunning. Lucy stroked the bed hangings.

"These are beautiful."

"My uncle always had the very best. Aunt Mary still has contacts in the trade. She's got several seamstresses working for her." Emma grinned at her. "If you should marry Mr

Lovell, you'll be close enough to buy things from her. She takes great pride in what she produces here and has all the latest fashion magazines. We even have a short trip to London at the beginning of every social season. Aunt Mary likes to check on the new fashions. People come from miles around to buy their gowns here."

"I'm not surprised. Your aunt sounds quite a business-woman. In the unlikely event that I do end up living in this area, I'll make sure to patronise her shop. Where is it?"

"Right in the middle of the high street. She supplies materials for the milliner's shop next door too. They have very good hats. There's everything in Dunsford for the fashionable woman at very reasonable prices. There's even a good haberdashery store a bit further along."

"It seems impossible at the moment, but if I can avoid marriage, I intend to set up my own establishment eventually. Perhaps Dunsford ought to be on my list of possible towns to move to."

Emma shook her head. "It's no good fighting it, I'm convinced you and Mr Lovell are destined to make a match of it."

Fiddlesticks. Why on earth did Emma keep going on about it? She could feel her face growing hot. It was simply because she was being teased. Bertie had been her childhood playmate and that's where he would stay in her mind.

"He's a good friend from my childhood, that's all."

Emma shook her head. "You'll come round. He's a man now. I think you need time to get used to the idea. I'll leave you to have a rest and I'll come in a bit later with some clothes for you to wear tonight."

That was the problem, Bertie was very much a man. She

would rather still think of him as a boy. If he was seeing her in a new light and she rejected him would that mean losing his friendship forever? Lucy suppressed a shudder and made herself answer.

"I realise it would be rude not to dress up for your aunt and mother, but I don't want you to go to too much trouble."

"Oh, it's no trouble, Miss Vaughan I know exactly what would suit you. Remember what I said about making sure you don't put Mr Lovell off. Let's go one step further and see if we can make him really notice you. I've seen his gaze linger on you longer than is necessary sometimes."

Lucy burst out laughing. "You're such a romantic. Have you been sneaking down to the library at Rugeley Hall to read those novels Mama's friend sends her? You're seeing romance round every corner."

"If you say so, Miss Vaughan. Make yourself at home and I'll be back in a while."

"Thank you, Emma."

Lucy watched her go and shut the door behind her. The bed did look inviting. Last night had been her first undisturbed night since they'd arrived back at the Hall and lack of sleep was catching up with her. An hour's nap would freshen her up. She pulled back the covers and climbed up into the large bed. It was the most comfortable bed she'd ever come across. Did Mrs Mitchell have contacts in the bed-making trade as well? She was certainly a redoubtable woman. There had been no need for Emma to find herself a job. Perhaps the ladies had rather naïvely hoped that a pretty girl like Emma might have found herself a husband from amongst the people Lucy mixed with.

In her experience maids were more likely to be violated by

well-to-do men than whisked off to church to marry them. Emma had been safe in London with her and Mama. The same wouldn't have been true at the Hall during one of Papa's house parties. The gamble had paid off though. Arthur was clearly a young man who was going somewhere, especially with Bertie's patronage. They would have a comfortable lifestyle. She drifted off into a deep sleep until an image of Lord Parfitt, looking even more depraved than normal, intruded upon her dreams.

They were in a shabby room with faded curtains, probably a seedy inn hidden away somewhere. She was lying on her back on the grubby looking coverlet of a bed so hard and lumpy she might as well be lying on the ground. Parfitt was throwing off his clothes. Once his chest was bare, he turned towards her and licked his lips. His grin stretched his features into a grotesque parody of a smile as he undid the buttons on the fall front of his pantaloons.

Her head threshed from side to side but she was powerless to get off the bed as if some invisible force was holding her down. Parfitt's leering face was getting closer and closer until his breath ruffled her hair. Still, she couldn't move and when she tried to scream no sound came out. With a superhuman effort she sat up and tried to push him off. His lips found hers. No! Lucy woke with a start, heart thumping. She was sitting up in bed with the breeze from a window Emma must have left open playing across her face.

Lucy shivered violently and pulled the covers round herself tightly. What a horrible dream, but one that could become a terrifying reality if she didn't avoid marriage to Parfitt. She breathed deeply for a few moments and the shivers subsided. There was a knock at the door and Emma came in creating a welcome distraction. Lucy gasped as she saw the gown that Emma was carrying over her arm. It was the prettiest rose pink silk evening gown she'd ever seen. Surely far too dressy for dinner in the country? Emma held the gown up for her to have a better look.

"This would suit you beautifully Miss Vaughan. A customer ordered it and then disappeared so Aunt Mary gave it to me as it was nearly finished and I was a similar size." Emma laughed. "I often get beautiful gowns from her for similar reasons or simply because she loved the fabric and wanted to see what it looked like made up. I've got a closet full of beautiful things. That's why I knew I'd have no trouble being a lady's maid. Betsy sometimes helps me with anything that's difficult to do up, but most of the time I look after myself."

"You make me feel guilty for employing a lady's maid. I'd be quite happy to go around in the sort of clothes grooms wear all the time. Peter used to give me his old clothes and we'd sneak off with me dressed like a boy. Peter taught me how to ride astride. Once you're used to it it's really liberating."

Emma put her head on one side. "I can imagine that. It feels very strange to me because I'm not used to it."

Lucy breathed hard. Perhaps this was a good moment to mention the plan to leave Emma behind.

"I hate to say this, Emma. But Bertie and I think it would be safer for you to stay here. Largely because, although you're a competent rider, we could tell you weren't used to riding astride. We've both had years of experience in the saddle. Bertie more than me but I rode all the time when I was at home as a child, right up to the age of seventeen. If it came to a chase, we'd have a good chance of getting away."

Emma looked crestfallen. "I was so looking forward to the

adventure. I know what you're saying though. It will be safer for you two if you don't have to worry about me." Her face brightened. "At least I'll be able to see Arthur fairly soon. He's bound to call on me once he's back at Mayford Castle. I do hope this Mr Roskelley wants to take him on. I know Arthur won't contemplate marriage until he's safely established. I'm really looking forward to us being together and having a home of my own to run. Aunt Mary has no other relatives but us and she's told me that she'll be leaving equal shares of her wealth to me and my brother. So, we'll be well set up."

"You certainly will. Thank you for being so understanding, Emma. It's for the best. I would never have forgiven myself if you'd come with us and something had happened to you."

Emma sighed. "These last few days have been so exciting. I suppose I've had my taste of adventure. Right. Let's get you dressed for this evening. I'm going to make it impossible for Mr Lovell to take his eyes off you."

Emma set to with a will. She helped Lucy into the gown and stood back to study it. "It looks every bit as good as I thought it would. It fits you well."

Lucy luxuriated in the feel of the shimmering, rose pink silk. The material was first rate. Emma settled her down in a chair in front of a small table with a large looking glass standing on it and tidied her hair. She brushed the hair at the sides out into longer curls framing Lucy's face but left the front tightly curled so that it hugged her head. She finished off by pushing a comb decorated with a matching ribbon into the hair at the back of Lucy's head to give an impression of height. Lucy gasped. The style was simple but effective.

"I think short hair suits me better." Lucy studied Emma. "It suits you too."

"I don't know about that, but it's going to be a lot less trouble. I don't suppose you brought a necklace with you, did you?"

"There's a string of pearls in an inside pocket of my coat, along with what money I'd got left to bring with me."

"Perfect. You find it out and I'll go and get dressed."

"I feel as if I ought to offer to help you."

"Oh, don't worry about that. I'll get Betsy to help. She would love to be a lady's maid and she's hoping that eventually I'll be in a position to employ her as one. You never know. Aunt will give me a sizeable marriage portion. If I know Arthur, he'll have all of that settled on me. He's determined to provide for me."

"That's very commendable. I'm sure you'll be really happy together."

"I'm sure you'll be very happy with Mr Lovell." Emma sashayed out of the room before Lucy could answer.

Lucy found her coat neatly folded on top of a chest and pulled out the pearls. They were of beautiful quality. She ran her fingers over them, the only part of her inheritance from her great aunt she had received at the age of one and twenty. She was grateful for the inheritance but even that wasn't fair. Peter had received all of his share as soon as the will was settled since he was of age. Why was a young man of one and twenty considered capable of handling his finances but not a woman?

But then life wasn't fair. She was a lot better off than so many people. Although somebody like Emma, from a comfortable background without all the society expectations on them, was perhaps the luckiest of all. She got up and walked around. There was no point wallowing in self-pity. There were people who didn't have enough to eat and children who couldn't read or write. Even children who spent large parts of their life living on the streets. She'd seen plenty of those in her charity work. She shivered and rubbed the top of her arms.

Emma bounced back in shortly afterwards. It was a shame Arthur wasn't here to see her. She too was wearing a silk gown; this one was of a soft shade of amber. A string of dainty polished amber beads hung around her neck. A silk, amber coloured rose attached to a tortoiseshell comb, nestled in her dusky curls.

"My word, Emma. You look quite beautiful."

Emma blushed a fetching pink. "Thank you. Not very warm these evening gowns though, are they? I'll go and fetch some shawls. I've got some lovely delicate woollen ones, a present from one of my uncle's friends who deals in them."

She ran from the room and soon returned with two shawls draped over her arm.

"Have you found that necklace?"

Lucy held out the string of pearls. "I inherited this from my great aunt."

Emma took the necklace from her and held it up. "This is lovely." She placed it around Lucy's neck and fastened the catch. Then draped a delicate, Paisley shawl, in a deeper shade of rose pink to the gown, around Lucy's shoulders. "There, you look perfect. Let's go down to the drawing room."

Lucy followed her out, being careful not to trip on the pair of evening slippers Emma had lent her, which were a size too big. When they reached the drawing room the door was ajar. Bertie was standing in front of the fire talking to Emma's mother and aunt who were seated on a sofa. Emma pushed her through the door.

"In you go. Try and make a grand entrance. Hold your head

high and try not to look at your feet, even if you don't feel very secure in my shoes."

Lucy laughed and walked through the door. Bertie looked up from his conversation and his mouth dropped open. He stood as if transfixed, staring at her, before he recovered himself and bowed to them both. A rush of heat swept Lucy from head to toe. Her fingers tingled and she felt lightheaded. She must be tired from all the worry. Her nervous state had absolutely nothing to do with the heat in Bertie's gaze as his eyes had rested on her.

Bertie rose from his bow. "Good evening, ladies. You look quite charming. What beautiful gowns you're wearing."

"Thank you, Mr Lovell," Emma said. "Some of my aunt's creations."

Bertie smiled. "Exquisite. Arthur will be a proud man when he places his ring on your finger."

It was Emma's turn to blush. She shook her head. "We're both young yet."

Emma's mother smiled. "Both you girls look very fine indeed. Why don't you take a seat until dinner is ready?"

Lucy sat next to Mrs Mitchell. "I've been admiring the fabrics in the guest room. Your husband certainly had wonderful taste. She stroked the skirt of the pink silk evening gown. I have to say this is beautiful too."

Betsy put her head around the door and bobbed a quick curtsy. She addressed Mrs Mitchell. "Cook says dinner is ready."

Mrs Mitchell took her sister's arm and they led the way into the dining room. Bertie held out an arm to both girls.

"Allow me to escort you, ladies."

He smiled down at Lucy and she missed her step, nearly

falling over. Bertie held her upright.

She looked at the floor unable to meet his gaze. "I'm sorry I'm so clumsy, these lovely slippers Emma lent me are a little bit too large."

Lucy had a feeling Bertie wouldn't believe that was the reason she had fallen any more than she did. She plucked up the courage to lift her gaze to his and he smiled at her. She held tight to his arm in case she tripped again and was glad when they finally reached the sanctuary of the dining room. Bertie released them and Lucy moved to sit next to Mrs Mitchell. Emma was too quick for her and manoeuvred her so that she had no choice but to sit in the chair next to Bertie.

Bertie pulled out her chair and his knuckle brushed the back of her shoulder as he pushed the chair in for her. Lucy closed her eyes. Even that briefest of touches seemed to affect her. He had a reputation for elegance that stopped just the right side of dandyism. Yet he had never had this effect upon her before. He was wearing riding clothes, the only things he had with him. Perhaps that made her see him differently?

Or was Emma right and he was becoming more than a childhood friend in her eyes? Bertie always looked elegant whatever he was wearing but she had never registered that before. He was simply Bertie. Perhaps it was the rugged cut of his riding coat emphasising his physique that drew her attention. In the country he was a man of action rather than a fashionable man about Town. Somehow, it made his masculinity more obvious.

A rather nervous-looking Betsy came in with a tureen of soup. For one awful moment it looked as if she might drop it. Bertie jumped up and took it from her and placed it in the middle of the table.

"Thank you, Mr Lovell," Mrs Mitchell said. "That will be all thank you, Betsy. We'll serve ourselves."

Betsy ran out and Bertie took charge of the soup. Allow me to help you ladies. That smells delicious."

"Thank you. This is Cook's own recipe for white vegetable soup. It's one of our favourites. The bread she bakes to go with it is excellent too. We prefer plain fare to what is generally served in smarter households in London. I hope you'll bear with us."

"My pleasure, Mrs Mitchell. I can't tell you how tedious some of the dinners in Town are. I much prefer plain whole-some cooking myself."

The soup was followed by roast chicken and a good selection of vegetables. Lucy forced herself to eat. Her appetite seemed to have deserted her this week and sitting so close to Bertie wasn't helping. If Bertie was feeling this strange tug of attraction to her then it certainly wasn't affecting his appetite. He tucked in happily to every course that came along and chatted away to his hostesses.

Lucy did her best to join in. Emma was surprisingly quiet, perhaps thinking about Arthur. She might be worrying about how he was getting on with Mr Roskelley. Assuming he had arrived on time. There was a gap in the conversation when Betsy arrived with a dish of pears cooked in brandy. When she left Lucy raised the subject.

"I wonder what time Mr Roskelley arrived."

"I was thinking about that," Emma said. "I do hope they get on."

Bertie laughed. "It would be difficult not to get on with Arthur. If Mr Roskelley should take against him that would give me serious pause for thought about Mr Roskelley. Don't worry, Emma. If Mr Roskelley has got someone he wants to take on as his assistant, I'll employ Arthur as my secretary. If he doesn't enjoy that and still wants to be a land agent, I'll find him a position with a friend I trust."

"Thank you, Mr Lovell."

Mrs Mitchell offered to leave him in the dining room with a bottle of port once the meal was over.

Bertie shook his head. "I need to keep a clear head. I'll be happy with a cup of tea with you ladies in the drawing room if you've no objection."

"I've no objection." Mrs Mitchell looked at the others.

Mrs Burnley shook her head. "I've no objection and I'm sure the others haven't either."

"Good. You carry on into the drawing room. I'm going to consult with Cook. I'll be back shortly."

Mrs Burnley took her daughter's arm and steered her towards the sitting room. Lucy found herself alone with Bertie. He smiled down at her and the warm expression she had noticed earlier was even stronger.

Bertie held out his arm. "There is no need to look so nervous. I was impressed by William. He'll help us stay safe. Let's go and sit by the fire. You're shivering. I can never understand why ladies' evening wear isn't designed to keep out the cold."

Lucy placed her hand on his arm and allowed him to lead her into the drawing room. Mrs Burnley looked at Bertie and gave him a slight nod towards the sofa by the fire. Heavens, even Emma's family were trying to match her with Bertie now. He looked completely relaxed and he allowed his arm to rest along the top of the sofa behind her. They weren't touching but she could feel the heat of him through the thin material of the shawl.

"You have an excellent team here, Mrs Burnley. William and Harry, with a lot of help from Buster of course, have had a really good look around. No one has been onto your property, but Buster got quite excited when he walked around the field that we crossed to get here. Harry suspects someone may have been following us."

Lucy tensed. "I know I should have been expecting we would be followed. . ."

"But it's come as a shock to have it confirmed," Bertie finished for her. "Of course, it may simply have been some random stranger taking a shortcut. We'll be on full alert tomorrow to be sure. Tonight, Harry and Buster will sleep with the horses. Harry informs me that if anyone comes within fifty yards of the house Buster will let us know in no uncertain terms."

Mrs Burnley laughed. "Oh, he will. One of the squire's cows got out and found its way into that field. Buster set up an enormous racket and woke the whole household. The cow was staring at him over the gate."

Mrs Mitchell came in and settled in the chair next to Bertie. "Yes, Buster is a marvellous guard dog. You can sleep soundly tonight. It will help having William with you but what do you plan to do tomorrow or would you rather not say?"

Bertie looked at Lucy. "If Lucy agrees I think we need to circle around a bit. I'm planning to make for London eventually. I have a good friend who lives less than twenty miles north of here. I think it will be a good idea to go and spend a few nights with him. I'm sure they'll be waiting for us to go south tomorrow."

"That's all very well but how do we get them off our trail if they do pick it up?" Lucy closed her eyes and soaked up the warmth of the fire. They were a long way from safe. "We could do with something to decoy them."

"Exactly what I was thinking," Mrs Mitchell said. "If William takes his own horse to ride with you, Robert could ride the horse that Emma was riding. He's not much taller than Emma. Dressed in similar fashion he might fool somebody who'd been following you yesterday. You can all ride together to start with. Robert can take a different direction if you suspect you're being followed. William is an expert at disappearing into a landscape. If anyone is following, they're more likely to pick up Robert if you split up."

"I wouldn't want to put him in any danger."

"If anyone catches up with him, he's my groom out on an errand. They will soon lose interest and you'll have put some distance between you and them."

Lucy sat forward with her chin on her hands thinking. "That has a chance of working but if they heard Buster and suspect we're on to them they'll be expecting something like that."

Bertie frowned. "Harry kept Buster quiet. He's confident that whoever had been there had retreated an hour or two before we walked around. It might be risky for Robert as you say."

Betsy arrived pushing a tea trolley. Mrs Mitchell thanked her and Emma stood up and went to help her aunt serve the tea. She handed a cup to Bertie.

"If I were you, Mr Lovell, I'd see what William says in the morning. He's a master at strategy."

Bertie smiled. "I noticed that. Your husband certainly had some good people around him, Mrs Mitchell."

Lucy swallowed the last of her tea and put the cup down on a side table. She lay back and closed her eyes. Much as she'd enjoyed the ride, her muscles were tightening up. Thank goodness Emma had persuaded her to have a hot soak. She sighed

Bertie placed a hand on her arm. "What's the matter, Lucy?"

"Nothing apart from having a madman chasing me." Lucy laughed. "If you must know I was thinking how much I'm aching now. Before I went to London, I lived on the back of a horse but five years is a long time not to ride and we've come quite a few miles today. Don't worry, I'm sure I'll get used to it quickly."

"We can stay with my friend for as long as you like so you can rest."

"It's a good idea as long as your friend's house is secure. I'm surprised you're not feeling stiff as well."

"Even when I'm in town I try and ride in the park every day, early in the morning when it's possible to get a bit of a gallop. You look tired and I admit to feeling a bit weary myself. Perhaps we ought to have an early night?"

Lucy smiled at Mrs Burnley and Mrs Mitchell. "Bertie is right, it's probably best to try and go to sleep early and then we can get off early in the morning if you don't object ladies?"

"Not at all," Mrs Burnley said. "Emma will come up with you and help you into bed."

"Thank you. If we brush through this safely and I end up back in London I would like to repay your hospitality one day when you come up for your annual visit." Lucy suppressed a yawn.

"That would be lovely, Miss Vaughan," Mrs Mitchell said. "Now why don't you get off to bed?"

They said their goodnights and Bertie ushered Emma forward to lead the way. He put Lucy's hand through his arm.

"It will all work out, Lucy, you'll see."

Lucy nodded and concentrated on keeping Emma's slippers on her feet. She really did feel bone weary. Her thigh muscles in particular ached. Bertie must have sensed she was struggling. He placed his arm around her waist and helped her upstairs. She was grateful for the support, but the feel of Bertie's body pressed closely against her side seemed to set her alight. She had never felt like this with any man before. She needed to face the fact that she had fallen for Bertie.

It would be mortifying if he found out. Men always took notice of attractive young women, and she'd had enough attention from men to accept that she was attractive. There was nothing to suggest that Bertie's interest in her was anything deeper than that. They reached the top step and Lucy lifted a heavy leg onto the landing. One of her slippers fell off and she staggered. Somehow, Bertie kept them upright with one hand on the banister and one hand round her waist. He almost threw her on to the landing and followed her up.

"You do look weary, Lucy." Bertie smiled at Emma who had turned back to see where they were. "Which room is she in?"

"Turn right and it's the second door on the left."

Bertie kept a tight hold around Lucy's waist and bent down. The next thing she knew she was swept up into his arms with a hand underneath her knees. For a man who was sometimes mistaken for a dandy, Bertie was incredibly strong. He carried her along the corridor as if she weighed hardly anything. Emma opened the door of her room and Bertie carried her through. He laid her down gently on the bed. She heard Emma's voice from the door.

"I'll be back in a moment. I'll go and find you a nightdress."

Bertie still had an arm around her waist. She was half sitting up with the support of the arm. Bertie bent down as if to release her and the next thing she knew he planted a kiss on her cheek.

"Sleep well, Lucy." He kissed her cheek again and then straightened up and strode out of the door.

Lucy rubbed at the cheek. Had he really just kissed her twice or was she imaging things? She did feel tired.

Emma bounced back in carrying a nightgown. "Let's get you into bed, Miss Vaughan."

"Thank you for the loan of your things, Emma." She smiled. "I'm looking forward to the day you become Mrs Reid and no one will think it strange when you call me Lucy. I look upon you as a friend rather than a servant after all we've been through."

Emma gave her an impish grin. "If you marry Mr Lovell, I'll have plenty of opportunities to call you Lucy."

A feeling of gloom spread through Lucy. "I can't see that happening. Heaven alone knows where I'll be living for the next few weeks and months. I'll probably have to stay in hiding."

Emma shook her head at her. "Let's have no more of that gloomy talk. If I had any doubts before, I'm positive Mr Lovell has fallen in love with you after watching him tonight."

Lucy winced and turned away from Emma. Had she seen Bertie kiss her cheek? "I'm like a sister to him, Emma, of course he cares about me." She sat up and swung her legs over the side of the bed. "I had better get undressed and try and get some sleep."

"Right you are."

Within minutes Lucy was tucked up in bed in a thick, long-sleeved cotton nightdress. Emma hung up the rose silk evening gown and snuffed the candle by her bedside.

"Off to sleep with you. The fire should stay alight for a while yet. If I'm not up in time to see you off tomorrow, I hope you find sanctuary very soon. Goodnight."

"Goodnight, Emma, and thank you again."

The door closed behind Emma and Lucy pulled the bed covers tightly around herself. Was Emma right and Bertie was developing a romantic interest in her? If he was, how did she feel about it?

CHAPTER FOURTEEN

Bertie ran down the stairs, his head in a spin. Lucy had looked so vulnerable but what had possessed him to kiss her, even briefly. He reached the landing and took a deep breath. He couldn't face going back into the drawing room straightaway. It wouldn't hurt to go and check on the horses and that would give him a good excuse to get some time to himself. He slipped out of the house and walked along to the barn housing the horses. Lucy looked horrified especially when he kissed her cheek a second time. What had he been thinking?

That was the problem he hadn't been thinking. He wanted to protect her and cherish her and the implications of that were scary. But not so scary as realizing that Lucy was a long way from seeing him as anything other than her old friend. He would push her away permanently if he wasn't careful. The door to the barn was slightly ajar. He clenched his fists and ran towards it only to relax when he heard Harry's voice talking to Buster. He pushed the door wide open and walked inside. The smell of horses and fresh hay lifted his spirits, even though it was a gloomy evening and some areas were in deep shadow.

"Hello, Harry. Thought I'd just check on the horses ready for tomorrow. Thank you for keeping guard with Buster."

Harry looked up from the bale of hay he was sitting on. "I like spending time in here. There hasn't been the slightest growl out of Buster. Whoever was around earlier is probably long gone now. I'll just take him out and walk around the periphery of our grounds while you look at your horses. They all seem quite happy."

Harry saluted and called Buster to heel. The pair of them disappeared outside. The light of two lanterns, set on shelves containing various items of horse equipment, gave the barn a cosy feel. Bertie walked around with interest. Mrs Mitchell's carriage horses were tied up at the farthest end. He wandered up to them. They were a decent pair of matched bays. It might be an idea to switch to hiring a carriage at some point. If the funds ran to it, perhaps with outriders. Then switch it up by reverting to horses and so on.

A couple of sturdy hacks were the only other occupants of the barn besides his own recent purchases. He went round each one of his horses checking every part of them and feeling their legs for any heat. They all seemed perfectly healthy. The long ride didn't seem to have affected them. They were sturdy animals. What he couldn't be sure of was how fast they would be if it came to a chase. Lucy's mount would be carrying a lighter weight and he wasn't particularly heavy himself, which might help. William too, wasn't a big man.

Harry came back in with Buster. "No sign of anyone about, Mr Lovell. I'm going to sleep in here tonight along with Buster. The slightest thing will wake him up."

"I'm much obliged to you. Once I've got Miss Vaughan to safety, I will make sure you all get a nice bonus. I'll say goodnight. We'll need to make an early start in the morning."

Bertie made his way back into the house and put his head

round the door of the drawing room. There was no sign of Emma but Mrs Mitchell and Mrs Burnley were chatting comfortably in front of the fire. They looked up as he walked in and both gave him a beaming smile. They must be happy to have Emma home.

"I'll take my leave of you, ladies. We're going to make an early start tomorrow. I want to thank you for your help."

"Not at all, Mr Lovell," Mrs Mitchell said. "You will let us know when you're safely in London won't you?"

"I'll keep in touch. I'm not sure that we will end up in London. I haven't decided that yet. My cousin and her husband will be helping us at some point. I'll see what they suggest, but don't worry I'll make sure you know we're safe."

Bertie's legs felt heavy as he made his way upstairs. He and Peter had always craved adventure as boys. Now he was about to embark on the biggest adventure of his life and it didn't feel like very much fun at all. He'd always known Mr Vaughan wasn't a particularly nice man. Peter had been open with him about his father's treatment of his mother. Even so he could never have guessed the depths to which Vaughan would sink. What kind of man tried to force his daughter to marry a man of Parfitt's stamp?

Bertie trailed up the stairs and threw himself into bed as soon as he was undressed. William had promised to wake him up at six o'clock and seemed reliable. All he had to do now was get to sleep. He tossed and turned and eventually fell into a deep sleep. He awoke bleary eyed to the feel of someone shaking him.

"It's time to wake up, Mr Lovell," William said. "Harry's getting the horses ready for us with some help from Robert. Cook's already up, determined to make sure we have some breakfast."

"That sounds promising. Any sign of trouble overnight?"

"Not trouble exactly. But Buster did get a bit agitated around five o'clock this morning. Harry waited till he calmed down and then they slipped out and had a skirt round. We reckon someone is watching here, but they've retreated to a distance."

Bertie sighed. "I was afraid of something like this but I was hoping it wouldn't come quite so quickly. Arthur Reid should be on the mail coach to London this morning but it will be days before my cousin and her husband will be able to send help. Still at least we know, thank you."

"Robert is slightly built. He's going to come with us wearing the clothes Miss Burnley was wearing yesterday, especially her cap. As you suggested, we'll ride together for a while. I think we'll probably have a start. Harry and Buster are out and about. Buster will soon let us know if anyone is nearby."

Bertie froze. "I don't want anything to happen to Buster. There's a chance they might try and shoot him."

"Never you fear, Sir. They won't get too close to the boundaries so they will be out of range of any shots. Robert will have the horses ready. As soon as we're out of the house we'll be away."

"Right. The sooner we start the better, let's get going."

William put a hand on his shoulder. Not until you've had some breakfast. Robert and I will be ready with the horses in twenty minutes. Where are we heading for?"

"To Kinsey Court, to join a friend of mine. We start off on the road to Stafford then head up north."

"Good. I know where Kinsey is."

Emma and Lucy were down in the kitchen eating breakfast when Bertie reached it. He smiled as his eyes fell upon Lucy and for a tantalising moment she smiled back, before looking away and concentrating on her breakfast. Now wasn't the time to try and fix her interest. Bertie sat down at the scrubbed kitchen table and accepted his plate of ham and eggs from Cook He munched his way through it as quickly as possible, downing a tankard of light ale as he did so.

William crept in so quietly Bertie jumped.

"The horses are ready as soon as you are, Mr Lovell."

"Thanks, William. We'd better get going."

Bertie smiled across at Lucy, who nodded. She gave Emma a tearful hug and moved towards the door.

William stood ready to open it. "As soon as you're outside, bend as low as you can and run into the barn." He glanced across at Bertie. "Just in case anyone is watching us."

Lucy's eyes widened and she looked at Bertie. He shook his head and Lucy nodded and stood by the door ready.

William opened it and Bertie grabbed Lucy's arm. They scuttled across the gap to the barn at breakneck speed and tumbled through the door, landing on a bale of hay. Bertie twisted in the air so that he landed first to avoid squashing Lucy. She landed on top of him with a thud. The air was knocked out of his lungs and he lay on his back unable to move. Lucy felt warm lying on top of him, but it was better not to think about that. Lucy struggled to her feet, bright red in the face. Bertie gasped in some air and managed to sit up.

"Are you all right, Bertie?" She sounded alarmed.

Bertie coughed. His breath was still coming in pants but he managed to answer. "I think so. I'm only winded. I'll be ready to go in a moment."

Robert helped him to his feet and William joined them. Robert cupped both hands under Lucy's foot and threw her onto her horse. Bertie managed to mount using the stepping stone, his breathing starting to ease.

William grinned at him. "I know I said keep low. I didn't mean you to throw yourself to the floor. Are you fit?"

Bertie laughed. "As fit as I'll ever be."

Harry opened the door and they rode out in pairs.

William pointed to some trees ahead. "Let's canter to the trees but keep your heads down low over the horses' withers." He signalled to Robert. "Ride on ahead as fast as you can and check there's no one lying in ambush.

They reached the trees and Robert circled back to them. "All clear so far."

"There's a path through the middle of the trees, follow me." William trotted in amongst the trunks of a stand of oaks.

They all followed in silence until they emerged on the edge of a wide field that looked as if it had recently held cows.

"We'll canter straight across the middle of this field," William said. "Give your horses their heads within reason. We'll see how pacey they are."

Bertie gripped his reins tightly and rode behind Lucy. Her horse was going well. He loosened his grip on the reins of his mount and soon ranged alongside her. His horse had a good action. He relaxed, enjoying the ride. Lucy was a joy to watch in the saddle. She had a natural balance and poise.

* * *

Lucy leaned forward in the saddle and enjoyed the feel of the wind in her face. She had always loved riding and five years was a long time not to be on the back of a horse. On top of which it was always more fun riding astride. Perhaps that was part of the reason why she never even considered hiring a hack to ride around Hyde Park when she was in London. Arthur was clearly a good judge of horses, this one was going well, as good as many a horse which had cost a lot more. She looked sideways at Bertie and laughed out loud. He gave her an answering grin. She let her horse have his head leaving Bertie behind.

They had been riding through fields for some time when a flash of light to her right caught her attention. The others might not have seen it. She pointed to her left and tugged at her horse's reins until he was running diagonally towards the far corner of the field that they were in. She glanced round to see Bertie following her. William and Robert ranged up along Bertie's right-hand side. Hopefully, they realised why she was leading them in that direction. As they neared the hedge, she tightened her hold on the reins and gradually slowed her horse.

There was a stand of trees around a hollow, which presumably held water when there had been more rain. The horse slowed to a trot and she rode him into the trees. Bertie was right behind her, closely followed by William and Robert. Lucy felt in her pocket for one of the pistols Bertie had given her.

"There's somebody by the right-hand edge of that field. I saw a flash of light. I think they might be carrying a pistol."

Bertie smiled. "I thought it must be something like that when you veered off course." He too pulled out a pistol and edged his horse closer to hers.

There was a whispered conversation between William and Robert. Robert wheeled his horse around and disappeared into a neighbouring field.

A grim-faced William rode up to them. "I was hoping whoever is tracking you wouldn't catch up with us quite so quickly. We've got some open country to get through." His expression brightened. "One good thing, those are decent horses and you can both ride much better than most people."

Lucy caught a breath at a rustling noise in the trees that turned into a low-pitched whistle. "I think there's somebody there."

William chuckled. "Don't worry that's Robert's way of letting me know he's there. We would never hear him if he didn't want us to."

Robert appeared from behind a tree trunk grinning. "Who-ever it is I think they're on their own and they've left their horse a good field away."

William tapped his chin." Let's make a run for it. We've got quite a bit of meadowland to get over once we get out of these trees. And if we're out in the open and they come after us we should be able to see them."

He wheeled his horse around and led them through the woods. "I'll take the lead. Robert will stay at the back. We'll keep him with us. Shout if you can't keep up."

They rode out of the trees and galloped across a large meadow. Lucy's heart thumped but she concentrated on watching out for anything that might trip them up like a rabbit hole or suchlike.

"Have a look behind, Robert," William shouted.

Lucy was tempted to look behind as well but she kept her eyes fixed on the ground in front of them.

"All clear behind us."

Lucy glanced to the right. "I can't see anybody to our right."

William's horse stumbled slightly. They slowed their pace a little until they were at a steady canter. William slowed to trot when they reached the hedge and led them through a gap into another large field.

"I intended to weave about a bit but I think our best bet is to take the most direct route."

This time William set off at a gentle canter. Lucy glanced at Bertie who seemed to be enjoying himself. Lucy smiled to herself. So many people in London underrated Bertie. Those who didn't think of him as a wild young rake saw him as something of a dandy. When she had landed on top of him, it was only too obvious that he was solid muscle. He must spend an awful lot of time in Gentleman Jackson's boxing saloon. Her pulse quickened at the memory of lying on top of him. For a brief moment she hadn't wanted to move. But now wasn't the time to think about the effect on her of Bertie's body being pressed against her.

She looked around as she rode but there was no sign of anyone. There was a big gap in the hedge looming in front of them and William rode straight through it and turned left. William pointed to a stand of trees in the far corner and set off at a canter that developed into a gallop. It was definitely the right decision to leave Emma at home. She would never have been able to ride at this pace. The question was, how long could the horses keep it up? William looked behind, frowning. He was worried about something even though she could see no sign of anyone. Once they reached the shelter of the trees William called a halt.

"We've got two options. We can go along a fairly busy lane for a short while or we can carry on across country. There might be some more of your pursuers covering it if we take the lane. If we go across country whoever is following us could take the lane and then cut us off at the other end."

Bertie tapped his pocket. "We're all carrying pistols. The

lane is probably our best bet. The horses still seem to be going well but at this pace we'll have to change them before we reach my friend's house."

William looked at Robert who nodded.

"I think Mr Lovell is right."

"Off we go then." William patted his horse's neck. "This boy will go forever let's see what yours are made off."

They rode through the trees and across the corner of a small field and out onto a lane. The hedge was quite low at this point. Bertie stood up in his stirrups and looked around.

"I can't see anyone." He turned and grinned at Lucy. "I can't remember when I've enjoyed a ride quite so much."

William shook his head at him. "It won't be so much fun if we get ambushed. Come on let's get going."

They cantered at a steady pace and it was some minutes before they came upon any other road user. The unmistakable shape of a large farmer's cart loomed ahead. When they got closer, they could see that it was packed with crates of cabbages and other vegetables, piled so high it was a wonder some didn't fall off. Robert and William circled it.

A red-faced farmer pulled out an old-fashioned blunderbuss. "You'll not be having my cabbages any time soon. Away with you or one of you won't be going anywhere."

Bertie joined William at the side of the cart. "We have no interest in your cabbages but you haven't got anything else on board, have you?"

The farmer's mouth dropped and he put down his weapon. "Like what?"

"It's a long story," Bertie said and fished in a pocket. "Here's a guinea if you let us check that you're telling the truth."

The farmer's expression was so comical that Lucy nearly burst out laughing. "I think if he was hiding anyone, they would have attacked us by now."

The farmer stared at her. "Now Missy, what be you up to dressed as a man?"

Lucy gave him her sweetest smile. "As my friend said it's a long story. But you would be doing us a huge favour by letting us check your cart."

The farmer narrowed his eyes but took the guinea and bit it before nodding. "Why would I hide anybody? Look if you'd like."

William took Robert's horse and Robert jumped onto the cart and checked through all the crates.

"There's no one here but there's plenty of room with a bit of moving things a round, if that's what you were thinking?"

Lucy nodded. "Why not?"

Bertie took out another guinea. "Where are you going?"

The farmer sighed and glanced at the guineas. "I don't know what game you're up to, but if I tell you I've been all the way to market with some of my produce and now I'm on my way to Kinsey Ford to deliver these cabbages to a friend will you let me go on my way? I've been up since four and I'm tired."

Bertie's eyes lit up. He grinned at William. "That's just where we need to go. We're on our way to stay with Lord Kinsey."

The farmer looked at them suspiciously. "Are you sure you ain't escaped from Bedlam?"

Lucy smiled at the farmer. "This is all a big challenge you see. We have to get there without being spotted."

Bertie was quick to follow her lead. "Yes, I laid a monkey that we can do it. I'll make it four guineas if you'll take us and promise not to mention us to anyone."

"That's the quality for you." The farmer sighed and shook his head. "I'll take you all the way for five guineas. What do you say?"

"Done. Just to prove I've got it…." Bertie showed the farmer the rest of the money. "But I'll give it to you when we arrive."

"Fair enough. He's a decent chap Lord Kinsey. I expect you're safe enough if you're a friend of his."

"I know him well. We were at Oxford together."

The farmer nodded. "In you get then, I haven't got all day."

CHAPTER FIFTEEN

Bertie secured the guineas in the hidden inside pocket of his coat and leaned towards William. "It might be a tight fit, but what a stroke of luck."

William chuckled. "She's a quick thinker, Miss Vaughan. It shouldn't be too much of a squeeze for the two of you."

Bertie raised eyebrows. "Aren't you coming with us?"

"No, there's an inn not much farther along called The Crown. I know the innkeeper well. I'll go on ahead with Robert and help him with your horses. Then I can stake it out to make sure there is no one in there, or around and about, who looks suspicious. I'll leave Robert there with the spare horses, if it's safe. I'll watch for the cart to go past and then follow you at a good distance. Robert will stay for a few hours and then take the horses back to Dunsford. Mrs Mitchell won't mind keeping them there for a while."

Lord that could prove devilish awkward, just him and Lucy hiding in the back of a cart. William's plan made sense. He handed the reins of his horse to Lucy and jumped in the cart to help Robert to make plenty of space for them. They soon had the crates stacked more securely, with a gap in the middle of the cart that could just about be reached from the side.

Bertie addressed Lucy. "In you come. We'll be hard to spot

in the middle of this cart, come on."

Robert jumped down and gave Lucy a hand climbing up and over the side of the cart. Bertie sat down in the middle. Lucy looked round obviously expecting William to follow. William edged his horse next to the cart.

"Let's not waste any more time. You two would be better to lie down. We don't want your heads being visible."

The farmer threw William a piece of sacking. "Here you are, Mister. Cover the pair of 'em with this. I don't want them losing their bet or me losing my money."

Lucy's eyes opened wide but she copied Bertie and lay down in the gap. The sacking landed on top of them and within minutes the cart rumbled off. Something landed on Bertie's shoulder, from the smell of it a cabbage. Instinctively, he put an arm around Lucy. Her body went stiff.

"I just got attacked by a cabbage. You'll be safer with me shielding you."

"But you won't," Lucy hissed in his ear. "If anyone finds us like this my reputation really will be ruined." She chuckled.

"At least you won't be bruised by the cabbages if I protect you."

"I wonder how long this journey is going to take. It seemed such a good idea hiding in a farm cart."

"Oh, it was a very good idea. I could see William was seriously worried. He was convinced somebody had tracked us to Mrs Mitchell's house last night. He wasn't too worried about one person, especially with Robert going with us at least part of the way. I think he was afraid there might be quite a few men following. We're not completely safe yet but this is definitely our best bet."

"I suppose so. But I've been in more comfortable transport.

I haven't been attacked by any more cabbages, have you?"

Bertie was strangely reluctant to remove the arm from around Lucy shoulders. "Not so far, but it's more comfortable to lie on my side. There's not that much room is there."

Lucy's voice sounded distant. "I suppose not but you won't be able to stay like that for long or you will lose the feeling in your arm."

"Ouch! I just felt another cabbage. We seem to be going round a corner."

The cart accelerated. "That's better we must be on the straight now."

He had spoken too soon. The cart veered to the left and Bertie was thrown more closely against Lucy. His whole body came alive. Despite the smell of the old piece of sacking, the scent of lavender and roses tortured him. This would never do. He edged away from Lucy. Her proximity was having an uncomfortable effect upon him. He managed to turn over onto his back. Better to risk being bombarded with loose cabbages than let Lucy realise just how attracted to her he was. He raised his arm to cover his face, which had the added benefit of lifting the piece of sacking off them a bit, giving them more air.

"That's better. I can breathe better now. Let's hope the cabbages behave themselves from now on."

Lucy giggled. "Try and keep your face protected."

She turned onto her side facing him and he felt another draught of air as she put her arm across her face.

"There, as long as we've got our faces protected it won't be so bad. We don't want to turn up at your friend's house looking like we've been in a fist fight. I wonder how long we'll have to endure this."

"I would say we have at least five or six miles left. By cutting across those fields, we saved some distance and we went at quite a pace so we've got to be at least half way there, probably a bit more. I wonder how fast a farm cart can travel."

Lucy sighed. "This one doesn't seem to be going much faster than walking pace. We caught up with it very quickly on horseback, even at a trot."

The cart slowed down and lurched to the right. Lucy fell forwards and landed on top of him, knocking the breath out of his lungs momentarily. That was the least of his problems. He tried to concentrate on something boring in a vain effort to control his wayward body.

"Let's hope we reach a straight bit soon." Lucy managed to roll off him.

Bertie took a deep breath. "That's better I can breathe now. This clearly isn't one of those lanes that were influenced by the Romans."

Lucy chuckled. "That's an understatement. Although we do seem to be going a bit faster now. We will be covered in bruises being bumped along on this lane. Doesn't seem that well-maintained, does it?"

"I don't suppose it's any worse than most country lanes. At least the drive up to Kinsey Court is in a good state of repair."

They hit a particularly bumpy bit of road. It would be so easy to throw his arms around Lucy in an effort to spare her the worst of the buffeting. Easy but not wise. At least they were spared any more cabbages falling on them. The bumping calmed down and the cart picked up speed. Bertie let out a huge sigh.

"We're going a bit faster now. Less than an hour to go by my reckoning."

"We should have brought our saddlebags with us. Then

we would have had something to rest our heads on." Lucy stretched and turned back on to her side.

"I never thought of that. William was getting edgy in case we were seen. He's going to follow us. I imagine he'll manage to bring them both with him."

"I've just had a thought," Lucy said in a small voice. "What if Lord Kinsey isn't at home?"

"There's no need to worry on that score, I had a letter from him last week asking me if I'd come and join him as he's alone and bored with his own company. The only thing that is worrying me is the possibility that other friends have accepted his invitation."

"Oh Lord, we really will be in the suds if he's got a house party." She sounded worried for a woman who had insisted she wasn't bothered about her reputation.

Bertie lay on his back and thought hard with his eyes closed and an arm across them. He knew what he wanted now. Was it worth sounding Lucy out once again to see if she could be persuaded to marry him? She was no fool. She must have noticed how aroused he'd become when they'd been thrown together. There had certainly been a reaction from her. But was that simply shock? There was only one way to find out? He burst out laughing. Perhaps lying in the back of a farm cart with some smelly sacking covering you wasn't the most romantic place to make a declaration of undying love.

"What are you laughing at, Bertie?"

"I was thinking what a weird situation this is. This will be something to tell our grandchildren about."

Why on earth had he said that? Lucy had gone very quiet. Was that a good sign or a bad sign? Perhaps he ought to ask her again despite the circumstances. Even Ralph Kinsey might raise an eyebrow or two with them arriving like this. If they could claim they were betrothed it might make things easier. Why not suggest a pretend engagement and see if he could gradually bring Lucy round to the idea of making it real?

"Lucy, don't take this the wrong way but I've got a suggestion to make."

"What's that?" Lucy sounded wary.

"Your suggestion about Kinsey having a house party has set me thinking. He's a sociable fellow. We could tell him we're betrothed and use your idea of calling this a challenge. Then if he does have anyone else in the house it won't cause so much talk."

"It would cause even more talk if we did that and then they found that we'd broken our engagement off."

"It probably would, but you wouldn't be there to suffer the comments. If you hide yourself away in the country somewhere it won't matter, will it?"

"I don't like deceiving people."

"It's a bit late for that." Bertie laughed. "Besides for someone who values honesty, you were awfully good at hoodwinking the farmer."

"I suppose so. It's not the same thing at all though."

"No, it's not. It might make things a bit easier for you." A pang of remorse hit him. He was trying to deceive Lucy. Perhaps he could put that at least partly right. "You do realise I'd be quite happy to make it a real engagement. If you married me the whole thing would be forgotten in a trice. One of the benefits of belonging to a powerful family like the Lovells."

"Oh, Bertie, you're so sweet. But I don't want you to sacrifice yourself just to save me embarrassment."

Bertie reached out and found her hand in the darkness. "It

wouldn't feel like a sacrifice, Lucy," he said softly. "I'm extraordinarily fond of you." He squeezed her hand and let it go.

"As I am of you. I just can't see myself as a married lady."

"I'd be gentle with you, Lucy."

"I know you would." She fidgeted and her voice sounded strained. "If I could feel comfortable about marrying anyone you would be at the top of my list, Bertie."

Well, that was something. Should he press home his advantage or leave her to think about it? The cart seemed to speed up and then slow down again. Bertie tensed. The cart rumbled to a halt and he pushed his right hand into his coat pocket, and closed it over a pistol. Lucy moved closer and he felt her body stiffen.

"Say nothing and keep still," he whispered in her ear. "We might have come to a tollgate but be ready to pull out one of your pistols."

They lay side-by-side listening intently. They heard a voice they didn't recognise and Bertie stiffened. He relaxed as he heard their farmer answer.

"What do you mean threepence? This ent a wagon, it be a cart." The farmer sounded indignant. "You're new, aren't you? Anyways not seen you before but it's about time you learned your job."

"If I say threepence, it's threepence."

A man's voice with a rough accent. It was a tollgate then but it was just their luck to come across a new man. The hairs on the back of Bertie's neck stood up. Or had something happened to the normal gatekeeper? He held himself tense, ready to spring if they were discovered.

The farmer sounded even more indignant. "I come this way

every week to market and I know the rules. Here's two pence. Now give me the ticket or I'll be reporting you to the trustees."

The other man gave a harsh laugh. "I'm covering as you might say for the usual man. I'll take two pence this time. If I find you're trying to cheat a new man I'll report you to the trustees."

Bertie waited, hardly daring to breathe. Lucy had such a firm grip on his arm it almost hurt. There was a sound of a coach pulling up behind them.

"Hurry up there, man. Some of us haven't got all day."

There was a rumble of the gate opening and the cart moved off. The farmer was muttering so hard under his breath they could almost hear him. The new gatekeeper sounded as if he was arguing with the carriage behind them. Bertie relaxed. They were on their way. Shortly afterwards there was a shout from behind and the cart swayed. The nearside dipped and for a horrible moment it felt like they might be tossed over as the cart bumped along. Bertie held his breath until their slide to the left stopped.

The cart's nearside wheels found solid ground with a thump, displacing yet another cabbage on to Bertie's leg. The farmer had kept them on the road somehow. Devil take it, he would be black and blue by the time they arrived. He smiled as he heard the string of expletives the farmer gave out at whoever had nearly put them into the ditch, presumably the coach behind them at the turnpike.

Lucy let go of his arm. "Heavens above. I thought we were going to overturn there. It seems a bit of a coincidence to have a new gatekeeper with us being on the run. Do you think it could be one of our pursuers?"

"It could be. Taking over the gate so they can check everyone out. I wonder if William has cut across country to avoid the gate. I certainly didn't hear his voice, did you?"

"No. It would make sense for him to go cross country to avoid any chance of being recognised. We don't know how close whoever was following got to us earlier."

Bertie felt for her hand. "In a way I hope Ralph Kinsey has managed to assemble a house party. We'd be less noticeable then. Especially if we were to be introduced as a betrothed couple. I was at university with Ralph and we have a lot of the same friends. No one would consider me turning up to be odd so there would be less likelihood of word getting out in the wider district. I do hope William's safe."

"William's a real expert at staying hidden from what Emma said. I'm sure he'll be somewhere. I don't know what to say, Bertie. I don't like deceiving people but if it's going to make us safer, it would make sense to say we're betrothed. Your friends are young enough to accept we're simply up to some sort of lark by arriving like this."

"If William gets there before us and manages to speak to Ralph privately, anyone who is there besides him won't need to know how we arrive. Ralph is a clever cove and he can be discreet when he wants to."

Lucy groaned. "Has it occurred to you that I haven't brought any gowns with me?"

"Devil take it, no it hasn't. Ralph's sister visits him sometimes. We'll have to hope she's left some clothes behind. She's a great gun. I'm sure she wouldn't mind you borrowing anything she has left."

The cart picked up speed and Bertie tried to relax. "We can't have much farther to go now, Lucy."

Lucy laughed. "I hope not. There isn't a bit of me that

doesn't ache."

A few minutes later the cart slowed down. Bertie made a mental calculation of where they were likely to be.

"I think we are approaching the turn into Kinsey Court's drive. I certainly hope so."

Lucy laughed. "So do I. Wait a minute, what's that?" She lowered her voice. "Did I just hear someone talk?"

Bertie reached for his pistol and they lay in total silence. They heard the furious voice of the farmer.

"You're not trying to cheat me out of my guineas, are you?"

Bertie relaxed when he caught the unmistakable sound of William's voice.

"You'll get all the money you were promised good and tight. You should be thanking me for saving you time." William lifted the piece of sacking covering them. His expression was grim. "Quickly, Mr Lovell. Give our man his reward and we'll be on our way. Lord Kinsey is waiting in his coach for you."

Bertie sat up, ignoring a moment's dizziness from the sudden change of position and pulled out the guineas from his pocket. He leaned forward so he could reach over to the farmer.

"Here's your money. Thank you for your help." He counted out two more guineas. "What did you say your name was?"

"I don't think I did say. Why do you want to know?"

Bertie held out the two guineas. "This is yours if you promise to keep this secret. I want to know your name so if it does get out, I'll know where it came from."

A head topped by a mop of well-cut chestnut hair appeared above the side of the cart. Bertie grinned. "Am I glad to see you, Ralph!"

Ralph grinned back. "We need to get you out of here fast.

Give Mr Wilson here his money and let's get you into my coach."

Bertie handed over the extra guineas and turned to see William helping Lucy out of the cart. He almost carried her to the waiting coach.

Ralph grabbed his arm. "Come on. There's no time to waste."

Pins and needles in the leg Lucy had been lying against made it hard to walk. Bertie was glad of Ralph's hand under his elbow urging him onwards. Ralph almost threw him into the carriage and climbed in after him. For some reason Lucy was sitting on the floor of the coach. Bertie went to help her up but was stopped by Ralph.

"Leave her there and get on the floor with her. Don't argue, I'll explain later."

Bertie's mouth dropped open of its own accord but he did as he was bid. He caught a glimpse of William and his horse disappearing into the trees lining the driveway, before his head dropped below the level of the window. Ralph banged on the roof and the coach took off at speed. Ralph lent over and pulled down the leather covers over both windows plunging them into darkness. The coach was going too fast for comfort especially for anyone sitting on the floor. Bertie moved closer to Lucy and put his arm around her shoulders to cushion her from the buffeting. She grabbed his other hand and held it tight.

"You're safe now, Lucy. We should reach Kinsey Court in a few minutes." It was a relief to get rid of the sacking. They could talk freely now.

"If you say so. Strange friends you keep, Bertie. I've never had anyone push me onto the floor of a coach before."

Ralph gave out a bark of laughter. "I like your style, Miss Vaughan. I imagine you've guessed you're in danger, but I'll leave it to William to explain it to you. Fortunately, there's only me at home today. My sister and her family went home yesterday. I'm expecting some more friends to arrive but not for several days. Which makes it much easier to keep your presence here secret. My staff are nothing if not discrete."

"As long as we can trust Mr Wilson to keep quiet," Bertie said, and raised his eyebrows in enquiry.

"I've no worries on that score. I've known him for years. He's a good tenant and he won't want to disoblige me. Kinsey Court buys a lot of his produce. He lives on his own and is not the sort to give away his business."

"I was pretty confident he was an honest sort. My biggest worry is that people will wonder where he's got his money from."

"He's more sense than to bandy it around. His daughter's got a big family and he thinks the world of them. I expect they'll get it at some future point. He'll tell them he saved it up from extra business I've put his way or some such. No, he's the least of your worries."

An awful thought struck Bertie. "Ralph, nothing has happened to the other man, Robert, who was helping us, has it?"

"Not as far as I know. But I can tell you there is a body involved. Who on earth have you been tangling with, Bertie? There wasn't time for William to explain it all to me, but I could tell a military man when I saw one and it was obvious from what he said that he was working for you. I did exactly as he asked."

"Yes, he's a good man. Let's just say I'm not Lord Parfitt's favourite person at the moment and he is definitely not a good man."

Ralph let out a whistle. "Parfitt is not a man I'd want to cross."

CHAPTER SIXTEEN

The carriage raced on for some minutes. Lucy leaned her head against Bertie's shoulder and closed her eyes. What a nightmare this was. Her head ached and her nose and mouth felt dry from being covered by sacking. At least they were safe and Lord Kinsey was happy to help them. Running away had seemed such a simple idea but it wasn't turning out that way. It was no good blaming herself for causing so many people so much trouble, she would never have expected Lord Parfitt to go to these lengths to try and capture her.

None of it made sense. She could only hope that Mama and Aunt Susan were safe. The coach swayed as it took a bend. They would surely reach Kinsey Court soon. Bertie tightened his hold around her shoulders and gave her hand a quick squeeze. She owed him a huge debt. The coach slowed and turned another corner before pulling up.

Ralph lifted the leather cover of the window by him. Lucy blinked in the sunlight. They had stopped near to a red brick stable block that looked fairly new.

"I've left my housekeeper waiting by the back door to whisk Lucy up to a guest room. Fortunately, my sister, Arabella, is a similar size and she always leave some of her clothes behind.

Mrs Adams is a lovely lady, Miss Vaughan. She'll look after you." He gave her an encouraging smile.

Lucy smiled back. Bertie's friend seemed a good-natured sort of man. "That's very kind of you Lord Kinsey. I'm sorry to put you to so much trouble."

Ralph laughed. "It's no trouble at all. I was feeling quite bored before you came and I can't wait to hear what's been going on."

Bertie helped Lucy out of the carriage. "I'll take you up to the house. Mrs Adams knows me well."

Ralph jumped down behind them. "I'll go and talk to my grooms. I can see William has made his way here already. I'll meet you in the library in a few minutes, Bertie."

"Thanks, Ralph." Bertie kept his arm around Lucy and led her towards Kinsey Court.

Lucy gasped when she saw the size of the building. It was certainly one of the largest houses she'd stayed at. It was constructed of reddish gold brick with pale stone edgings and castellations. As they drew closer, they walked past a well-maintained kitchen garden. Beyond that she could see red brick walls with an open gate behind the main part of the house. Most likely a walled rose garden. Part of the back of the house looked older, which suggested this was one of those country houses that had been rebuilt in the previous century on the site of a much older dwelling.

Bertie smiled at her. "You seem very quiet. Are you too tired to talk?"

Lucy shook her head. "I was taking in the magnificence of your friend's house. You move in more exalted circles than I do."

"I wouldn't say that. After all you're best friends with Grace

Bamford."

"Yes, I suppose so, but most of my friends live in more modest accommodation."

"Your uncle and aunt live in some style."

"Yes, they do, but I don't have any other well-connected relatives. I imagine most of your family live in places like this." She looked up at the castellations. "Very impressive and several floors high. I'm sure the servants will look down on me dressed like this."

Bertie caught her hand and she felt colour flooding to her cheeks.

"Don't worry about them. Ralph will have them well trained. We used to get up to all sorts at Oxford, Ralph won't turn a hair. You'll see, it will work out perfectly well. Ralph keeps a lot of servants. After what's happened today, I think our safest bet might be to stay here until we hear from the Cathlays." He looked embarrassed. He opened his mouth as if he was about to say more but closed it with a snap.

"What is it, Bertie?"

"The thing is. I mean.... Dash it all, Lucy, are you sure you wouldn't like to marry me?" Bertie's voice quivered. His face went redder than Lucy's felt. "I have an overwhelming urge to protect you and I could do that much better if you were about to become part of my family. I'm not convinced it's safe for you to stay in London with the Cathlays for long. There are two or three of my Lovell cousins you could stay with whilst we arrange the wedding."

"Oh, Bertie. I don't know what to say. You've been so kind to me."

Bertie squeezed her hand. "Don't worry, I don't expect you to answer me now. I know I'm not much of a catch."

Lucy caught his arm. "Never say that. You're a splendid catch. Too splendid for me, I don't deserve you."

"Now that's not true. I think you're feeling a bit blue devilled after all the problems you've had. Once you've had a day or two of rest and good food, you'll feel a lot better. I realise it's a big decision for you, especially with your views on marriage. Don't give me an answer until you feel ready." He gazed into her eyes. "The thing is, Lucy, the more I think about it the more I think what a good idea it would be."

Bertie's voice was gentle and she felt safe with his arm around her. It would be so easy to say yes now and hope for the best. But what if she couldn't cope with marriage. Bertie deserved better than someone as damaged as she was.

"All I ask is that you think about it, Lucy." He smiled at her and the look in his eyes made her shiver.

"I will." They reached a door and Lucy looked upwards at the towering building. "This place is impressive but it's intimidating as well. I can't stop worrying about what the servants will think of me turning up dressed like this."

"Whatever they think they won't say anything. Try and walk in looking like women dressed in breeches are an everyday occurrence." Bertie grinned at her. He opened the door and guided her inside with a hand on her arm.

Lucy's fear returned with renewed strength when she spotted the housekeeper waiting for them. Mrs Adams was tall and angular. The sharp planes of her face were set in a prim expression, almost as if she was looking down her nose at Lucy.

Bertie whispered in her ear. "I see what you mean. Do you want to go ahead with the pretend betrothal? It might make things easier for you."

Lucy closed her eyes for a second. When she opened them, Bertie was smiling down at her and she could see the housekeeper staring at them. She nodded.

Bertie nodded back and led her forwards. "How pleasant to see you again, Mrs Adams. Allow me to introduce my fiancée, Miss Vaughan."

Mrs Adams face relaxed slightly and she bobbed a curtsy. "I'm delighted to meet you, Miss Vaughan. Congratulations, Mr Lovell."

"Thank you, Mrs Adams," Bertie said. I'll leave her to your care, I'm sure you will look after her well."

"Of course, Mr Lovell. Follow me, Miss Vaughan. I've had the maids prepare the best guest bedchamber for you. At least the best one that isn't reserved for the family."

Lucy forced a smile. Mrs Adams valued honesty highly from that comment about the family bedchambers. If it got out that theirs was a false engagement, she'd be even more disapproving. They would be best moving on from here as soon as they safely could. The Lovells had always struck her as a delightfully informal family, despite Max Lovell being the Marquess of Hargreaves and the formidable exterior his eldest sister Augusta and her husband, the Duke of Cathlay, showed to the world at large. She would feel much more comfortable with one of them. Especially if she arrived correctly dressed of course.

Mrs Adams led her down a narrow corridor which opened out onto a spectacular hallway. A wide staircase rose up from the centre of the hall and then split into two halves further up. She almost walked into a suit of armour, so busy was she taking everything in.

"What a delightful hallway. I imagine it's quite hard to heat though."

Mrs Adams pointed to a magnificent fireplace. A huge log burned away merrily, surrounded by smaller logs. Even from several feet away she could feel the heat coming from it.

"That's most impressive."

Mrs Adams nodded. "Lord Kinsey is the heir to an earldom. This is the main family seat but his parents prefer to live in one of the smaller properties these days."

Her voice was full of pride. And of course, she had done very well to become the housekeeper at such an establishment.

They climbed the main stairway and took the left-hand fork into a wide corridor. Mrs Adams opened the fifth door along.

"After you, Miss Vaughan. The master says your luggage has gone astray. You're a similar height and size to his sister, Lady Lovering. I've sent one of the maids to look out some of her clothes. They should fit you until your own arrive." She looked Lucy up and down. "I imagine you'll want a bath first."

The disapproving edge to Mrs Adam's voice made Lucy grateful she had agreed to the fake betrothal. "Thank you, I would appreciate that."

A young and rather nervous looking maid was waiting for her in one of the finest bedrooms she had ever seen. It looked as if it had been recently decorated. A gold striped paper covered the walls and the drapes and bed hangings were a beautiful shade of rose pink, adorned with gold embroidery. It could have been overpowering but the furniture in the room was so delicately made that it softened the effect.

Mrs Adams nodded at the maid. "This is Hannah, Miss Vaughan. I'll leave you to her care."

"Thank you, Mrs Adams."

Mrs Adams nodded and left the room. Lucy swallowed and

smiled at the young maid to try and put her at her ease. The poor girl looked every bit as nervous as she had felt with the housekeeper.

"How do you do, Hannah. I'm grateful to you for looking after me at such short notice."

"It's no trouble, Miss. We have lots of people turn up here who are not always expected. Lady Lovering arrived with her entire family a few days ago. The first we knew about it was when she sent a groom on ahead to warn us, no more than two hours before they arrived. Mrs Adams was so cross." Hannah went a fiery red. "Lawks Miss, I shouldn't have said that. You won't say anything to Mrs Adams, will you?"

"Of course not, Hannah. I would hate to get you into trouble. Not that I think Mrs Adams would take any notice if I tried. I don't think she's taken to me."

Hannah giggled. "She's like that with everyone, Miss. Don't you worry. Mr Lovell is a bit of a favourite with her. Are you going to marry him?" Hannah clapped a hand to her mouth. "Oh no, I shouldn't have said that either. My tongue does run away with me. Mrs Adams says it will get me into big trouble one day."

Lucy cringed. What could she say? If she said no, it would give the lie to their pretend betrothal. And yet lying sat heavily with her. She took a deep breath, she had no alternative but to lie, at least by omission.

"You're young yet, Hannah. You'll get used to being more careful about what you say. Mr Lovell and I are betrothed." She hesitated as a thought struck her. "How did you know about that?"

Hannah grinned at her. "Don't tell Mrs Adams. The senior maids were given the afternoon off after Lady Lovering left because of all the extra work. Some of us junior maids were watching the two of you together from an upstairs window. It was obvious."

Lucy felt her face go red. She was saved from the necessity of replying by a knock at the door. Hannah opened it and two footmen came in carrying a large bath. They placed it in front of the fire. What a luxury to have a fire in her bedroom at this time of year.

"Hot water will be up in a few minutes, Miss," the elder of the footmen said, once they had set the bath down.

Hannah grinned at her and waited for the footmen to leave. "I'm so pleased for you, Miss Vaughan. We all like Mr Lovell. He's very kind to us servants but he never causes us maids any bother if you know what I mean."

"I'm sure he doesn't but I fear Mrs Adams is correct, Hannah. That is something you should keep to yourself," Lucy said, her voice gentle.

Hannah looked crestfallen. "Lordy, my tongue does run away with me sometimes. I meant no offence."

"There's no harm done this time. Remember to be more careful in future. What if Mrs Adams had come back and heard you?"

Hannah hung her head. "I do try and remember but it's harder with someone nice and friendly like you."

Several more footmen arrived with cans of hot water and the bath was full very quickly. Lord Kinsey kept an extensive staff. Hannah locked the door.

"Let me help you undress, Miss. Some of the maids were angry that I got the job of looking after you but, if you ask me, it was a good thing. I got young brothers and I'll soon have you out of those clothes."

She was as good as her word and Lucy sank into the warm bath with a satisfied sigh. Hannah handed her a bar of lavender fragranced soap. Another advantage of having her hair cut short was how quickly it dried. She ducked her head under the water and rubbed soap through her hair. That way she would feel clean after being underneath that old sacking. Lord, if her hair felt dirty was her face grubby as well? Hannah was sorting through a pile of clothes over by the window. Lucy rubbed her face hard with the soap and ducked her head under the water. Hannah must have seen her. She came across and held out a towel.

"Here you are, Miss. Close your eyes until you've dried your face or you might get soap in them."

Lucy accepted the towel with a word of thanks and rubbed her face dry. On impulse she soaped her hair for a second time and ducked it under the water again. Anything to make sure she got rid of the smell of those cabbages. She surfaced and dried her face and rubbed at her hair with a fresh towel from Hannah. Ah, that felt so much better. She luxuriated in the bath until the water cooled down and climbed out feeling much more relaxed. Once she was dry Hannah helped her into a soft, cotton dressing gown.

"You look tired, Miss. Why don't you have a lie down on the bed and I'll sort some clothes out for you to wear now and for tonight at dinner."

The bed did look inviting. A few minutes rest wouldn't hurt but she did want to find out what had happened to William and Robert as soon as she could. Hannah folded the covers back and Lucy gave into the urge to lie down. It had been an eventful morning. She closed her eyes.

She was woken by the sound of a knock at the door. Hannah

entered carrying a tray. She placed it on a small table by the bed.

"That's the ticket, Miss. You've had at least an hour's sleep. I thought it best to wake you though to make sure you had something to eat and drink or you might get a headache."

Lucy sat up. "I do feel hungry now you mention it. That was very thoughtful of you, Hannah."

Hannah blushed with pleasure. "Cook has sent you some of her Shrewsbury biscuits and a nice pot of tea."

"That sounds wonderful." Lucy climbed out of bed. "I'll sit in that chair by the fire if you don't mind."

"Of course not. I'll pull that little side table closer for you."

Lucy sat by the fire and watched as Hannah poured the tea. The girl was quick and nimble fingered. Which was, perhaps, why a stickler like Mrs Adams put up with her overfamiliar attitude. Hannah might make a good lady's maid. A lot more latitude would be allowed with a trusted personal maid like that. She smiled to herself. Perhaps she could poach her from Lord Kinsey.

Two cups of tea and several biscuits later, Lucy felt much more awake. "I'd like to get dressed now, Hannah. I need to talk to Mr Lovell."

Hannah nodded and held up a stylish day gown in blue crêpe. "This one would suit you. I think it will fit, but I can adjust it if not. I'm handy with my needle. My Ma is a dressmaker."

Which was perhaps another reason that Mrs Adams had used her as a lady's maid to an unexpected guest who might need some clothes altered. Would Lady Lovering be cross at them taking liberties with her things? She chewed at her bottom lip. It was bad enough borrowing Lady Lovering's gowns. As long as they didn't look too bad, she would wear them as they were.

When Lucy was ready to get dressed Hannah picked up a shift from a pile of white linens, lying on a sofa next to the blue gown. Heavens, she ought to marry Bertie then she would be in a position to buy Lady Lovering a new wardrobe. There was nothing she could do about it. With Mrs Adams as housekeeper there was no way she could wear her groom's outfit.

Once she was in the gown, Hannah gently took her shoulders and turned her around. "I thought so. You are almost the same size as Lady Lovering." She narrowed her eyes. "Slightly slimmer but I if I tie the ribbon a fraction tighter at the back it will be a reasonable fit."

"That's good. I feel really bad about borrowing Lady Lovering's clothes without her permission."

"I wouldn't worry about that. She's a very kind lady and I'm sure she won't mind."

Hannah put a chair next to the window. "If you come and sit here in the light, I'll see what I can do with your hair."

Lucy sat down and tried not to worry about their problems. Lord Kinsey had said Robert was safe and they'd seen William. So, who did the body he had mentioned belong to? It might not have anything to do with Lord Parfitt and yet she had an awful suspicion that it did. She had never liked Lord Parfitt and despite rumours that he was well off none but the most desperate of doting Mamas had tried pushing their daughters in his way. There was something repulsive about the man. Hard to say what.

He was well enough looking but his style of dress was flamboyant, in keeping with a person who always wanted to be noticed. Which tended to hide his excellent physique. She had never liked the way he looked at her but it wasn't only women who kept out of his way. There was often a cold, hard expression in his eyes which suggested more than a hint of cruelty in him. Perhaps other people saw that. Most members of the Ton did their best to avoid him. She had overheard people warning their friends, in hushed tones, when he was at an event. He was a peer of the realm and as such he could have got away with behaviour that would get other men banned from social events.

Peter had said Parfitt was a dreadful bully at school, which was why Bertie hated him. A shiver went through her. Her arm and shoulder still ached from the way Parfitt had dragged her into the dining room at Rugeley Hall. He had enjoyed hurting her. Yes, she could believe that he was the sort of man who would commit murder in an effort to get what he wanted.

"I've nearly finished," Hannah said. "I'll find you a shawl in a minute."

Lucy smiled at her, even though she didn't feel like smiling. "Thank you, Hannah."

"There. I've brushed your curls out and threaded a blue ribbon through to match the gown. You look lovely." She sounded pleased with herself. "Come and have a look in the glass."

Lucy gasped when she saw herself in the looking glass. Emma had been correct, short hair suited her and Hannah had dressed it beautifully."

"You have a way with hair. Have you ever thought of being a lady's maid?"

Hannah blushed and gave her a speculative glance. "I'd love to do that, Miss Vaughan. I'll go and fetch that shawl. You sit by the fire."

Lucy couldn't resist doing another turn in front of the looking glass. Would Bertie have the same reaction to her as he had done when he'd seen her wearing Emma's beautiful rose silk gown? Or was she reading too much into what had only been surprise at her transformation? Hannah came back with a fine, cream coloured, woollen shawl and placed it round her shoulders.

"I don't suppose you have any jewellery with you?"

"I did bring my mother's pearls. What happened to my saddlebag?"

Hannah opened the cupboard. "It's in here."

"It's a bit early in the day to wear pearls but I can wear them at dinner. I think Mr Lovell and Lord Kinsey said they would be in the library? I need speak to them."

CHAPTER SEVENTEEN

Bertie sat back in a leather armchair in Ralph's huge library, trying to find a position that eased his aches and pains from his journey in the farm cart. He absentmindedly nibbled at another one of the gingerbread biscuits Cook had sent in for them. It wasn't much past noon but it already felt like a long day. They had been on the road before seven o'clock and it had been a trying few hours.

"These are excellent. Remind me to get the recipe for my cook." He drained the last of his coffee.

Ralph smiled at him. "For someone who's just found out that you're in a far bigger fix than you thought you were, you're taking this very calmly. What about Miss Vaughan?" Ralph's relaxed tone changed to a sharper note and he fixed his attention on Bertie's face. "Are you just being chivalrous to a childhood friend or do you intend to marry the chit?

Bertie looked at the floor. "I've a nasty feeling that persuading Lucy to marry me is going to be harder work than seeing off a madman like Parfitt. That said, I do want to marry her."

"Why should it be difficult? You're her knight in shining armour, slaying a dragon for her. Surely any girl would find that romantic and you're not without your own personal charms, are you?"

"Thank you for the ringing endorsement." Bertie laughed. "I'm not sure why I'm laughing. Lucy's father has treated her mother abominably for as long as I've known the family. I think that's why Lucy is so vehemently opposed to marriage. There were times, when I was staying with Uncle Ambrose, when Vaughan hit his wife. I don't think he beat Lucy but he did hit her brother more than once. This was when Peter was older and tried to protect his mother when he realised what was going on.

"When we were younger, we noticed that Mrs Vaughan was a different person on the occasions when Vaughan deigned to visit his home. Mrs Vaughan would be really cheery one day and very quiet and withdrawn the next if Vaughan arrived. The turning point was when Peter noticed bruising on her arms. He challenged his father and got his ears boxed."

"I can see why Miss Vaughan might be wary of marriage then. Even so she's known you a long time and I can't imagine you attacking anyone, let alone a woman."

"I'm sure she knows that but it's hard to put her fears behind her. I'm hopeful, but it's best not to force the issue." Bertie hesitated. Ralph might be offended but it was best to tell him the truth. He kept his voice neutral. "We decided to say we're betrothed because Miss Vaughan was embarrassed by your housekeeper's attitude to her turning up in men's clothes."

Ralph nodded. "I see. Mrs Adams is a wonderful housekeeper but she does have very strong views on the proper conduct of women. I hadn't thought of that. I expect she was shocked seeing Miss Vaughan wearing breeches."

"I think that was part of it, but Lucy expected that sort of attitude." Bertie shook his head. "It seems to me we don't realise how lucky we are to have our freedom. Life is very different for women."

Ralph threw back his head and laughed. "You're sounding just like my sister, Arabella. It's a pity she's not still here. She might put some heart into your Lucy. Besides which, Arabella is living proof of how much more freedom happily married women have than single women. Lovering absolutely dotes on her. In his eyes she can do no wrong. It means she has freedom to do exactly as she wants." Ralph shook his head, his affection for his strong-minded sister obvious from his amused expression.

"Now there's a thought. If I can get Lucy to safety with some of the Lovell women, perhaps they can help me."

Ralph coughed and his eyes twinkled. "Surely you can be a bit persuasive yourself?"

Bertie grimaced and cleared his throat. "I'm not sure that would be the right approach. I have a feeling that things weren't always good in the bedroom between her parents. That may well be part of her worries. Cousin Augusta is probably my best hope. It's come upon me gradually but I think I was already having warm feelings towards Lucy when I suggested we contact the Cathlays for help."

Ralph raised his eyebrows so much they almost disappeared under his hair. "You must know the Duchess of Cathlay better than I do then. She terrifies me. She's the last person I'd think of to try and reassure a nervous maiden."

"Augusta is the best of the bunch. She puts on a fierce exterior but underneath she's very warm and caring. She was the only one of the Lovells who ever had any time for me when I was growing up. The others disliked my mother so much it rubbed off on me. Augusta always made a point of talking to me and being encouraging."

"You've shocked me there, but I'll take your word for it. Besides which, I can't think of any other people I would want on my side in a case like this than the Duke and Duchess of Cathlay. The pair of them have a formidable reputation. I'm surprised Parfitt didn't back off when he realised your interest in Miss Vaughan." Ralph gave him a playful smile.

It was Bertie's turn to be surprised. "Parfitt was pursuing her way before this current how do you do."

Ralph shook his head. "If you want to know the truth, several of us guessed it was you who saw Parfitt off at the beginning of the season when he was hanging round Miss Vaughan at every opportunity. We never quite worked out exactly how you pulled off that trick."

"There are times when it's useful being known as something of a fool." Bertie smiled. "I came across him in my club one evening and he challenged me to a game of cards. He chose piquet, a game I played regularly with Uncle Ambrose. I jollied him along for the first few rounds, then I started playing seriously. He didn't notice at first, probably thought I was just having a run of luck. Then he started getting angry. He must have thought he'd be able to turn the tables on me. That's when I started playing at full stretch. In no time at all he owed me a fortune. He asked for time to pay when some friends of mine came in. I didn't want Lucy's name bandied about and said I would give him until the following evening to settle with me."

"But how did losing money to you stop him going after Miss Vaughan?"

"I remembered what a nipcheese he is despite being fabulously wealthy. When he came to my house the following night, I offered to let him off his losses as long as he left Lucy alone."

"I'm surprised he didn't simply accept your offer but still pursue her."

Bertie grinned. "He did but I anticipated that. Parfitt is the sort of man everyone's known forever but they try not to mix with. I had a quiet word with Cathlay who spoke to Parfitt. He told him that if he didn't stick to the terms of our agreement and additionally leave London, he would personally ensure that word spread all around the Ton that Parfitt didn't honour his gambling debts.

"Cathlay said Parfitt huffed and puffed a bit but once he realised Cathlay was deadly serious he capitulated. Parfitt didn't want to be ostracized and he took himself off. I was hoping he'd leave Lucy alone after that."

Ralph scratched his ear. "That's interesting. I'd always thought Parfitt was as rich as Croesus but I did hear a few rumours earlier in the year that he had driven himself aground. Some rather bad investments."

"Ah. I hadn't heard that, but it makes sense."

"I presume Miss Vaughan is an heiress." Ralph wrinkled his brow. "Which is surprising considering her father is well known to be a reckless gambler, always living on the edge."

"Lucy said she's got an inheritance from a great-aunt which will come to her when she's five and twenty or presumably when she marries, whichever is first. So yes, she has got expectations but she's never mentioned being a great heiress."

"It's possible that Miss Vaughan doesn't know the extent of her inheritance. Which might explain why her father is pushing the match. He is probably expecting a share once she's married."

Bertie rose and stood with an arm on the mantelpiece

looking at the fire. "I have wondered that myself. Lucy's mother thought the inheritance was a lot bigger than Lucy realised. "He gave a harsh laugh. "I don't think Vaughan is particularly clever. It's probably never occurred to him that the chance of Parfitt honouring an agreement once he had a ring on Lucy's finger would be nil."

"What do you propose to do now? You're welcome to stay as long as you like. I've got an extensive staff and some of the male servants have spent time in the army. Parfitt won't be able to get at you here."

Bertie smiled at the determination in Ralph's voice. "Thank you. Ralph. I knew I could rely on you."

"I should think so. You would do the same for me."

Bertie stared into the fire. What was he going to do? He heard voices in the hall and the sound of the door opening into the library. He turned to see Lucy entering. He caught his breath. How was it that he had never realised just how beautiful Lucy was? The blonde hair framing her face in loose curls shone and the blue gown she was wearing showed off every curve of her figure. The thought of Lord Parfitt getting anywhere near her made him feel physically ill. Ralph stood as she entered and ushered her to the sofa, the nearest seat to the fire. She thanked him prettily and sat down with the natural grace which he must have always been aware of but only now was noticing. She smiled at them both.

"I do hope your sister doesn't mind me borrowing her clothes, Lord Kinsey."

"Arabella won't mind at all. All in a good cause. I wish you would call me Ralph. Bertie and I have been best friends ever since we met at Oxford on the first day we were there."

"In which case, you must call me Lucy." Lucy's gaze turned

towards Bertie. "Where's William, has he gone back home?"

Ralph put a hand on Bertie's shoulder and almost pushed him onto the sofa next to Lucy. He took Bertie's place standing in front of the fire.

"Yes, William has gone back." Ralph looked at Bertie. "You can probably explain what's happened better than I can."

Bertie nodded. "William followed the cart we were in at a good distance. He decided to skirt round the tollhouse and watch what happened to us from beyond. He said he had the feeling something untoward was going on. Nothing he could be sure of. Simply more people lurking on street corners and what have you than usual."

"Emma said William is incredibly good at searching out danger so he was probably right, which is worrying." Lucy stared at him, wide eyed.

Bertie slipped an arm around her waist. He hated to see her upset.

Ralph coughed. "If you will excuse me, I'll go and sort those clothes out for you, Bertie." He left the room, winking at Bertie from behind Lucy's back on his way out.

Lord he could do without Ralph matchmaking. Lucy rested her head against his arm and he pulled her closer.

"William went on a detour around the tollbooth and tied his horse up in a spinney. He crept around the hedge to the back of the tollhouse. The cart was going so slowly that he could see it approaching the tollhouse. He crept into the house to check how many people were there and found the body of a man in the kitchen. He'd been knifed. William reckoned from the way he was dressed that he was probably the official keeper. He could see no one else and crept around the side of the house and watched.

"A gig came along driven by a clergyman and the man on the gate engaged him in conversation. William said he got close enough to peer inside the gig. Presumably to make sure there was no one else hiding. He waved that one through and when the cart drew up you remember there was an altercation about the price. Then a coach came along in a tearing hurry and the man let our cart carry on. You know the rest."

Lucy shuddered. "The coach that nearly overturned us. That was close."

"A bit too close for comfort with all the cabbages it dislodged." Bertie grinned at her.

"We can laugh now but if that coach hadn't come along, the gate man might have found us."

"William said he was ready to pounce if needed, but he's not sure the man would have moved crates around and we were well hidden, especially after all the cabbages that had already fallen on me. William watched a few more vehicles arrive. Every time, the man on the gate kept them in conversation and appeared to have a good look at their vehicles and inside them sometimes. He was definitely looking for us I would say."

"We can be sure it was one of Parfitt's men, can't we?" Lucy chewed at her lip, concern clouding her eyes.

"I think we can, what we don't know is how many men he had out and how many routes they were watching."

Lucy gasped and her eyes shot wide open. "I do hope they didn't follow Arthur?"

Bertie instinctively reached for her hand and she grasped it tightly.

"It is a concern. I thought Parfitt was the sort of loose screw who might lash out in a rage when thwarted. It hadn't occurred to me he could be ruthless enough to have a band of hired thugs ready to kill anyone who stands in their way."

"What can we do?"

"William's gone back. Ralph lent him a fresh horse and he's going to ride a different way home. He'll go over to Mayford Castle as soon as he can and try and find out whether Arthur caught the coach or not."

Lucy's face went paper white. "I do hope he's safe."

Bertie grimaced. "So do I! There's always a chance Mr Roskelley would have ridden to the coaching inn with him, to help him get the lie of the land. My man of business said that he'd had a spell in the army. I wish I'd paid more attention now. At the time I was just relieved to know he'd found me an agent. I have the feeling he mentioned that Roskelley had been trained by Mr Bright."

"He'll be good if Mr Bright trained him?"

"Yes. Bright's father was a land agent. I remember now. Roskelley had started training for that job with Bright before he went into the army, when an uncle left him enough money to buy a pair of colours and keep himself. Bright trained him up after he sold out and recommended him, I think."

"If Mr Bright trained him, I'd be surprised if he didn't go with Arthur. Mrs Hobbs would have been bound to tell him how seriously you're taking the threat from Lord Parfitt."

Bertie squeezed her hand and moved closer to her. The warmth coming from her was comforting.

"I hope you're right. I can't bear the thought of Arthur getting into any difficulties. Arthur is a resourceful young man. I did give him some pistols, although I don't think he's had much training with them." Bertie frowned.

Lucy lifted her head and gazed at him. "Don't look so

worried. It's not your fault Lord Parfitt is like this. I've struggled to make sense of it all. The only thing I can think of is that Mama is right and there's a lot more money coming to me than I imagined. I wish Peter was here. He had a legacy from our great-aunt too, which he received straightaway."

"I saw Peter just after Christmas. He did say how happy he was to be completely independent of your father. Did he realise your inheritance was tied up like it is?"

Lucy shook her head. "I don't think he did, I remember him saying I could do what I wanted now and Mama could always live with me."

"Peter was still his usual frugal self, but that doesn't prove anything."

"It's a puzzle, isn't it? Mama said she was sure my great aunt would have left me half." Lucy wrinkled her nose. "When Parfitt was pestering me early in the year, he asked me about Uncle James more than once. He's a real toad eater. I assumed he was hanging around me hoping to get an introduction, with Uncle James being so influential in government circles. Never occurred to me he might be after my money. Oh Bertie, what have I dragged you into?" Lucy looked near to tears.

"Don't worry about that. I've been enjoying your company no end. The risk to other people besides us does concern me. We'll be safe here with Ralph for a while. Assuming Arthur did get through, Cathlay will send us some of his people. They might even be able to find out where my new grooms have got to. Anyone Bright has trained will be handy to have on our side."

"You look tired. Let's try and forget about it for tonight and relax. There's nothing we can do until William returns." Lucy sounded exhausted.

Bertie pulled her close and dropped a kiss on her forehead. Lucy stared at him for a moment and he tried to pull away. He didn't want to frighten her. A tremulous smile spread across her features and she raised her face to his. His breath hitched.

"May I kiss you, Lucy?"

"Yes please," she said in a small voice.

She looked almost surprised at herself. He mustn't rush this. Ralph's words of encouragement came back to him and he put both arms around her and touched his lips to hers. She clung to him and kissed him back. He teased her lips with his tongue. She froze and he stopped immediately. Then she closed her eyes and clung to him even tighter. Her lips pressed against his. Flames of desire shot through him more fiercely than he had ever known.

Like most men of his social group, he'd had plenty of adventures with women. None of them had affected him like Lucy did. It was obvious she was a complete innocent but all her worries seemed to fall away from her. Their tongues tangled in a frenzy of wanting. He lay back against the arm of the sofa and pulled her closer so she was almost sitting on his lap. If he didn't stop this soon heaven knew where it would lead. He gently pulled away from the kiss and held her a little away from him.

"We had better stop there, sweetheart." Whatever he did he mustn't rush her. He longed to marry her but the most important thing was to do what was best for her.

"I suppose so." Lucy blinked up at him. "I never expected to feel like this about anyone. I suppose it's happened to you before."

Bertie smiled and shook his head. "I'd be lying if I said I'd never been with a woman. No woman has ever affected me as much as you do. Will you marry me?"

Lucy sat up and moved a little away from him. He held his breath. Why had he listened to Ralph? It looked like he had over played his hand.

Lucy took a deep breath. "I don't feel like I deserve you. Are you sure you want to marry me?"

"I've never wanted anything this much in my life. Is that yes?"

"Yes, I will."

"Thank you. It's me who doesn't deserve you. I always thought I'd struggle to find a bride. Who'd want to marry a man with a mother like mine?"

"She's not exactly the ideal mother-in-law."

Lucy grinned at him and he felt giddy with happiness.

"Still now she's married I don't suppose we'll see much of her. At least she hasn't tried to sell you off to the highest bidder like my father."

"In a way she has. She was always trying to push me onto Max Lovell as his heir, she thought I should be treated with more respect by the family to improve my social standing. She's been trying to find me well-connected young women ever since I left university. Preferably the daughters of dukes, or marquesses at the very least. Let's not talk about our parents."

"Let's not. Now I've found the courage to say yes surely another kiss is in order."

"I'm more than happy to comply with that."

A few moments later the door opened and they sat up. Giggling like schoolchildren.

Ralph came in. He took one look at them and walked across to Bertie and slapped him on the shoulder. "Congratulations, old man. I take it you've made your betrothal official?"

"Yes, we have."

"I'm sure you'll be very happy. My cook appears to be working on something of a banquet. The staff seem excited at the prospect of celebrating your betrothal. I'm glad it's a real one now."

Bertie grinned at him. "So am I. Now all we have to do is see off a murderous madman."

CHAPTER EIGHTEEN

Lucy slipped into a happy daze, listening to Ralph teasing Bertie. Had she really just agreed to get married? She ought to feel terrified and yet it was a relief. If truth be told she had been fighting her feelings for Bertie for some time without acknowledging it to herself. It hadn't seemed quite right since she had always thought of Bertie as a brother. She didn't see him in that light now. It was a scary thought giving up her independence but somehow, with Bertie at her side, she'd work it all out. Seeing Emma so happy to be marrying her Arthur had helped.

Ralph sent a footman to fetch some wine to toast the happy couple. Lucy found a glass pressed into her hand. She sipped at it. Ralph certainly kept a good cellar. After two glasses she was feeling a little foxed, not being used to alcoholic drinks. Ralph offered to refill her glass.

"No more for me thanks. I'm not much of a drinker, especially at this time of day. If you don't mind, I think I'll go and have a lie down before dinner."

Bertie squeezed her hand. Her cheeks went hot as he caught her gaze.

"That's the ticket. There's nothing we can do at the moment. Ralph's invited us to stay for as long as we like. It will do you good to have a rest from all the stress." He dropped a kiss on her forehead. "Off you go and have a lie down. We'll see you later."

Ralph called for a footman to show her to her room. "I'll have a maid sent up to help you, Miss Vaughan."

"May I have Hannah again?"

Ralph nodded at the footman. "Once you've escorted Miss Vaughan to her room, can you find Hannah and send her up."

Lucy floated up the stairs behind the footman. Perhaps this happy feeling had more to do with the promise of being able to stay with Bertie rather than the alcohol she had drunk. The fire still crackled merrily in her room. She curled up in the armchair next to it and waited for Hannah to appear. It wasn't long before Hannah rushed into the room all smiles.

"I'm so happy for you, Miss Vaughan. I've sent for some hot chocolate and toast. It will be a while until dinner. Cook is determined to do the occasion justice. It's chaos down in the kitchens."

Lucy sat up. "Oh dear, I don't want to put her to so much trouble."

"Don't worry about that, she's enjoying herself. She said catering for a betrothal dinner is much more fun than pandering to Lady Lovering's children." Hannah grimaced. "I shouldn't have said that."

"Perhaps not, but I appreciate the sentiment from Cook. I like your initiative too. I've had two glasses of wine and some toast will be just the thing to mop it up. And I love hot chocolate. You must be a mind reader."

* * *

Lady Lovering must be very fond of blue. The evening gown Hannah helped her into was a shade of deep sapphire blue. She had always tended to pick pink and pastel colours for her gowns but the blue seemed to suit her. Hannah bubbled over with excitement.

"You look wonderful in this, Miss Vaughan. I found some ribbon to match the dress. If I brush your hair upwards, I can make it look as if it's a little bit longer than it is. Then thread the ribbon through. Did you find your pearls?"

Lucy pointed to the bedside table. "They're on there."

Hannah fastened the pearls around her neck and draped the shawl around her shoulders. She stood back and looked at Lucy from all angles, walking all around her.

"Perfect. Mr Lovell won't be able to take his eyes off you. You look a bit pale though. Perhaps you're cold, come and sit by the fire until the gong goes for dinner. That should put some colour in your cheeks." Hannah danced over to the window and closed the drapes. "I've got the afternoon off tomorrow. I can't wait to tell my mother I've been dressing a fine lady like you."

Lucy wrinkled her brow. "You will be careful, won't you? There is a rather unpleasant gentleman who wanted to force me to marry him. We think he may have followed us. If you see anybody strange keep well away from them when you go and visit your mother. I would hate anything to happen to you."

"How romantic. Two men fighting over you." Hannah's eyes brimmed with excitement.

"It's not romantic at all. My father was pushing for the match and we've had to flee."

"What's the point of him following you if you've agreed to marry Mr Lovell? I don't understand."

"Neither do I." Lucy closed her eyes. "I can't bear to think about the other man. I'm of age so my father couldn't force me to marry him but we didn't trust this man not to try and kidnap me. And that would not have been romantic at all. You be careful that's all I'm saying. He's the sort of man who doesn't take no for an answer. He's very angry at the moment. He's also got quite a few people working for him trying to trace us so please be careful what you say tomorrow."

Hannah's mouth dropped open. "I'll be careful. I'll just say that some of the friends Lord Kinsey has staying have recently become betrothed. He has a lot of visitors and nobody will think anything of that. My ma is quite a gossip. She is bound to tell me if there are any new people in the village. I can investigate for you."

Lucy shook her head. "Please don't. I don't want you putting yourself in danger."

"It's you that's in danger, why would anybody bother about me?"

"We are talking about a madman here. No one knows what he might take into his head. You be careful."

"Don't you worry, I expect it's all a fudge. Men can say all sorts of things when they're angry."

Hannah might well be right but not if Parfitt was responsible for the death of the tollgate keeper. There was nothing more to be gained by warning her. She had probably said too much already. They would have been better hidden if Ralph's other visitors had already arrived. But if they had she wouldn't have had any time alone with Bertie. She shivered. When she was with him it all felt so right. Now she was alone all the difficulties closed in on her. How would they get away from Parfitt's malignant influence? How would she cope with marriage after watching Mama's suffering?

"Don't look so sad. You're going to your betrothal party. You should be smiling."

Lucy stared at Hannah. "Have some more people arrived then?"

"Oh no. No one else is expected for days. It's still a betrothal party though, even with only three of you to celebrate."

"Of course. It all feels a bit strange."

"Just you concentrate on Mr Lovell. You do look lovely." Hannah bit her lip. "I don't suppose you need a new lady's maid, do you? Meaning no offence. My ma says you should never ask for anything but I think that's humbug."

Lucy couldn't help but smile. Hannah was such an original. "I suppose you're right. If you don't ask nobody knows you want something. If I should have a vacancy in the future, I will bear you in mind."

Hannah grinned at her. A loud gong sounded.

"Time for you to go downstairs. You'll be so impressed with the dinner table. I think Cook is afraid that Lord Kinsey might be tempted to take on a fancy male chef. She wants to impress him."

Hannah gave her one more look-over. "You'll do. I'll wait up for you so you can tell me how it went."

Lucy smiled and shook her head. "There's no need to go to the trouble of staying up late. I'll be able to manage."

"Oh, it's no trouble at all. Anyway, if I really was your lady's maid it would be my job to stay up late."

"I can see you're determined to wait up for me. I'll see you later."

Hannah opened the door for her and Lucy walked slowly down the stairs. Would Bertie think she was fast from the way she had responded to him in the library? She heard voices coming from one of the drawing rooms and hesitated. Bertie and Ralph sounded really happy. But then Bertie had said they were good friends. He would be enjoying the company. It must have been quiet for him at Mayford Castle after the hustle and bustle of London. Would Bertie find he wasn't as keen on the country as he thought he was after a while?

She took a deep breath and walked into the drawing room. Both men stood and Bertie walked towards her and placed her hand on his arm.

"You look delightful. Blue really suits you."

"Why don't you to lead the way into dinner," Ralph said, grinning at Lucy.

Lucy gasped when they entered the dining room. The highly polished wooden table sparkled in the light of a huge chandelier. Everything was of the first quality and the silver had been cleaned by an expert. It looked beautiful. A wave of sadness hit her.

Bertie bent down towards her. "What is it, Lucy?"

"It's nothing. I felt a bit sad that Mama and Peter couldn't be here that's all. This feels like a betrothal party."

Bertie rubbed the hand resting on his arm. "Once we've got you safe, we can find your mother and aunt and have a proper party. You never know, Peter might be back soon too."

"Perhaps. I think this is a proper betrothal party. I can see your staff have really worked hard, Ralph. I don't want you to think that I'm ungrateful."

"I'll pass your compliments onto the staff. I can understand you feeling sad that your family aren't here. Much as she infuriates me, I would hate it if Arabella wasn't at my betrothal party. My people were so keen to help you celebrate that I let them have their head. Perhaps I should have reined them in a bit."

"Not at all. I do appreciate it and as Bertie says there will be nothing to stop us having a big party later on."

Bertie led her to a seat on the right-hand side of the head of the table and pulled out the chair for her. He took the seat opposite her, leaving Ralph to take his place at the head of the table. He grinned at Ralph once they were settled.

"Are you saying that a betrothal might be imminent?"

Ralph burst out laughing. "Absolutely not. I'm not even going to think about matrimony until I'm at least thirty years old, whatever my mother might say about the subject. My cousin would make a perfectly good Earl, in the event of me never having a son. I don't know why she makes such a fuss over me finding a bride."

A shadow crossed Bertie's face. "What's wrong, Bertie?" Lucy said.

"I suppose I was wishing I had a mother like Ralph. However much he complains about her, she's a gentle lady. She wouldn't dream of pushing every well-connected young woman at him simply to improve the family standing."

Ralph smiled at him. Sympathy written across his face. These two were close friends.

"I suspect it was more my reference to my cousin. Mama has always included him in family events and we're almost like brothers. I'm glad to hear you and Max Lovell are on much better terms now."

"We are. He admitted my mother's attitude had affected the way he reacted to me. He's mellowed a lot since he married. I doubt we'll ever be close but we are friends now." He smiled across at Lucy. "Lucy won't mind me telling you that in her case it's her father who has treated her shabbily. We have a lot in common."

Two footmen came in with the first course, a soup made of spring vegetables - a favourite of Lucy's. This was followed by trout baked to perfection. Several courses later a dessert consisting of a variety of nuts, fruits and sweetmeats was laid out for them. Cook's marzipan candies were every bit as good as her biscuits.

When they had all finished eating, Lucy smiled at Ralph. "Please convey my thanks to Cook. That was a superb meal. I'll leave you to your port and go and sit in the drawing room"

Both men stood.

"We won't leave you alone for long," Ralph said and smiled at Bertie.

Lucy thanked him and strolled out of the dining room. They were laughing as she went into the hall and Ralph's voice reached her clearly.

"You're a lucky dog. Lucy is a treasure and I'm sure you'll be very happy together."

Lucy moved away quickly in case he looked up and saw her in the hallway. It was reassuring to know that one of Bertie's good friends approved of her. She pulled a face. Bertie's mother was likely to cut up stiff. Apart from Uncle James, who was only a relative by marriage, there wasn't a hint of a title in her family. Never mind. It was what Bertie thought that mattered. Mrs Adams came out into the hallway as she reached the door to the drawing room.

"Would you like a tea tray, Miss Vaughan?"

"That would be lovely. I'd like to congratulate the staff on a wonderful dinner. I really appreciate how much everyone has put themselves out for some surprise visitors. Tonight's dinner was splendid."

Mrs Adams blushed faintly and smiled. "Thank you, Miss Vaughan. Mr Lovell is a bit of a favourite with us. We wanted to mark his betrothal. I'll bring the tea tray myself."

Mrs Adams bustled off and Lucy smiled to herself. Mrs Adams's attitude had certainly changed since she had first arrived. It was amazing the difference clothes made. She looked down at the blue gown. Lady Lovering had taste.

Mrs Adams arrived with the tea tray a few minutes later. She put it on a side table next to Lucy.

"There you are, Miss Vaughan. Ring if you want anything else."

She had barely left the room when Bertie and Ralph joined Lucy. Ralph took a chair near the fire, leaving Bertie to share the sofa Lucy was sitting on.

"That was quick. Would you like tea?"

"Yes please," Bertie said. "We only had one glass of port. We need to keep clear heads." He was smiling but there was a sober expression in his eyes.

"Why is that? Are you expecting some sort of trouble?"

"Nothing to alarm you, Lucy," Ralph said. "Some of my men are patrolling the grounds. There do seem to be one or two newcomers in the district but then there usually are. I'll have my dogs sleep in the house tonight. If anyone should try and get in, the dogs will raise a real dust."

Lucy glanced across at Bertie. "I'm sorry to be putting you to all this trouble."

Ralph waved a hand at her. "Believe me, I'm more than happy to help. I'm delighted to see my friend here happily settled, with a lovely lady like yourself."

"Hold on there, Ralph. You'll be making me jealous if you

don't watch it."

Lucy shook her head at them and prepared the tea. She handed it round, taking her seat next to Bertie with her own cup.

"You pair are like a couple of schoolboys. I thought you said you met at university."

"We did." Bertie smiled at her. "You ought to know after seeing me and Peter together that boys never grow up."

"That is very true. Never mind Bertie. You'll be able to get your own back on Ralph when he finds a wife."

"Oh no. Now you two are ganging up on me." Ralph downed the last of his tea. "I'll say good night. I need to go down to the stables and fetch the dogs."

Bertie made to rise but Ralph put up a hand. "Don't worry I'll take a couple of footmen with me. You stay here and guard Lucy."

He strode out of the drawing room, whistling to himself.

CHAPTER NINETEEN

"I've been thinking. Now we are properly betrothed, how would you feel about a quick wedding?" Bertie moved closer and put his arm around Lucy's shoulder. "Once we're married there won't be any point in Parfitt pursuing you."

Lucy rubbed her hands together. "I suppose so." Her voice quivered.

"You don't seem very sure."

"Something you said made me think. If this is more than Lord Parfitt losing his temper over being bested, wouldn't you be in danger once we're married?"

He didn't like to see her looking so worried. Was he letting his enthusiasm override caution? He couldn't afford to let himself be distracted by a wedding until he was sure it was safe.

"I know what you're saying. What could be Parfitt's motive? We suspect it's your money he's interested in but there are plenty of other heiresses. Why doesn't he search amongst them? Of course, we can't be sure that the murder of the gatekeeper is anything to do with Parfitt. It's possible it was simply a coincidence."

Lucy rested her head against his shoulder. "I doubt it. I

won't feel safe until that man is behind bars. I can't see how that can be achieved."

Bertie sighed. "I wish he would take himself off and leave us alone. I've always wanted to be part of a proper family and now I have the chance I'm impatient. We can make a decision when we get to London. I'm hoping we'll find your mother and aunt are there."

"I would be glad to know that they're safe."

"Have you any idea where your uncle is?"

"Aunt Susan said he was detained in London, working on government business. Joining him would be the obvious thing for them to do."

Bertie grimaced. "I still can't believe that your father rented out your London house without consulting your mother. What a thing to do to you both. You'll want the rest of your family at our wedding of course but what about your father?"

Lucy jerked away from him and shook her head. "I'd rather have Uncle James give me away. He cares far more about me than my father ever has."

She was shaking, poor girl. "We have to get to London first, which may not be easy." He dropped a kiss on her forehead.

"I know. I wonder when Peter will be back." Lucy gave him a tremulous smile. "I would love him to be there with us."

"So would I. If your mother has any idea where he might be staying, we could try and get a message to him. Let's forget about it for now."

Lucy nodded. "I hate to think that Lord Parfitt could be nearby."

"Try not to worry. I don't think Ralph was seriously worried about the people he mentioned. I think it's his way of tactfully leaving us together. I notice he left the door closed."

Lucy smiled. "All we can do is take each day as it comes."

She moved closer until their legs were pressed together and raised her face to his. The invitation was obvious and he was not the man to ignore it. He took her in his arms.

Lucy suddenly jerked away from him, looking stricken. "You don't think I'm fast, do you? Letting you kiss me, I mean."

"Of course not. We are betrothed, aren't we?"

"I know. Women aren't supposed to enjoy that side of things though, are they?"

"Who told you that nonsense? There's absolutely nothing wrong in wanting to kiss your fiancé. In fact, it's obligatory. Why are we wasting time?"

Lucy snuggled up against him and kissed him on the cheek. "I'm relieved to know that. I can't explain it but I feel different when I'm next to you."

"I'd be worried if you didn't. I won't rush you. I want you to enjoy it as much as me."

Lucy wound her arms around his neck. "I like the sound of that."

He nuzzled her neck and gave himself up to the sensations being close to her aroused. She was eminently kissable. This time when he teased her mouth with his tongue, she knew what to do and the strength of her response to his kisses almost overrode his self-control. This would never do. She would be mortified if somebody like Mrs Adams came in now. He gave her one last kiss and pulled away.

"We need to leave it there, Lucy. I can't wait for all this to be over and for us to be together at Mayford Castle. It's the only place that has ever felt like home to me and you and Peter were a large part of that." He sat up listening. "It sounds like quite a rumpus in the hall."

Bertie got up and went into the hall to find Ralph chatting to some of his men, whilst holding the leashes of his two wolfhounds. The dogs started whining and tried to pull away from him. Ralph looked up and saw him. He nodded at the tallest of the men who seemed to be the leader of the group.

"Tell Mr Lovell what you've just told me."

"We found the two men some of the villagers were talking about. When we approached them, they ran off. The next thing we knew, two horsemen cantered off into the distance. I couldn't swear to it, as moonlight can play tricks, but although the men were roughly dressed their horses looked the sort you or Lord Kinsey would ride."

"Hmm. Why did they run off if they had nothing to hide?" Ralph said and exchanged a glance with Bertie. He turned back to his men. "Still, I don't think we'll see them again tonight but increase patrols around the house in case there are any more. I'll keep the wolfhounds in the house tonight. Take the rest of the dogs out with you."

Ralph waited until the men had gone out then he locked and bolted the door behind them.

"I don't like the sound of this, Ralph." Bertie's mouth was so dry his voice came out as a hoarse whisper. Should he tell Lucy? The decision was made for him when he felt her move beside him. He put an arm around her shoulders. "Come on in and tell us all you know, Ralph."

"Some more tea would be good," Lucy said.

Ralph signalled to the footman standing by the door, who nodded and disappeared through a servants' door.

Bertie guided Lucy back inside to the sofa and Ralph followed. He took the chair nearest to them.

Bertie grinned at him. "There was me thinking you decided

to listen to a mere trifle simply to give us some time alone."

"There was an element of that. I was concerned though. Several people had reported to my steward that they had seen some men hanging around who nobody appeared to know. Not unusual in itself, there is a good inn in the village, but people whose judgement I trust thought there might be something shady about them."

"What made them think that?" Lucy said.

"A good question. One of the men who came to see my steward this evening was Mr Wilson."

Bertie and Lucy exchanged glances.

"The farmer who brought us here in his cart?" Bertie asked.

"The very same. He's no one's fool and he realised that the story you told him was hiding something else. Since it was clear to him that you were friends of mine, whatever you were up to, he felt obliged to come and say something. He was sitting in a quiet corner of the coffee room at the inn, as he does some evenings and overheard two strangers talking. He couldn't make much sense of it but he had a feeling it was connected to you two."

Lucy's mouth dropped open. "Are you saying that they have worked out we are in the area?"

"Mr Wilson wasn't sure. He was convinced that these men were trying to track someone down and he thought it sounded like they were part of a bigger group. It seems likely that they are out looking for you but not that they particularly suspect this area."

Bertie pulled at his earlobe. "It's worrying though, isn't it? I don't want to put you and your staff in danger."

"Don't bother about that, old man. I haven't enjoyed myself so much in ages."

Bertie burst out laughing. "If you say so. Let's try and work out the earliest we might hear from the Duke of Cathlay. If I'm being honest, I immediately thought of the Cathlays as much to protect Lucy's reputation as anything. Now it's clear there is something bigger afoot, I can't think of anyone else I'd rather have on my side."

"Assuming the message got through to him," Lucy said in a small voice.

Bertie shuddered at Lucy's words. "Oh Lord, that means Arthur is even more likely to have faced danger then we thought, doesn't it?" A cold chill ran down Bertie's spine. He tried to ignore it. Lucy was worried enough without him showing his anxiety too obviously.

"There's nothing we can do tonight," Ralph said. "That man who was helping you, William wasn't it, might get back to us tomorrow with any luck. If not. . ." Ralph stroked his chin. "I could send a couple of my men to Mayford Castle if he's not back by lunchtime tomorrow."

"Thanks Ralph, now let's try and work out how long the mail coach would take to get to London from Mayford. I haven't been on one since my school days."

"Neither have I, old man. Mrs Adams might know how long the mail coach takes to get here. That would be a start."

Mrs Adams arrived with the tea tray, which she placed on a table near to Lucy. She lingered, looking concerned.

Ralph smiled at her. "Ahh, Mrs Adams. You know this area well, have you any idea how long the mail coach takes to get to London. We're trying to work out when Mr Lovell might hear from a messenger he sent by mail."

Mrs Adams tilted her head slightly to one side. "It's faster than it was when I was a girl but it still takes more than a day.

It's a long way to London."

"It is indeed. Thank you, Mrs Adams."

Bertie waited until the door closed behind her. "If Arthur caught the coach from Mayford this morning, he should be in London tomorrow. He's got to find the Duke or Duchess. Let's say it takes him a day. Another day back, we can't look to see him for two or three days at the earliest." He rubbed the back of his neck, unable to hide his anxiety about Arthur any longer.

Lucy let out a strangled cry. "I do hope he's safe. That's a long time to wait to find out. Perhaps I'm being selfish running away from Lord Parfitt and putting everyone in danger. I should have simply stood up to him and Papa and refused to marry him."

Bertie exchanged a glance with Ralph. "No, you weren't selfish, you were sensible. There is something about Parfitt that really disturbs me. I've never liked him but the way he haunted you in London earlier in the year was nauseating. I won't rest until I've got you safely back to London under the care of your uncle. Preferably with assistance from the Duke and Duchess of Cathlay. I don't think even Parfitt would want to tangle with that trio."

Ralph laughed. "I don't know why I'm laughing. Parfitt is definitely a man to keep well away from. You'll be much better off with Bertie here, Miss Vaughan."

"I'm sure I will." Her voice broke and she stared down at her hands. "That doesn't stop me wishing it could have been done without putting people in danger. It sounds like Parfitt is far worse than I had imagined."

Bertie shuddered. "I was at school with him. He was a dreadful bully. He was the boy everybody in the school kept away from. There's always one."

Ralph grimaced. "There is, isn't there. He must have been one of the worst, going on all the rumours I've heard about him in Town. Strong men now doing well in the army shudder at his name. I don't envy you being at the same school as him."

Bertie's expression took on a faraway look. "He's a couple of years older than me and he attacked me for standing up for one of my new classmates when I had just started at the school. He smiled at Lucy. "Lucy's brother, Peter, and a group of his friends, a year older than me and used to Parfitt, heard the commotion and rescued me from a real pummelling. That's when I first met Peter. And Parfitt too. I can't bear to think of Lucy with him."

* * *

Lucy shivered so hard her teeth chattered. "I couldn't believe it the night he arrived and Papa left me alone with him. I swear he would have ravished me on the spot if two footmen hadn't come in, followed by Mama, and I managed to break away."

Bertie put an arm around her shoulders and she felt the hot sting of tears running down her face. He pulled out a handkerchief and wiped them away.

"You'll be safe with me."

Lucy nodded and gulped in a breath. "I know but I can't help worrying about Mama. She had bruises on her face the next morning. The first time Papa has hit her where it would show that I remember."

"I hope that your aunt got her safely away. Let's drink our tea and try to forget about our worries for now. There's nothing we can do tonight."

Lucy rested her head on Bertie's shoulder for a moment. "Thank you, Bertie." She lifted her head and managed a weak smile. The concern in his expressive grey eyes nearly had her crying again. Now wasn't the time to give in to weakness. She smiled harder and accepted her teacup from him. How had it taken her so long to realise that she loved him?

"I'll be alright in a moment. I'm tired that's all."

"That's my girl." He kept an arm around her shoulder and continued his chat with Ralph.

She studied them as they talked. Could Parfitt hold a grudge against Bertie? If Parfitt had noticed Bertie had developed an interest in her he might be doing this to get back at him. It made some kind of sick sense. Parfitt was the sort of man who would hate to be bested. Bertie was the sort of man who would stand up for the underdog. He was slimmer in build than Parfitt but he had always been keen on boxing. Underneath his elegant Town exterior was a powerful man that many people would be surprised at if they knew. Yes, he would have defended boys who were bullied. The question was, would Bertie be in more or less danger from a revenge driven Parfitt rather than one with a monetary motive?

Lucy poured the tea and tried not to think about Lord Parfitt. Her thoughts strayed to Arthur and Emma seeming so happy together. Whatever Bertie said, she would never forgive herself if anything happened to him. If only she was more resolute like Grace Bamford, she would have persuaded Mama to ignore Papa's summons and go into hiding somewhere until Aunt Susan arrived back in London. It seemed she was the same as her mother in being conditioned to do whatever her father expected of them.

She leaned back and sipped her tea. Bertie was chatting

quietly with Ralph. What was it that Mama had said to her once about men? That was it. Don't be taken in by a man's obvious attraction to you, it doesn't necessarily mean he loves you. It might simply mean he's a man. She took another sip of tea and sat back with her eyes closed. Bertie was a good, kind man. How could she be sure that he loved her in a romantic way? Yes, he was attracted to her that much was obvious, and yet he hadn't said he loved her. He'd said he'd always wanted a proper family life. Was his proposal one of a marriage of convenience, with his main motivation being his urge to protect her in deference to the friendship between him and her and Peter. And how could she know?

She sat up with a start. Was she really wondering whether or not Bertie was offering her a love match? Yes, she was. If Bertie loved her, marriage might be something she could cope with after all. It was one thing telling yourself that not all men were like your father. Believing it deep inside was another matter. But Bertie had been so caring and kind towards her how could he ever be anything like her father. And she was in love with him.

CHAPTER TWENTY

Two days later Lucy arrived in the breakfast room to be met by total silence. There was no sign of Bertie or Ralph. She walked over to the window and scanned the area around the stables, hoping for a glimpse of them.

Mrs Adams came in with a fresh pot of coffee. "Lord Kinsey and Mr Lovell have gone out to help with building that new bridge near the home farm, Miss Vaughan."

"Did they say how long they would be?"

"Lord Kinsey said not to expect them much before dinner. He intends to show Mr Lovell around the home farm once they've finished the bridge. I suppose they think it's safe to be out now. They told me they saw or heard nothing about the strangers they were worried about yesterday."

Lucy studied Mrs Adam's face. Could she trust Bertie and Ralph to tell her everything? "I hope they haven't made a mistake going out."

"I shouldn't worry, Miss Vaughan. The talk in the servant's hall was the same yesterday. I expect those unknown men were simply travellers."

Lucy forced a smile, a long day stretched ahead of her. How she envied Bertie and Ralph being outdoors. Riding around the countryside on sunny days like this was one of the things she had missed most since living mainly in London. The prospect of choosing a book from Ralph's extensive library didn't appeal as much as she'd expected, knowing they were out and about. Why couldn't they have taken her with them? No, she was being selfish. No one would look twice at Ralph showing a friend around. She would be far too conspicuous.

"I expect you're right. I'm seeing shadows where there are none. She squared her shoulders. That coffee smells wonderful."

"Let me pour you a cup. The eggs on the side table should be hot and Cook will send in some fresh toast."

"Thank you, Mrs Adams."

Lucy helped herself to eggs and a slice of ham and took a chair at the polished breakfast table which gave her a view of the kitchen gardens and stable block. The pitter patter of paws on the wooden floor announced the entrance of one of Ralph's wolfhounds. He sat down beside her.

Mrs Adams tutted. "I'll send one of the footmen to take him down to the stables out of your way."

The tension in Lucy's shoulders eased. She relaxed against the back of her chair and fondled the dog's ears.

"No leave him. I feel safe with the dogs around." The temptation to get some fresh air was overwhelming. "I might take them out for a walk later."

Mrs Adams looked dubious. "If you're sure, Miss Vaughan."

"They've taken to me and I'm convinced they would protect me if anyone was lurking."

The dog put his head in Lucy's lap and looked pleadingly up at her. The second one came in and padded up to her.

Mrs Adams shook her head at the dogs' antics. "You should be safe out with them if you stay close to the house. They do look intimidating. Not that I think these two could catch anybody but they are good at begging for food. No one would believe they have recently polished off a huge breakfast. I'll send a footman along to shut them in the scullery until you've finished your breakfast, so you can eat it in peace."

"That might be best. I'll take them out once I've eaten."

Another grey furry head landed in Lucy's lap. She laughed and stroked both dogs at once. "Naughty pair. I enjoyed your company yesterday. Don't worry, I'll rescue you in a little while but we don't want to upset Mrs Adams now do we."

Mrs Adams shook her head at the dogs and smiled. "I don't know what Lord Kinsey sees in you two."

She bustled out and two footmen arrived minutes later. Lucy watched the dogs go as the footmen led them away.

Ralph's wolfhounds seemed quite biddable. Perhaps she ought to stay indoors but if she kept to the gardens of Kinsey Court, she should be safe enough. It would be a brave man who attacked her if she had the wolfhounds with her and a walk in the sun would lift her mood. She sighed. All this worry was wearing her down. She could only hope that Parfitt had given up and gone home. Surely, he and Papa must have realised she'd escaped with Bertie and drawn their own conclusions.

Lucy worked her way through a substantial breakfast. The waiting was interminable but at least she felt safe at Kinsey Court. Ever since Papa had made his outrageous demand for her to marry Parfitt, she had been too upset to eat much. She had hours to herself before Bertie and Ralph returned and might as well take her time over breakfast now her appetite had returned.

Eventually, she could stretch it out no longer and she rose from the table. Voices came from the hallway and she went to investigate. Perhaps Bertie and Ralph had come back early. She quickened her pace only to stop abruptly. A smartly dressed young man, who looked vaguely familiar, walked through the front door opened by one of the footmen. He must be a friend of Ralph's but the fewer people who knew about Ralph's unexpected visitors the better. She hung back in the shadows and studied him carefully.

Oh Lord, she recognised him now. He had been at several Ton parties she'd attended earlier in the year. She would be lucky to escape without him seeing her if the footman invited him in. Thank goodness Mrs Adams had insisted on having one of the maids alter some of Ralph's sister's clothes to fit her. Fortunately, her skirt was too long for the sturdy boots she was wearing to be visible. With a fine Norwich shawl around her shoulders, also borrowed, she would pass as a society lady on a country visit.

He was one of the Ton smarts who had been hanging around the ballrooms. A rather surprising friend for Ralph, with his no-nonsense attitude, perhaps? But then men in Ralph's position always attracted hangers on. They were often distant relatives, making them hard to shake off without being uncivil. The man glanced around the hall before addressing the footman again. Lucy tried to steady her ragged breathing; it would be so much easier if she could avoid him noticing her. She edged further back until her shoulders met the cold resistance of the hall wall.

"Have you any idea when Lord Kinsey will be back? He is expecting me." The man's voice was pleasantly deep.

The young footman looked uncertain and a blush stained his cheeks. "I don't rightly know, Sir. He went out with another guest some time ago. Let me show you to the drawing room and I'll go and find Mr James, the butler. I'm sure he'll be able to help you." The footman looked ready to scuttle off but he remembered his manners. "Who shall I say has arrived, Sir?"

The man removed his hat and tapped it against his thigh. Ralph must have forgotten he had his friend coming. A friend who looked rather put out about it. Ralph was a good friend to Bertie to willingly put up with this sort of disruption to his life without even any notice. The footman hovered from foot to foot looking ever more uncomfortable and the forgotten guest gave a smile that looked forced.

"Mr Gillett. I've been invited to the house party but Lord Kinsey suggested I come a day or two early." He pursed his lips and looked down his nose at the scared-looking footman.

Lucy took pity on the boy. He must be new to answering the door. She moved forward, as if she had just stepped out of the doorway of the breakfast room into the hall, and smiled at the footman.

"Perhaps you could tell Mr James that Mr Gillett is here. In the meantime, I'll show him the way to the drawing room."

The footman gave her a nod and a grateful smile and almost ran to a partially concealed door which must lead to the servants' quarters.

Mr Gillett went into a theatrically deep bow. "How delightful, Miss Vaughan. We were introduced at a musical soirée if I remember correctly."

"You are very good to remember my name, Mr Gillett."

"How could I ever forget such a charming lady as you, Miss Vaughan?"

Lucy sighed inwardly. Why so many young men in London thought this sort of overdone charm was attractive she would never know. For her part she'd rather have somebody straightforward like Bertie. Not that he didn't have plenty of town bronze of course, his manners were impeccable, but he had none of this exaggerated courtesy towards women that felt more like an insult. She gritted her teeth.

"How kind of you to say so."

"Not at all. Tell me, do you have any idea where Ralph has gone? I have rushed, at far too fast a pace for the good of my horses, to get here to give him the latest news from Town. I'm desolate to find he has forgotten me." Mr Gillett dipped into another theatrical bow.

Lucy suppressed a giggle and fought to keep the smile off her face. He cut such a figure of fun but he would be mortally offended if he noticed how amused she was. London was full of men of his stamp, charmers who lived on the fringes of society. Generally harmless, although some of them were known to hang around any heiresses who weren't too hideous. Papa would have told Parfitt about her expectations. There was no reason this man should know she was an heiress. She was rather surprised herself having expected no more than a comfortable competence.

Gillett straightened up and bestowed another of his smiles upon her. "I suspect you have a good idea. Won't you take pity on me and point me in the right direction. Knowing Ralph, he will be tramping over the countryside somewhere and a good walk is just what I need after all this travelling."

Lucy glanced at Mr Gillett's gleaming boots. Boots that stylish must have come from the hands of Hoby, no less. Still, it was his affair if he wanted to risk ruining them. He wasn't the only one who would be better for a good walk.

"They've gone to help with a bridge near the home farm. Ralph mentioned last night that it's being replaced. It's a fine day. I'll walk part of the way down the drive with you and set you on the right path. Then by the time you come back Mrs Adams, the housekeeper, will have your room prepared for you. I have a feeling the butler is down in the wine cellar and probably won't be here for some time. I'll explain the situation to him on my return."

Mr Gillett swept her another bow, much sketchier this time. Perhaps even he was finding it a bit too much. He held out his arm. "Let us be gone. There is no need for us to wait for a footman to open the door. I'm sure I can manage. I confess I am eager to find Ralph."

Lucy put her hand on his arm and he tucked it into the crook of his elbow, crammed his hat back on and swept her up to the front door. He wrenched it open and led her outside. Heavens, he was in a hurry to find Ralph. The sweeping driveway split into three directions. Lucy pointed to the farthest one.

"That way. The lane to the home farm leads off it a bit farther on. I believe the broken bridge is just beyond there. Once we've turned onto the lane, you'll see the farmhouse. They'll point you in the direction of the bridge." Lucy smiled up at him. He was a tall man and, like Bertie, looked as if he spent at least some of his time in London keeping himself fit.

"If Lord Kinsey isn't there the farmer's wife may know where he is. If not, you will have had a walk and won't have too far to get back to the house."

"Indeed, Miss Vaughan. Lead the way," he said in a light tone of voice.

Lucy started walking but the satisfied smile that played around Mr Gillett's mouth when she glanced up at him unsettled her. She stopped and tried to pull away from him. He tightened his hold on her arm, an ugly expression on his face.

She opened her mouth to scream. Something cold pressed against her side. Her legs wobbled as the end of a pistol dug into her flesh. Good Lord, how could she have been so stupid? At the very least she should have brought the dogs with her.

"I wouldn't make a scene if I was you, Miss Vaughan. I won't hesitate to shoot if I have to. Start walking smoothly but down the pathway to our right."

Frozen with fear, Lucy allowed herself to be half dragged by the arm towards the driveway to the village and the lane that led to the main road. Reason reasserted itself. He must be connected to Parfitt and shooting her would be the last thing he would want. Parfitt needed her alive if he was to force her into marriage. Although, he might not be too bothered about keeping her alive once he had his hands on her fortune.

A shudder went through Lucy at the thought. She screamed in earnest even though it was unlikely anyone from the house would hear her. Gillett pocketed the pistol and clamped a hand over her mouth. She kicked and bucked. They were close to a bend in the driveway. He was too strong for her. The muscles in his arm felt like iron where it clamped her arm to his side and her shoulder hurt from him almost lifting her off the ground.

She twisted and turned in a desperate effort to break free, despite the pain in her shoulder. Gillett swore in fluent French when a kick from one of her sturdy boots caught him full on the shin. He dropped his hand from her mouth and scooped her up. She kicked and flailed at him with her legs and twisted around so she could pummel his chest with both fists. Trying to escape him was a hopeless task and in minutes Monsieur Gillett had carried her around the bend in the drive.

Why hadn't she noticed his slight French accent before? Was he connected to Parfitt or was this some sort of attempt to blackmail Uncle James into giving him information to pass to France? Uncle James must be working on something important to have left Aunt Susan to rescue them from Papa's matchmaking scheme on her own. An icy shiver ran all the way down her spine and she screamed at the top of her lungs at the sight of a shiny, dark blue travelling coach.

The four sturdy bay horses harnessed to the waiting coach looked as if they could keep going for a long stretch. Gillett threw her through the already open door onto the floor, where she landed awkwardly, knocking the breath out of her lungs. He climbed in behind her and they took off before he had closed the door. Lucy rolled around the floor as they gathered speed on the twisty drive, her breath coming in pained gasps.

CHAPTER TWENTY ONE

Ralph gave a satisfied sigh as the last nail was hammered home in the new bridge by the home farm. "That's a good job done. There are several streams around the estate, each with more than one bridge. We've got a programme of replacing them all. Not many left to do after this. This one should have been the last one done but an awful storm we had a few days ago brought a tree down on it."

"We had that as well. Quite a storm and it seemed to come out of nowhere." Bertie smiled at the memory of cannoning into a sodden Lucy as he raced for cover.

The farmer strode across to them, a big smile on his face. "I'm glad that's finished, my lord. It's a really good bridge, wide enough to take a big cart. It will be much quicker to get our vegetables to market now. My wife has been baking if you would fancy some home-brew and a hot bun."

Ralph looked at Bertie. "Mrs Harper's baking is legendary. Do you want to sample some?"

"That's a very good idea. Thank you, Mr Harper."

They emerged from the farmhouse half an hour later, well-fortified with home brewed ale and hot buns. It was a beautiful spring day, and Bertie took a deep breath.

"I'm so glad to be out of London. The air is always so much

fresher here." It was a sunny day. Bertie looked around him. Green leaves were sprouting on hedgerows and trees. "From the direction of the sun it's not even noon yet. I'm glad all the visitors to the area seem to have disappeared. I'm looking forward to our tour of this part of your estate. A good walk is just what I need."

"Let's walk round first then and come back to have a look at Mr Harper's breeding stock. There's a path we can take that goes through the fields rented by Mr Wilson, the farmer who took you up in his cart the other day. We can ask him if he's seen any more unusual activity, assuming he's about. Then we can go the back way into the home farm and walk home using the main road."

They set off in good spirits, with Ralph pointing out local landmarks. Bertie always loved this time of year. There was no sign of Mr Bailey so they started back to the home farm.

"Your land looks in good heart. I can't wait to bring my new estate up to modern standards. Once I've shaken off Parfitt. I should hear from Cathlay's people soon. With luck he'll send some men up to help us." Bertie looked at his boots as they tramped along the country lane. "I'm hoping to find a way for Lucy and me to marry quickly. I want to put an end to all this nonsense. I don't trust her father any more than I trust Parfitt."

Ralph frowned. "I can see your point, but has it occurred to you that Parfitt is such a rum customer you might be putting your life in danger?"

"Surely not even Parfitt would be that evil."

"Are you sure, after that dreadful bashing that he gave you when you started at the same school as him? I've heard it said that he's got a grudge against you."

"Parfitt beat me several times. Peter and his friends saved me from him more than once. Then I started shooting up in height and gaining strength and was able to fight back a bit more. Cousin Augusta arranged for me to have boxing lessons one summer holiday. When we arrived at school for the following autumn term Parfitt started on me, showing off what a strong man he was for the school's new arrivals."

"I think I can guess what's coming."

Bertie grinned. "With everything I'd been taught over the summer Parfitt got a surprise. I planted him a perfect facer and he landed in the mud at my feet. He lay there like a stranded fish and couldn't get to his feet for some time, with a crowd of much smaller boys laughing at him. He's never forgiven me for the humiliation."

"I would have loved to see that." Ralph tilted his head to one side and studied his face. "His hatred of you must have got even worse recently after the way you warned him off chasing Lucy in the spring. Especially with the Duke of Cathlay threatening him." Ralph let out a long whistle.

"Good Lord, man. It's a wonder he didn't have you stabbed in some dark corner. Parfitt could never stand a humiliation like that."

"I thought of that. When I went to visit my cousin, Max, Mr Bright, his friend Overton's major-domo, gave me some serious self-defence and awareness of danger training."

"Hmm. It seems to me you've had your eye on Miss Vaughan for a long time."

Bertie felt himself go hot. "Not knowingly, but she and her brother were close childhood friends. I felt this intense urge to protect her and it's grown from there. I'd heard her father had got himself into debt and didn't think anything of it when he called her and her mother back home. It never occurred to me the old devil would get himself tangled up with a wrong 'un like Parfitt. I feel partly responsible for Lucy's predicament."

Ralph stopped walking and turned to face him, with a worried look on his face. "Are you sure you've offered for her for the right reasons? Guilt is no basis for a happy marriage."

Bertie went hotter still, even his ears burned. "Absolutely sure. The thought of any woman in Parfitt's clutches would make me want to rescue her. But I realised I would feel almost as murderous if any man was marrying Lucy. It was a while before the whole truth dawned on me."

"I'm glad to hear that. I like Lucy. Judith, one of my young cousins, is a friend of hers. In fact, Judith worships her because of all the charity work she's done amongst other things. But then Judith is very keen on good causes. Her mama is afraid she's showing bluestocking tendencies."

Bertie grinned. "There is nothing wrong with bluestockings. At least they've got a good brain."

"Very true and Judith has always shown good judgement. I'm very happy for you. Right, now I've established that my best friend is getting married for the right reasons, let's get going." Ralph pointed to a stile at the side of the path they were on a little way ahead. "That leads to the main road. It's a quicker way back to the home farm and then home."

Bertie smiled to himself as he followed Ralph along the path to the stile. He couldn't wait for all the nonsense with Parfitt to be over so he could marry Lucy and introduce her to all his friends. He drifted into a happy daydream, only to be brought back to the present with a furious shout from Ralph from the other side of the stile. He followed Ralph over to find him shaking his fist at the fast disappearing back of an expensive looking travelling carriage.

"Imbecile. Did you see that? That coach was going so fast it was all over the road. It was a miracle it didn't hit me." He pointed to some wheel tracks on the grass verge. "Anyone would have thought he was trying to run me down the way he veered across as I jumped down onto the verge."

"Perhaps it was driven by one of Parfitt's minions who was hoping it was me." Bertie struggled to keep his voice light. "We need to get back to Kinsey Court quickly."

"Yes, we do." Ralph squeezed his shoulder. "Although it's probably just some fool in too much of a hurry."

They set off at run, past the turn off to the home farm and on towards Kinsey Court. Bertie was glad of the physical exertion to take the edge off his anxiety. If it was one of Parfitt's men, why was he driving away from Kinsey Court at such a pace? Surely, they couldn't have broken in and stolen Lucy away? Ralph stony faced stare suggested he was having the same thought. Bertie stumbled but recovered quickly. He had better keep his eyes on the road. Oh Lord, he should have stayed behind and kept watch.

Deuce take it. He was letting his imagination run riot. It was an expensive looking brand-new carriage. It probably carried some wild buck who had told his coachman to spring the horses just to show off. All the same, he was glad when they reached the driveway. Even at a steady run it had taken them nearly twenty minutes. He gulped in some air and quickened his pace, overtaking Ralph. Ralph caught up with him, blowing heavily, and pointed out a side door.

"That's the quickest way into the house from here."

They reached the door to find it locked and Ralph banged hard on it. He turned to Bertie. "The household staff have been told to take all precautions. This door is usually open at this time of day. I often use it as a shortcut to the house from the stables. Especially if I have the dogs with me. Then I can rub them down in the scullery, which is the first room you come to."

Mrs Adams herself opened the door to them. Ralph's dogs were howling in the background. Ralph led him into a passageway that appeared to lead to the kitchen.

"Oh, Miss Vaughan was going to let the dogs out of the scullery once she'd had her breakfast. She must have forgotten. I'm sorry about that, Lord Kinsey."

"Where is Miss Vaughan?" Bertie exchanged a glance with Ralph. "At least she can't have gone out if she didn't take the dogs with her."

"I don't rightly know, Sir."

Bertie's whole body stiffened. "I'll get these boots off and go and look for her."

"Don't worry about the boots." Ralph opened the scullery door and his wolf hounds tumbled out. "Now you two, where has my other guest gone."

Mr James, the butler stormed in with a hand on the shoulder of a nervous-looking footman, who trotted along beside him. "Tell Lord Kinsey what happened."

The footman stumbled and stuttered hopping from one foot on the other. The butler glared at him.

"Out with it boy."

"I... I... I... think she might have gone out with your friend, Lord Kinsey. I was supposed to fetch the butler but I got waylaid by the head footman and I forgot until a few minutes ago." The lad sounded terrified.

Ralph stared at him. "What friend?"

"The one you were expecting. I think he said his name was Gilbert, no it was more like Gillit. Very smartly dressed he was. Not as tall as you, dark hair, looked as if he might have been out in the sun a bit too much. He said you were expecting him and he was most put out that you had forgotten."

Mr James opened his mouth to say something but Ralph put his hand up.

"You're not making sense, lad. Why were you supposed to fetch the butler?"

The boy's eyes darted from one to the other. "Uhm, Miss Vaughan asked me to."

Bertie gasped and the room did a circle around him. "Were you expecting someone else this week, Ralph?"

"Not until the weekend. Quick. James, send someone to fetch an item that Miss Vaughan has worn recently. We'll let the dogs loose in the house in the meantime in case she is still here."

Mrs Adams looked at him in alarm. "Oh no, you don't think something's happened to her, do you? I'll run upstairs myself."

Bertie ran around the downstairs rooms looking for Lucy, although he knew deep in his gut that she wasn't there. He had to do something or he would go mad with the worry. He came out of the library and nearly fell over the wolfhounds as they bounded towards the front door. One of them started pawing at the bottom of the door and let out a deep throated whine. Ralph came up to join him.

"Mrs Adams has had all the maids checking upstairs and there is no sign of Lucy." He pointed at the dogs milling about by the front door. "I'd lay you odds that Lucy went out that way from the way those two are performing. Perhaps she's just gone for a walk."

Bertie shook his head. "She would have taken the dogs. She loves dogs and Mrs Adams said she had promised to let them out once she'd eaten."

A footman ran into the hall and handed Ralph a pair of gloves. "Mrs Adams says Miss Vaughan has worn these regularly since she's been here.

Ralph took the gloves and held one out to each of the dogs who obliged him by sniffing hard at them and whining. One started pawing at the door again.

"They've got Lucy's scent." Bertie had the front door open before Ralph could reach it. "Let's see if we can pick up her trail. We'll soon know from that whether she's out walking or not."

The dogs surged out and ran down the right-hand fork of driveway. Bertie charged after them, barely aware of Ralph just behind him. They reached the bend in the drive that led to the path to the main road. The dogs came to such an abrupt halt that Bertie fell over one of them. Ralph grabbed his arm to keep him upright and called the dogs to heel.

Bertie stood stock still, stunned. Ralph had a quick look around. He pointed to some tracks on the side of the drive.

"See, someone has turned a coach round here."

"She's in that blue coach. She must be." Bertie jerked into action and ran towards the stables. "We've got to get after them. Can you lend me a horse?"

Ralph shouted at a groom sitting outside cleaning a bridle. "We need two good horses quickly."

The door to the stables opened and Bertie nearly bumped into Arthur. "You're back! Are you on your own?"

Another man stepped out from behind Arthur. "Neil Roskelley. There is a man called William with us too."

Ralph shouted at his groom, who had disappeared into the stables. "Make that five horses. The best you can find. We want ones with plenty of stamina as well as speed." He looked at Arthur. "I presume your horses have already covered some distance."

"Yes, we've ridden them for a couple of hours or so. William is settling them down. I'll go and help saddle up some more." He put a hand on Bertie's arm. "I take it despite all your efforts they've somehow got hold of Miss Vaughan. There's about a dozen of the Duke of Cathlay's men in the area. At least I think they're his men. Some of them could be Miss Vaughan's uncle's men. We can send William to find them once we know which way they've taken her." He ran into the stables.

Bertie forced himself to behave logically and shook hands with his new agent. "Glad to see you again, Roskelley. Arthur is right. We think Parfitt's men have got Miss Vaughan. We could be going into something very dangerous. You don't have to come with us. I doubt anything would stop Arthur joining in since his fiancée is a great friend of Miss Vaughan's."

Roskelley grinned at him. "I'm sure the estate can manage without us for a while longer. I haven't enjoyed myself so much since my army days. Sorry if that seems unfeeling. From what Arthur has told me, Miss Vaughan could be in real danger if she's been captured. I've done a fair bit of army intelligence in my time. It might be difficult to persuade him but it would be better to take William with us and send Arthur for reinforcements. He's a good lad but he doesn't have military experience. Don't worry we'll find her. There's a lot more going on here than you know. Her uncle will leave no stone unturned and with the Duke of Cathlay helping we'll find her. Right. I'll start saddling up too."

Bertie exchanged glances with Ralph. "I knew Roskelley had been in the army. Didn't realise he was in intelligence. I don't know what's going on here but I don't like the sound of it. But for now, all I care about is getting Lucy back."

CHAPTER TWENTY TWO

The coach was modern and well sprung, even so Lucy took a buffeting lying on the floor. They must be travelling at some speed. She could see Gillett's legs on the side of the coach farthest away from her head. He was humming loudly enough for her to hear over the pounding of the horses' hooves. How much was Parfitt paying him? He must be pleased to have caught her with so little effort. How could she have been so easily taken in? She tried to sit up but Gillett lent over and pushed her back down.

"Stay where you are or it will be the worse for you. I only have to deliver you alive. A few bruises won't matter." His voice was hard.

Lucy lay back down and shuffled across the floor of the coach until she was up against the opposite seat, as far away from her captor as possible. She turned onto her side and tried to roll with the movement of the coach. This proved a successful strategy until the coach veered to the side so sharply that she was rolled almost completely over, adding a searing pain in the shoulder Parfitt had hurt to the general bodily aches caused by bracing herself to take the movement of the coach. They slowed up and came to a halt which gave her body relief but her mind started working overtime. Had they come to their destination?

Fear swamped her. She had absolutely no idea where she was. She closed her eyes and concentrated on her breathing. In and out, nice and steady. If any opportunity to escape arose she wanted to be calm enough to take it. They must have been travelling for an hour or so and at some speed. She lay still and tried to think. The road through the village went in two directions. She had been so stunned for the first few minutes she had no idea of which way they had turned. Even if she had it wouldn't help. The road they had travelled had so many twists and turns it would have been impossible to be sure if they had taken any side roads. No wonder Gillett had made sure that she couldn't see out of the windows.

Gillett wrenched open the door and jumped down. "Stay where you are. I'll be back in a minute." He gave her a triumphant look.

She didn't answer him but craned her neck to try and catch a glimpse through the door. They were on the sort of driveway, with rolling lawns beyond that suggested a country house of some size. Gillett slammed the door shut behind him. Before she had time to scramble up, the door behind her head opened. Rough hands were shoved under her armpits and dragged her into a sitting position. Her effort to get a proper look at where she was failed when a rather dubious smelling scarf was tied around her head. A man who reeked of stale ale picked her up bodily and carried her away from the coach and up a flight of steps.

She was being taken into a substantial house from the sound of the door opening on well-oiled hinges and the number of steps she'd been carried up. Which reinforced her impression of being in the grounds of a big country estate. But which one?

Possibly, one with its own chapel. She shivered. Did Parfitt live somewhere in the midlands? This might be his home. Was she doomed to a marriage with a man even worse than her father? Parfitt was probably waiting to drag her into his private chapel with a special licence tucked into his pocket. Any clergyman in his pay would be unlikely to aid her. Even if she refused to make the vows, they would say she had.

The sound of another door being opened made her catch her breath. The man carrying her slowed down. He swore as he caught her foot on the door frame and had to turn sideways to carry her through. She was tossed onto what felt like a leather sofa. There was a definite smell of old books, strong enough to get past the scarf. They must be in a library. She heard the sound of two sets of footsteps entering and something being poured. She held her arms tightly to her side and lay as still as she could. If this was Parfitt, she had a feeling that the more fear she showed the more he would enjoy attacking her. Perhaps he would leave her alone for a bit if he thought she had swooned.

"Here you are, Sharp. Off you go. And make sure you keep this to yourself, or it will go badly with you."

That was definitely Gillett's voice, but with a hard edge to it. Having her eyes covered seemed to make her hearing more acute. She really had been stupid to miss the hint of a French accent in Gillett's voice, which would have made her more wary. It was obvious now. Sharp muttered something and from the sound he made almost ran out of the room. Gillett swore fluently in French and heavy footsteps made for the direction of the door, slamming it shut. The next thing Lucy heard was the sound of a key turning in a lock.

Another man in the room said something she couldn't catch.

They must have moved further away. She didn't recognise the second voice but it definitely wasn't Parfitt. Perhaps he wasn't here yet, which would give Bertie more time to find her. A wave of desolation washed over her. It might be ages before Bertie realised that she was missing. When he did, there wasn't much chance of him finding her. If she was going to get out of this, she had to find some way to escape. It wasn't going to be easy.

She tried to gather her scattered wits. The room had a musty smell to it. That could be coming from the scarf over her nose but if it wasn't it suggested somewhere that had seen little use in recent times. A property Parfitt didn't visit very often perhaps. Which would suggest the place would have no more than a skeleton staff. Perfect for Parfitt's purposes. It didn't have to be his own property. All the better for him if he was unknown in the area.

If only she had been born a man she wouldn't be in this mess. She had been naïve to think a well provided for young woman of her station could keep away from men. How ironic that Great Aunt Agatha had left her a large sum and tied it up in a trust to keep her safe from fortune hunters, only for her own father to use that knowledge for his own ends. The man who should have been the person to protect her above all others. Everything bad in her life always came back to him. If she had married one of the sensible men who she had come across she'd be safe now. She'd had offers enough.

Bertie was more than sensible. He was good and kind and fun and she loved him. If only she had realised what he meant to her sooner. She tried to blink back the tears seeping into the blindfold. It was no good thinking about Bertie. He would try to rescue her but she didn't want him to be hurt, or worse.

She had got herself into this mess and she wasn't worth Bertie risking his life for. Would Parfitt be any worse than Papa? Should she just capitulate and accept that her plan of forging a different sort of life for herself had been nothing more than a dream?

Not that Bertie would have any chance of finding her in time if Parfitt arrived soon. Parfitt had enjoyed the idea of defiling her first so she went through with a marriage without a fight. If he did take her virginity first, would even Bertie want to marry her if he found her before a marriage had taken place? He was the sort of man who would stand by her but if it got out, which it was bound to, he would be shunned by the Ton at worst or ridiculed at best. Either way his social standing, which she knew was important to him, would be gone. She couldn't ask that of him. As long as she could avoid marrying Parfitt, her fortune would be intact and she could go and live quietly in some remote spot.

Before getting to know Bertie better these last few days, setting up her own establishment had been her firm ambition. Somehow the prospect had lost its appeal. Surely a few days of Bertie's company and support couldn't have changed her that much. It had though. That day when she thought he was Parfitt she had run into she had put her joy at finding it was Bertie down to relief. She had shied away from the truth at first. The friendship between them had sparked into something much deeper after being held in his arms as he reassured her. She was in love with him.

There was no point worrying. It would all be academic if she couldn't escape from Parfitt. If he managed to force her into marriage would Uncle James help her to escape somewhere and support her? It was so unfair that a woman's possessions all became her husband's property on her marriage. Lucy tensed as footsteps approached and she heard the sound of curtains being drawn. The footsteps drew nearer. How long could she keep up her pretence of being in a swoon?

Two large hands grabbed her shoulders and shook her none too gently. She gave out a groan that ended as a whimper and she was pulled up into a sitting position. Her pulse hammered in her ears and she felt as if she was spinning. She groaned loudly and this time without forcing it.

"Where am I? My head aches."

"She's still alive, Gillett. Lucky for you." A cultured and very English voice, but not one she recognised. "I'll leave you to revive her. Best give her some of the brandy."

"She'll survive. These society misses are useless. I didn't even tie her up. She must have swooned from the shock." He sounded irritated.

"Hmm. Make sure she does survive. And in one piece if you take my meaning."

"Yes, Sir." Gillett's voice dripped with outrage. He didn't like his superior. Interesting.

"I'll be back later. Give her some brandy and have her carried up to a bedroom. Don't take the blindfold off until she's ready to be locked in there. And make sure the room doesn't have a view of the stables or driveway. I don't want her seeing me."

It didn't sound like Parfitt was here yet and Gillett's superior didn't want her seeing him. Meaning he was likely to be a member of the Ton. She heard someone snort, probably Gillett. Footsteps stomped away and the door slammed shut. There was definitely no love lost between Gillett and his superior. She would recognise Gillett of course but he must be banking on Parfitt keeping her quiet once he had married her. There must be some doubt about Gillett's reliability if Parfitt had someone checking up on him. In which case it might be worth trying to buy him off by offering him more to release her than Parfitt was paying him.

CHAPTER TWENTY THREE

Ralph called his dogs to heel and sent them for a walk with one of his grooms. Arthur led out the first of five horses and they were on the road in no time at all. Ralph led the way down the lane that ended at the main road. Ten minutes later they came to the junction. There was a cosy-looking country inn on one corner. Ralph left his horse with Bertie and ran inside. He was out again very quickly.

"They're making for the road to London. The landlord happened to be outside when he saw what must've been the coach that she was taken in. Very new and shiny and a dark blue colour. It was going at a frantic pace apparently."

Roskelley rode up to Arthur. "I want you to see if you can find that group of the Duke of Cathlay's men we bumped into on the way here."

A mulish expression flitted across Arthur's face and Roskelley's voice took on a forceful edge. "They said they were heading south later today and shouldn't be far from where we saw them. Tell them what's happened and see if some of them can join in the chase. They might have some idea where Miss Vaughan is likely to be taken."

Arthur glanced across at Bertie who nodded. "I'll see what I can do. If I don't find them, where shall I go?"

Roskelley looked at Bertie.

"You had best make for Mayford Castle," Bertie said. "There's always the chance that the kidnappers have set a false trail and doubled back. Parfitt might still be in the area of the castle, so be careful." Bertie said.

Arthur nodded. "I'll do that. I think Miss Vaughan's uncle has some men in that area. I'll try and contact them as well."

Bertie watched him canter off along the main road in the direction of Mayford Castle. "I think that was the right decision, Roskelley, to send Arthur. Right let's get going."

They turned onto the road to London. William and Roskelley took the lead. Ralph rode up beside Bertie and cleared his throat.

"Don't worry old man. We'll find her. I was listening to those two. They seem to have plenty of experience of tracking between them." For all his encouraging words Ralph looked worried.

"I know how good William is and Roskelley comes well recommended. I just can't stop thinking about Lucy in the hands of a kidnapper. I think he could be that Gillett fellow from your footman's description."

"I remember coming across a Mr Gillett hanging around the fringes of the Ton earlier in the season."

"Yes, that's when I noticed him. One of those charming types who try and attach themselves to anyone with good connections. I think he has French relatives. I'm not sure what his link to Parfitt is."

"Paid lackey most like."

"That was my first thought but I'm surprised Lucy's Uncle James, Lord Hampton, hasn't arrived sooner to rescue her. I have a strong suspicion Lord Hampton might be involved in secret operations with one of the departments of government at times. Possibly connected to the War Office from something my new stepfather let out. I don't like the sound of all this. Can we even be sure that Gillett is working for Parfitt?"

"Good heavens. Lord Hampton is very high up in the War Office. My mother knows the family. Do you think Lucy could have been kidnapped for political reasons?"

"It would be a coincidence but I can't rule it out." Bertie grimaced.

They settled down to their ride. About twenty minutes later they came to a fork in the road and turned in the direction of London. A while later they came up to a farm cart and Roskelley hailed the driver.

"We looking for some friends of ours. They left something important behind." He pointed to his saddlebag. "Travelling in a new, dark blue coach."

The cart driver scratched his head. "I reckon it must have been that coach that charged through a while back just before the road forked. Going so fast I didn't see it clearly. I was too busy trying to keep my cart on the road. My old mare was so startled she tried to bolt with me. It was a dark colour and smart looking."

"That will be it. Did you notice which direction it went in at the junction?" Roskelley pulled out a coin.

"I noticed alright. They turned for London. I was expecting them to end up in the ditch the speed they were going at. It lifted onto two wheels but righted itself."

Roskelley threw him the coin. "Thanks. That'll be him, the idiot. He was in such a hurry he forgot to pick up what he came for."

They surged past the cart. Bertie's brain was working

overtime.

"Don't look so worried," Ralph said. "We know we're on the right road so far and this sounds more like Parfitt's style to me. If the French were involved, they'd want to stay inconspicuous. Not go charging about the countryside making everyone look at them."

"I can't help but worry. This mad dash does have Parfitt's stamp on it." Bertie gritted his teeth. "If that swine has forced Lucy into marriage, before we can catch up with him, I swear I'll make her a widow on the spot."

"I don't doubt it, old man. We'll cover for you. Let's hope it doesn't come to that."

They rode on in silence for several minutes. Bertie felt increasingly agitated. He rode up beside Roskelley and William.

"I wish it wasn't so quiet today. We need more sightings of that coach to be sure it hasn't turned off."

Behind him Ralph gave a shout and rode past them towards a lone traveller approaching on a grey horse.

"Geoffrey, old man. We're trying to catch up with a smart, dark blue coach. You haven't ridden past it by any chance, have you?"

"You're in luck. I saw it take the turn towards Tennant Manor about a quarter of an hour ago. Driving like a madman the chap on the box. He didn't look like a regular coachman to me and the horses were really lathered up. He'll ruin them. Shame, they looked like four prime goers." He sounded angry.

"Oh, good man, Geoffrey. I've no time to explain now. Can you tell us exactly where Tennant Manor is? I know the place but I haven't visited it since I was a boy."

"Keep going past Tennant village followed by a farm. There's a gated turn off to the left just after the farm. Mind you, if you want to catch up with them, you'd be best riding across country. Take the lane on the left before you reach the village. Follow the lane round, it's full of twists and turns with lots of trees on both sides, until you come to open parkland on your right. There's a side entrance to the estate. You can't miss it."

"Does it have a gatekeeper?"

"No, it's just a bridle path."

"Perfect. Don't mention you saw us to anyone will you."

"I won't tell a soul but I'll be expecting a dinner from you sometime soon so you can tell me what's going on." Geoffrey saluted and rode on his way.

Ralph gave a whoop. "Come on. I know where he means."

Roskelley caught up with Ralph. "I wonder if we can turn off the main road before we get near to the village and still find the lane to the park. I'd like us to be as invisible as possible."

"It's a long time since I came this way but I know there's a bridle path to our left through woodland a bit farther on. We could try going down there. I'm pretty sure it comes out near to Tennant."

Bertie threw up a hand. "We can't risk getting lost and losing time."

"If their destination is Tennant Manor, which seems likely, we'd be unlucky if they don't stay there for at least a while," Roskelley said. "The kidnapper was probably sent on a scouting mission and grabbed an opportunity when he found Miss Vaughan alone."

"That makes sense. We think we're dealing with a Mr Gillett from the description my footman gave us. I know the man vaguely. He would have some story ready to fish for information, to find out if I had unexpected visitors." Ralph looked at Bertie. "I've come across silver tongued men like him before. They can sound so plausible."

"Indeed. Parfitt probably has several scouts out searching for you, Mr Lovell. They'll be meeting up later today to compare notes. My best guess is they will stay at Tennant Manor tonight."

Bertie groaned. "Guesses aren't good enough. I've got to rescue Lucy."

"At the very least they will have to change that team, Bertie. Geoffrey knows his horses. If they push on much farther with them in that state they'll come to grief. I agree with Roskelley. We need to find them without being seen to have the best chance of rescuing Lucy."

Bertie allowed himself to be persuaded and they carried on. When they reached the bridle path, Roskelley took the lead and they trotted down it in single file. The path twisted round and once they were hidden from the main road Roskelley stopped.

"There's a spinney up ahead and this path seems to go through the edge of it." Roskelley grinned at them. "Have you had much practice at climbing trees, William?"

William laughed. "Just the sort of thing I like."

"Good. We'll ride through and stop when you see a suitable tree with a good vantage point. We should be able to get our bearings if you can see the village."

The spinney proved to be large enough to be called a wood. The trees to their right started to thin out. William called a halt near to a fairly young, healthy looking oak tree. He dismounted and handed his reins to Roskelley.

"That oak looks perfect."

Bertie squinted up at it. "It is once you've reached that first branch. Hold my reins, Ralph. I'll give William a leg up."

With Bertie's help William was soon on the first branch. He picked his way to the top, keeping the trunk between him and the open ground to the right until he was partly hidden by the emerging leaf canopy. Bertie shielded his eyes from the sun and watched. For the first time in hours, he felt calm. With any luck they would soon have Lucy with them. A few minutes later a pair of feet emerged from amongst the leaves.

William swung himself down from the bottom branch and dropped the last few feet to the ground. "We're in luck. This path does come out on the lane to the back entrance and I can make out what looks like a coach next to what must be the stable buildings."

Bertie sagged with relief. His instinct was to go charging in but he knew Roskelley was right. The safest way was to go in by stealth. They joined the others who had dismounted and tied all the horses up to branches. William drew them around in a circle.

"There's a coach by the stable block with no horses harnessed. I can't see it clearly but I'm confident it's the dark one we're following." William caught Roskelley's eye. "We're not the only ones hiding out in woodland. There are some men in the woods near to the entrance to the park. There's a stream in the woodland a bit farther along this path. I suggest we walk the horses there and you wait while I scout around and try and find out who is also about."

"Good idea." Roskelley studied Bertie. "Whatever we do we don't want to be seen at this point."

Bertie nodded. "I've calmed down now. I can see the wisdom in that. I'm carrying a set of ladies' muff pistols in my pockets, ready loaded. Do you want to take them?"

"No, too noisy if there are a lot of them." William bent down and pulled out a wicked looking knife. "I've got this."

"I've got one too." Roskelley tapped his calf and laughed. "I wonder if we were trained by the same team. Let's hope it's nothing more than some boys on a day out."

"Some of Cathlay's men would be useful," William said.

"Or some of Miss Vaughan's uncle's men. Lord Hampton, that is."

"Don't worry I'll work out who they are before I do anything. We have no idea how many men are inside Tennant Manor. Any reinforcements would be useful."

William disappeared into the trees and Bertie watched him go. Ralph walked up to him and put a hand on his shoulder.

"What is it, Bertie?"

"I'm worried that there's some sort of political game going on here. I don't want Lucy used as a bargaining tool."

"It's far more likely to be Parfitt and his games. Besides even if there is some political motive behind Lucy's capture, Lord Hampton is her uncle for heaven's sake. He'll want her kept safe. Don't worry, you're bound to be nervous until we have Lucy back."

Bertie nodded but his stomach clenched when he glanced at Roskelley who didn't meet his gaze and walked off towards the horses. Bertie shook his head and followed Roskelley. What on earth was going on, it was torture being in the dark. The more he thought about it the stranger it seemed that Lord and Lady Hampton had taken so long to respond to Mrs Vaughan's plea for help.

Lord Hampton was a well-known figure on the London social scene. He must be fully aware of how nasty Parfitt was. Apart from a few close friends and hangers on, Parfitt was generally hated. Was he thinking too much? It might simply have taken a long time for the message to get to the Hamptons. He untied his horse and followed Roskelley who was leading his own horse and William's. They found the stream and led the horses down to it for a drink. Once they had finished Roskelley and Ralph found some dry grass and gave them a cursory rubdown before tying them up again where they were well hidden from any passers-by.

Bertie walked up to Ralph. "All this waiting is killing me. Give me a leg up and I'll climb the tree that William did."

Ralph stared at him in horror. "William looked to be an expert. Climbing oak trees is a dangerous game. Besides which we'll be in trouble if anyone sees you."

"Ralph, think. You've been to Mayford Castle. It's surrounded by trees. I spent most of my childhood holidays staying there. I know how to climb a tree. Lucy and Peter were good climbers but I was the best. Come on. If I can get high enough, I'll keep a watch on who's coming and going. At least then we'll have an idea of how William is getting on."

Ralph looked at Roskelley who nodded. "I was going to volunteer myself but, if Bertie is a good climber, it might as well be him and it will give him something to do. The waiting is the worst part. It was always like that before a battle when I was in the army."

"I do a good impersonation of an owl," Bertie said. "If I catch sight of Parfitt arriving, I will hoot once. If I spot William getting into trouble I'll hoot twice."

They soon had him on the bottom branch of the oak tree. Bertie studied the branches above. Yes, it was easy to see the best route to avoid being visible. He swung himself up to the next branch and was soon high above the ground. There was no sign of William but he could see evidence of horses tied up in the trees much further along. He had a good view of the road when he turned the other way. Knowing Parfitt, if he did turn up, it would be in a coach and even this high up he should be able to hear it. He turned his attention to the area William must be in and concentrated hard.

Try as he might he couldn't see any movement of men. William was right, whoever was in these woods with them was unlikely to be connected to Parfitt. Even the horses were well hidden, you'd have to be high up to see them. He wished now he had pressed Roskelley harder to explain what he meant about more going on in the background. Was he himself simply speculating or did he know more than he had told them? Bertie sighed and concentrated on his surveillance. There was no point worrying about things he could do nothing about. He had to believe that he would soon see Lucy again. Anything else was unthinkable.

CHAPTER TWENTY FOUR

After some muttering in French, Gillett scooped Lucy up with an arm under her knees and shoulders. She froze and then let her arms dangle down as if she was still in a swoon. It seemed her best defence for now. He carried her for a few strides and then kicked at something which was probably the door. When nothing happened, he shouted.

"Somebody, open this door and give me a hand, now."

Gone was the smooth voice of a society gentleman, replaced by an angry tone, with a strong hint of a French accent. He was a good actor to be able to change his voice so much. The hinges of a door creaked and footsteps stomped in. Two sets of rough hands grabbed her. One taking her legs and the other under her armpits. The one taking her arms smelled of onions and beer. Lucy tried not to retch as they carried her up a set of stairs and stopped.

Gillett swore at them. This time in English. "In that first room over there, imbeciles."

Lucy was dumped unceremoniously onto a soft bed. One of the guest rooms then. Someone, probably Gillett, chafed her hands.

"Hand me that brandy decanter and then get out. I'm going to take her blindfold off and the fewer people she can recognise the better. She must have come round by now but it won't hurt to get some brandy down her. It might keep her quiet if nothing else."

One of the men muttered something.

"You can join the grooms keeping watch. I'll call you if I need you again."

Lucy heard the men march out. She winced as the blindfold was yanked off pulling a few hairs with it. She blinked rapidly, opened her eyes and looked up straight into the face of a smirking Gillett. He picked a glass off the nightstand and splashed liberal quantity of brandy into it.

"I see you're with us now." Gillett glared at her. "Not that I'm convinced you weren't before. Don't play clever with me. If you know what's good for you, drink this."

He put an arm under her shoulders and yanked her into a sitting position. Lucy let her head loll back and tried to get a glimpse of the men before the door closed behind them. One of them looked like the man who had carried her out of the coach.

The next thing she knew, Gillett poured brandy into her mouth until she gagged and spat some out.

"Stop that you little hellcat. If I can get you insensible so that you do what you're told without kicking up a fuss I'll get a bonus." His voice was almost a growl.

She jerked her head from side to side as he put the glass back to her lips and managed to knock it out of his hands so it spilled onto the cover of the bed. He put the rest of the contents of the decanter into the glass and tried again. She managed to spit some of it out but swallowed a fair amount. How lucky she'd had a large breakfast. It should mitigate the effects. She thought back to the first time she'd seen Peter foxed when he had found her father's drinks cupboard as a young boy. If she acted like that perhaps Gillett wouldn't bother to go and fetch some more brandy. She started giggling.

"Ooh, I feel like I'm floating. I've never tasted brandy before. It's not so bad after all. More. I feel a bit queasy though."

Gillett peered at her. "I'll leave it at that for now. We can give you some more later when he arrives."

Lucy gritted her teeth against the impulse to ask him who. If she did, he would guess she was exaggerating the effects of the brandy. Besides it had to be Parfitt. Who else would it be?"

Two pillows were pushed roughly under her shoulders.

"Stay propped up like that and behave yourself." Gillett marched out of the room and slammed the door shut behind him.

She heard the sound of a key turning in a lock. At least she was rid of Gillett and his henchmen for now. She looked around the room. Fiddlesticks, there didn't seem to be any furniture light enough to pile in front of the door to buy some time for rescue to arrive. Assuming it did arrive. Would Bertie and Ralph have been back in time to pick up her trail? She had to act as if they had. Lucy looked around the room again. The furniture was well kept but old and solid. Tudor? There was a second door which probably led into a big closet or even a dressing room.

The walls were covered in wooden panelling. She glanced around the room again. Casement windows. Yes, this was a Tudor house. The place felt cold and damp, as if it had been neglected for years. It would help her to sober up more quickly if she moved around. From the state of the bed cover and her gown she had managed to spit out a lot of the brandy that Gillett had tried to force down her throat. Even so her head spun when she swung her legs over the side of the bed. She sat still for a moment until the dizziness subsided. A shiver ran through her.

There was a pitcher of water and a glass on a side table near the bed. Gillett seem to have taken the empty decanter with him. She poured some water into the glass and sniffed at it. No smell at all. Could she risk drinking some? Parfitt would need her awake for a marriage ceremony after all and it might help to sober her up. Then she noticed a tray covered by a cloth at the back of the table. She lifted a corner of the cloth. There was a plate containing bread and cheese. The bread smelled freshly baked. The room had been prepared for her to be in there for a while. Did that mean they weren't planning a wedding straight away?

Lucy sighed. That didn't seem likely. She walked over to the window. There was no sign of the drive, so this was the back of the house but on the opposite side from the stables. Interestingly, there was woodland to the left as she looked out. If only she was wearing her breeches, she might have been able to climb down the ivy clinging to the wall under the window, assuming she could open it. Even the reek of the brandy wasn't enough to mask a strong musty smell. There was a fair chance the casements would be jammed shut from lack of use.

Still, it was worth a try if she could find something to tie up her skirts with. She walked over to the window. It looked to be in poor condition but she managed to open one of the casements. Good. It was big enough to climb through and near to the ivy. She closed it quickly in case there was anyone below who could see it. The curtains were hanging in tatters. She tried to tear a length off but the material disintegrated in her hands. No use for tying up her skirts.

Lucy wandered about the room until she came to the second door on the wall around the corner to her right, as she faced it, from the wall with door to the corridor. Towards the side of the house and nearer to the woods. Was it too much to hope for that there might be a secret passage on the outside of it? Her chest felt tight, making it hard to breathe. There was a key in the lock. It was stiff with age but after a concerted effort, it finally turned with a bit of a grating noise. The mechanism must be stiff from lack of use.

The door led into a large dressing room with cupboards on either side. There was a candlestick, candles and a tinderbox on a small table near to the entrance. She set to with the tinderbox and managed to light a candle and fix it in the candlestick. Now she could see more clearly. Her hands felt clammy as she opened the first of the cupboard doors. Would there be anything left behind that she could use to tie up her skirts? Or even some discarded men's clothing.

It was full of gowns from decades before. There wasn't a pair of breeches in sight. She glanced in a couple more of cupboards. They contained nothing but female clothes. Perhaps it was a shared dressing room. She tried one of the cupboards on the opposite wall but again it was all women's things. It looked like it hadn't been touched for years. The wall opposite the door was covered in the same oak panelling as the bedroom. On closer inspection the panelling had a more elaborate design than that in the bedroom, with carved flowers in places. She had seen similar before and not just at Mayford Castle. Surely there must be some sort of hidden passageway here? Excitement coursed through her.

Lucy went back to the table and picked up the candlestick. Her hands were shaking and she took some deep breaths to steady herself. When she was calmer, she shielded the flame and walked across to the end wall. She held the candlestick higher and concentrated on running her hands over the panelling. If there was some sort of opening mechanism, it would most likely be in the elaborate parts of the carving. Eventually she found what she was hoping for when she pressed on the centre of a carved rose and part of the panelling slid open.

She stumbled back a few steps and stared at the gap in the wall. It led into an identical dressing room with cupboards either side. To have any chance of escape, she needed to work fast. She rushed back to shut the door of the first dressing room behind her. She pulled the key out and locked it from the inside If anyone came for her now, they would assume she was hiding somewhere in the bedroom she had escaped from. It might be a while before they noticed the second door in the bedroom. Then they would have to find a way to force it open.

That done she hurried across the dressing room, shielding the candle flame carefully with her hand, and walked through the opening in the panelling. She put the candlestick down on a matching table near the door to what was probably another bedroom and checked the cupboards. They were empty until she came to the last one. Inside there was a selection of men's clothes, more exactly probably those of a youth.

They were old-fashioned but more recent than the gowns. She found some riding wear and scrambled into a pair of breeches. They were a little large but that gave her room to tuck her gown and pelisse inside them. The coat hung loosely but it was wearable. And there, sitting on a shelf at the top of the cupboard, was a selection of caps. She found one that looked promising and rammed it on her head. It covered all her hair and pulled down low the peak covered some of her face.

Her mouth went dry and a buzz of energy ran through her. Her body was tight with tension and it took her a few minutes to find the mechanism to close the panelling behind her. Once it slid into place some of the tension in her shoulders eased. She put her ear to the door but could hear nothing. This was no time to freeze. She pulled the door open and peered into another bedroom. This one was shrouded in holland covers. It wasn't the passageway out she'd been hoping for but what she had been expecting. Another bedroom made sense from the layout.

There was no tinderbox or candles in this second dressing room so she left the lit candle on the table and went into the bedroom to investigate. There was a key in the external door. She thought quickly. It was best to douse the candle and leave it in the dressing room. If she had to double back, she should be able to find her way by feel. Even if it did mean being in the dark for a while. It was a risk she had to take. Pointless to get this far and not try to find a way out. And preferably a safer one than climbing down the ivy, with the risk of being seen.

Once she had put out the candle in the dressing room and closed its door, Lucy ran across the bedroom. There was no sound coming from the corridor. She took some deep breaths, opened the door and slipped out, closing the door gently behind her. This was the last bedroom on the corridor. There must be a servants' staircase somewhere nearby. A quick glance at the panelled end wall showed her what she was looking for. She took another glance around and ran towards the outline of a door in the panelling. It was interesting that this one was clearly visible to anyone looking for it, whereas the ones in the dressing rooms had been completely hidden. So typical of some of these Tudor homes. Lucy held her breath as she reached the door. Would it open?

Heart pounding, she turned the key in the lock and pushed the door open. Yes! She slipped through it and closed it behind her. It opened onto a small landing with a steep flight of stairs leading down from it. It was partially lit from light streaming into a corridor below. She ran down the stairs and stopped abruptly near the bottom. The door to the kitchen stood open on her left but all was quiet and the musty smell of damp and decay reached her. She crept down the last few steps. There was no one in sight. It was quite a short passageway. With any luck it led to a door to the outside.

Another door to her right stood open. It appeared to lead into a scullery, again empty of people and festooned with cobwebs. The place seemed deserted. She dashed along the corridor, catching her foot in a worn rug. Somehow, she managed to stay on her feet. She half expected someone to come running but nothing happened. She carried on, carefully this time, towards a big sturdy-looking door.

Her hands felt clammy but she managed to turn the key in the lock. It opened with a grating sound. Lucy ran through and closed it behind her, frantically looking round to get the lie of the land. It led out into an overgrown kitchen garden. If she crouched down in amongst some of the shrubs it would be difficult for anyone looking out to see her.

Beyond the garden there was the start of extensive looking woodland. She ducked her head down and ran along the edge of the garden nearest to the woods until she came to a gate. She rushed through that and ran headlong into the trees. Now all she had to do was find out where she was and try to get back to safety, without Parfitt's men finding her. She took in gulps of sweet fresh air. Freedom. A large hand clamped itself over her mouth and a long arm hooked around her, holding her captive against a giant of a man. Lucy squeezed her eyes shut in a vain attempt to stem her tears of frustration.

CHAPTER TWENTY FIVE

Bertie shuffled around on his perch to get a good view of the coach as it drove onto the driveway leading to the Tudor mansion. A man pushed his head through the window of the coach and shouted up to his coachman. That had to be Parfitt. They could set about rescuing Lucy at last. He shinned down the tree for the second time that afternoon. This time as fast as he dared and ran towards the woods nearest the mansion. Overton might have been put in charge of the operation to rescue Lucy, but there was no way that he was going to stop him being involved. Bertie ran at full pelt till he reached the trees. Overton had said he would watch by the kitchen gardens. William and Roskelley appeared from a spinney to his left.

Bertie pointed in the direction of the woods next to Tennant Manor.

"It's definitely Parfitt in the coach coming up. Come on, we need to join Overton. He should be by the kitchen garden."

William and Roskelley caught him up. William tapped his arm. "Steady now, we don't want Parfitt to hear us. There's a short cut through the trees up to the house. Follow me."

Bertie ran after William, with Roskelley close behind him. He felt his coat pockets. His muff pistols were still there. He'd kill Parfitt before he would let him harm a hair on Lucy's head. William skidded to a halt in front of him. Overton was standing in a clearing with his arm around what appeared to be a youth. Something about the youth's stance hit Bertie. Good Lord, his clever wonderful Lucy had managed to escape all on her own. He ran towards her. She appeared to be wiping her eyes with the backs of her hands. When she saw him, she threw herself into his arms.

"How on earth did you manage to escape?" Bertie whispered. A surge of relief hit him so hard that his legs felt too weak to hold him for a moment.

Lucy gave him a watery smile and leaned close to his ear. "You'll never believe this, there was a dressing room off the bedroom they put me in with a secret opening at the back going into the dressing room of another bedroom. Very similar to the mechanism to your secret room at Mayford Castle. The key to the corridor was in the lock of this room. I found these clothes and escaped down a servants' staircase and out through the back door nearest to the kitchen."

"Clever girl. Parfitt's coming up the drive." Bertie felt Lucy tense in his arms.

William and Roskelley were in conference with Overton. There was an air of suppressed excitement about them as they came over to join them.

"I'm sorry you won't be able to act as Sir Galahad, Lovell. Miss Vaughan's clever escape does make life a lot easier for us though. More complicated but easier." Overton clapped Bertie on the shoulder.

"Bright is covering us with the rest of my men and the grooms we've brought for your approval. Lord Kinsey is with them. Lord Hampton's men are watching the front approaches."

Lucy gasped. "Is Uncle James here then?"

"He's had to go back to London on government business. I'll tell you what I know about it later. It was your uncle's men who were keeping watch over you when you were staying with Lord Kinsey." Overton looked at Bertie. "I'll leave you with William. I know the two of you will keep Miss Vaughan safe." He raised his eyebrows at them.

Bertie nodded. "We won't let her out of our sight. They must be getting close. I'm sure it's Parfitt in that coach."

"If any of my men need to contact you Lord Kinsey will be with them, so you know for sure who they are. Right. Roskelley you're with me. "

They heard the sound of the coach drawing closer. Overton saluted and disappeared into the trees closely followed by Roskelley.

William signalled to them. "Come on. We need to put you somewhere safe."

Lucy pointed to a stand of trees. "We should be well hidden in there."

William shook his head. "You'd be vulnerable if someone found you."

Lucy smiled at Bertie and pointed to a young oak. "Not if we climb that tree. We'll be able to see what's going on from up there as well."

"There's a better look out tree near to where we tied up the horses," William said. "You can see the front of the house from it."

"Good idea, it's not far. Quickly." Bertie pulled Lucy through the trees to where the horses were tethered.

They were all there and difficult to spot until nearby. He

pointed to the oak tree and lifted her up so she could reach the first branch.

"I'll patrol this area and keep an eye on you and the horses," William said.

They heard shouting in the distance. William gave Bertie a leg up into the tree. Lucy had found a sturdy branch where she could rest her back against the trunk. Bertie followed her until he was sitting on the same branch, with a branch from a nearby tree close by if he needed to hold on. The trees around covered them from view, but there was a big enough gap for them to see the whole of the front of the manor house and the stables to the right. The stables were a hive of activity.

Someone got out of the dark coloured coach, presumably Parfitt. He stood watching a group of horsemen galloping up the drive and waited until they reached him. They were too far away to be sure but one of the new arrivals appeared to be fashionably dressed in a green riding coat. He dismounted and handed his reins to one of the others. The rest of the men disappeared into the stable buildings with their mounts. The smartly dressed man joined Parfitt and walked up the drive towards the front door of Tennant Manor with him. They appeared to be in animated conversation.

"There's quite a few of them." Lucy sounded worried.

"Overton will be ready for that. He had a reputation as a master tactician in the army. I like the look of Roskelley too. It sounds like there are plenty of men with them."

Lucy sighed. "I was so stupid getting taken in by Gillett. But he said he had an invitation to Ralph's house party and seemed annoyed that Ralph had forgotten about him. Ralph had been so good to us I didn't want one of his friends to be put out."

"I've come across Gillett before. He's a plausible rogue. Try not to blame yourself." Bertie struggled to keep the anger out of his voice at the mention of Gillett. He pointed at the two men waiting at the front door. "Something about that man with Parfitt looks familiar. He's much shorter than Parfitt but the way he walks suggests a man of consequence. I'm sure I've seen him before somewhere."

"Try not to think about it for a while and it will come to you."

"It may be nothing but yes, I'll leave it to simmer and see if I remember who he reminds me of."

Lucy tapped Bertie's arm. "Look, that's Gillett opening the door to them. He didn't seem the sort to do anything menial like open a door to visitors. Which suggests there's no one but him inside. They're being very careful to avoid too many people knowing what they're up to."

"They are. Try not to feel guilty about Gillett. If he mentioned Ralph's house party you were entitled to believe he was a friend of Ralph."

"Oh, he was very plausible. I can't believe after this that he's really a friend of Ralph but he must know at least one of his friends well."

"Why?"

"It could have been common knowledge that Ralph was arranging a house party but Gillett said Ralph had invited him to come a few days early. I remembered Ralph saying he had invited a few close friends to arrive early if they were free but no one seemed to have taken him up on it."

"You're right. If they knew about that anyone would have been taken in by Gillett."

"It was still stupid walking out with him on my own in the circumstances. I didn't think. I do hope no one gets hurt because of me."

"This is not your fault. I don't know what's going on here but it sounds like your uncle is deeply involved in it." Bertie frowned.

"I know what you mean. It might even be a matter of national security. Uncle James is involved in some top-secret things. I've had an awful thought." She went quiet.

"What is it, Lucy?"

Lucy wouldn't meet his gaze. "We know Papa was in financial trouble, that's why he wanted to marry me off."

She paused and looked into the distance. Bertie sat quietly and waited.

"Papa used to do everything to avoid spending Christmas with Uncle James and Aunt Susan but last Christmas he seemed keen. Peter and I thought he wanted to save money. Peter said his gambling had been getting worse. The point is Uncle James was working on some paperwork over Christmas. Is Papa a traitor?"

Oh Lord, what was he going to say? It seemed all too likely that Vaughan was involved in something shady. He wouldn't put anything past Parfitt. Lucy was too intelligent not to be honest with her. His mouth felt dry.

"It's a possibility, Lucy. It's no good speculating until we know exactly what's been going on. If your father was involved in something, then I expect Parfitt was the prime mover. He'd taken quite a shine to you this season and that might have given him the idea."

"What do you mean? Did you have any part in Parfitt's sudden disappearance early on when he was driving me insane with his unwanted attentions?"

Bertie laughed. "You wouldn't believe me if I denied it would you."

"No. Oh, Bertie. What would I do without you?"

"You and I are meant to be together. I should have realised that a lot sooner." He watched in satisfied silence as Lucy's cheek went pink.

The three men went inside and the door closed behind them. Lucy grinned at him.

"If Parfitt's come to collect me for a wedding, he's about to get a nasty shock."

"Agreed. You did well to escape."

"I've Mayford Castle to thank. Remember how it got the three of us interested in secret rooms and passages. Gillett kept me on the floor of the coach and put a blindfold on me once we arrived, before they carried me out of the coach. I couldn't catch a glimpse of the building and had no idea where I was. Once I saw all the panelling on the walls of the bedroom Gillett locked me up in, I was hopeful."

Good Lord, what a way to treat her. Bertie struggled to contain his anger. If only he could get his hands on Parfitt, he'd teach him a lesson he'd never forget. "I'm glad you found a way out. It was unbearable thinking of you in the power of a kidnapper."

"I would have climbed down the ivy under the window in the bedroom if I'd had to. The windows were in a state, but I managed to open a casement that was big enough for me to get through in case I needed to escape that way. The rooms I saw both looked seriously neglected. Like no one had lived there for years. I wonder who owns it."

"I'm not sure. Ralph might know. He said it was called Tennant Manor. Parfitt's main home is somewhere near to the south coast. I suppose he might have been left this one and left it to rot. That would be just like him."

Lucy stretched her back against the tree trunk and sighed. "This waiting is awful. I don't see what they can do with Parfitt if they catch him. He had Papa's permission to marry me and I'm sure my family won't want me to press kidnap charges because of the scandal. Doesn't seem right that he should get off free. The next heiress he tries it on might not be as lucky as me."

Bertie grimaced. "Or as resourceful as you. I agree that with your uncle being in public life your family will be more averse to publicity than most. Not that any family would want to let the world know their daughter had been kidnapped." He balled his hands into fists. "I'm hoping they'll give me a few minutes with Parfitt."

Lucy squealed in alarm. "I don't want you tangling with him and getting hurt."

"Don't worry. I'm not the wastrel people think I am. I spend a lot of time at Gentleman Jackson's."

"I know that, stoopid. I just don't expect Parfitt to fight fair. He would probably pull out a hidden knife or something. I can't see Nat Overton letting you loose on him, thank goodness. I ran straight into Lord Overton with my head down and didn't see him for a moment. It was such a relief when I realised who he was."

"You have been through the mill. And we don't even know what it's all about yet."

"My imagination keeps trying to run riot, this waiting is awful. I wonder what Uncle James will do with Papa if he has been colluding with Parfitt. Surely, they couldn't have been selling secrets to the French, could they?"

"I suppose it's possible. If your father was trying to see Government documents the French would be the most likely foreign power to pay for the information on them. I wonder where Gillett comes in?"

Lucy put her head on one side. "I noticed he has traces of a French accent, especially when he gets agitated. I wonder if the man who's gone in with Parfitt was the man telling Gillett what to do. He was lording it over Gillett, who didn't take too kindly to it."

"Interesting. I don't suppose you got a look at this man, did you?"

"Gillett didn't take the blindfold off until he threw me on the bed in the bedroom. I did listen to them talk for quite a while though. I pretended I'd swooned. The man had a deep voice with an upper-class accent. I think there might have been a trace of a Highland Scottish accent in it somewhere. Great-aunt Agatha's husband was Scottish."

Bertie stroked his chin. "You've got a good ear. That narrows it down. An upper-class Englishman with Scottish relatives perhaps."

"Oh look." Lucy pointed in the direction the stables. "There are men running everywhere. They must have found out that I'm missing. I wonder how long they'll search for me."

"For quite some time I expect. It's not that comfortable up here. I could go down and find out what's happening if you like."

"I'm not letting you out of my sight, Bertie Lovell. I don't want you getting hurt. Besides, Lord Overton seems to know what needs to be done and there's no point interfering because you don't know the whole story yet."

"I suppose so. You're right. The waiting is dreadful. I just want to get you somewhere safe and away from all these people." Bertie smiled at her.

"About us, Bertie. Uncle James is good at burying scandals when it matters to the government. He'll keep me out of it and make sure my reputation is unsullied. I know he will. You don't need to feel honour bound to marry me now. I will understand if you want to pull out." Lucy looked away from him. "Whatever happens you will always be my best friend."

"Lucy Vaughan, marrying you is the most important thing in the world to me at this moment. What makes you think otherwise?"

"Because we've always been like brother and sister and I'm sure you only offered to marry me to save me from Parfitt."

Bertie hesitated. Lucy deserved the full truth. "At the time I first made the offer that was what I thought my motivation was. Now I've had time to reflect I'm not sure that was true. I believe I've been in love with you for some time and simply didn't realise it." He grinned at her. "After that ride in a farm cart I can assure you my feelings towards you are no longer those of a brother."

"Well, we were in close proximity." A shy smile played about Lucy's mouth. She blushed and looked away from him.

Bertie's stomach did a leap.

"I still think you should have some time to think if marriage to me is what you really want. You're young for a man to marry. I would hate it if we rushed ahead and then you realised you had made a mistake." She looked worried.

"I know my own mind, honestly. You're not put off by my wild behaviour in recent years, are you? "

"Of course not. I've always known you've been rebelling against your mother and her constant efforts at social climbing." Lucy smiled at him. "I'd be very surprised if even half of the tales going around about you are true. I'm sure you've been deliberately spreading them to upset her. I've seen the distaste in your face that even your impeccable manners can't mask, when she's pushed you under the nose of yet another Duke's daughter. "

Bertie raised a hand. "Guilty as charged. I realise now how childish I was by acting like that. I was letting my mother carry on running my life even as an adult. It's more than time I took responsibility for my own future. I want you to be a central part of that future."

"You think that now but I want you to have time to be sure. That's all." She laughed. "It's a strange place to be having a discussion like this."

"It certainly is and a very inconvenient place." Bertie laughed so hard he had to grab a hold of the nearby branch to keep his balance.

"It's not funny enough to nearly fall out of the tree for."

"It occurred to me that if I set about proving to you how sure I am of my feelings we would both end up falling out of this tree."

"Oh Bertie, those sorts of feelings don't mean you're in love necessarily."

An awful thought struck him. "Lucy, are you having second thoughts? I know you've always had an aversion to marriage. Which is hardly surprising with the way your father treats your mother and the offhand way he's always treated you and Peter. Compounded by his selfish attempt to marry you off to Parfitt. Not all men are like that. I'm certainly not." He kept his voice gentle.

"I know that. You're the kindest person I've ever met."

"Are you put off by the social implications of my bad reputation? I haven't got a title to temper it like Max. I had a long chat with Max when I was down at Hargreaves. He said that he had come to realise, helped by Cousin Augusta I'm sure, that I was no wilder than most young men let loose on the Town. But that a bad reputation isn't always easy to throw off even for a man. It might make things awkward for us socially but with the Lovells on my side it should soon pass."

Lucy shook her head. "That doesn't worry me at all. I'm not really a Town person. I can think of nothing better than living quietly in the country most of the year. Making sure tenants are properly supported and given every opportunity to improve their lot. I'd like to set up a school for the children."

"I'd like that too. You haven't answered my question though. Are you still frightened of marriage?" His voice shook.

"I don't think I am now. I think deep down part of it was that I was worried about what would happen to my mother if I left her alone with Papa. I was her excuse to set up in London away from him for most of the year."

"I've plenty of money of my own. Between your uncle and me we could help your mother come to a financial settlement with him and separate. She would always be welcome with us."

"Uncle James and Aunt Susan wouldn't let her go back to him after this. She hid a lot from them."

"There you are then. For my part I would love to get married quickly. There is so much to do to get my estates as I want them. There is nothing I would like more than to have you at my side, setting up schools and whatever you think is needed. Let's get this affair sorted out and then talk again. What do you say?"

"Yes. We'll talk again."

Bertie smiled at her. "That's one yes from you. Now I'll get to work on the most important yes that I want from you."

They heard a strange whistle. Bertie peered around the bottom of their hiding place and could see nothing. Then a head poked up from behind a bush and William laughed at them.

"Down you come. Some scouts have arrived and it's safe to get you out of here and back to Kinsey Court."

Bertie climbed carefully down the tree. His limbs were stiff from perching there for so long. He hung from the last branch by his hands and dropped the two or three feet to the floor. Lucy followed him. Once she lowered herself from the branch Bertie lifted her down with a hand on either side of her waist. She landed on his chest. A wave of longing rushed through him as he set her on her feet. He should have realised years ago that Lucy was the only one for him and then they wouldn't be in this mess. Ralph and a young man Bertie didn't know appeared at William's side.

Ralph pushed the young man forward. "This is Edward, one of the grooms Mr Bright has trained and sent for your approval. Overton said for you to go and join him. Edward will show you the way. William and I will escort Lucy back to Kinsey Court. There's a couple of scouts waiting by the turn onto the main road from the back road we came down. They'll join us."

Bertie looked longingly at Lucy. The last thing he wanted to do was leave her now, but curiosity won. Never say Overton was going to let him have a go at Parfitt. He could live in hope.

"Are you happy with that, Lucy?"

"Not really but I trust Lord Overton. If I need to get away to safety, we had better start out soon." She grinned at Bertie. "It would be a dreadful waste of all my efforts if I was recaptured."

"I couldn't bear that, perhaps I should stay with you."

Lucy shook her head. "No, you get off. We should be back at Kinsey Court fairly quickly."

Bertie gave a rueful smile. "You're right of course. I'll see you off on your, or rather my, horse first."

Ralph ran on ahead and untied the horse Bertie had ridden. Bertie threw Lucy up into the saddle and handed her the reins. She pulled the brim of her hat right down so that her face was largely obscured. Ralph and William were mounted in a trice and the trio set off through the trees. Bertie's heart turned over when Lucy turned back and gave him a wave. He waited until they were lost from view.

"You're one of my new grooms then, Edward."

Edward blushed scarlet. "I hope so, Sir."

"I can't imagine anyone Mr Bright has trained not giving satisfaction. Come on let's go and join Lord Overton. I'm hoping to find out exactly what's been going on."

Edward nodded and led the way at a fast pace. He halted every time they came to open ground and checked carefully before carrying on. Yes, Bright had certainly trained this young man well. What a clever idea making sure that all the grooms he trained up were well versed in security. Eventually Edward called a halt near to the stable buildings.

"There's a barn set a way back from the stables. I left Lord Overton and Mr Bright in there."

Keeping to the shadows, they ran round the stables and stopped near the barn. Edward pointed at a large bush. "Hide in that and I'll check if they're still here."

Edward ducked around the side of the barn and soon returned. "Yes, they're still there."

They slipped inside the barn to find the two men tucked behind some bales of hay. Overton signalled to them to join them. Bertie shook hands with him and sat down on a nearby bale.

"Two things. Do we know where all Parfitt's men are and is there time to tell me exactly what's been going on?" Bertie leaned forward, eager to hear from them.

Nat Overton gave him a lazy smile. "To answer your first question, I've got men tracking all of them, in pairs. We'll soon know if they double back here. They seem to be fanning out. Several of them went off in the direction of the village in a dark blue coach. The logical place for a girl on her own to make for of course, but it helps us. As to your second question we can make a start." He glanced at Mr Bright who grinned at Bertie.

"I took some men down to the village after Miss Vaughan joined us. It was the obvious place for them to start a search for her and one of your new horses had cast a shoe. We left him with the blacksmith and went to the posting inn there.

"There were some locals in the taproom who were laughing at an old lady who'd just left, making a dreadful fuss to her maid because a new companion she was supposed to be picking up hadn't showed up. She suspected she'd travelled on the stagecoach, which was due, instead of the earlier mail coach to save some of the fare and wasn't prepared to wait for her." Bright laughed out loud.

"The best bit was the stagecoach was early and one man thought he saw a woman standing by it after the passengers got off who could have been a lady's companion. There was no sign of a lone female in the inn. They decided she must have been in time to go with the old lady whose coach left a few minutes after the stagecoach arrived."

Bertie rested his elbow on his knee with his chin in his hand

and nodded. "Let's hope they think that Lucy went with the woman. A stroke of luck if they do."

"I expect they will. We stayed in the inn for a good while before we went back to the blacksmith for your horse. Some men had pulled up in a dark blue coach and were asking him if he'd seen a young woman looking lost who they were late collecting. I told them about the old lady and her missing companion and let them draw their own conclusions about mistaken identities." Bright gave a satisfied grin and rubbed his hands together. "They went haring off to the inn to find out where the old lady was going to."

"Oh well done, Bright. A lucky chance but you made good use of it."

"He would have thought of something else if that hadn't happened. But if the other coach is hard to trace it should get them off our trail for now. Once we've seen what Parfitt, Gillett and the other man do we can go and join Lucy at Kinsey Court. Ralph said we're welcome for the night. I'll have our three villains all followed. I thought you would want to see this bit."

"Thanks, Overton. I do, but you might have to hold me back if Parfitt gets anywhere near me."

Overton gave a throaty chuckle. "I know that. Now prepare for what could be a long wait. If we go up to the top floor, we've got a good vantage point." He pointed to a rickety wooden ladder in the corner. "One at a time, mind. It's a bit ancient."

They climbed up the ladder and settled down on some more bales of hay in the loft to wait, which gave Bertie time to think. Was Lucy right about her father being involved in something treasonous? The answer was really important to him. It didn't worry him if there was a big scandal but he knew Lucy. It might well be one of the reasons her reluctance to commit to marriage had resurfaced. Even without that he had never thought it would be easy when it got to the point of her actually taking the vows. His own mother had been bad enough with her social climbing but what Vaughan had done to his family was horrible.

CHAPTER TWENTY SIX

Lucy waved at Bertie. It was an effort to look away from him and listen to what Ralph was saying.

"We're retracing our steps through the woods onto a side road into this back entrance to Tennant Manor. It won't be long until we reach the main road. It's lucky you managed to find a disguise."

"Thank heaven for secret doors and passages in old houses and for the previous occupants who left clothing behind. I lost all track of time in Gillett's coach. Do we have far to go back to Kinsey Court?"

"About two hours, but the horses have had a long rest and they should be well able to carry us back."

They picked their way through the woods and Ralph called a halt. He sent William on ahead to find Lord Overton's men. William was soon back.

"They are waiting for us just before the main road. Two good military men." William beamed approvingly. "One of them was in the same regiment as a friend of mine. They'll keep you safe, Miss Vaughan."

Lucy tried not to smile when they found the two men. They both looked to be tall, riding big rangy horses, but their hard-bitten faces would be enough to keep anyone away from them.

One had a scar running all the way down his cheek, probably from a sabre cut. The other man had a patch over one eye. They had seen some action that was for sure.

The one with the scar rode up to Ralph. “It will take a while longer but I’m from round these parts and there’s a bridle path that will take us across country and comes out much farther up along the main road. Follow me.”

They followed him in single file onto a path on the opposite side of the lane. After a few minutes it widened out into a full width bridle path.

Ralph rode up alongside Lucy. “I don’t know this area all that well, despite growing up at Kinsey Court. We had friends farther north and tended to travel that way or else to London and the south coast for the summer. How are you feeling? You’ve had quite an eventful day.”

How was she feeling? Stunned, relieved? “It’s hard to say. This whole adventure has been strange.” Lucy smiled. “I do hope we don’t drag you into a nasty scandal.”

“It wouldn’t worry me if you did, but from what Overton said the Duke of Cathlay is taking a hand in the affair. He and your uncle together will surely be able to keep your name unsullied.”

“I’m glad that Cathlay is involved. Let’s hope they can keep this all quiet.”

Lucy concentrated on the back of her horse’s head as they cantered along. In normal circumstances she would agree with Ralph but, if her father was involved in treason, even Uncle James and the Duke of Cathlay, for all their political influence, would struggle to keep the Vaughan name unsullied. It was no good dwelling on it. If the worst happened, she and Mama could set up home somewhere where they weren’t known.

Ralph moved up to talk to William.

Lucy wiped her eyes with the back of a hand. Sometimes there was no other way to escape society expectations than run away. It would be ironical now that she was ready to marry someone she wholeheartedly loved if that future was snatched away from her. And yet she couldn't drag Bertie down with her. Coming from a powerful family all sorts of scandals around him would soon subside but treason was something that would never be forgotten.

They settled down to the ride with William and Ralph behind her and Lord Overton's two men in front. At times they had to drop back to single file and sometimes slow to a trot where the path was rough. It did have the advantage of being completely empty with no sign of anyone in the fields to either side. Eventually the path widened out and they came to a junction with a proper lane. Two men at the front called a halt. The one with the scar seemed to be the leader. He waited for them to catch up with him.

"Jack will ride up to the main road and see if it's clear. We'll wait here."

"Who is it that you're worried about?" Lucy asked.

"I can see how you were sharp enough to escape." The man smiled at her. "We've had dealings with Lord Parfitt before. He's no one's fool. We've had a lot of men around Tennant Manor. I don't expect him to hang around when he arrives at the Manor to find you gone. He'll have scouts with him."

He grinned. "Ones that might even be as good as us. He'll guess something is wrong, especially if his men who Mr Bright tricked into following the old lady from the village inn catch up with her coach and find out you're not with her. He's been staying at Rugeley Hall. My guess is he'll return there."

Lucy shivered. Papa had even moved Parfitt into their home then. "I definitely don't want to be seen by him. Apart from anything else I don't want anyone getting hurt because of me."

The man patted his coat pockets. "I'll shoot him before he lays a hand on you or anyone else, you needn't worry. Besides with that cap pulled down he's not likely to recognise you. But we try not to take unnecessary chances."

"I'm a lot smaller than the rest of you. I'd stand out to him for that reason alone. I've always thought of him as a clever man and a dangerous one. It's only recently I've found out just how dangerous."

Jack came back. "All clear. I got chatting with a farm labourer and a group of riders he didn't know passed down the main road only a few minutes ago. We'll set off but quite slowly to give them the chance to get in front."

They rode on in silence with Ralph and William on either side of her, as if determined to shield her from casual view. The rest of the ride passed uneventfully but it seemed a very long time before they arrived back at Kinsey Court. Lucy sighed with relief as they turned into the drive. There was a lot of activity around the stables. Ralph signalled to them to go to the front of the house. The butler was waiting with the door open, a smile hovering on his normally impassive features as they pulled up. Lucy could see Mrs Adams peeping out from behind him with several footmen.

"Excellent." Ralph smiled at his staff. "You get inside, Lucy. The rest of us will ride round to the stables and see what's going on."

The butler sent a footman to help Lucy dismount. He himself walked up to Ralph.

"There's no need for alarm, Lord Kinsey. We've had some

new guests arrive and I'm sure you will be glad to see them."

"That's a relief. Let's get Miss Vaughan inside. She's had a long tiring day. I'll ride to the stables with the rest of these men."

The butler ushered Lucy into the house, where the housekeeper was smiling at her.

"Let's get you upstairs. We'll soon have a hot bath ready and you out of those clothes. Then you'll be ready to greet your guests." Mrs Adam's eyes shone.

Lucy followed Mrs Adams upstairs to her bedroom. She had never seen Mrs Adams be so animated. Could the Cathlays have arrived? Once the door closed behind her, she turned to Mrs Adams.

"Tell me who's arrived."

"The most important ones for you are your mother and your aunt. We'll soon have you presentable so you can go down and greet them."

"Oh, that's wonderful, but Mama and Aunt Susan won't worry about what I'm wearing."

"They will when they're in the company of a Duke and Duchess. You need to make a good impression on them."

Lucy laughed. "If you mean the Cathlays, I've known them forever. The Duchess is Bertie's cousin."

"I didn't know that. Yes, it is the Duke and Duchess of Cathlay. They arrived first. And a duchess is a duchess, no matter how well you know them. Let's get you tidied up."

CHAPTER TWENTY SEVEN

Bertie concentrated hard on the view from the hayloft at the top of the barn. How long would it take Lucy to get back to Kinsey Court? How was she feeling? He wouldn't rest until this was done and he could get back to her to see for himself. They could be here for hours. Next to him Nat Overton let out a soft whistle.

"Did you hear that bird call? It was one of my men telling us someone is on their way."

All seemed still with no sign of movement. Just as Bertie was beginning to think it was a false alarm, they heard the sound of hoof-beats. Nat pointed to the house.

"I haven't met him socially, is that Gillett coming out?"

Bertie squinted into the late afternoon sun. "Yes, that's him definitely."

They watched Gillett walk towards the stables. His shoulders drooped and his steps dragged. He must be expecting trouble. Parfitt wasn't the man to take the failure of his minions lightly. Bertie shuddered at the thought of Lucy in his clutches. Gillett walked past the stables and waited, shading his eyes with a hand and watching the group of horsemen as they rode up the drive. His pockets look suspiciously bulky and Bertie noticed him pat one of them.

"Tell your men to be careful, Overton. It looks like Gillett is expecting trouble and he's armed."

Overton stood up and whistled. "That will warn them. From what I've heard Parfitt would be the sort to lash out in temper. It's clear Gillett doesn't trust him. He'd be better to hide. I would in his shoes."

Bertie closed his eyes for a minute. "With Lucy free, Gillett is a liability to Parfitt since she will have recognised him. I've known Parfitt since my school days. He's evil. There's no other way to describe him. Anyone who's been around him for any amount of time would realise that. Gillett is wise to arm himself, but you're right he would have been wiser still to escape before Parfitt arrived. "

"I suppose he was hoping she would have been recovered beforehand. Ideally, we won't have to reveal we're here at all. As long as they don't know for sure where Miss Vaughan is they'll waste resources looking for her. My men are under orders to do nothing until I give the order. As you say we don't want anyone getting in the crossfire."

Even from the distance of the barn they could hear an argument rage between Parfitt and Gillett. Bertie strained to hear but they were too far away to make out what was being said until Parfitt moved a few steps closer and roared the word, "Imbecile!"

Gillett threw up his arms and stamped a foot. Bertie saw Parfitt wave at one of the men with him. The argument started up again with Parfitt and Gillett standing almost nose to nose. Bertie gasped as Parfitt's man circled round behind Gillett, who was too busy arguing to notice. Gillett dropped to the floor. A knife glinted in the late afternoon sunshine as Parfitt's man wiped it on the leg of his dark coloured breeches and hid it inside his boot. Parfitt spat on Gillett then called to two of his men who walked towards the body. The rest mounted up and trotted after Parfitt down the drive towards the main road.

"Gillett wasn't clever enough to watch for an attack from behind or pull out his guns first, was he?" Overton said.

Bertie shook his head. "His persuasive tongue let him down when he needed it. Over-confidence did for him. What do we do now?"

"I'd like to check if there is any life left in Gillett. We'll have to wait and see what happens next first. I'm not sure if there are any of his men still around here besides the ones Parfitt's left behind."

Parfitt's men carried Gillett's body into one of the stable buildings. They ran back to where they had tied up their horses and cantered after the rest.

"With luck, they'll ride to the village. I'm hoping Bright's ruse with the old lady's party will keep them occupied for a good while." Overton paused when a shadow flitted along the hedge separating the stables from the kitchen gardens and the tall figure of Roskelley slipped into the stable building where Gillett was. He emerged and gave out a piercing whistle. A few minutes later they heard a whistle from the floor below them and Roskelley's head appeared at the top of the ladder.

"We can't find any sign of men left behind here. I've checked and the man in the stable, Gillett I presume, is still alive."

Overton gave a satisfied grunt. "Ah. I did wonder if he was stabbed hard enough to penetrate far through that thick coat he's wearing. Well done. Yes, that's Gillett."

"I've sent in an ex-army medic to patch him up. He might survive. His pulse seemed fairly strong but he has lost quite a bit of blood."

"If he does, Lord Hampton's men will want to interrogate him. The Duke of Cathlay has found a billet for any of our men who need one with the local magistrate, another retired army man, Colonel Harper. We need to get Gillett to his house." Overton grinned. "Let's hope Gillett does survive."

"There's an old carriage in one of the outbuildings. I'll have some men clean it up and see what horses we have to pull it." Roskelley laughed. "From what I've seen, the Duke of Cathlay is definitely a man to have on your side."

"He is indeed. Right. We've got carriage horses among the ones that we're delivering to Mr Lovell. Bright will find you a couple of quiet ones. Send your medic with Gillett and a driver. One of my men will show them the way and act as an armed guard up front with the driver. If the coach is large enough, put another armed guard inside," Overton said, his voice brisk.

"Do you want me to go with them?" Roskelley asked.

"No, my men will manage. Once you've organised that I have a better use for you." Overton grinned at Roskelley. "Find a mount for Mr Lovell and collect a couple of his new grooms, would you. You escort Mr Lovell back to Kinsey Court and we'll move the rest of the horses and men to the Colonel Harper's house. I'll join you at Kinsey Court later."

"Very handy finding Colonel Harper. I know him from my army days. A good man." Roskelley laughed. "Any particular grooms, or horses?"

"I'll leave it to your discretion. See what Bright thinks if you like. He'll know the most suitable ones."

"Oh, I will. Mr Bright is another man I like the look of." Roskelley disappeared back down the ladder.

"How did Cathlay know you needed to stay here?" Bertie asked.

"Cathlay knows Colonel Harper well and when he got your note, he made a detour to stay with him on the way. Between you and me I think the Colonel is part of some sort of government network of intelligence reserves."

Bertie laughed. "That wouldn't surprise me at all knowing Cathlay. Lord Hampton is a close friend of his and I've always thought he was a bit more than a diplomat."

"The previous owner of Tennant Manor died some months ago and the new one hasn't moved in yet. The Colonel was keeping an eye on the place and got wind of some comings and goings immediately before Cathlay arrived. Cathlay told him all about Miss Vaughan's pursuit by Parfitt. They sent some of Cathlay's men to investigate Tennant Manor and realised something clandestine was going on there."

"Which made Cathlay wonder if Parfitt was behind it, I imagine. He always was a downy one. Gillett must have heard the house was empty and found a way to break in when they needed to. Without Colonel Harper's efficiency they were unlikely to be noticed before they left the place." Bertie shook with anger and his hands formed fists. Gillett was as bad as Parfitt.

"Yes. That's about the size of it. Tennant Manor was close enough to take Lucy to whilst Parfitt arranged a wedding, away from anyone who knew her. Cathlay had us billeted with the Colonel to await developments. At that point we hadn't found you."

"I see. That still doesn't explain why you're here Overton. Grateful as I am to you."

Overton laughed. "Two of Eliza's sisters have arrived in London, one all the way from Scotland. They've both got daughters that they intend to bring out next season. The

Scottish family have come down to get the girls used to London. I escorted Eliza to our London house and left her very happily enjoying her sisters and nieces. Bright and your new grooms and horses travelled with us as far as London. We arrived just as the Duke of Cathlay received your letter. He recruited us to help and when I heard what was going on I was determined to join in."

"Oh, I see. You thought you'd make good your escape."

"That's about the strength of it." Overton grinned at him.

"Was it your men who scouted out the area around Kinsey Court?"

Overton hesitated and glanced at the floor. "No that was Lord Hampton's men. Once he knew Miss Vaughan was safe with you, he went back to London leaving his men in the area keeping watch from a distance. He called in to brief the Colonel, in case his men needed his help, on the way."

"Which explains why the Colonel was keeping such a close eye out for any unusual activity in the area." Bertie scratched his head. "But I'm surprised Lucy's uncle went back to London without rescuing her? That seems odd." He couldn't keep the surprise out of his voice.

Overton wouldn't meet Bertie's eyes and stayed silent. Lord, was Lucy right about her father being involved in espionage? He looked around and through the hatch with the ladder. There was no one about.

"Lucy is afraid her father has been involved in something," Bertie kept his voice to little more than a whisper. He hesitated. "Shall we say, against the national interest."

Overton finally met his gaze. "I'm not privy to all of it but I would say she's right."

Bertie closed his eyes and rested his chin in his hands with his elbows on his knees. He jerked his head upright. "She'll take it very hard. I hope Lord Hampton can scotch any scandal. Otherwise, she'll break off our engagement. I know she will. And the stupid thing is it wouldn't bother me if I never set foot in society again." Frustration flowed through him.

"Sensible man. Come on. I can see Roskelley headed this way. It's time to get you back with your intended." Overton gripped his shoulder briefly. "You'll work it out with her, trust me."

"I hope you're right."

Roskelley arrived with four men and a spare horse for Bertie. All the horses were good looking animals, Bright was certainly a good judge. Bertie jumped onto the smart bay that Roskelley held out to him.

"Are we going to follow Lord Kinsey's cross-country route back to Kinsey Court?"

Roskelley shook his head. "I think it will be safer going back along the main route. If Lord Parfitt is in the area he'll be hidden somewhere by now."

"Do you think that's likely?"

"I don't know but it is something we must be prepared for."

Bertie rode alongside him down the drive to the main road. "I understand you were in the army for some time."

"Yes, I was. I'll be open with you, I spent some time working for Colonel Harper just after I was promoted to captain, in army intelligence."

Bertie raised his eyebrows. "You know him well then."

"Yes. He's a good man and I learnt a lot from him." Roskelley jerked his head towards the grooms behind them. "The grooms Mr Bright has given me were all in the army and they are all armed. When we reach the main road, we'll spread out."

"Isn't that a recipe for being seen if Parfitt's men are around?"

"Don't worry. Some of Cathlay's men have been sent ahead. They will be dotted along the route. I don't think we've heard the last of your Lord Parfitt."

They reached the main road and Roskelley sent one man on ahead. He and Bertie rode together with two men immediately behind them and one further back. They rode on in silence for some time. The man in front suddenly doubled back.

"Looks like some men ahead, Captain. No more than three or four."

Roskelley signalled to the men behind. "When I give the word we break into a gallop, the horses are well rested, in case they are Parfitt's men. If we take them by surprise, we should be able to get past them. If they're strangers, no harm done." Roskelley waved an arm. "Let's go."

They gave their horses their heads and Bertie relished the feel of the wind through his hair. If this was Parfitt, perhaps he could have it out with him. Lucy wouldn't feel safe until he'd been dealt with one way or the other. Perhaps Cathlay could get him sent to the West Indies. He was good at that sort of thing. There was a sudden movement from a spinney ahead and several horsemen spilled onto the road. Roskelley signalled to them to slow down.

"I can see some of Cathlay's men coming towards us behind this lot making for us," Roskelley said. "Let's tell Cathlay's men we're here." He gave out a battle cry. "Charge."

Bertie asked his mount for more and it flew effortlessly upsides Roskelley. Good Lord, this was some horse. The men from the spinney circled around, caught between their party and Cathlay's men galloping towards them. Bertie looked around in alarm at the sound of more horses approaching them from behind.

Roskelley grinned at him. "More of Cathlay's men."

There was an ear-splitting war cry from Cathlay's men behind them and the men from the spinney tried to make their escape back the way they had come. Bertie's horse accelerated of its own accord and Bertie found himself upsides the escaping men. The next thing he knew, one of them had grabbed his bridle and he was powerless to stop his horse going with them. He could hear Roskelley shouting from behind him. They came to a clearing and there was Parfitt with a dozen or more men. Bertie ducked as Parfitt pulled out a pistol. Before Parfitt could fire it, Roskelley led a charge straight at the group. Some of Parfitt's men circled around and started peeling off into the woods.

Parfitt roared at them. "Come back you lily-livered cowards. I've paid you well for this."

Most of his remaining men ignored him and disappeared into the trees. Bertie pulled his horse round and rode close enough to Parfitt to knock the pistol out of his hands with his whip.

Parfitt snarled at him. "You've been a thorn in my side for as long as I can remember. Don't think you can get away with this, I'm a peer of the realm."

Rosskelley joined them. "The Duke of Cathlay's men have been waiting for days for this moment. You might as well come quietly. His men are loyal."

Without warning, Parfitt rode at Bertie and grabbed his reins. Bertie's horse reared and he landed on the ground with a painful thump. He managed to roll out of the way of flying hooves and spring to his feet. Parfitt jumped off his own horse and ran towards Bertie before Rosskelley could stop him. Bertie stood his ground and landed a heavy punch to Parfitt's head as he reached him, sending Parfitt spinning to the ground with the force of it.

"Come on then, Parfitt. Let's have this out man to man." Bertie kept his fists in front of his face and waited, trusting Roskelley to keep any of Parfitt's men who had stayed away from them. Parfitt lay perfectly still. Bertie's shoulders quivered with the tension of waiting. Parfitt would play dirty. He took a step closer keeping his eyes firmly on his opponent.

"Who's lily-livered now, Parfitt? Up with you, man."

There was no response. Roskelley walked past him, pistol in hand. He bent down and turned Parfitt over.

Roskelley pointed at a bloodstained rock, where Parfitt had lain. "He must have hit his head on that as he landed. He's dead."

CHAPTER TWENTY EIGHT

Lucy allowed herself to be escorted upstairs by Mrs Adams. She refused a bath and made do with a quick wash. She was barely aware of what gown one of the maids helped her into. Thank goodness for Lady Lovering's generous nature. Mrs Adams had a point. She would hate to present herself to the Duke of Cathlay dressed as she had been. The maid brushed her hair into order but Lucy refused any further ornamentation.

"As long as it's tidy, that's all that matters. I'm in a hurry to go down and meet the new guests."

She almost ran down the stairs to find Mrs Adams hovering in the hallway.

"I've put your guests in the gold drawing room, Miss Vaughan. It's the one opposite to the library."

"Thank you." Lucy hurried across the hall and walked in. The first person she saw was her mother.

Mama stopped in midsentence. "Lucy! We're so happy to see you. Come and tell us about your adventures." Her voice shook with emotion.

The Duke of Cathlay rose to his feet. "Bertie's new assistant land agent managed to catch up with some of my men to tell them you had been kidnapped, Miss Vaughan. I have a feeling you must have played a part in your own rescue to arrive so quickly. Come and sit down and tell us about it. Then I'll leave you ladies to go and see what your escort can tell us." His eyes twinkled as he smiled at Lucy.

Mama and Aunt Susan made room for her on a large, gold striped sofa. Lucy sat down between them with a huge grin on her face.

"Getting caught was my own silly fault. I was stupid enough to accept Mr Gillett, the man who abducted me, as a friend of Ralph's - that is Lord Kinsey. I agreed to point him in the direction Ralph and Bertie had gone. I can't believe I didn't immediately pick up on the slight French accent he has. He bundled me in a coach and took me to a place called Tennant Manor, not that I knew where I was at the time."

The Duke raised his eyebrows. "Ah, I had a feeling there was something happening there."

"I was blindfolded until I was put into a bedroom." Lucy hesitated when Mama cried out. "It wasn't too bad. Once I was locked in a bedroom, I soon realised I was in a Tudor house. I went exploring and, as luck would have it, I found the secret doorway into another bedroom. The key was in the lock and it opened opposite a servants' stairway. I escaped through the kitchen corridor almost directly into the arms of Lord Overton - who was extraordinarily glad to see me!"

The Duke laughed. "I can imagine he was. Well done for escaping. I wouldn't be too hard on yourself for being taken in by Mr Gillett, you're not the first. We've had our eye on him for some time. Let's hope Overton manages to catch him."

Mrs Adams arrived with a maid bearing a tea tray.

"Would you all like tea?" Mrs Adams looked at the Duke. "Lord Kinsey is in the library if you'd like to join him, Your

Grace."

"Thank you. I'll see you at dinner, ladies."

Lucy accepted a cup of tea and made inroads into a plate of biscuits. Breakfast seemed a long time away. Once she had eaten and been fussed over for a few minutes, Lucy's buoyant mood faded.

"Bertie is still there. I do hope nothing happens to him or to anybody else for that matter. I feel awful about leading them all into danger with my stupidity this morning."

Mama took her hand and gave it a squeeze. "They'll come back safe; you'll see."

The Duchess smiled at her. "I was glad to hear young Bertie had pitched in to help you. I've always had a soft spot for that young man. It can't have been easy for him given his mother's attitude. I'm sure he would have been the first to help anyway, but I have wondered lately if Bertie was developing a tendre for you." Her voice rose on a questioning note.

Lucy's cheeks burned. Lord, she had forgotten just how direct the Duchess of Cathlay could be. Words failed her.

The Duchess patted her arm. "I'm sorry to put you to the blush, child. I'm afraid I was fishing for information. I'm confident Bertie has feelings for you and if those feelings are reciprocated, marriage would help you out of your current difficulties."

Lucy's cheeks went even hotter. She glanced at her mother. This was a conversation she would rather have had in private with her but there was no sense annoying the Duchess.

"Bertie has asked me to marry him. I'm not sure if he is just being chivalrous and I told him he needs time to think about it. I want to see what sort of scandal comes out of this. I'm determined to refuse Bertie if I think I might drag him down with me."

The Duchess smiled at her. "Don't worry about any scandal. If you end up married no one will even think of it."

Lucy shook her head. "It's not that simple. I'm not at all sure what my father has been doing to get himself into debt to Lord Parfitt. Bertie's never been comfortable within the Lovell family until recently, I would hate to jeopardise that by pulling him into a scandal that might be beyond even your social powers to smother."

Mama and Aunt Susan exchanged a glance. Mama looked close to tears. The Duchess pursed her lips and looked around at them all.

"Bertie will always be welcome within the Lovell family as long as I'm a member of it. There's no need for you to worry about that. Is it perhaps that you're not sure about marrying Bertie yourself?"

Lucy sighed and closed her eyes briefly. "I do have reservations about marriage but I feel safe with Bertie. I'll be frank with you. I have a feeling my father might have been dabbling in something that's against the national interest. The man who abducted me this morning, Mr Gillett, has connections who are French. I may be making too much of it but I have theories about what has been going on."

"Bertie is not such a social animal as you might think, you know. Even if there was a scandal that became common knowledge it would fade eventually. I don't see why you and Bertie should suffer for your father's sins. I won't tease you any more now. The two of you will have to work it out between you. Rest assured, anything that is in my power to smooth your path will be done and the same goes for Cathlay."

"The same goes for me and your Uncle James," Aunt Susan

said.

Lucy hesitated. What on earth could she say? She had a feeling Uncle James was connected to it all. She glanced at Aunt Susan who was looking pensive. There was the sound of an arrival in the hall and the door to the drawing room burst open. Bertie strode in and Lucy's pulse quickened. She raised her eyes to his.

"I'm so glad to see you safe. Is anyone hurt?"

"Not from our side." Bertie looked around the room. "Excuse me bursting in like this without even changing but I knew Lucy would want to know what has happened."

Aunt Susan jumped up to make room for Bertie on the sofa next to Lucy. "We don't mind at all, Mr Lovell. We are all keen to hear what's happened."

Bertie almost flopped onto the sofa and ran a hand over his eyes. He seemed really shaken which wasn't like him.

Lucy took his hand. "What is it, Bertie? What's wrong?"

"Nothing's wrong, in fact in one way it's good but I feel awful. We were ambushed by Parfitt and some of his men on the way back. Most of his men deserted him when some of Cathlay's men came to our rescue. Parfitt tried to attack me by pulling me off my horse. I managed to roll to safety. He dismounted and charged at me. I connected with an almighty punch to his jaw, sending him to the ground."

"Surely that serves him right after what he's done? I assume the Duke's men managed to capture him."

"He landed awkwardly and hit his head on a rock. He's dead. Colonel Harper, the local magistrate, is known to the Duke. His men have taken Parfitt's body for the Colonel to deal with." Bertie's face was filled with remorse.

Lucy chafed his hand. He was shaking. "There's no need to

blame yourself, it was clearly an accident. Parfitt would have shown you no mercy, I'm sure."

"I know, but I've never killed a man before even accidentally and it's weighing on my conscience."

"Lucy's right," the Duchess said. "It's not your fault but I understand it's a difficult thing to deal with. I expect you'll feel better when you had a good night's sleep. It's been a very stressful time for you and Lucy." She smiled at Bertie and glanced from him to Lucy.

"That's what Rosskelley said. He was in the army and he said it's never an easy thing to realise you've killed a man but you do come to terms with it. At least Lucy doesn't need to worry about him anymore." He gave Lucy a lopsided grin. "I might not have taken you up on my charger but I did slay your Dragon."

Lucy blinked back tears. "I won't deny it's a relief but I'm sorry it happened like that."

Bertie grimaced. "To be honest it's perhaps as well it did. I'll never know now whether I really would have killed him to spare you any more distress, if I'd had to. I'd said so in anger."

"So now you feel even worse."

Bertie nodded. "More news. We watched when Parfitt arrived at Tennant Manor and Gillett came out to speak to him. They ended up having a furious argument, presumably because you had disappeared. Parfitt signalled to one of his men to attack Gillett with a knife. Gillett was still alive when we reached him after Parfitt had gone. He's been taken to Colonel Harper's house with an army medic looking after him. Rosskelley said they'll try and keep him alive to see what information they can get out of him. Rosskelley's gone into the library to talk to the Duke. I just had to come and see you first."

"And quite right too, Bertie." The Duchess looked at the other two ladies. "Why don't we go and dress for dinner and leave these two to talk."

Lucy waited until the Duchess pulled the door closed behind them and threw her arms around Bertie.

"I'm so sorry I managed to get myself captured. If I hadn't you would have been spared this. I tell you what, why don't we forgive each other. It feels strange that we no longer need to worry about Lord Parfitt but I expect we'll get used to that."

Bertie laid his head on her shoulder. "I hope you're right. Will you marry me now?"

"I don't know. I was quite frank with the Duchess of Cathlay about this. I told her I didn't want to drag you down if the whole thing created a huge scandal, quite possibly connected to national security. I think we need to wait and see what happens. The Duchess said they would do their utmost to scotch any rumour but even she can't guarantee anything."

"Bertie took a few deep breaths. "I don't care about scandals. All I want to do is set up home with you and keep you safe."

"We'll talk about it when you're rested. I'm so glad you weren't hurt. Why don't you go and have a soak in the bath and get ready for dinner. Mrs Adams is determined to enjoy having a duke and duchess staying. The least we can do for Ralph is to make tonight into a bit of a dinner party for him after messing up his week."

"If you say so. But won't you give me a kiss first."

Lucy nodded and Bertie took her in his arms, at first gently but then almost as if his life depended upon it. Lucy kissed him back with equal fervour. Her whole body seemed to tingle. Eventually Bertie pulled away, his breathing ragged.

"I'll go and see about that bath now and see you at dinner." He kissed her on the cheek and strode out of the room.

Lucy could understand him wanting an answer but she didn't feel ready to give one. It was all very well him thinking he wouldn't mind about a huge scandal but he was a social animal at heart. She would be perfectly happy in the country but she couldn't see him not wanting at least a few weeks in Town during the season. Her head ached with all the worry. She waited a few minutes. Bertie was bound to have a word with Ralph before he went upstairs. She heard the library door open and shut and footsteps heading towards the stairs. Right. Why not go and have a word with the Duke of Cathlay.

Lucy knocked on the door of the library and Ralph's voice bade her enter. A man she didn't recognise was sitting around a large desk with Ralph and the Duke. Lucy hesitated but they all stood and Ralph ushered her into the room.

"Come on in, Lucy." He pulled up a chair for her.

"I don't want to interrupt your meeting but I wanted to thank you for all your help, Ralph. Mrs Adams says she is happy to be giving a dinner party for a Duke and Duchess tonight. I hope we haven't put your staff to too much trouble."

Ralph smiled at her. "It's been no trouble at all. I've thoroughly enjoyed myself. Mrs Adams and Cook seem very happy with the opportunity to show off their skills. I was a bit disappointed at the lack of response to my house party invitation, probably because of the time of year. You and Bertie have more than made up for that so there is no need for you to feel beholden."

Lucy smiled at him. "I can see why Bertie thinks such a lot of you." She turned towards the Duke. "I don't suppose I could have a few minutes private conversation with you, Your

Grace?"

Ralph jumped to his feet. "I should have introduced you to Mr Rosskelley, Bertie's new agent. I'll show him upstairs to his room."

Rosskelley bowed low. "I'm delighted to meet you, Miss Vaughan. Don't worry about Mr Lovell not appearing to be himself this evening. His protestations that he would like to wring Lord Parfitt's neck were said in anger. It's ironical that a freak accident caused Parfitt's death at Mr Lovell's hands. It's a very strange feeling the first time you kill someone. For most of us in the army it's something you never really get used to. Rest assured though he will soon come to terms with it." Rosskelley grinned at her. "Parfitt's death will make life easier for the two of you. I'll take my leave of you now and see you at dinner."

"Thank you, Mr Rosskelley."

Rosskelley nodded and left the library chatting away to Ralph. The Duke of Cathlay led her to a sofa in front of the fire.

"What is it that's worrying you, Miss Vaughan?" He looked at her with so much concern on his face that Lucy felt close to tears. She took a deep breath.

"I have to know. Is my father a traitor?"

The Duke sighed and looked at the floor for a moment. "We have no proof, but we believe he's been helping Lord Parfitt to steal information from your uncle. As far as we can work out Gillett was the go-between with the French government. We're hoping he survives so we can get more information out of him."

"Was that why Uncle James was out of London?"

"I think you've guessed the whole. Your uncle came under suspicion himself when the War Office worked out a certain leak must have come from him. He thought someone at his main residence was behind it at first."

"So, he went home to investigate to clear his name?"

"Yes. There were several staff members who could have had access to his private rooms. He spent a while investigating but no one appeared guilty."

"Until the awful truth dawned on him that it must have been Papa?"

The Duke nodded. "When he got back to London and read the message from your Mama about your father trying to marry you off to Parfitt he knew for sure. Parfitt was a known associate of Gillett and another person on our watch list. Your uncle and I were already in consultation when Mr Reid and Mr Roskelly arrived to see me."

"I see," Lucy said in a subdued voice. Her own father a traitor. What an awful thought. Even the Duke seemed lost for words. At least she had information that might be useful.

"Bertie thought he recognised one of the men who came with Parfitt to talk to Gillett. If he's the man Gillett spoke to in my hearing then he had an upper-class accent with a faint but definite trace of a Scottish accent. I was blindfolded which seemed to make my other senses more alert. I might recognise his voice if I heard him again. Between us we might be able to identify him for you."

"Ah I have an idea who that might be. Keep it between yourselves. If anyone else were to find out about your suspicions you'd be in danger." He smiled down at her. "Is there something else you are bothered about?"

"Bertie wants to marry me and I think it's what I want, despite always thinking I would never marry. What I don't want to do is ruin his social standing if there is a huge scandal around my family. What do you think?"

"It's all down to your father. If we can bring him about and we're confident he will behave himself we can brush through this. Parfitt being dead makes things easier. But whatever happens, are you sure it's your decision to make?"

"What do you mean?"

"All you need to decide is whether you love Bertie enough to put aside all your doubts about marriage and accept his offer. It's for him to worry about the chance of scandal ruining his reputation. If he wants to take that chance, have you considered that perhaps you ought to let him? Think about it. As soon as I find out any more, I'll let you know I promise."

"Thank you. I'll leave you in peace now and see you at dinner."

"I look forward to that. I do hope you decide in Bertie's favour. Augusta has been saying for quite a while that you two are made for each other. If you decide to accept him, I too think you will be very happy."

Tears came to Lucy's eyes. She dropped a curtsy and ran out of the room. Once she reached her bedroom she lay down on the bed and fell into an exhausted sleep.

* * *

Lucy woke to Hannah gently shaking her.

"I left you as long as I could, Miss Vaughan but it's time to get you ready for dinner." Hannah's voice bubbled with excitement. "Imagine, a Duke and Duchess to dinner. It was my afternoon off. I'm so glad I'm back in time to dress you."

Lucy waited until the last minute to go down to the dining room. She could see Bertie hovering near the door in the drawing room as the other guests waited for her. She slipped in and went straight up to Mama and the Duchess of Cathlay. She couldn't give Bertie an answer until she had slept on it. Fatigue was clogging her brain. She went into dinner between the two ladies and managed to resist Ralph's efforts at seating her next to Bertie.

The Duke seemed to understand her dilemma and manoeuvred her so that she was sitting next to him. He kept up a string of easy conversation. Lucy was so tired that she couldn't do justice to a lovely meal. At one stage her head nodded forwards and she only managed to jerk herself awake seconds before she disgraced herself by falling asleep in her lemon cream dessert. It was a relief when the Duchess led the ladies into the drawing room to leave the men to their port.

Lucy excused herself from taking tea with them and made her way up to her bedroom where Hannah was waiting for her. For once Hannah curbed her love of chatter and had her prepared for bed mercifully quickly. Lucy gave a satisfied sigh as she pulled the covers over her head and fell into an exhausted sleep.

CHAPTER TWENTY NINE

The following morning Bertie woke up quite late. He dressed quickly and went down to the breakfast room, where Ralph was waiting for him.

"How are you feeling? That was quite a day you had yesterday."

Bertie grinned at him. "Not one I'd like to repeat but I feel a lot better after a good night's sleep. Have you seen Lucy about?"

"No not at all. Did you manage to get some private conversation with her last night?"

"No. I'm still waiting for an answer." His voice sounded flat even to his own ears. Waiting was torture.

"Your Lucy seems to have a great deal of integrity. I gather she's worried about dragging you into a scandal. Much to her credit, but no help to you. Never mind I'm sure you'll come about. Did you want to have some breakfast then come out with me and the dogs or would you rather wait for her?"

"I'll come with you. If I push her for an answer, I might push her away."

Half an hour later Bertie and Ralph collected the dogs.

"I thought we might wander down to the home farm. You still haven't seen those breeding stocks have you."

Ralph called the dogs to heel and they set off at a brisk pace. They hadn't been walking for long when Bertie glanced back at Kinsey Court and stopped so abruptly one of the dogs cannoned into him.

"I can see two horsemen coming down your drive."

"I wonder who they are. Do you want to go and meet them?"

"Yes. That could be Arthur riding the grey."

The riders must have seen them. They waited for them to catch up. Bertie broke into a grin when they were close enough to see that it was Arthur.

"Arthur. What brings you back? I thought I sent you to Mayford Castle."

"I got there yesterday and turned straight around to tell you the news once I'd confirmed it. I stayed with Emma's family last night and set of for here early this morning. They've sent Robert with me for safety. There wasn't enough moon visible or I would have ridden through the night. Mr Vaughan is seriously ill."

"What with?"

"He's broken his leg. The Rugeley butler, Drake, said his master went out early in the morning with Lord Parfitt a couple of days before. They were arguing. Drake thought Mr Vaughan might have changed his mind about forcing Miss Vaughan to marry Lord Parfitt. Drake doesn't know if Parfitt was involved or Mr Vaughan simply fell. One of the footmen found him lying in the gardens soaked to the skin but not until the evening. He wasn't able to get himself back to the house and they'd had heavy rain. They don't know if he'll survive. He turned feverish and the doctor said he's got an inflammation of the lungs, besides the broken leg. I thought you would want to know." Arthur smiled at him.

"Good man. You did the right thing. I'm going back to the house. Join me there once you've stabled your horses."

"Of course."

Bertie watched them go. Good Lord, if Vaughan didn't pull through then Lucy would go into mourning. Perhaps for as long as six months or even more.

"Are you thinking what I'm thinking?" Ralph said.

"I expect so. I'm going to have another try to see if Lucy will marry me straightaway."

"I would if I were you. Despite the man being something of a rogue you can bet your life his female relatives will go into mourning if anything happens to him. Off you go and best of luck."

Bertie ran all the way back to the house. He found Lucy alone in the breakfast room. He sat next to her and took one of her hands.

"Arthur has just arrived with a message from Rugeley Hall. Your father is seriously ill. He was found with a broken leg in the gardens a couple of days ago. They think he was lying there most of the day and they had rain. The doctor says he has an inflammation of the lungs."

Lucy gasped. "This might sound strange but, despite what Papa tried to do to me, I don't like to think of him being ill."

"That sounds just like you, Lucy. The most kind-hearted girl I know."

"He is my father. From his red complexion and worsening temper, I think he had been drinking a lot, even for him, lately. His general health can't be good."

"Which won't help him. Arthur said Drake saw him go out early with Lord Parfitt and they were arguing. No one saw what happened after that. I wondered if Parfitt pushed him but if he was drinking heavily, he could have simply fallen over. Drake thought your father had changed his mind about trying to force you to marry Lord Parfitt, if that's any comfort to you." Bertie smiled at her sympathetically. He could have sympathy with Lucy's feelings but it was hard to have much sympathy for her father.

Lucy was still for several moments. "Yes, that is some sort of comfort."

Bertie squeezed her hand. "I don't think there is going to be a scandal. Why don't we get married straightaway? I could go to the bishop and get a bishop's licence."

"I don't know what to say."

"Lucy, I love you. Please say yes. I don't want anything to come between us now. I really don't care if there is a scandal or not. The most important thing to me is to be with you."

Bertie held his breath as he watched the emotions flit across Lucy's face. Then she broke into a huge grin.

"Yes, I love you too. I will marry you."

Bertie kissed her soundly. "You've made me the happiest of men. Do you want to get married in Rugeley church?"

Lucy shook her head so vigorously her curls bounced. "I don't trust the vicar of Rugeley. Why don't we get married at Mayford church? I suppose Mama and Aunt Susan will want to come back with me to Rugeley but Mayford is nearly as close."

"I'm not sure I want you in the same house as your father but we'll worry about that later. I'll go and find Ralph; he'll know where to go to get a bishop's licence I expect."

Ralph not only knew where to go but offered to take Bertie there.

* * *

Lucy watched them set off. The Duke of Cathlay was right. It was Bertie's decision not to worry about any scandal. Bertie loved her and that was all that mattered. Bertie loved her. A surge of joy swept through her. Perhaps it was wrong of her to be so happy with Papa gravely ill but she deserved a little happiness after what Papa had put her through. If he died, they would have to wait for months to marry. How long would it take to get a bishop's licence? She went to pass on the news to Mama and found her with Aunt Susan, chatting over their breakfast.

"I've got something to tell you, Mama."

"You've agreed to marry Bertie!"

Lucy smiled. She couldn't help herself. "Well yes but Arthur Reid, Bertie's new assistant agent, has arrived and Papa is gravely ill. Bertie's ridden off with Ralph to try and get a bishop's licence for us to marry at Mayford church straightaway."

Mama looked confused but Aunt Susan clapped her hands.

"Oh, what a wonderful idea. Bertie Lovell is a gem." She put an arm around Mama's shoulders. "If anything happens, you'll have to go into mourning. It will look strange if you don't. This way they can be married first. Since people in London assumed you had been summoned home because of Vaughan's health, a private family wedding will be unremarkable. Perfect." A satisfied smile spread over Aunt Susan's face.

Mama nodded but her expression suggested she was having the same ambiguous feelings as Lucy. Mrs Adams bustled in leading Uncle James. Aunt Susan explained the situation to him.

"What do you think, James? Will it work?"

Uncle James smiled at her. "It will work very well if Vaughan survives until after the wedding. We had better get across to Rugeley Hall straight away. I've just come from Colonel Harper's house. Gillett is talking. He's mentioned Lord Parfitt but said nothing about Vaughan. I don't think he knows about Vaughan's links with him, apart from Parfitt wanting to marry his daughter. It was all over Town that Parfitt was making a cake of himself over Lucy. Since Colonel Harper will report that Lord Parfitt has died in a riding accident," Uncle James's eyes twinkled at Lucy, "there is no need to worry about a scandal."

By midday they were on the road to Rugeley Hall. It was well into the evening when they pulled up by the front door. A young man ran down the steps to greet them. Lucy jumped from the top step of the coach into his outstretched arms.

"Peter, you're back from Scotland!"

Peter set her down, grinning. "I am. It sounds like I should never have gone on that holiday. I've been told some fantastical tale that Papa tried to marry you off to Lord Parfitt of all people."

Peter helped his mother and aunt down. "I'm sorry I went off like I did, Mama. Papa angered me so much I thought I would be best out of the way for a while. If I'd known what he was planning for Lucy I would have stayed here."

Mama smiled at him and then grinned at Lucy. "It's all turned out well in the end. I'll leave Lucy to tell you about her news."

Peter's eyes glowed. "Never tell me you and Bertie Lovell have finally realised you're made for each other. I heard that he rode to the rescue."

"Yes, we have. But how is Papa tonight?"

Peter grimaced. "Arthur Reid found you then. Papa's not

looking too well. Been hitting the bottle hard from what Drake said. He thinks he was foxed when he fell and broke his leg."

Mama put a hand on Peter's shoulder. "Let's get inside and we'll tell you all about it."

CHAPTER THIRTY

Two days later Emma put the finishing touches to Lucy's hair. "My word you look beautiful, Miss Vaughan. Mr Lovell is a lucky man."

Lucy smoothed the skirt of the pale blue gown she was wearing and twirled in front of the looking glass in her bedroom at Rugeley Hall. "You've done a wonderful job. Don't you think you should start calling me Lucy now?"

Emma shook her head. "Not until Arthur and I are married. If I'm going to train your new maid, I don't want to slip up by calling you Lucy in front of her."

"I suppose so. Are you sure you want to stay as a maid. It could be for a few months."

"I'd be bored stuck at home and this way Arthur and I can still see each other regularly. Mama is insistent we don't marry until he's one and twenty. Now let's get you to your wedding."

Peter was waiting downstairs to drive her to Mayford church in his curricle. Lucy felt a buzz of happiness to have her brother with her.

Arthur was waiting in a borrowed gig to take Emma to the church. Peter helped Lucy into the curricle and waited until Arthur had settled Emma in and driven off. He jumped up into the driver's seat and accepted the reins from his groom.

"Are you ready, Lucy? I'm so happy to be giving you to Bertie." His expression became sombre. "I know he will treat you kindly. Not like Papa."

Lucy felt like singing. The sun was shining and she was about to marry her knight in shining armour. Peter set his horses into motion and they were on their way to her future.

"I'm going to try not to think about Papa any more today," Peter said. "At least he's had the decency to cling on to life long enough for you to marry straightaway."

Lucy caught her breath as the church came into view. Every person in the village and for some way beyond was waiting outside to greet her. They cheered when Peter helped her to the ground. She smiled around at them and waved. The crowd gave another cheer and Peter led her into the church. It took a moment for her eyes to acclimatise to the darker interior after the sunshine outside but there was no mistaking the beautiful scent of spring flowers that hit her as she walked in. The church was awash with flower arrangements, more of the villagers' work. Bertie was so popular.

Tears sprang to her eyes as Bertie turned around from his position near the altar to smile at her. The front pews were taken by Peter, Mama, Aunt Susan and Uncle James on one side and The Duke and Duchess of Cathlay, together with Lord Overton on the other. Emma and Arthur, Mr Roskelley and various members of the local gentry were behind them. The rest of the seats were taken by staff from Mayford Castle and Rugeley Hall. The best wedding that she could have.

The wedding service took on a new meaning now that it applied to her. When Bertie placed a ring on her finger, she smiled up at him with tears running down her face. He pulled out a handkerchief and gently wiped her cheeks dry. The vicar pronounced them man and wife and Bertie kissed her.

Bertie lent so close that his breath tickled her ear and whispered. "I'll do better than that later." He grinned down at her.

Lucy laughed and allowed him to lead her back down the aisle. She smiled at Mama and Aunt Susan, both of whom were wiping their faces with wisps of lacy handkerchiefs. Bertie took her out of the church and handed her up into his curricle and climbed in beside her. The crowd cheered yet again as they waved to them. Bertie signalled to the groom at his horses' heads to let them go and they were on their way.

Lucy sank back against the swabs and savoured the sun on her face. "It was very kind of Mrs Hobbs to offer to organise a wedding breakfast. There are hardly any staff left at Rugeley Hall."

Bertie laughed. "I think she would have shot me if I hadn't agreed. She's hired half the young people for miles around to help. Quite a few permanently. She's enjoying herself hugely. For my part I shall be glad when everyone has gone home."

A bubble of happiness escaped Lucy in the form of a joyous laugh. "I will too. I find strange things happen to me when I'm near you."

"That sounds very promising. If I wasn't driving, I would kiss you now."

"Perhaps we had better change the subject for a bit. These are excellent horses. Some of the ones Mr Bright brought for you?"

"Yes. He's brought some great horses. There's a beautiful chestnut mare you might want to try the paces of. If you like her, you can have her as a wedding present."

Lucy clapped her hands in delight. "I'm sure I'll love her. It will be wonderful to have my own horse again."

They arrived at Mayford Castle to the cheers of a row of servants Mrs Hobbs had lined up outside. Lucy and Bertie exchanged a word with each one of them. Bertie led her into the grand dining room, which had a baronial hall look about it.

Lucy grinned up at Bertie. "I hadn't thought about you living in a castle before. It's the perfect home for my knight in shining armour."

They laughed together as they moved forward to greet their guests. Lucy caught a glimpse of Mama accepting a larger handkerchief than the wispy one she'd had in church from Peter. She ran forward and hugged her.

Mama blinked hard and hugged her back. "I'm so happy for you, Lucy."

Aunt Susan and Uncle James came forward to greet them. Bertie ushered them all to their seats as soon as it was politely possible. Lucy suppressed a grin. He was afraid of another bout of feminine tears. Cook had prepared a banquet fit for a king and Mrs Hobbs must have trained all the new staff for hours, so smooth was the service. The wedding breakfast passed in a blur for Lucy. She smiled so much her face ached.

It was early evening before the last of the wedding guests left. Lucy hugged Mama and Peter clapped Bertie on the shoulder. They watched as Peter helped Mama into his curricle and drove off.

Bertie sighed. "Thank goodness for that. What would you like to do now? A walk around the grounds to relax or shall we go upstairs?"

Lucy grinned at him. "Upstairs please. I love you, Bertie Lovell. I think I've loved you ever since the day you rescued my kitten."

In answer, Bertie took her hand and they ran upstairs laughing.

THE END

Afterword

If you enjoyed 'The Rake's Rescued Bride' I would appreciate a review, which helps new readers to find my books.

Previous books in my Reluctant Bride Series of stand-alone novels linked by character,
in order:
A Good Match For The Major
The Viscount's Convenient Bride
The Marquess's Christmas Runaway
The Duke's Bluestocking

To find out more please visit my website
https://josiebonhamauthor.com
or follow me on social media
Facebook: @josiebonhamauthor
Twitter: @BonhamJosie
Instagram: @josiebonham

I love it when readers get in touch to talk about my books.

Printed in Great Britain
by Amazon

28106982R00193